PRAISE FOR THE

ISLES OF

STORM & SORROW

TRILOGY

'Hogan builds a vivid world, and her descriptions of life aboard ship evoke the taste of salt in the air … visceral battles and bristling prose'
*SFX*

'A rip-roaring, swashbuckling adventure that left me breathless'
Kat Dunn, author of *Dangerous Remedy*

'Every line held me captive. Bex Hogan is a master storyteller!'
Menna van Praag, author of *The Sisters Grimm*

'Pulse-pounding fantasy pirate adventure – I loved it'
Kesia Lupo, author of *We Are Blood and Thunder*

'Full of twists and turns that kept me on the edge of my seat with my heart in my mouth'
Katharine Corr, author of *The Witch's Kiss*

'A powerful story about sacrifice, the
and the painful

ORION CHILDREN'S BOOKS

First published in Great Britain in 2021
by Hodder and Stoughton

1 3 5 7 9 10 8 6 4 2



All characters and events in this publication, other than those clearly in the public domain, are fictitious and any resemblance to real persons, living or dead, is purely coincidental.

In order to create a sense of setting, some names of real places have been included in the book. However, the events depicted in this book are imaginary and the real places used fictitiously.



A CIP catalogue record for this book
is available from the British Library.

ISBN 978 1 51010 587 4

Typeset in Adobe Garamond by Avon DataSet Ltd, Arden Court, Alcester, Warwickshire

Printed and bound in Great Britain by Clays Ltd, Elcograf S.p.A.

The paper and board used in this book are made
from wood from responsible sources.

Orion Children's Books
An imprint of
Hachette Children's Group
Part of Hodder and Stoughton
Carmelite House
50 Victoria Embankment
London EC4Y 0DZ

An Hachette UK Company

www.hachette.co.uk
www.hachettechildrens.co.uk

ISLES OF
STORM & SORROW

# VULTURE

BEX HOGAN

Orion

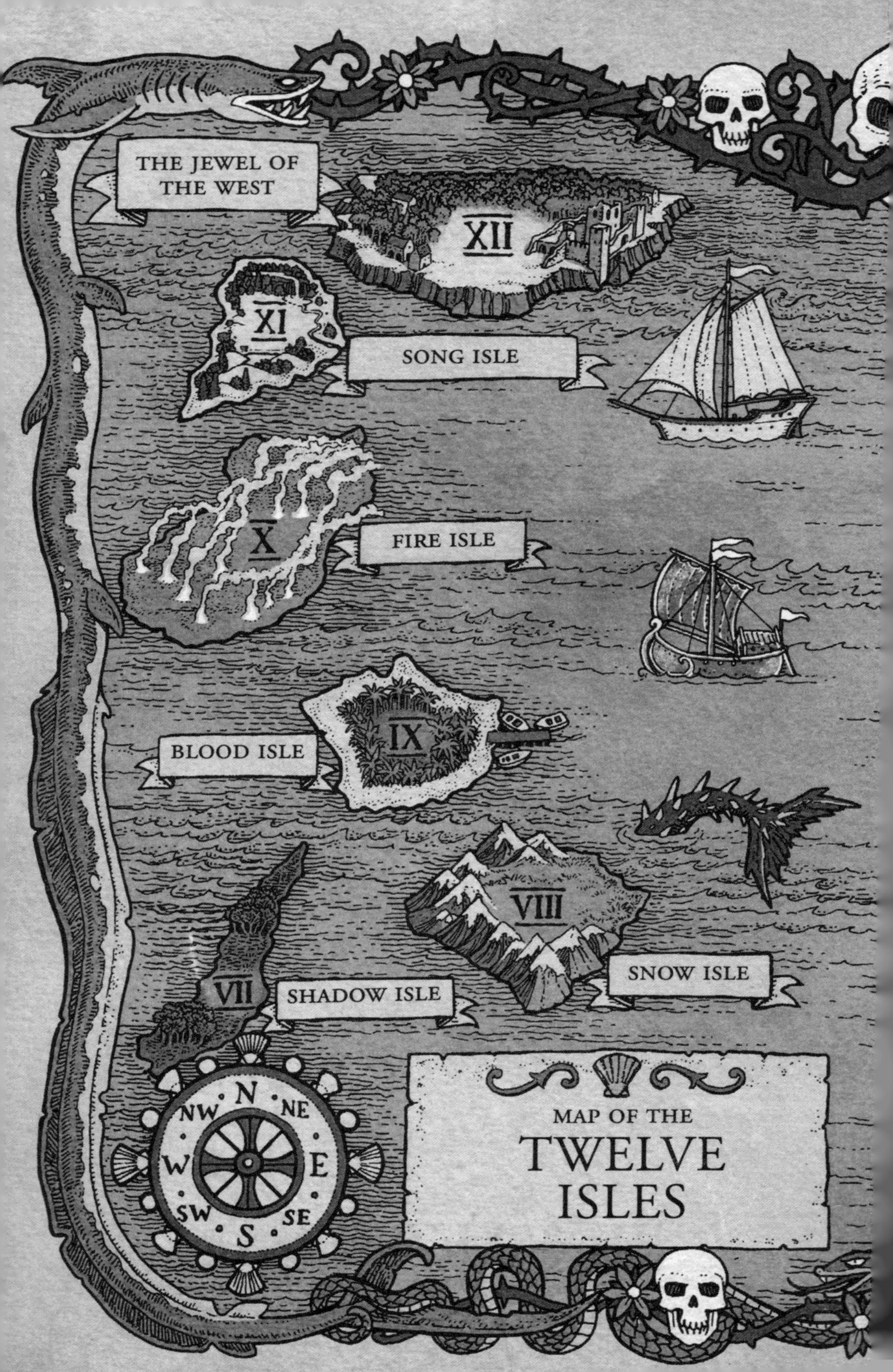
THE JEWEL OF THE WEST
XII
XI
SONG ISLE
X
FIRE ISLE
BLOOD ISLE
IX
VIII
VII
SHADOW ISLE
SNOW ISLE
N
NE
E
SE
S
SW
W
NW
MAP OF THE
TWELVE ISLES

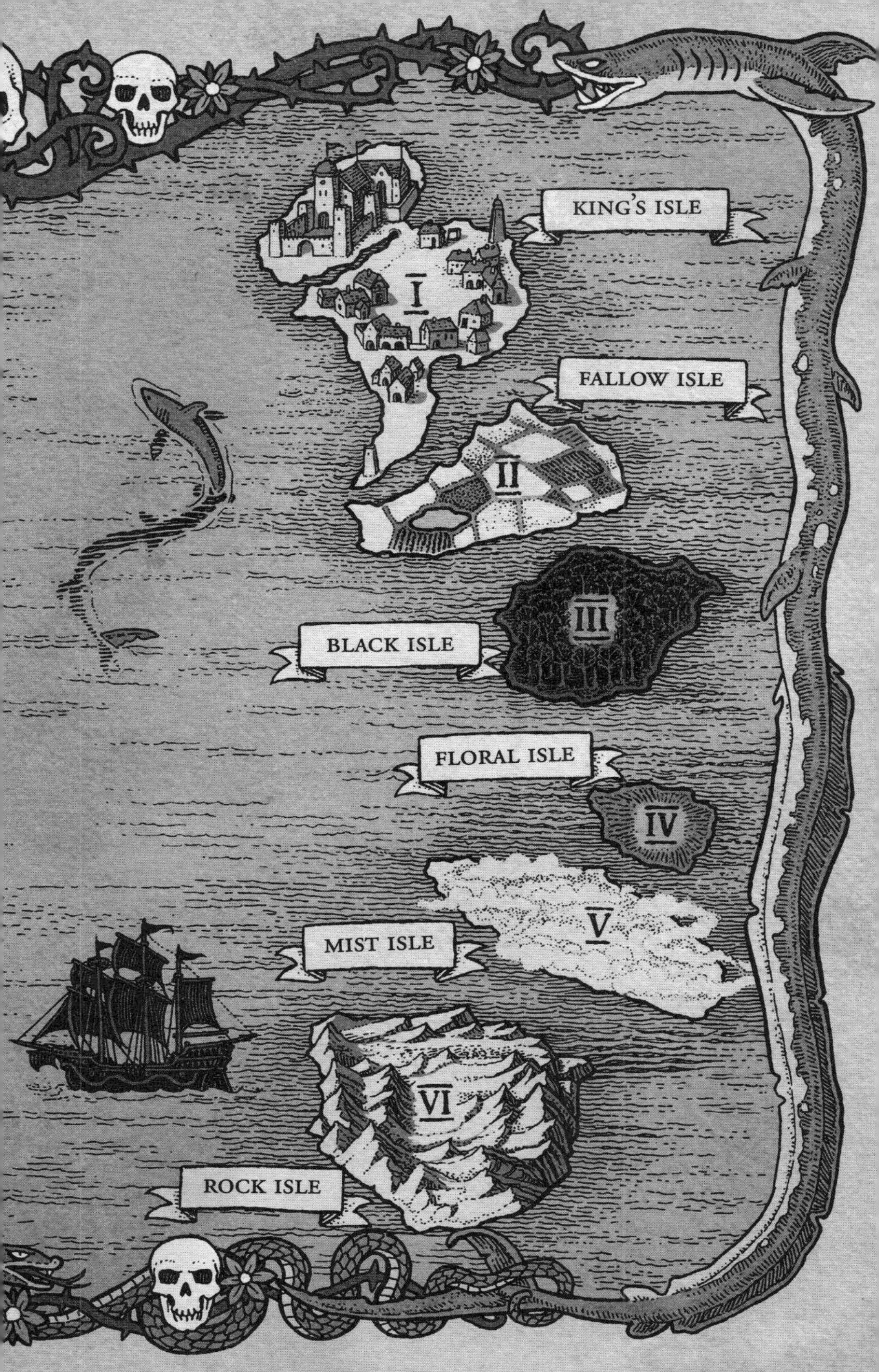
KING'S ISLE
I
FALLOW ISLE
II
III
BLACK ISLE
FLORAL ISLE
IV
V
MIST ISLE
VI
ROCK ISLE

For Mum and Dad.

*People I love. People I trust.*

*People who accept me just as I am.*

*I'm struggling to stay upright . . .*
*It's time to end this . . .*
*Bronn glides his blade across my neck . . .*
*Heat blazes through my whole body . . .*
*I slide down . . .*
*I gasp for air but choke on blood . . .*
*I'm dying alone . . .*
*I'm afraid.*
*I'm so very sad.*
*I'm . . .*

# PART ONE
# AWAKE

There's no peace. Just pain. Cold and lonely despair that shatters every nerve, every bone, every fading heartbeat. It should be no surprise that dying hurts, and yet here I am, cursing the agony that consumes me. The crushing weight of finality rushes to meet me, my body empty of essence, nature declaring I've reached the end. All I have to do is let go.

It's so tempting. I'm not afraid of death, but I'm so very tired of living. I could surrender myself to the sands, soak into the island, become one with the earth, until not even a stain remains to betray my presence here. My life would be a forgotten whisper carried on the wind. I would be free.

But I cannot abandon the Isles. I will not.

And so I resist. In the space after my final heartbeat fades, when my body has stopped but my soul remains, I watch as the threads of my spirit drift upwards away from me, separating from my flesh, ready to sever permanently. This is the final test to pass. I must be quick, or it'll be too late and this last remnant of who I am will leave my body. I have never succeeded in doing this before, but while I've hesitated with others, now there is no fear. If it goes wrong, then I simply stay dead. I alone will suffer, and that knowledge gives me comfort, resolve.

The strands are familiar as I weave them with my mind, and I have an advantage because I can feel them fit into place as I reconnect them to the body lying cold on the sand.

My confidence grows and warmth buzzes through me. It's urgent but peaceful, and so very *right*.

But the heat escalates beyond my control, and a blinding light surrounds me, scorching the peace away, eviscerating my confidence, pain consuming me until all my previous failures seem like merciful escapes.

There's no relief as the light thickens into an impenetrable blackness that forces itself down my throat and nose, choking me, destroying me, ripping me to pieces with ferocious intensity. Still the heat burns, flowing with the darkness. I can't survive this, won't survive this. I am being obliterated.

And then I understand.

Not obliteration.

Not even simply revival.

I am being *remade*.

Great power is forged in fire. Its flames engulf me now. The sacrifice has been given, the test passed. All that remains is to endure.

My bones shatter and mend, flesh melts then cools, all of me destroyed and reformed from the inside out.

The essence of who I was knits around this new form, a physically familiar shell with something new at its core. Pure magic.

And then, after a minute, after an eternity, I take a breath. Deep and long. It fills my lungs, and restarts my heart.

I'm alive.

For a moment I don't move. I just lie staring up at the sky, wondering if it is looking back in disbelief, an astonished witness to my resurrection. But the clouds roll over with indifference. As if nothing happened. As if I didn't just bleed to death.

I lift my hand to my throat, hardly daring to touch the wound, fearing what I might find, but feel only soft, warm skin. Healed.

I look down to where before fingers were missing. Then at my feet, where toes had been severed. They have been restored as completely as my life.

Cautiously I sit up, and in place of the pain that not long ago coursed through every fibre of my being, there is nothing but magic woven into the fabric of my soul. Its physical presence contradicts itself. It's hot yet cold, heavy yet light, sharp yet soft. It's familiar but strange, a perfect fit, yet too much to contain.

I am a Mage.

But there's something else. Something beyond the magic. Something altered. I can't identify it, the thought intangible and moving fleetingly from my grasp, but I sense it nonetheless.

Is it possible that maybe, just maybe, I haven't quite restored myself to who I once was?

But that uncomfortable thought is pushed aside by more urgent ones – can I still sense Esther's protections? Do I remain hidden here? Am I safe from the man who imprisoned and tortured me? Despite the fact that my body is fortified with magic, it recoils in fear at the mere memory of him. Of Gaius. But Esther's enchantments hold strong, her familiar magic resonating with my own.

I need to focus. I fought past death for one reason and one reason only. To protect the Isles and the people I love. The blood moon is coming, I can sense it on the air, which means there isn't time to waste.

I have to get back to the East. To Torin.

I flex my fingers, both old and new, the power moving through them, through me, as though it has replaced the blood in my veins.

Who am I now? I stand, unsteady as a newborn fawn, faltering to find myself. There is the woman I was, I recognise her within me, but this pounding force that is also now a part of me demands attention.

Yes, I must return east to save Torin. But something else whispers inside me, persistent and strong, like the promise of a storm on the wind. For all those I love, there are those I hate. And now vengeance might just be within my grasp. I cannot face Gaius, not yet, not until I'm certain of my capabilities – but he's not my only enemy.

I try to quiet the thought, but it worms its way in, burrowing deep.

*You can kill the King.*

Once Torin is safe, I can finally take revenge on the man who tried everything he could to kill me. I thought I needed an army to defeat him, but maybe I just needed magic.

And when the King's gone, there will be one confrontation remaining for me in the East.

Bronn.

I position the stones carefully along the edge of the beach. This will be the first test of my new power and I'm nervous. Once I'd allowed myself a moment to bask in the fact that I could walk properly again, I'd set straight to work. While I'm certain that Esther's protective magic continues to shield this place from Gaius's view, I can't be too careful. I've imbued each smooth stone with magic, whispering the incantation *felra* – hide – over every one, so they may create an invisible barrier around this corner of the island. I don't want anyone to see what I'm about to do.

I walk to the water's edge and take a breath,

wondering if my plan will work. There's only one way to find out. When I summon forth the magic it answers differently to before, now coming as easily as words to the tongue. A rush of heat rises inside me. My blood is boiling in my veins, until it runs dry to pure magic, a world of untamed power harnessed in skeleton and flesh. I have never been so alive. Or so unpredictable. The wild nature of the magic grips me tightly, and it's wonderfully freeing. I'm no longer restricted by anything, not my past, not my future. I am no longer Marianne, but so much more.

My fingers graze the water and call out for the one I seek.

*Rysa vatfa fugda. Veitja mi flutni.*

The last time I did this, I was foolish, commanding what wasn't mine to command, trying to wield a weapon that could not be harnessed. But not now. Now I whisper to an ally, one who understands the tongue I speak in, the language of the islands, the royalty, the Mages.

I do not fear her any more, do not wish to control her. I simply ask for her help.

And almost immediately she answers.

Ripping the fabric of the ocean wide open, the water raptor emerges, soaring straight upwards and stretching her four colossal wings wide to hold her in the air. She screams out with delight, a sound that reaches inside me, connecting with my magic, shivering through my bones.

I hold my arms up, focusing all my energy on shielding the sight from Gaius's eyes.

The water raptor circles in the sky several times, drinking in the air, the sun on her feathered back, before she descends and lands on the beach before me. She holds her head high and proud, and I walk slowly towards her, the exertion of using my magic to keep us hidden taking an unexpected toll.

After a moment, she lowers her neck, her massive head stretching to meet mine, until we're so close that our breath and thoughts mingle as one.

When she hears what I desire, she grunts in understanding, unfurling a wing so that I can climb up on to her back. Her feathers are slick like oil and thick as rope, and I coil my hands around them to keep a grip, positioning myself just behind the first of the massive fins that run down her spine.

As soon as I'm secure, she senses it, and pushes away from the ground. We're rising towards the clouds and I can feel the world falling away beneath me. The sense of freedom is so acute I could almost forget the islands beneath us, and fly away with the raptor to explore the wider world. But, alas, I cannot. Nor can I even fly to the Eastern Isles, not without attracting a lot of unwanted attention. I cannot keep us hidden as we travel at such a speed.

Though I'm braced for it, the raptor's descent is sharp and swift, throwing me forward so that I'm forced to grab handfuls of feathers to stop from falling. She plunges back into the water with such speed and grace, I barely have time to fill my lungs before we're deep enough for all the light to disappear.

Slowly I release the air I swallowed. Once this would have terrified me. For so many years the ocean kept me captive on a ship because I feared it more than Adler. But now, in these still depths, I find a peace I hadn't expected. The world of water does not belong to me or any other human; it has no mistress but the moon and its elemental enchantments call to the magic now fused to my bones.

As my lungs begin to dangerously empty, the raptor resurfaces, allowing me time to breathe, and the moment I'm ready we once again submerge.

I revel in her speed and embrace the thick nothingness of the deep. In this moment I am not at war, not running for my life, fighting for my islands. There is no heartbreak, no pain. Nothing beyond the raw power of the raptor, and the crushing strength of the ocean. If I can harness even a fraction of their might, the Isles stand a chance.

*And your enemies will fall at your feet.*

Just like that, the need for vengeance rushes into the

space created by the stillness. So many have sought to do me wrong, to steal my life, to silence my voice. How I long for my very name to drive fear into their hearts. For them to regret ever betraying me. To have my revenge. This time I don't try to silence the thought.

I relish it.

The veil of mist that shrouds the Fifth Isle has always kept its secrets hidden. Tonight we become one of them. It's hard to say how long our journey has taken, for time moves differently on the back of a water raptor. Deep beneath the waves, the rising of the sun and moon meant little and my fleeting moments of air passed so quickly it was hard to be sure of the measure of light. I couldn't even judge by my hunger, for it had been so long since I'd eaten anything, the sharp pain had dulled to a constant ache.

All I know is no ship could ever have traversed both Western and Eastern waters with the speed of the raptor.

Her only moment of hesitation was when we reached the West–East divide. She had been bound to the Western Sea for her whole existence and feared what might happen if she were to break across.

I sensed her reservations as if they were my own and, in truth, I had no idea what might happen if we were to cross the boundary. But believing that if we simply were brave, nothing could hold us back, I'd stroked her feathers and willed her forward.

A defiance had stirred inside her, one that mirrored my own. Too long she had been shackled, too long a prisoner. Both of us were ready to tear all the walls around us to the ground, and together we'd hurtled through the ocean, defying ancient laws.

Since then we haven't looked back.

And now, finally, we are here, returned to the islands I've sacrificed so much for.

Under the protection of the moon, the water raptor delivers me safely to the shallows of the Fifth Isle, the mist concealing us from prying eyes. I slide down from her back, and tread water beside her.

She bends her neck, bringing her head close to mine.

'Thank you,' I say, leaning to press my forehead against the shell of her beak. 'I am grateful to you. Go now, be free. Be safe.'

She rears up, stretching her magnificent wings, and then, with a respectful nod of her head towards me, she dives, disappearing into the depths and leaving me quite alone.

I stare at the still water, momentarily bereft. But then I steel myself and swim towards land. My journey east may be over, but my mission has only just begun.

The island is cloaked in an eerie silence, as though the ground itself is holding its breath. As I walk up the cove and on to the thin grass, I press my palm against the earth and close my eyes. Somewhere deep below me, I sense ancient traces of magic lying dormant and ready to be awoken. It's reassuring to know that while most of the magic was purged, it was impossible for a single man to eradicate it entirely. For all his best attempts the old King Davin only suppressed magic, not destroyed it. But I can also sense the island is sick, as clearly as brushing a fevered forehead. It's rotting from within, the disease spreading. It sings a mournful song of sadness that moves me to tears.

I've been gone too long.

A lot has happened to me since I last came to this island, when I'd first become the Viper, when my crew and I were doing our best to undo the damage caused by Adler. But it's not only my life that's changed. The island has too. Harley warned me that the grazing lands weren't replenishing, that the animals were dying, and now I see for myself how true that is. Where once plains stretched from the coast to the mountains, there is now dusty earth, with a few weeds poking through the exposed soil. Where before woolly beasts roamed as far as the eye could see, now only skeletons remain. If this island isn't already dead, it soon will be.

I trudge inland, in search of a settlement. While this was the safest place to bring the raptor unnoticed, my final destination is the First, and I'm going to need some supplies to get there. Though looking around, I'm not sure there'll be much on offer.

It's about an hour before I reach the first sign of

habitation, a farming settlement for those who, at least once, tended to the flocks.

As I approach, I wonder if it's already been abandoned. The cottages on the outskirts have at some point been boarded up – though they look like they've since been ransacked.

And then I see the bodies. Hanging from crude gallows, swinging lifelessly from ropes, left for the birds to pick to pieces. Some are badly decomposed, others are not – there's at least one that looks like they died within the last day.

A blaze of fury flares in my gut at the sight. What has happened here?

Like a shadow, I enter the settlement, silent and unseen. At the centre of the small community, though it's the middle of the night, some sort of collection is taking place. A group of hard-looking men stand at the front of a line of bedraggled people, collecting everything from food to coins.

Bandits.

My rage is quick to rise, and I quietly approach a tiny woman near the end of the queue. Her skin looks like it's been stretched over bones, no flesh left to fill it out. She's been starving for some time.

'What is happening?'

She glances at me, but if she's surprised to see a strange woman, with hair and clothes still damp from the ocean, then she doesn't show it. I think perhaps she no longer cares.

'Daily offerings to the King's Guard.'

'Where are their uniforms then? They don't work for the King.'

'Anyone willing to take his money works for him now.'

So the King is using criminals to rob those who clearly have nothing left to give. I guess that's one thing that hasn't changed. The King is still a bastard.

'What are the offerings for?'

'Protection from those who wish to kill us for our land.'

'And do they? Protect you?'

This time when the woman looks at me, I see the flash of fury spark within her. 'My son is hanging out there. It was the King's Guard who strung him up.'

My anger, always simmering below the surface, rises up my throat like bile.

'What was his crime?'

'He did not make a sufficient contribution.' She spits the words with contempt.

Raised voices cause me to look up the line. An old man is crying out as the bandits wrestle with his companion.

'What are they doing?' I ask the woman.

She closes her eyes. 'His husband has not paid his

dues. He'll join the others on the gallows.'

I start to walk further up the line, watching as these so-called King's men hold the man down and loop the rope around his neck while his husband sobs and protests.

I know I came east for Torin. I know I shouldn't be drawing attention to myself. But when has that ever stopped me? A memory of the cave where I was a prisoner invades my mind, the thought of all the children I abandoned to save myself. Guilt and shame stoke my fury; my magic swells until I fear it might overflow.

*Stefta pokla.*

I don't even say the words out loud, merely think them; it's not even a conscious summons. But the mist of the island hears my call, sweeping in from the coastline to the settlement. I stare at it in wonder. My newfound power is exhilarating. My body hums with energy that ebbs and flows like a tide, rising up then down inside me. Ready to be unleashed.

*Do it.*

I give the mist my instructions, and it branches into tendrils, advancing on the King's bandits and weaving nooses round their necks.

The men are shouting, screaming, clawing at their own flesh in a vain attempt to free themselves. The islanders are shrinking back, terrified, seeking shelter and safety. But they needn't fear. They're in no danger.

I stride through the fog, unseen, and up to the man who seems to be in charge, before commanding the vapour around me to melt away.

'You work for the King?' I ask him as if he didn't have a rope of mist tight around his throat.

'Yes,' he gasps, his eyes wide with fear, hardly able to believe what's happening. He will never have seen magic before.

'But you're a bandit, no?'

The man nods, his skin starting to turn purple. 'I was recruited.'

'By whom?'

'The Viper.'

*Bronn?* My eyes narrow. 'What role does he play in this?'

'He does whatever the King asks of him. Recruiting mainly. Found me looting on the First and sent me here.'

Did he indeed? 'And he told you to hang those who can't pay what you demand?'

'No, that's King's orders. To set an example.'

I'm almost blinded by my rage. At the injustice. 'Then consider this me setting one of my own.'

*Rysa. Dregar.* With a clench of my fists the mist responds to my request. It rises, lifting the bandits off the ground and into the air, tightening around their necks. They dance in the sky, legs flailing, bodies shaking until they fall still, hanging over the settlement like ghosts swinging from gallows of mist.

For a moment I stare up at what I've done. I killed them. Executed them. It takes me a while to notice I'm trembling, breathing hard. But not from exertion. Not from guilt.

From the rush of power. And the uncomfortable realisation that I enjoyed it.

I steal a boat from the Fifth, and travel to the Second Isle. Before I left the settlement, I shared the coin of the King's Guard among the villagers, keeping only a little for myself, for my journey. I need more information before I approach the First, to build up a picture of what's been happening while I've been gone. As I travel across the Fallow Isle, nights at inns prove fruitful, tongues loosened by ale, spilling secrets I hoard like treasure.

Word of my death has reached the King and bled out over the islands, Talon delivering the message faster than Bronn could. Doubtless he rejoiced. The King left the mountains not long after my trial, returning to his main palace with Torin where the best healers were sought out to tend to the Prince. Meanwhile he's done little to help his people, and much to continue persecuting them. With every passing day my need to kill him builds like thunderclouds.

The Viper has still not returned from the West, but it won't be long before he does. I dread our inevitable reunion. No part of it will be pretty.

News of my retribution on the Fifth Isle doesn't seem to have travelled as quickly, though, and I pass unnoticed from town to town. A wisp of cloud. A thought slipped from memory. A lingering trace of nightmare.

From time to time I hear familiar names in conversations. Names I recognise from my trial. Governors and friends of the crown who sat on the jury and sentenced me to death for crimes I didn't commit. At every utterance the temptation torments me.

*Hunt them down and make them pay.*

It would be so easy, and remembering how the mist obeyed me makes me ache to do it again. To see what else I'm capable of.

Only the thought of Torin stays my hand. I must focus, continue to gather knowledge that will enable me to rescue him.

Which is precisely what I do. But on the very night I plan to leave, when I've harvested enough information to form my plan, a man walks into the inn where I'm staying. I'm in the corner, lost in shadows, but his drunken voice carries and I would recognise it anywhere. The lies he told about me were the most damning at the trial. The most heinous.

Lord Pyer, governor of the Sixth Isle, who stood at my trial and dragged my name and reputation through the mud, accusing me of deliberately sabotaging the mines, directly causing the suffering since. He assumed I would die, felt safe spewing blatant lies, and now here he is, laughing, drinking, gambling – while I have been to hell and beyond.

He's rowdy and vulgar, groping the serving woman, and I stare at him with loathing.

*He deserves it.*

I fight the thought. I mustn't get distracted. I always get distracted.

*He's right here. What's the harm? You can sail to the First tomorrow.*

I close my eyes, trying to stifle the memory of how I felt at the trial, how weak, how exposed. My mind wanders inevitably to the cave. Nowhere left me as broken and as vulnerable as my prison there. My torture.

But I survived. I'm here. And I'm not weak any more.

I can taste my desire for my enemies' blood, the need to crush them almost overwhelming. The woman I once was believed in justice. The woman I am now lusts for vengeance. And it's within my grasp.

They tried me as an assassin. So that is what I shall be.

When Lord Pyer retires for the night, I follow. He's

far too inebriated to notice as he stumbles up to his room. Moments later, I try the handle – he's so drunk he forgot to lock the door, and I enter the room unchallenged.

Lord Pyer, distant cousin to the King, has collapsed in a drunken stupor on his bed. I could kill him in his sleep, but why should he receive such a merciful end?

Instead I shove the wooden frame hard. 'Wake up.'

He stirs, shuffling upwards in confusion, and groggily staring at me until recognition drops.

'You?'

'Hello, Lord Pyer.'

He glances at the dagger resting at his bedside.

'Go ahead,' I say. 'Pick it up.'

Pyer hesitates, then lunges for the blade. It amuses me to see he feels safer with it in his hand, as if I could be remotely threatened by it or him.

'You're supposed to be dead,' he says, his voice trembling a little.

I smile. 'Who says I'm not? Can your ghosts not return to haunt you?'

'What do you want?'

I take a step towards him, want him to know I am not afraid. 'Revenge.'

He strikes first, leaping from his bed, jabbing his dagger blindly back and forth at me with pitiful skill. The privileged fool hasn't had to fight a day in his life.

I barely have to shift my weight to dodge his attacks, laughing as he loses his balance and falls to the floor.

'Is that the best you can do?' I say, discovering I wish to taunt him. 'Pathetic.'

He looks up at me, eyes wide with terror.

'Come on,' I say, holding up my hands in mock surrender. 'I'm not even armed.'

He scrambles back to his feet, and tries once again to plunge his dagger into my chest. This time I grab him by the wrist and twist it hard so that the bone snaps beneath my fingers.

With a cry he drops to his knees.

I lean down until my mouth is close to his ear. 'Tell me, Lord Pyer, why did you lie about me at the trial? Was it fear of the King, self-preservation or sheer malice?'

'I did nothing wrong. I only told the truth.'

I look him deep in the eye. 'Oh, Lord Pyer, that was unwise.' I twist the already shattered wrist a little further. 'Perhaps you should learn to separate fact from fiction before I break every part of you.'

He glares at me with undiluted hatred until, with a sharp jerk, I dislocate his elbow, and he finally yields. 'The King knew I'd been allowing your father to take crystal for himself, after taking my cut. It was testify against you or be ruined.'

'You would have let an innocent be executed to cover your own sins?'

Pyer's face creases with contempt. 'You are no innocent. Nor was your father. No one aboard that ship can claim honour when savagery runs in your veins.'

'You look down your nose at the Viper and his crew because they are so beneath you in station?'

'I am a cousin to the King. I am royalty. Of course my blood is worth more.'

A burst of magical outrage surges from my fingertips and scorches into his flesh.

'You. Are. Worth. Nothing.' With every word, I tighten my grip and his cries grow louder.

Eventually I release him, and he clutches his arm protectively to his chest, which heaves from the sobs he's suppressing.

'And you are nothing but the she-devil offspring of a dead man.' Despite his pain and terror, he's still able to be outraged at my existence.

'You want to know who I am?' It's rising now, the magic, and with it the cruel part of me that's so longed to be unleashed, like a heat that is burning from the inside out.

*Lifya byndi*. The thought is directed at the cords holding back the bed's drapes. At my command they unknot themselves and slither snake-like towards him, coiling round his arms before dragging him on to the bed, until he's splayed out, tied so tightly to the four posts that he can barely breathe.

Pyer stares open-mouthed in disbelief. I stand over him. 'I am not Adler's child. I am the rightful Queen of the West. I am a Mage. And I am tired of men like you. You value wealth over truth, justice, morality? Then you shall have it.' I throw a coin on to the bed.

*Meirpa*. A thought is all it takes. One coin becomes two, and then four. They multiply, slow at first then faster, the pile growing up around his trapped body and I watch with both awe and satisfaction as they bury Pyer, the weight crushing him so that he cannot even struggle, and his mouth, wide in shock, soon fills, until he is drowned by the coins he valued so much.

I stay even after he is silenced by such a fitting death. When I release the enchantment, the gold disappears in a moment, only the original coin remaining. I pick it up, and walk away, snaking back through the inn, where the drunken din has drowned out all Pyer's screams. As I disappear into the night, I find myself smiling. For so long I've denied wanting power, but now its presence intoxicates me.

I can't pretend any longer. I'm not going to the palace. Not just yet. I still have time. My enemies don't. I've tasted revenge and my hunger is far from sated.

The truth is, I'm just getting started.

I become a huntress. I track my prey over the islands with a dogged determination, counting down the days to the blood moon. A lying jury member here, a corrupt official there, and with every kill, every wrong avenged, my magic strengthens, making me more powerful, more unstoppable.

Every step has brought me closer to Torin. Tonight I shall save my prince. And kill the King.

Under the watchful eyes of the stars I easily scale the ivy rooted in the palace walls, stealing my way in like a disease.

When I reach the room I'm looking for, the windows are bolted shut, but metal is no concern to me. I learned that in Gaius's cave. *Brena, hyrri.* Once again, I only have to think the incantation for the magic to work; the bars, the chains, the locks all melt, trailing like molten vines down the rock. The shutters open for me and I enter the room unchallenged.

As the moonlight spills from behind the clouds, I look to the bed. But it's empty. In the same moment I hear the shuffle behind me and spin round in time to grab his wrist as he tries to bring down a vase upon my head.

'Sharpe, it's me,' I whisper.

His grip relaxes and I catch the vase before it smashes on the stone floor. 'No,' he says, shaking his head in disbelief. 'You're dead.' His hands reach for my face, seeking out my familiar features. 'Yet you don't feel like a ghost.'

'I'm not. Or at least, I don't think I am.'

For a moment he doesn't speak, but then he pulls me towards him, holding me tight in an embrace. 'I thought we'd lost you too.'

The warmth of it burns and only then do I realise how cold my heart has become. Cruelty is all my body has known for the longest time, since the Hooded captured me in the West, and this act of friendship sears into me, reminding my soul of things lost in my previous life.

I pull away, not wanting such reminders. I don't want my ice to melt, don't want to turn away from the quenchless need for revenge. It drives me, sustains me, strengthens me.

A flicker of confusion passes over Sharpe's face. Even without sight he sees I'm different.

'How are you here? *Why* are you here?'

'Because it's time for us to wake Torin up. Together.'

He clutches me tightly, the hope rising in him. 'They haven't let me see him these many months – not since your trial.' He hesitates. 'I do not know if he's still alive.'

'He is,' I say, taking his hand. 'He has to be. Come on, let's find him.'

'How can we?' Sharpe asks. 'I'm locked in.'

'Is there a guard stationed outside?'

'Not for some time now.'

'Then let's go.'

He pulls me back again. 'I'm unarmed.'

A crooked smile tugs my lips at the thrill of danger. 'So am I.'

Once again I see it, the look on his face, a frown of concern. What would he say if he knew what I did on the Mist Isle? Or to Pyer and the others? Would he agree that I had no choice?

My magic makes short work of the lock, and I open the door. All my senses are on alert, heightened by the magic coursing through me. The corridors are quiet in this wing, and I hold Sharpe's hand tightly as we slip unseen towards the healing room. I've heard that Torin is being kept close to the healer at all times. I guess if they're having to keep him in an unnatural sleep, they need constant access to medicines.

The castle has been still, its residents' slumber not yet disturbed by the sun, but as we reach the healer's room, our luck runs out. It is guarded by two men. But I realise I'm not disappointed. My skin is tingling with the need to fight. To draw blood.

I make no effort to conceal myself, walking straight up to them, watching with satisfaction as their mouths drop open in horror, their brains trying to make sense of my presence.

'Let us pass,' I say, my voice deep with warning as I let go of Sharpe's hand and step forward.

To their credit the men stand their ground.

'Let us pass and I will let you live.' It's their last chance.

They don't take it.

I don't need a weapon or magic. Swiftly, before they can move, I swing out at the guard on the right, jabbing my elbow hard into his throat. He buckles in pain, and his companion turns to defend him, only I'm faster, and pull the man in front of me as a shield, so that the sword slips into his belly and not mine.

While the guard gapes in shock at what he's done, I snatch up the dead man's weapon and thrust it into his friend's chest. With a strained grunt he falls forward, his body landing on top of the other.

'Marianne?'

I can hear the doubt in Sharpe's tone. But I don't care. I gave them a chance and they refused to take it. Their deaths are on them, not me.

I hand him the sword. 'Here, you might need this.'

I'm half expecting him to object, but he doesn't. His grip tightens round the hilt as if his hand has been incomplete without a weapon in it. I watch the tension mount in his jaw and realise he's afraid. Not for himself, but for Torin. Afraid that we might be too late.

'Come on,' I say, leading him so he doesn't trip over corpses or slip on blood.

Again the door is locked, but with one thought it

swings wide and I take in the sight before me.

The healer is leaning over Torin, his hand poised to pour an orange liquid into the lifeless prince's mouth.

'Don't come any closer!' he says, holding his other hand up in warning. 'Or I'll make sure your beloved prince never wakes up.'

Before I can do anything, Sharpe surges towards the sound of the healer's voice and grabs him by the throat, so that he spills the contents of the vial.

'Don't even dare touch him again,' Sharpe says murderously, and just like when he hugged me, I experience that distant sense of warmth. Of affection. It's like the memory of a faded fragrance, beautiful but sad. Because I realise that I cannot afford to linger in the comfort it offers. Not if I want true power. And I must have power, I've been through too much to turn away now.

While Sharpe restrains the quivering healer, I stride over and crouch beside Torin, resting my hand on his cheek.

The last time I saw him, he was bleeding out on our wedding bed, fading from one life to the next. Now he is pale and lifeless, but the faint touch of breath assures me he's not gone yet. My heart tightens with fear for him. I've left him for so long. Too long. Perhaps I was wrong to assume he was safe until the blood moon. Perhaps this is a prophecy I can't cheat.

'Torin?' I speak the word softly into his ear. 'Wake up.' When he doesn't stir, I try again, this time with magic. '*Vakja*.'

Still nothing.

I spin round to the healer and pull him from Sharpe's grasp. 'What have you been giving him?'

The healer is too afraid to answer, but his gaze shifts to the vial still clutched in his hand. I snatch it from him, and inhale the smell.

The bitter scent of woodflax burns my nostrils, and my eyes narrow. 'How long have you been poisoning him?'

Woodflax is pernicious and unpredictable. If the healer has been dosing Torin with it for months, it's no wonder he didn't respond to my words alone. To counteract such a toxin will take all the skill I possess.

The healer has the ingredients I need, and I begin to snatch up jars and bottles, mixing together a tonic that will reverse the effects of the poison and bring Torin back to us.

'What are you doing?' Sharpe asks, still holding the healer to prevent him from running.

'Saving our prince.' After that I don't speak, concentrating entirely on mixing up the potion. To make it work, I'll need something from the one who's been responsible for the sleep, something offered, not taken. I don't expect cooperation, but I'm unconcerned.

When it's almost ready, I walk over to the healer, and without warning, thrust my hand into his mouth and, with a sharp crack, wrench out a tooth.

He screams in pain, but I ignore him, holding up his tooth, root and all, in front of his bleeding face.

'Give this to me freely.' It's not a request. When he says nothing, I step closer towards him. 'Or I'll take them all.'

'Have it,' he sobs. 'I give it freely.'

Permission granted, I punch him hard in his bleeding jaw, rendering him unconscious. I have no further use for him.

Ignoring Sharpe's frown, I take the tooth to the pestle and mortar and grind it up until it's nothing but dust. Then I stir it into the potion.

Once it's ready, I carry the liquid to Torin. Cradling his head, I slowly pour the tonic down his throat, whispering magic over him as I do so.

When I've done all I can, I stand up and I rest my hand on Sharpe's arm. 'Go to him.'

I guide him to the edge of Torin's bed and then step away. My part is over.

Sharpe gently moves his fingers over Torin's body, mapping his way up to his face, where he cups Torin's head in his hands.

'Come back to me, my love,' he whispers with such tenderness I think my cold heart might break.

Sharpe leans forward, his lips brushing Torin's. 'Please come back.'

Nothing happens. And then, just when I'm losing hope, when I fear nothing can undo what has been done, Torin's eyes flicker open.

‘Am I dreaming?’ Torin’s voice is raw, barely a whisper. But it’s there.

Relief floods through me with a force to rival the magic. He’s alive.

Sharpe is smiling down at Torin with undisguised joy. ‘Not any more.’ And the kiss they share speaks of all they’ve endured: the pain, the heartache, the separation and the sheer bliss of finding each other again.

When their embrace ends, Torin tries to move but winces.

‘It will take a while for your strength to return,’ I say. ‘Give the tonic time to heal you.’

Torin turns his head at the sound of my voice, noticing me at last. ‘Marianne.’ He sounds so happy to see me, it hurts. ‘What happened?’

‘Do you remember anything?’ Sharpe asks him, helping Torin sit up.

Torin’s forehead creases, and the lines only deepen as his memories return. ‘I was stabbed.’

I nod. ‘Yes.’

‘I feared you were dead,’ Sharpe says, resting his head against Torin’s.

Torin presses his palm to Sharpe's cheek. 'You can't get rid of me that easily.'

'I thought losing my sight was the worst thing that could happen to me, but I didn't know true darkness until I lost you.'

Torin looks at Sharpe in a way that makes my chest ache. I remember when Bronn used to look at me like that. *Bronn.* The thought of him is a physical pain and my fingers absently brush my neck. He should be in Eastern waters by now. And soon I shall have to face him. I close my eyes, and try to block out the thought, turning my back on Torin and Sharpe, leaving them to their reunion. Let them have their happy moment; there will be precious few others.

While they talk, I drag the guards' bodies inside the room, not wanting them to be discovered and the alarm raised. I ignore the way Torin stares over at me as I do so, and say very little when Sharpe fills Torin in on the events directly after he was stabbed. It feels like a lifetime ago. No, it's more than that. It feels like it happened to a different person: one who was weak, afraid of the darkness always shadowing the corners of her being. I see now how wrong that was. As I embrace the magic a little more with every breath, I understand that it's not me who should fear it, but others.

Starting with the King.

As soon as the sun has risen, I turn on my heel and

leave the room without a backwards glance. With Torin safe I can turn my attention to his father. It's time for the King to answer for his crimes.

I'm done hiding. This palace should be Torin's and mine. I will not creep about our home like a common thief. My eyes are blazing with the fire that burns inside me, the bloodlust that runs in my veins.

The corridors are not as empty now. Courtiers and advisors are taking early-morning strolls through the palace halls and when they see me they scream. A ghost returned for vengeance, spattered with blood.

Some soldiers appear at the commotion and raise their swords, though I can see their hands shaking. I could fight them; I would win. But I'm in a hurry, and don't want to waste my time with people insignificant to my mission. *Brena*. A simple thought is all it takes, and their swords glow red-hot, scorching their hands before clattering to the ground. The soldiers shrink back from me in terror, and do nothing to stop me walking past. The power is dizzying, my craving for it only growing.

No one else is stupid enough to challenge me as I stroll towards the throne room. Some freeze to the spot as I pass, others flee. Is this how it feels to rule? Because for the first time I'm starting to understand what motivated Adler, what turned the King into a man willing to go to any lengths to keep his power.

And, with a start, I realise I can even see what drives Gaius. The thought makes my stomach lurch. But no. I am nothing like Gaius.

Still, I can't pretend I don't enjoy the sensation of control as I sweep unchallenged into the room of the most powerful and protected man in all the East.

The guards turn to face me as the heavy doors swing open at my command. Blades are raised to point at me. I ignore them; my eyes are only for the King.

'Surprise.'

He's staring down at me from his throne, eyes narrowing with irritation. 'So the Viper didn't kill you after all.'

'Who says he didn't?' I say with a cold smile.

Hesitation flickers across his face before he regains his composure. 'No matter, I shall finish the job. Seize her!'

I tut at him as I shake my head. Poor fool. He mistakes me for the girl he imprisoned many moons ago. He has no idea who he's dealing with now.

I think the words: *rysa stejot.* As if sensing some unseen danger, the King stands, his hand moving to his sword, but when he tries to step forward he gasps in horror.

The stone floor is rising, over his ankles then up his legs, entombing him in solid rock, along with every one of his guards. Only my body remains free. The stone is eager to do its part to help me, tired of witnessing centuries of injustice and being powerless to stop it. Though the men shout for help, no one comes. There's no one to save them from their fate. When the stone has encased them as high as their waists, I command it to rest.

I stride up to the King, and a thrill of pleasure spikes through me to see fear in his face. Finally. Finally he understands who I am. What I can do.

'We have a lot of catching up to do, Your Majesty,' I say, my voice laced with danger.

The King is staring at me like he's woken from a nightmare only to find it hasn't ended. 'Why didn't you die?' he says, still struggling to accept what's happening.

'I did,' I say, and I walk closer to him. 'But what makes you think death can stop me?'

The King swallows hard. 'What do you want? Gold, jewels? Titles? I'll grant you a full pardon, restore you to your ship if you wish.'

The King would sell me his soul right now if I asked. I simply have no use for it.

'Have you dreamed of this moment, as I have?' I ask him, ignoring the audience of half-statues watching me.

The King doesn't answer. He doesn't have to. I doubt any of his dreams ended like this.

'I have imagined the many ways I might kill you.

With fire? Should I scorch the sins from your flesh?' I unfurl my fist, and a flame dances on the palm of my hand. Though I can feel its heat, it causes me no pain. 'Or with ice? To match your frozen heart.' And the flame crackles as heat gives way to cold and an icicle forms in its place. 'Before you die, I want you to suffer the same depth of pain that you inflicted on me. Retribution. Moment for moment.' I take a step closer. 'A cruel death for a cruel king. After all, you are at least partly responsible for making me a woman capable of the long, excruciating torture that will be your end. A woman without mercy.'

'Marianne, stop.' Torin's commanding voice cuts through the air. He's walking slowly but surely into the room, Sharpe standing beside him.

The King looks at his son in astonishment, as if he had already been thinking of him as dead too. 'You're awake.'

Torin glances at me. 'Only because of the woman you tried to execute.'

The King feigns innocence. 'That woman,' he says, pointing at me, 'should have been put down a long time ago.'

I step forward, flames spontaneously forming in the palms of my hand.

'Marianne.' Torin touches my arm gently. 'Don't kill him.'

I swallow back the rage and the flames diminish. I'm not even sure where they came from; I gave no command. They simply formed from within me.

Torin glances around at the guards, still encased in stone. 'Can you free them?' he asks me. 'I want to talk to my father alone.'

I silently ask the stone to release them all, including the King, and the moment the guards are free, they run. Not one of them remains to defend their ruler. Not one even considers it.

'My son,' the King says when they are gone, with an unconvincing attempt at affection, 'I thought I'd lost you, truly. But you're here; you're alive. It's time we took back control of the island from those who seek to steal our throne. We can rule together, you and I, as it always should have been.'

'You're right,' Torin says to his father's delight. I eye him sideways. 'It *is* time to take back control. I've lost months of my life and I don't intend to waste another moment.'

He reaches and takes Sharpe's hand in his own. The King's eyes narrow at the sight.

'Marianne wanted to dispatch you as soon as she returned from killing Adler. I persuaded her otherwise, intending to give you a chance to step down with dignity. But you refused that chance. I should have known what lengths you would go to just to cling to power. After all, you've never hidden your true colours from me. And in return for my goodwill, what did you do? You drugged me into silence. You put my wife on trial and sentenced her to death. You allowed bandits to run riot over the islands, and you have forsaken our people.'

Now Torin steps forward, away from Sharpe and towards his father and I have never seen such anger blaze in his eyes. Judging from the apprehension on the King's face, neither has he.

Torin's voice drops low, menacing. 'But do you know the worst thing you did? The reason I am going to take your throne from you without a moment's hesitation? You hurt the man I love. You tortured him, nearly broke him, and I will never, ever forgive you for that.'

Torin turns his head towards me, his beauty only enhanced by his righteous anger. 'He's all yours,' he says.

The King whips his head between us, as I smile with anticipation.

'You told her not to hurt me,' he shouts.

Torin looks at the man who has done nothing but mistreat him since he was born. There is no pleasure in his expression, but nor is there regret. 'I told her not to kill you. Beyond that I don't care what she does.'

And giving me a nod of permission, Torin returns to

Sharpe, and they walk out together, the door slamming behind them. The King and I are alone.

The first time we were alone I was weak and isolated. When I asked for help, he assaulted me, blackmailed me and then betrayed me.

The last time I saw him, I was stronger, I had allies. Yet he forced people to lie about me, made people believe that I had committed his and Adler's crimes and condemned me to death.

Now we are alone again. But this time there is no weakness.

There will be no mercy today – and he knows it.

The King backs slightly away from me. As if somehow he can escape.

'Marianne,' he says. He's going to plead with me, the fool. 'Everything I've done has been for the good of the islands.'

Does he actually believe that? Or is he just saying what he thinks I want to hear?

'Everything you've done has been for the good of one person and one person only,' I say, stepping towards him, my prey in my sights. 'It's time to pay the price for your villainy.'

'If you hurt me, Torin won't forgive you, whatever he may say. The boy's always been too soft.'

Unbelievable. Even now he cannot bring himself to think well of his only child. He should be so proud of his son but can only dismiss him as inferior.

'You don't deserve Torin,' I say, advancing towards him until he backs up, tripping and stumbling into his throne. 'He is good and he is kind and he is wise. He is going to be the best king these islands have ever known. I do not think he will weep for you, or even think of you beyond today. But if he doesn't forgive me?' I crouch before the King, amused by how his fear has paralysed him. 'Well, here's the thing. I don't care.'

There's panic in his eyes now, as if he can see the magic rising up in me like a snake about to strike. My fangs are laced with venom and I shall sink them deep.

I reach forward and lift the crown from his head. I can smell his sweat as I do so, feel his ragged breath warm on my face.

'This no longer belongs to you,' I say, crouching to place it on to the ground. I look up at the King, drinking in his confusion. 'You know, when I came to you all that time ago, wanting to help you – I was genuine. If you had only worked with me, rather than selling me out to Adler, then all of this could have been avoided. I want you to remember that – that it was you who made me your enemy.'

'Then give me another chance.' He's frantic now. 'I'll do as you and Torin ask, I swear. I'll abdicate, disappear from public life, you'll never see me again.'

'You really will say anything to save your sorry skin,

won't you?' I say. 'That's the problem with men like you, men who've always had power, always abused it and never been held to account. You think you can bargain your way out of anything.'

'I'll hand over everything to you. All that I have.'

I narrow my eyes at him. 'Even now you fail to understand. There is no way out. Not this time. Because you would slither away for a while, but you'd return. Drawn back to power like a drunk to his bottle. And I can't allow that.'

'There must be something!' The King is desperate. 'Anything!'

I stand up, wanting to look down at him. Wanting him to look up at me. 'There is only one thing I desire.'

'Yes, it's yours,' he says eagerly.

'I want you to suffer.'

He cries out, squirming away from me in the throne that has become a prison. Like all bullies, the King is a coward. And there's nowhere left to run.

'Your head looks so empty without a crown,' I say. 'Let's fix that, shall we?'

There's a spider scuttling along the arm of the throne, and I take it into my hand. I whisper the word *meirpa* over it, before placing it on the King's head. It scurries around his forehead, and then, just as the coins did before, it doubles to two spiders, then four, until a whole cluster of them spin their silk, creating a crown of their own. The magic barely needs prompting any more; it's always there, ready to serve. It's exhilarating.

'Behold, a crown befitting you,' I say to the King, who whimpers as I make the spiders disappear. 'A web of your lies. A web of your betrayals.' I pause to ensure he's listening. 'I am going to take your most dangerous weapon. Your mind.'

And as he screams in terror, vainly struggling to evade my touch, I place my fingers on to his web crown, merely thinking the word *takarr* – steal – and summon his memories, his dreams, his ambitions, his every thought until his body is still and nothing remains in his head. It has all been absorbed by the web crown.

The room is silent. The King remains on his throne, staring forward with blank eyes and an expressionless face. Breathing but not living.

I lift the crown from his head, and blow over the fragile strands. Instantly they disperse like dust. Gone for ever. The King no longer poses any threat to his son or the Isles. And I inhale the victory like air.

*Look what I did!* It wasn't even hard. It was magnificent.

A glint at his waist catches my eye. I pull a dagger from his belt and hold it up in disbelief. I had thought I'd never see this again – the blade he took from me the first time I visited. Bejewelled and beautiful. My eighteenth birthday gift. I tuck it into my own belt, relishing the irony of being reunited with it now.

Because there is only one person left for me to face here. The man who gave me this dagger: Bronn.

I watch as the *Maiden* glides silently through the still Eastern waters towards the First Isle. Word is yet to reach them of the King's reckoning or Torin's awakening. With Talon as my faithful accomplice, I have intercepted every sea vulture that Torin has sent to the *Maiden* to warn her I was coming. Because despite the fact that I left without telling him where I was going, he knew exactly where I was headed.

But the only message I want Bronn to receive is mine.

The night water is like silk grazing against my skin as I glide through it, the cold a caress to the ice crackling in my veins. I scale the side of the *Maiden*, my touch gentle as I greet her. There was a time I didn't think I'd ever stand upon her deck again, and despite everything, I'm glad to be here. The ship is my ally, ready to welcome me home, content to hide me in her shadows as I creep towards the nearest night watchman.

My blade is at his neck before he knows what's happening. He's new. Bronn's been recruiting. What stories has he been told about me? Is he afraid?

'I have a message for your captain,' I say softly in

his ear. 'Tell the Viper I do not wish his crew any harm; it's him I seek. Tell him to come to where the moon lies on the ground, and to come alone. Do this and I'll spare you. Should you refuse . . .' I press the dagger closer to his skin. 'Well. Consider this a warning.'

The moment I summon the thought to my mind, all the ropes on the ship – from the rigging and the masts to unused coils on the deck – transform into living black vipers. They slither and slide their way along the deck, their fangs bared, poised to strike.

I can smell the man's fear, I savour it – and then I'm gone as quickly as I appeared, retreating first into the shadows and then the sea.

When I hear the shouting grow louder, I smile to myself, imagining the surprise on the crew's faces when they try to kill the vipers I've left for Bronn. Because for each one they cut down with their blades, two will spring back in its place. I learned in the West that you cannot fight magic with steel.

It's only as the sun rises that I release the enchantment and free the *Maiden* from the vipers. They've served their purpose. My message will have been well and truly received.

In a different lifetime Bronn drew me a picture of a crystal-clear lake on the Second Isle. He knew how much I loved that drawing, and he'll understand where I am now.

I'm waiting on the shore, and, just as in Bronn's sketch, the moon is perfectly reflected in the still pool, giving the impression that it's fallen to earth, a small orb lying in the clearing. But tonight its waters are crimson in the light of the blood moon.

There will be no barbaric rituals to ward off its evil influence this time, no murdering of silver seals. There's only one thing the Viper will wish to hunt. Me.

Bronn will come, I'm certain of it. He'll want to protect his crew above all else, and I'm using this to my advantage. I had to be sure he'd come.

I'm standing in the bloody moonlight, not bothering to hide. The time for deception is long past. Tonight only truth and consequences matter.

I hear him before I see him. His tread, though soft, is one I've listened out for all my life, sometimes with longing, sometimes with dread. My fingers tingle to reach my blade, but I resist for now, though I know what's coming.

Bronn makes to strike, thinking me unaware, but I've heard the shift in his weight, felt the movement in the air, and I duck away, his fist sailing through nothing, as I throw my body into his chest, knocking him backwards. Catching him off guard makes me smile, because the last time we fought I was at a serious disadvantage and far from my best. Tonight I've never been better.

Bronn recovers quickly, and he grabs me hard, shoving me against the rocks, his arm pinning me still, and for the first time since he cut my throat we are face to face and staring at each other.

Uncertainty flashes in his eyes, but then he blinks and it's replaced with a torrent of emotion. Fear, confusion . . . relief.

He hadn't really believed it was me who left the message. Thought I still lay dead where he left me in the West. But now . . . now he knows.

His grip relaxes just a fraction. 'It's you,' he whispers. And just as quickly, doubt makes his grip tighten tenfold. 'How?' His gaze moves swiftly to my throat, to my perfectly healed skin. 'I killed you.'

'I know,' I say, my voice cold. 'I was there.' And I push him away from me with an unnatural force, my strength taking him by surprise.

He looks at me in a way he never has before. Like he has no idea who I am.

I'm not sure any more either.

Recovering quickly, Bronn brings himself to his full height. 'Tell me how,' he demands. 'How are you still alive?'

A wave of anger consumes me. Irrational, vengeful anger. At him, at me, at how horribly unbearable this is . . . at *everything*. 'How do you think?' My shout bounces off the rocks, my rage echoing through the night.

This time, when Bronn stares at me, he sees it. The difference. And it only fuels *his* anger. 'Magic? You used *magic*?' He vents his frustration on the nearest stone, kicking it hard, so that it flies through the air and shatters the surface of the pool. But before the spray has even settled, his mind has moved on, and his head whips back to look at me. 'You planned this?'

When I don't answer, not trusting myself to speak, Bronn does the only thing he knows will provoke me. He attacks.

My dagger is in my hand in time to block his blow, and the next, until we're locked in a desperate fight fed by betrayal and heartbreak. Each strike of steel is a reminder of what we've done to each other, the tangled mess of love and lies that have brought us to this place.

'You bloody planned it all, didn't you?' He spits out the words as he tries to corner me.

'I asked for your trust.' I slip past him, so now he's the one close to being cornered.

'You asked for far more than that, and you know it.'

He's right, of course. But he was the only one I could ask. Even though I knew what the cost would be: his hatred, his wrath, and never his forgiveness.

My guilt makes my blood run as cold as ice. 'You got your reward.'

I may as well have struck him with the blade.

'You think I give a damn about being Viper?' He swings hard, so that I only just avoid his dagger this time, and the taste of his fury excites me. I want this fight to be bloody. I want it to hurt.

'You'll thank me one day.' My words sound more like a hiss.

'You asked me to kill you!'

We're standing pressed together, blades at each other's throats, bodies heaving from exertion and rage, breath mingling. And in that moment none of it matters. There's nothing but me and him, and the fact that we're alive. Together. Alone.

Our lips meet hard and fast, passion overriding every other emotion. It's as if we've been suffocating and now we can finally breathe, our kiss the air in our lungs.

Our blades fall to the floor, forgotten; all that exists is our need for each other, our hunger, our pain.

But just as quickly as our embrace began, Bronn ends it, pulling away, shattering the moment.

He sits down beside the pool, defeated. Leaving some distance between us, I settle to the ground too.

'You asked me to kill you,' he says again, this time in a whisper.

It's true, I did. And honestly, I hadn't expected it to work. It was the plan of a desperate woman. To fight him on the sands of the Eighth Isle, which had always spoken to me, to be killed in a way that would take long enough for me to work my magic at a time when I was guarded by Esther's protective incantations. To have a chance to save myself. To have a chance to become a Mage.

I knew it was a lot to ask of Bronn, especially after I'd broken his heart. To trust me. To kill me. But he did as I asked and now I see what it's cost us both. We've lost each other.

'It was the only way,' I say quietly. 'I had to die.'

I tell him everything. Everything that happened since I left him in Western waters, even though some of it he knows from Rayvn. His face remains emotionless, even when I tell him what Gaius did to me.

'I've fought the magic inside me for so long,' I say, exhausted by it all. 'But, Bronn, Gaius is incredibly powerful. He cannot be fought with a blade. Only a Mage can hope to beat him. I know it was a risk, but I had to try.'

'Then why not cut your own neck? Why drag me into it?'

'So you could legitimately become the Viper. So that Gaius would believe me dead and not search for me.' I sigh. Bronn's not going to like this next bit. 'And so

Gaius would believe you a potential ally.'

I knew Gaius would be searching for me, for any trace of my magic, and by lifting Esther's protection around the beach for a short while, I was inviting him to watch the stage I'd set. To see Bronn and me fighting. To see him slash my neck. I wanted Gaius to think I was dead, needed him not to be looking for me. I wanted him to look instead to Bronn, and see a shared hatred for me. My fragile plans depended on these things being witnessed – and believed.

Bronn is glaring at me. 'Is that all I am to you? A player on a stage?'

'I did what I thought was necessary.'

'Do you know what it did to me?' His voice is low. 'I've barely slept since that day, believing you were dead, and at my hand. I have seen that moment over and over until I've wanted to tear my own eyes out.'

I daren't look at him, not wanting to carry his pain along with my own.

'You told me to trust you, and I did, but you could have trusted *me*.'

'I couldn't risk it.'

He's silent for a moment. 'Why do you want him to think of me as an ally?'

'Gaius has a history of using the Viper to do his dirty work. He used one to wipe out the Western royalty, another to steal a secret princess. I'm hoping he might want to utilise your skills now. Having a spy could help us fight him.'

'Us?' He shakes his head. 'You made it very clear to me that there is no *us* any more.'

'And yet you came anyway. You came West for me.' My voice is so soft it's barely audible. But I know he hears it.

He just chooses to ignore me. He rises to his feet and throws a pebble into the pool, and I count the ripples as they spread. Each one is another second in which Bronn's silence grows louder.

'What exactly do you want me to do?' Bronn says eventually. There is no warmth to his voice.

'I want you to go West. He has children, Bronn. He takes them from their families, locks them in cages, steals from their souls. I want you to ally yourself with Gaius. Find out where the children are, who exactly is working with him and what he intends to do. Then we're going to stop him.'

Bronn laughs. It's a hollow, humourless sound. 'You're not my captain any more. I'm done taking orders from you.'

'This isn't about me,' I say, and I can hear the anger rising in my voice. At least it disguises the sting of the implication that he had only come to the Eighth Isle because I was still his captain. 'This is about the Isles. You think Gaius will stop at consuming the West? Once he's done with them, he'll come here and everything we've fought for will be lost.'

'You have some nerve, pretending you care about the East,' he says. 'You haven't been here. You left.'

'And then I came back.'

Bronn turns on me. 'For what?'

'For revenge!' I shout the words without meaning to. They haunt the air between us. 'I came back to make my enemies pay, to make them rue the day they betrayed me and end the King once and for all. And that's exactly what I've done.'

'What happened to you?' Bronn's looking at me like I'm a stranger. 'Killing for revenge? That's not you.'

'It is now.' I'm too angry, too defensive, and he knows it.

'And has it made you feel any better?'

'You were the one who told me we didn't have the luxury of making right choices. That sometimes we have to get our hands dirty.'

'And you were the one who left me rather than do that!'

Finally. His pain explodes from him, raw and unguarded. He bends down to pick up my dagger and then strides towards me, his arms stretched wide, his chest exposed.

'If revenge is what you came for, then take it.'

He grabs my wrist, pushing the blade into my hand and positioning it against his heart. 'Kill me as I killed you.'

Though he'd only done it because I asked him to, though nothing that happened on that beach was his fault, for a moment I'm tempted. The tip of my blade grazes his shirt, and I imagine the skin beneath, the muscle behind it, and then his heart beyond that, beating in time to my own.

Magic swells inside me, urging me on. *End it.*

My own heart seems to freeze at such an impulse.

Shocked by the thought, I lower the dagger. 'You are not my enemy, Bronn.' I step away from him, and he drops his arms. Is he relieved? I can no longer tell. His face is as impenetrable as it was in the years we did not speak. 'I didn't seek you out for revenge. Believe what you will, but I care for the East just as I always have.' *And for you. I still care for you.* 'I will fight for the islands and I'd rather do it with your help. But if you want, I will leave now, and you'll never see me again. It's up to you.'

Bronn stares at the ground, his weight shifting. He's tempted too. Tempted to walk away, from me, from us, from the tattered mess of our relationship. He rubs the back of his neck, and sighs deeply.

'Tell me, Marianne, why should I do anything you ask of me?'

He's asking for a reason to trust me, to trust us.

But just moments ago, I nearly slid a blade into his chest, and I look him square in the eye. 'You shouldn't.'

The walk back across the island is filled with torturous silence.

I'm not sure why he's made this choice. For the islands? For his new king? Out of guilt? The only thing I can be certain of? It's not for me.

We reach his boat, banked in the sand, and push it into the water together. He grabs the oars before I have a chance, and starts rowing us back to the *Maiden*.

He still doesn't speak a word.

I decide to ignore him, and lean my arm over the side, trailing my fingers in the water. The coolness spreads up to my hand, and I close my eyes, feeling something close to calm. And with dismay I realise how the anger that's fuelled me has diminished since Bronn kissed me by the pool.

Panic twists my heart. I can't be the same girl who was in love with Bronn. She died alone in a hopeless cavern. She wasn't enough to win this fight. Whatever I've become, I have to be stronger than she was.

But that kiss. It was more intoxicating than magic, more vital than air. And more final than death.

From now on it seems I shall have to learn to exist without breath.

When I open my eyes, we've emerged from the cove and the *Maiden* awaits us beyond. The black beauty that once was briefly mine. How will it feel returning as a guest, no longer a member of her crew? I try not to think about seeing the Snakes I used to command – especially the ones who stood on the shore and did nothing while Bronn took a knife to my neck. They saw him betray me and chose their side – it wasn't mine.

The hurt feeds into my anger and it's good to feel my magic stir inside me. I *am* stronger than I was. I don't need the crew's respect any more. Now I want to be feared.

By the time Bronn steers us alongside the jet-black hull, I'm almost crackling with dangerous energy. When the rope ladder is thrown down for us, Bronn reaches for it.

'Safest if I go first,' he says. I'm not sure whose safety he's most worried about – mine or the Snakes'.

But I don't argue, burying all my conflicted emotions beneath the blaze of magic that keeps me strong. I follow him up and lightly leap over the side on to the deck to fall just behind Bronn.

The crew – his crew – stand ready to defend him, eyeing me with fearful caution. Apart from Harley. I don't see the sailing master anywhere.

Bronn raises his hand to reassure them. 'She's with me. I'll explain everything, but right now we need to continue to the First Isle.'

He glances my way, but can't bring himself to actually look at me. 'I'll have quarters prepared for you. Make yourself comfortable.'

His cold indifference is no less painful for knowing I deserve it. I watch as he strides away, and see how Rayvn steps out from the crowd to touch his arm and speak softly to him. Her eyes are liquid as she gazes at him with concern, and with a jealous pang I realise what is all too obvious. My cousin is in love with Bronn.

I look for his response. I cannot hear his words, nor can I read his expression. But he does rest a hand on her shoulder, a gesture of affection clearly meant to comfort, and it stirs bitter envy inside me.

Does he love her? Did he so easily replace me once he thought me dead? Has he kissed her the way he kissed me at the pool?

I turn my gaze away, and seek my other friends. Ana, the level-headed boatswain, is watching me warily and when I nod at her in greeting, it takes her a moment to reciprocate. Trying not to let it bother me, I scan the crowd until I find the cabin boy, Toby, up on the quarterdeck. He, at least, looks happy to see me. I almost manage to return his smile, but his father Ren steps forward and puts his arm protectively round Toby's shoulder, steering him away.

I don't have time to feel the sting because Rayvn is approaching me now, her eyes shining with uncertainty.

'Is it really you?' she says.

I don't bother answering. 'You've made yourself at home,' I say, and my voice is so sharp it could cut flesh.

Her brow knits tighter. 'I thought that's what you wanted for me.'

'I asked you to give Bronn a message. I didn't ask you to keep the bed warm.'

Rayvn's skin flushes red; she is used to being the hard one between the two of us. I simply raise an eyebrow in response.

'Bronn invited me to join the crew,' she says, clearly confused that she's having to defend herself.

'And invited you to watch my death.' My anger won't be tempered any longer. 'You just stood there. You didn't try to stop him.' They had watched as their first mate stole my title and not one of them lifted a finger to help me; I'm furious at their lack of loyalty.

'Because you told me to trust him!'

It's not the answer I was expecting. 'What?'

'When we parted ways, you told me to trust Bronn, no matter what. So I did, because I trust *you*.'

I stare at her in disbelief, a tangle of emotions snatching at me.

Rayvn sighs. 'I am glad you're not dead,' she says.

'And I assume at some point you'll explain everything to me?'

All I can manage is a curt nod. Shame and guilt prickle behind my anger, but I cannot bring myself to be kind. To be honest, I'm not sure I know *how* any more.

'Where's Harley?'

At that Rayvn affords me a small smile. 'I think you'll be pleased. She's in the brig.'

Why would that please me? 'What was her crime?'

'Ask her yourself,' Rayvn says, gesturing for me to lead the way.

I appreciate her not escorting me to the brig, for remembering this ship was my home long before it was hers, and again I'm ashamed of the way I spoke to her. I have few friends left. If I carry on like this, I'll have none.

'How's Olwyn?' Rayvn asks as we make our way through the ship, the crew eyeing me with fear as we go.

'She was alive the last time I saw her,' I say too harshly. In truth, I try not to think about Rayvn's sister. Or Jax and Astrid, my guardian friends. My disappearance will have made things difficult for them at best, dangerous at worst. I'm afraid for them, even as I can't be with them. But I see the worry flash in Rayvn's eyes and force myself to add, 'And she was happy.

She's found her place as surely as you have.' The words stick in my throat, not wanting to be said, but I spit them out in an attempt to comfort. I think my bitter tone somewhat undermines it.

It's enough to silence her, though, and I'm glad of it. I'm struggling to keep steady, my mind as volatile as the ocean. Always the magic is rising, like the tide washing in. I slip and stumble inside myself, trying to stay upright against the constant assault.

We arrive at the brig. My eyes are slow to adjust to the gloom, and without a conscious summons the magic comes to my aid, illuminating my vision. It gives me a sharp thrill to possess such ability.

Harley is sitting on the floor of her cell, eyes shut, though I don't think she is sleeping. I'm quick to take in the folded blankets left unused by the door, a half-empty bowl of food beside them. Harley has been well looked after, despite her crime, but for some reason has chosen to reject the comfort and warmth of the blankets.

'Harley?'

I see the shock ripple across her face at the sound of my voice, and slowly she opens her eyes.

'Bilge-swilling devils! I thought you were dead.'

'Not any more.'

She gets to her feet, moving stiffly, clearly suffering the effects of imprisonment.

'Why are you here?' I ask her.

Harley looks surprised, and glances at Rayvn. 'You didn't tell her?'

Rayvn folds her arms, but there's a hint of a smile dancing on her lips. 'Thought you'd want to.'

Harley narrows her eyes, trying to figure Rayvn out. Which I can understand. She's almost as unreadable as Bronn.

When Harley looks back at me, her gaze is softer, but more than a little suspicious. 'I'm here because of you.'

'What?' Now it's my turn to be confused.

'Not everyone had been told to trust Bronn,' Rayvn says to me quietly.

Harley straightens her back with pride. 'I don't stand for mutiny,' she says. 'Or the murder of my captain.'

Her words are a light penetrating the walls of my rage.

'When Bronn came back, declaring your death and his title, I didn't believe him. I still can't. But there were witnesses. What was I supposed to do?'

'You refused to accept him as your Viper?'

'To this day. Nor will I accept his attempts to win me over.' She gestures at the blankets.

Now I see them for what they really are. A sign of Bronn's respect that Harley stayed loyal to me when no others questioned his betrayal.

I reach my hand through the bars, and take Harley's. 'Thank you.' I mean it more than I can say.

'So tell me,' she says more gently now, 'if you died on a beach in the West, how are you standing before me now?'

'It's a long story,' I say. 'The main thing is, I *am* standing here.'

Harley has always been one to hear the unspoken, and she considers me carefully.

'And Bronn? Was he really the one who killed you? Because I find that hard to believe. The boy I knew loved you more than his own life.'

'He did,' I say softly. 'But it was at my request. He slit my throat because I asked him to, because he would do anything for me – even that. He is your captain by right. And with my blessing. Please make your peace with him and get out of here, because I need you more than ever.'

And I press my hand to the lock, releasing it, before I've even realised what I'm doing. The door swings open and I try to ignore the look Rayvn's giving me. One full of uncertainty. Laced with fear.

Harley, on the other hand, looks typically unfazed. 'Strange girl,' she says, shaking her head in disbelief. 'Whatever you are, whoever you are – Viper, Queen or ghost – you can count on me. And if you wish for me to reconcile with that blackguard?' She hugs me so tightly I can barely breathe. 'Well, consider it done.'

When we emerge from the brig, Bronn is addressing the crew, explaining that we remain allies despite appearances to the contrary. He gives them no real information about what I'm doing here and, his speech made, the Snakes continue about their work. I am not assigned any tasks, and so have nothing to do but watch.

I climb the main mast, until I reach the first spar, and sit on it, my fingers twisted through the ropes. I'm instantly calmer away from everyone, with the breeze in my face. When I was a child, I always found dark corners of the ship to hide in, but I should have come up here. I feel invisible and free all at once.

Beneath me, a group of Snakes are training hard, swords glinting in the sunlight. I watch them with a half-smile. Memories flood back of doing the same with Grace, of being young and struggling to bear the weight of a blade, of tripping over my own limbs. It seems forever ago. Looking back, I realise how naive I was, how innocently I viewed the world. But I had to be. It was my way of protecting myself from the horrors I lived with. Sitting here, the shifting discomfort of unreleased magic tugging at my innards, I almost miss the blind, foolish child I once was.

I stay watching until night begins to edge out day,

and the crew head to the mess hall, then return with their stomachs full and their tankards fuller. It occurs to me that no one has come to find me, or offered me food, but I would rather be alone anyway. Or so I tell myself, as I watch the Snakes drinking beneath me, laughing and gambling.

When the words reach my ears, I think I'm imagining them, and look down in amazement at the crew toasting their victories.

'STRIKE FIRST!' one shouts.

'DIE LAST!' the rest cheer in reply.

The motto I etched into the Captain's desk before I left the *Maiden* for my voyage west. I hadn't thought of it since and certainly hadn't imagined that Bronn would do anything other than score it out to carve words of his own.

Did he take my saying to heart? Did he pass it on to the Snakes as my legacy?

A scratch of sorrow runs across my heart as I think of Bronn sitting behind the desk, brushing his fingers over the marks I'd made. As I imagine him returning to the ship after that day on the beach. Had he scrubbed my blood from his hands with anger or grief? How had it felt to see the awe of the Snakes who admired his actions? Was it easier to be confronted by Harley's disgust? How many nights has he turned to drink to help him slip into a black abyss?

*What did I do to him?*

As if my thoughts summon him into being, Bronn emerges on deck, a bottle in his hand. Even from this distance I can tell he's drunk. Which perhaps answers one question.

For a moment I forget the magic, the need to save the Isles, destroy Gaius, all the horrors – I am simply a girl who wants to be with the boy she loves. To erase all the hurt I've caused, to forgive all that he has. Without thinking, my feet begin to climb down the rungs, urgent to reach him. Then I stop.

Rayvn has come to find him.

I pause and watch with barbed envy as someone other than me tries to ease Bronn's suffering. I can't hear what they say, can only watch as Rayvn moves to stand beside him. She says something and in response he shakes his head. I cannot see their faces, and imagining them is somehow worse. Would I see affection there? Desire? Love?

Instead all I see is him resting his hand on her shoulder, just like he did earlier, a gesture that could mean so many things. After a few moments, and more than a little hesitation, Rayvn leaves, though I notice the way she glances back at him before she disappears beneath deck.

I should be pleased for my cousin. For finding someone after so many years of loneliness in the mountains. But she found *my* someone. And even if I can't have him, I'm not sure I want anyone else to. Not yet. Not when the pain is as raw as flayed skin.

Bronn doesn't follow her. He stays looking out over the waves, drinking his rum, and talking to no one. Only when the sky darkens and Bronn is the only person left on deck do I descend the mast.

I'm wondering whether to clear my throat to alert him to my presence, but before my feet can touch the ground he asks, 'Done spying?' He doesn't even look round and that's when I realise he's known I was up there all along. I wonder if that's why he's stayed, and my heart constricts at the thought.

'I wasn't spying,' I say, joining him at the railing, though I keep a certain distance. 'I was trying to stay out of the way.'

'There's no escaping you on this ship,' he says, every word spoken as if it tastes bitter. 'Your presence invades every inch of the space.'

'It isn't much fun for me to be back either,' I retort. 'This is no longer my home.'

'Well, whose choice was that?'

*What choice did I have?* I want to scream at him. In fact, when have I ever had a choice? Should I have surrendered to Adler? Bowed to the King? Joined Gaius? Given up, given in? I will not apologise to Bronn, nor to anyone, for the path I've taken. I've fought, I've wept, I've bled for these islands and their people, and I've sacrificed everything to imbue myself with my own power, one that can finally match the enemy I face.

But I would give anything – *everything* – to be free from this nightmare. How can he not know that?

I bite my tongue, though, and instead simply say, 'We'll arrive at the First soon enough. I'll keep out of your way until then.'

I want him to fight back so badly, but his silence is deafening. He has given up on me entirely.

The best thing to do would be to leave now, go below deck and keep out of his way like I promised. But I cannot seem to will my body to move away from his, and so I stay, tormented by the void between us.

'Do you love her?' I say the words without meaning to, the jealousy eating me alive.

'Who?' He seems confused.

'Rayvn.'

He glances at me for the briefest of seconds, before scoffing and shaking his head, draining his bottle dry. 'What's it to you?'

'Only a question.'

'She's a good Snake, and loyal too.' I think that's all he's going to say, but then he adds, somewhat reluctantly, 'But, no, I don't love her.'

'She loves you.'

Bronn frowns. 'She shouldn't.'

'You're kind to her.'

'Because she's your family.' He says the words harshly, betraying his anger. He tries to drink liquid that doesn't exist, and throws the bottle aside.

I should be pleased he doesn't love her. But I can take no pleasure from seeing him hurting.

'I meant what I said. On the beach.'

Bronn looks at me properly for the first time since our kiss. I burn under the intensity of his gaze.

Does he remember how I told him I loved him? Did he believe me?

His conflict is obvious; I see how my words pierce him, and perhaps I'm imagining it, but I think I glimpse a longing to come to me, to hold me. But then it's gone, smothered by overriding anger.

'Yeah, well, it doesn't matter. I no longer feel anything for you. In fact, I can't stand the sight of you.'

His words cut deeper than the blade he took to my neck. I walk away from him, cursing Gaius, cursing magic, cursing love. I ignore how the ship has started to rock, the waves sudden and violent, the skies thunderous and fierce. As the tempest rages, Snakes emerge from below deck, frantically trying to secure the *Maiden*. Only when I escape to oblivion, curling up in my old favourite corner in the darkest part of the ship, does the tumult outside subside.

But not mine, not my storm. Not my wild, untameable rage.

It will never be still again.

The remainder of the journey to the First is as tempestuous as my thoughts.

Bronn avoids me entirely, which is both a relief and an agony. Harley makes sure I eat and offers a little company, but I know I'm not easy to be around. My thoughts are haunted by memories of Gaius's cave, of my body being dismantled, of children staring at me, voiceless. Their eyes accuse me for abandoning them, leaving them behind. I welcome in the magic, as it takes the pain of those memories away. I can lose myself to the white rage, obliterate Bronn from my heart with razor shards of vengeance.

I don't want to *hurt* any more.

Making port at the First doesn't bring any relief. Though I'm glad to leave behind the suffocating misery of the *Maiden*, I'm not entirely looking forward to what lies ahead either. I left the palace without a word to Torin. He'd have every right to be annoyed with me and I'm not sure I can bear to lose him too.

A handful of crew accompany me and Bronn to the palace, but I walk ahead of everyone else alone. The wind is still strong, tearing at our clothes, our hair, luring them to dance away. The others curse it, but the storm is calling to me, and my magic is answering.

Soon there'll be no Marianne left. Only a wild woman who looks like her, who breathes pure power and danger.

And how her enemies shall fear her.

When we arrive at the palace, we're escorted by guards to the war room, and I smile to myself as they keep their distance from me. They haven't forgotten my last visit.

Torin, however, greets me with a hug. 'You need to stop leaving me without a goodbye,' he whispers in my ear, so softly no one else can hear him.

I breathe a sigh of relief. He's not angry – not yet – and it goes some way to calming me. I offer him only a hint of a smile, though, in response, and take my seat at the table where we will decide the fate of the islands – and our own.

I'm expecting Bronn and Torin to shake hands, or some other formal gesture, but to my complete astonishment, Bronn pulls Torin into an embrace. They express delight at seeing each other again, and I wonder when I missed these two becoming such good friends.

Torin asks the others to wait outside, and then there are only the three of us. Just like old times. Nothing like old times.

I tell Torin everything. It's like I'm simply telling a story, as if none of these things happened to me, but I see the way his expression shifts as I talk, the glances he sends Bronn's way. When all is told, Torin looks a little paler than he should.

'And you two . . .? Torin asks, trying to wrap his head around all the horrors.

'Are working together. Nothing more.' Bronn's voice is ice.

Torin blinks at him, before looking at me. 'And you were—'

'Dead, yes.' I lift my chin defiantly.

Torin sighs. 'And I thought what happened to me was bad.'

'There will be a time when we can try to process all we've endured,' I say. 'But right now, stopping Gaius is what matters most.'

'Stabilising the East is more urgent,' Bronn argues.

'I have a plan for that,' I snap back, irritated he's picking a fight.

'It's the first time you've mentioned it.'

'You didn't ask.'

'Perhaps—' Torin politely tries to intervene and diffuse the tension, but Bronn and I ignore him.

Bronn is glaring at me. 'Is that how our alliance is going to work?'

'Oh, so we have one? I wasn't sure after the way you've been ignoring me.'

'I've brought you to your husband, haven't I?'

'He's not my husband any more.'

The words come out too loud, and hang awkwardly in the air.

'What are you talking about?' Torin asks.

I sigh. This isn't how I planned to tell him – I wanted to speak to him in private first. 'We vowed to honour our marriage until death parted us. Well, it already has. Bronn saw to that.'

That last part is unfair, but I want to hurt Bronn the way he keeps hurting me, even though I deserve it and he does not.

Reluctantly I show them my wrist. 'See? No binding.'

They stare at my skin, no longer scarred with the burns given to me by Adler.

'How?' Bronn's voice is thick as fog.

'I healed it when—' I stop myself from saying *when I died*. I turn to Torin. 'I can heal yours too, if you want. Because you're free now. There is nothing to stop you from openly being with Sharpe – no wife, no father who would rather see you dead than happy.'

His eyes glimmer with gratitude. 'Thank you,' he says. 'But I don't mind keeping my scar. After all, I chose to have it. You didn't.'

When he says things like that, it reminds me I still have a heart beating inside my chest. I allow him a very small smile.

'This is all very touching,' Bronn says, sounding as far from moved as possible. 'But can we focus on why we're here? Are you going to explain your idea?'

All softness evaporates as I glare at him. 'There are three things that have to happen now. First, you need to be crowned,' I say to Torin. 'There can be no delay in having a legitimate ruler on the throne, to ensure stability here in the East.'

'Couldn't agree more,' he says. 'Preparations are already under way.'

'Fine.' I turn to Bronn. 'I hear you've been consorting with bandits in my absence. Recruiting them for the King's Guard?'

Even Torin looks taken back by that. Bronn's jaw clenches with tension. 'I was in the unenviable position of having to keep the King onside while also trying to protect the Isles. I had little choice.'

'Did you find Karn?'

I flinch inwardly at the memory of our argument in the West, after Bronn tortured Ferris for information on the notorious bandit's whereabouts.

'I did.'

'And? Did you kill him?'

Bronn shifts awkwardly. 'No, we established an alliance.'

'Good.'

Now it's Bronn's turn to look surprised. 'What do you mean "good"? He's scum. I hated having to pretend to like the man, but it was the King's expressed wish.'

'Does he trust you?'

'I think so. We haven't spoken since I returned from the West though.'

'Then make contact with him. Send word to all the bandits to meet you just north of the First. Say that you have new orders to share with them.'

His eyes narrow. 'And then what?'

'Then we do the second thing: have the Fleet close in on them and end them for good.'

If it's possible, his eyes narrow even further. 'What does that mean?'

I wave my hand in a vague gesture. 'Kill them, capture them, I don't care. We just need them neutralised so we can head west without abandoning the East to terror.'

There's an uneasy silence before Torin says, 'And what's the third thing?'

A smile creeps unbidden to my lips. 'I'm going to build an army.'

Torin shuffles uncomfortably, and Bronn gets to his feet, pacing as he does when he's furious.

'Didn't you say what's-his-name in the West can only be destroyed by magic? Isn't that why you went to such lengths to gain it?' Bronn cannot even begin to disguise his bitterness.

I face him calmly. 'Gaius,' I say, emphasising his name, 'can only be destroyed by magic. But he has plenty of people on his side who can die by the blade.' I speak slowly, as if I was explaining to a child. 'The Fleet need training. What awaits them in the West couldn't be more different than what they've come up against here.'

'And who's going to train them? You?' Bronn scoffs, which is a bit rich considering how many people I've killed, with or without magic. I am more than capable of training anyone.

'You have a problem with that?'

'We'll need more soldiers,' Torin says, ignoring our bickering again. 'You can't take the entire Fleet and leave the East completely without protection, even if we rid ourselves of the bandits.'

'Then we recruit.'

'I suppose you're going to do that too?' Bronn practically rolls his eyes at me.

'Yes. Right after I've paid a little visit to the Third Isle. It's time the Seers joined this fight.'

'The Seers?' Torin's ears have pricked up.

'For the Twelve Isles to heal, everyone needs to be united. The Seers may want to wait out the war, but I have other plans for them.'

Bronn looks doubtful. 'They've been in hiding for a long time,' he says. 'How do you intend to find them?'

'Leave that to me,' I say, and don't miss the glance exchanged between Bronn and Torin. One that tells me they no longer trust me – either of them.

'I'll come with you,' Bronn says, though he sounds as if he'd rather rip his own arm off.

'No. I'll go alone.' Right now, I want nothing more than to be away from him, from everyone.

'Marianne,' Torin says, tentatively trying a different approach, 'why don't you stay here and rest – let me send men out to search for the Seers?'

The look I give him should, by rights, turn him to stone. He knows it too, and shrinks away from me a little.

'Your men won't find them. I will.'

Again they share a glance, and the heat of my annoyance rises quickly.

'Stop,' I say too loudly. 'Stop doubting me. Stop fearing me. I'm the same Marianne I've always been. Trust me as you once did.'

It's Torin who's brave enough to answer. 'We do trust you,' he says. 'But you're lying to yourself if you think you're the same as you were. The Marianne I knew was no assassin. She believed in justice, not vengeance.'

The magic flares inside me, and it takes all my control to keep it contained. 'While you slept, things changed. I did what was necessary.'

I instantly regret my words when I see the hurt flash across his face. Torin has suffered plenty, and nearly all of it is because of me.

But it's Bronn who answers, his voice as sharp as a blade. 'We've all done things because they seemed necessary. Doesn't bloody well make them right.'

We stare at each other, and I wonder if they're thinking the same as me.

*What happened to us?*

When did fighting for the East turn into us fighting each other?

I remind myself who these men are. What they mean to me. And I choke down my fury.

'I am not your enemy.' My voice sounds so weary, so small. 'I know a lot has happened and that things will never be the same as they were, but our fight hasn't changed. Protect the East. Protect the Isles. We three are King, Viper, Mage. What I'm asking is nothing more than our duty.'

Maybe my words find their mark, or maybe in my tone they hear an echo of the old Marianne, but something shifts.

Torin nods. 'You're right. I've always known that to reunite East and West would mean paying a price, possibly the highest one there is. And this Mage, Gaius? He will come for us in the end, as surely as the sun will rise. So yes, I'm with you.'

We both look over at Bronn, whose internal conflict is plain to see, as he paces to the window and stares out. Eventually he hangs his head with a resigned sigh.

'Torin,' he says, his voice flat. 'You are the King; I am your Viper. Are your orders for me to gather the bandits into a trap?'

I turn my head away so no one can see the tears pricking at my eyes – I hate how much it hurts that he trusts Torin's judgement but questions mine. But I still feel Torin's gaze searching me for a moment.

'Yes,' Torin says finally. 'That is my order.'

'Then consider it done.'

And without a backwards glance, Bronn strides out of the room.

I say nothing, arranging my features to mask my feelings.

Outside, the storm howls.

I'm not expecting a warm greeting from the island where outsiders are unwelcome, but I walk up the black sands of the Third Isle towards the forests of nightheart trees regardless. It's time the Seers stopped cowering away and played their part.

Besides, I'm not just here for them. It's time to visit some old friends.

The weather is foul, the storm growing more violent by the minute, but I'm so lost in thought I barely notice. It's hard not to remember the time I arrived here with Grace almost two years ago, wide-eyed and excited. Such a child. Everything changed that day.

*You're the girl who didn't shoot.*

I haven't forgotten Raoul's parting words to me the day he helped me flee the King, and I still want to know how he could possibly have heard about what happened in that ruined building, the day I refused to kill a man in cold blood for Adler. But that's not the only answer I'm hoping to find today.

For all my newfound power, for all my plans, one problem remains: Gaius. He must be destroyed. I must sever every mortal tether he has stolen for himself. But I have no idea how. He's been a Mage for hundreds of years. I've been one for the blink of an eye. The truth is, I'm hoping the Seers will help me. Tell me what I must do.

I follow the same path that Grace took me on and can almost hear the echoes of our laughter haunting through the forest, the shadow of her figure guiding my way. In fact, I'm so caught up in the past, that I don't notice at first how the trees seem to be shrinking away from me, their leaves curling, their branches lowering. It's only when I see the tree I used for target practice before my initiation, all scarred and splintered, that I understand.

The forest is afraid. Of me.

Stepping towards the trunk, I run my fingers over the damaged bark, sensing a weak but ancient power within the tree – it recoils from my touch.

'I'm sorry,' I whisper as I rest my cheek against it. 'I didn't realise I hurt you. Forgive me.'

I hadn't been aware of the magic when I was here before, but now I can hear its faint hum beneath the howling winds and hammering rain. Like the Mist Isle it's fading, the island weeping softly as it's slowly consumed by sickness.

I carry on walking through the forest, with no idea how to find Raoul or anyone else, but soon realise that I won't need to find them. The atmosphere shifts, my skin prickles with the familiar sensation of being watched, and I know *they've* found me.

'Show yourselves!'

There's a movement in the shadows, and I become aware of their presence. I'm surrounded.

A deep voice reaches my ears. 'You should not be here, Mage. It is not safe.'

'I've been to far more dangerous places than this,' I call back, though I still cannot see anyone.

'You mistake my meaning. It is your presence here that is not safe for us. Even the trees fear the power you carry within.'

So it isn't just because I'd once shot at them. Maybe the forest senses how volatile my magic is. Or simply the vengeance in my heart. Either way, it stings to be rejected by the nature I hold so dear.

'Where is Raoul?' I ask, ignoring the tightness in my chest. 'I wish to speak with him.'

It's then that they emerge. Two men, two women, dressed in long black robes, all four of them with hair hanging past their waists. One of the men, the eldest by some margin, has a beard that comes almost to his knees, and in contrast to his clothes and skin, his hair is a shining silver.

Though no one else can be seen, I am certain there are still many hidden weapons aimed at me, should I threaten these four – clearly important – people.

'You're not Raoul,' I say, unwilling to make any

more small talk.

'We are the Elders,' the oldest man says. 'My name is Agon. We know the prophecies that surround you, child of the ocean.'

'Did Raoul tell you? Because I'm not sure he's actually that good at reading rúns.'

Agon ignores me, instead holding out his hands to the downpour. 'I suppose this storm has nothing to do with you?' he asks calmly.

His suggestion unsettles me, but I try to refocus on my reasons for being here. Sidestepping his question, I say, 'There is a Mage in the West who threatens the existence of the Isles as we know them.' I pause, expecting some flicker of reaction, but they say nothing. The four of them just stare impassively at me, which only feeds my irritation.

'I need your help,' I continue. 'Your foresight.'

Once again, it is Agon who replies. 'We chose long ago not to involve ourselves in your wars.'

'Hiding won't save you from Gaius. He will hunt you down and take your magic for himself. You'll be wiped out and your island with you, all your power residing in the hands of an evil man.'

My plea is met with silence and my heart sinks.

Eventually Agon says, 'It is not our fight.'

I look at him with disgust, before I turn my attention to the other three. 'And what about you? Don't you have anything to say? Can't you speak for yourselves?' I'm being rude, but I've long ceased to care.

Still they remain silent.

Agon steps forward, and gestures towards the forest path. 'Walk with me.'

I don't want to go with him, but I also don't want to give them cause to shoot at me. Because then I'll have to kill them all, and any hopes of an alliance will be over for good.

So I fall into step beside him and we stroll deeper into the dark woods. This time I can't help but see how the flowers wilt as I pass, and the branches pull protectively inwards. This was how the animals and birds behaved in that vile cave when Gaius appeared. They recognised him as someone who would steal their energy, their power, for his own. The thought that I'm now seen as a similar threat is chilling.

When we reach a small clearing, Agon stops walking and faces me. 'Let me speak plainly. You must leave this place and never return.'

'Why won't you help me?' Though my voice is still hard, I can't disguise my despair. Because I know what's out there in the dark, the terrible monster waiting to feed off us all.

'I'm not sure what Raoul told you when you met, but we Seers have foreseen the end that's coming. It is why we live beneath the trees, among their roots. It is the only chance we have to survive the destruction that will sweep over the land and sea. There must be someone left to rebuild. People who know the past *and* the future.'

Frustration strangles my throat. 'That end doesn't have to come. We can stop it from happening altogether. Just tell me, how do I destroy him?'

Agon considers me closely, with a sadness in his eyes, which quickly fades to disappointment. 'There was a time when I thought you might be our hope. That maybe you could be strong enough to harness the magic required to save us all. But you're a fledgling Mage and already you're losing yourself.'

Now my magic flares defiant with outrage. 'I have been fighting for these islands with all that I have. I've sacrificed everything, even my own life, while you hide away in your holes – and you dare to judge *me*?'

'Yes, you faced your own death. But you brought yourself back, didn't you? And unless I'm much mistaken you failed to restore every part of your former self, just like you couldn't bring all of Lilah back. Am I right?'

I'm utterly thrown by this accusation. I want to dismiss it, but he's seen the truth about Lilah. Could he be right about me too? I sensed at the time when I awoke on the beach that I wasn't quite the same, but is it possible it was more than that? That I left a part of myself behind?

'You know nothing about me,' I spit, hating myself even as I say the words.

'Maybe, maybe not,' he says with infuriating calmness. 'But I will not risk my people to fight your war.'

'It's not *mine*; it's everyone's. Gaius will come for your magic too, that I promise you.'

'For all I know that's why you're here. Perhaps it isn't this Gaius I should be fearing but you, for you seem to hunger for our magic too.'

'Don't ever compare me to him!' I clench my fists and a burst of energy shoots out from me, across the ground, so that all the trees around us drop their leaves in a sudden convulsion.

My magical tantrum unfortunately only serves to prove his point.

He nods wryly. 'Get off my island, girl,' he says. 'And never come back.'

As I storm down the sands towards my boat, I remember the last time I left this Isle, fleeing for my life with no idea where to go, or what to do. All I knew then was that I had to survive. In some ways things are no different this time. Maybe even worse, because while now I'm desperately trying to save everyone else from the pain that awaits them, they seem apathetic to their fate. Sometimes it seems the whole world would rather look away, close their eyes and hope the inevitable horrors won't materialise. And sometimes I wish I could do the same. I still dream of the life I could have had on the Fourth, with Joren and Clara, watching Tomas grow from boy to man as he should have. I would gladly have lived in denial to stay there with them.

Remembering them comforts and burns at the same time, an ache of grief clutching at my heart. The darkness threatening to destroy me is curbed by their memory. But I can't forget Clara's dying words that set me on this path.

*Make them pay*.

Adler's dead, the King is as good as, but Gaius is guiltier than anyone, for he was the one to set things in motion two hundred years ago when he helped one king to slaughter another.

Too many families have been torn apart, too many loved ones lost. So no, I won't run away from this fight; I will never give up because I won't break the promise I made to a dying woman who I loved as a mother. For her husband who I loved as a father. And her son who I loved as a brother. Love will always be more powerful than hate, no matter what Gaius believes. No matter what my own fury says.

'It was you?'

Raoul's angry voice fills the air, and my heart sinks, the warmth of the previous moment evaporating. This confrontation isn't going to be pretty.

I turn slowly to see him marching towards me, his pistol pointed straight at my head. His face is contorted with rage, and I know he's spoken to Agon, has learned of my part in Lilah's loss of memory.

'All this time you let us believe you rescued her! But you're the reason she forgot me!'

What pity I have for him is swiftly silenced by my ever-present anger. 'I'm the reason you still have her at all.'

Raoul shakes his head. 'To think I helped you when I could have handed you over to the King.' He shoves the gun hard against my chest, the sharp pain at my ribs rippling through me like a violent invitation. My eyes twitch with anticipation.

'And why didn't you?'

'Because I trusted you.' The bitterness of betrayal spills from his lips and I can see that he means to kill me here and now. But even as his finger curls round the trigger, I've flicked my wrist and an invisible force sends it hurtling from his hand. He falters, not believing what's just happened, but he doesn't need a weapon to hurt me.

His fist drives hard into my guts, but I can play this game too, and match him blow for blow. The exhilaration I experience from the taste of blood, the sound of bone crunching on bone, should concern me. But there's no room for that part of me, not now. The pain reminds me I'm alive, and all it costs to continue to be so. Inflicting it on someone else is just a bonus. No, that's a lie. I enjoy it.

The realisation surprises me, as I land a punch to Raoul's jaw, knocking a tooth out. The power to inflict pain is addictive, and with every swing of my fist I crave it more and more.

To find myself revelling in such casual cruelty pulls me up short.

I look down at Raoul, now lying in the sand, covered in ash and blood, and remind myself he's my friend. Whether or not the feeling's mutual.

'Go back to your people,' I say, stepping away from him and wiping my own bloody nose. 'Hide with them if you must. You'll die eventually, but it won't be today and it won't be by my hand.'

And I walk away from him, from his people, from an island that has never brought me anything but misery. They're on their own now.

As am I.

Though the Snakes are used to working in every condition, even they are beginning to grow weary of the relentless torrential rain.

The strong winds make for difficult sailing conditions as the *Maiden* heads for the open sea, where the bandits should join us by the morning. I could help, both practically and by trying to control the tempest with my magic, but I offer neither. If the crew are busy fighting the weather, then they don't have time to glare at me.

Torin and Sharpe have joined us aboard the *Maiden*, and Talon is standing by to carry Torin's orders to the Fleet, who are hidden a safe distance away. Once the bandits have congregated, the Fleet will close in and trap them. Though no one has said it out loud, I'm fairly certain my friends are here to keep watch over me. Between them and Bronn I'm being treated like a wild animal that needs muzzling.

When I'd returned to the *Maiden* after the disastrous visit to the Third, Bronn had taken one look at my bruised face and my bloodied knuckles, and sighed. 'What went wrong?'

I'd tasted the blood in my mouth from where Raoul's fist had made its mark. 'The Seers refused to help.'

Bronn had watched me closely. Could he hear the incessant tumult in my head?

'Care to elaborate?'

I'd considered it, just for a second. Imagined sharing the weight of my misery with him, like I used to. But that time was long gone. 'No.' The word punctuated the air harshly. 'What about you? How did you get on with the bandits?'

I could tell he wanted to dismiss me as cruelly as I had him, but he'd said, 'They'll be there.'

To my annoyance I hadn't been able to disguise how impressed I was. 'How did you manage that?'

Bronn had looked at me then, and a shadow of a smile brushed his lips. 'Told them I had myself a prisoner they might want to help me dispose of.'

'You used me as bait?'

Bronn had shrugged. 'My orders were to make sure the bandits all gathered together in the same place at the same time. You never specified how.'

And he'd walked off before he could see my smile. Because if things had been the other way round, I would have done exactly the same.

'Ship approaching!'

Rayvn's voice carries down from the crow's nest, interrupting my reverie, and I look over at Bronn who's already holding his spyglass to his eye.

He lowers it and glances my way, before reluctantly

coming to join me. 'Friends of yours?'

I take the spyglass he's offering and look for myself. The last ship I'm expecting to see is *The Black Nightshade* and I can't imagine Raoul's motives for seeking me out.

'I'm not sure,' I say cautiously. 'But if he had wanted to conceal himself from us, he could have. I think it's a good sign he hasn't.'

Bronn sighs, like everything to do with me exhausts him. Like I'm ruining an otherwise perfect existence. It bothers me far more than it should.

'Bring her to,' he orders, and the crew start hoisting the sails.

The rain becomes heavier as does my heart. I don't want to fight Raoul again. I hardly even notice that Torin has come to my side, or that his hand is resting on my shoulder.

'You OK?'

*No*. I want to scream it from the deepest part of myself to the highest sky. I can barely remember a time when I was OK.

Instead I say, 'I'm fine.'

Torin is not my friend for nothing, though, and I know he hears the lie. 'We've got your back,' he says, his free hand resting lightly but purposefully on the hilt of his sword, and I give a small nod in gratitude.

By the time Raoul's ship pulls alongside ours, Torin has been joined by Sharpe and Harley. Bronn waits at the rail, ready to receive our guest, Ren just behind him, and hovering nearby is Rayvn.

But Raoul comes on board alone. And, to my surprise, unarmed.

'You must be the Viper,' he says to Bronn, holding out a hand of friendship. 'I'm Raoul.'

For an awful moment I don't think Bronn's going to accept his hand, but after a heartbeat of consideration, he shakes it.

'Welcome,' Bronn says. 'What brings you here?'

Raoul searches the faces about him until he finds mine. 'A friend.'

He glances at Bronn for unspoken permission, and Bronn grants it with a cautious nod.

I don't move as Raoul strides towards me, intensely aware of Torin and Harley at my back, of Bronn's hand ready to strike at the first sign of trouble. I don't need them, but it startles me how much I appreciate knowing they'll still fight for me.

'I owe you an apology,' Raoul says as he comes to stand before me.

'For your accusations, or for trying to shoot me?'

I hadn't told Bronn about that, and before he can stop himself, he steps forward protectively. From the corner of my eye I can see how the impulse has bothered him.

'For all of it. Lilah put me straight. Made me see that she'd be dead without you, and she loves me despite losing her memories. Said if she doesn't care, why should I?'

'She doesn't hate me?'

Raoul smiles. 'Not at all. I want to fight for my family, Marianne. My island. The other Seers may want to hide, but not me. We're here to join you. My ship is your ship. My crew are your crew. My rúns are yours.' And he unfolds his hand to reveal the stones.

Their power calls to me. It would be so easy to reach out and take them, another valuable weapon for the fight ahead. If my friends weren't flanking me on all sides, I'm not sure I could resist.

Instead I reach forward, and close his hand. 'Your rúns are yours. Always. I have not come to steal your magic. But your support is most welcome. And if the rúns speak to you, I'd be grateful for any knowledge you can share.'

Our eyes meet and I wonder whether he heard the way my voice shook, stumbling over the lie that I wish wasn't there.

If he did, he shows no sign of it. Raoul simply nods once more, and then returns his rúns to his pocket, before turning to talk with Bronn. No doubt discussing whether the *Nightshade* is of any use to us right now.

I step backwards, wanting to slip away from so much attention and flee beneath deck before anyone can speak to me.

I don't emerge until the sun has set and flashes of lightning are all that illuminate the sky. Most of the crew are asleep, and I seek some solace in the quiet darkness. The rain is still persistent, puncturing the ocean beneath us like gunshots. The ominous atmosphere matches my mind, which brims with dark thoughts that forbid peace.

'When did you last sleep?'

I turn slightly to see Bronn watching me, keeping his distance as always. I'd forgotten he doesn't rest much any more either.

'I can't,' I say, staring back out to the ocean.

Even without looking, I can sense his conflict. He wants to leave me. He wants to be with me. Always I torment him. In the end, though, his curiosity wins and I hear the gentle thud of his boots on the deck as he comes to join me.

I glance over at him, before lowering my eyes to the water. Would I be able to rest if I was safe in his arms? Curled up against him, the solidity of his body something real to tether me to who I once was?

'Talk to me,' Bronn says, looking down at the sea too, both of us avoiding meeting the other's gaze. 'Tell me what's wrong. And don't say nothing, I know you too well.'

And maybe it's feeling that there's no one else in the world but us in this moment that allows me to finally lower the defences I've had up since I awoke in the sand on that beach.

'When I brought myself back . . .' I no longer want to hurt him with his part in my death. But he knows what I mean. There's the same awkward flinch at the mere mention of it. 'Well, I didn't entirely succeed.'

Bronn frowns. 'What do you mean?'

'I didn't bring all of myself back. Something's missing. Or maybe I brought too much back, something different, I don't know exactly. But you were right to say I'm not who I was before. And every day I'm drifting further away from that person. She's like a fading memory, slipping from my mind. I'm afraid she'll soon be gone for ever.'

He doesn't speak, and I glance over to see his reaction. The sadness on his face undoes me.

'I'm so angry, Bronn,' I say, my voice rasping with the fury brimming over in me. 'All the time. I want to hurt people, make them suffer—'

'Like you suffered.' He says the words softly, finishing the thought I didn't even realise was there.

But he's right, of course, and I nod. 'Yes. Like I suffered.'

Bronn sighs heavily, and I know I'm not the only one shouldering unbearable weight. He carries the fate of the Isles with him too. 'Maybe you didn't leave something behind on that beach,' he says. 'Maybe I took something.'

At last our eyes meet and then I know; the force that has connected us all these years is not lost. There is nothing that can sever the bond between us. 'What happened on the beach was necessary,' I say. 'It was not your fault.'

His eyes shine with emotion. 'It wasn't yours either.'

What little heart that remains beating in my chest is left in tatters. 'And yet we pay the price.'

Bronn's smile is achingly sad. 'We always have.'

I think he's going to say something else, something important, but the sound of someone nearby clearing their throat interrupts us. To my surprise Rayvn is standing there, shuffling awkwardly, and I find myself feeling sorry for her. No matter the utter mess of my relationship with Bronn, it carries a weight of history she will never possess.

'We're nearly at our destination, Captain,' she says, and I find it hard to imagine a time when Rayvn wasn't a Snake. She looks so perfectly at home here, despite the tipping deck, the lashing rain that sticks her hair to her skin. I suppose compared to the harsh environment of the Eighth Isle, it's not that bad.

Bronn looks at me and raises his eyebrows. 'The bandits will be here soon. Ready to be my prisoner?'

He claps me in irons, and then gestures to Rayvn to come and guard me. 'I'm going to talk with Torin, see if there's any update from the Fleet,' he says, 'but I'll be back shortly.'

I'm not sure which one of us he's talking to, but I find I'm relieved when he's gone. The tension between me and my cousin slips away with him.

'You're happy here,' I say. It's not a question.

She lifts her dark eyes to meet mine. 'I am. It's like . . .' She pauses, searching for the right words. 'It's like I can breathe. I love the open sea, the vastness of all of this.' And she stretches her arms wide. 'I finally found my home.'

'I'm glad for you.'

Her forehead creases into a frown. 'Why then, since your return, have I felt like it'll soon be over? That my time here was a dream, and I'm soon to wake up?'

Guilt stabs at my heart. It's true. I want to take her home to the West. I want her to risk everything for the war that's coming.

'You were born to protect the snow mares,' I say. 'Born to duty, not desire. Though I am sorry for it.'

'That's it? That's all you have to say?' Her pent-up anger finally breaks through.

'What do you want me to say?'

'I want to know what happened to you!' Her voice carries on the night air. 'When I left you, you were so different. Kinder, gentler, less . . .'

'Less what?' Now it's my voice that's raised. 'Less powerful?'

'Less bitter.'

'Yeah, well, after you left things deteriorated quickly.'

'So tell me what happened! You've barely spoken to me since your return, and Bronn tells us nothing. The crew are afraid of you, they whisper about you and I tell them to shut their mouths, but all the while I agree with them! You want to lead us all to war, but no one will follow a ghost who's keeping secrets.'

'Is that what they think of me? Is that what *you* think?'

'I think something changed and I wish you'd share it with me. Why isn't Olwyn here with you? What really happened on that beach? I saw Bronn cut your throat and then watched him torture himself every moment since. How did you survive?'

That's a lot of questions, most of which I have no intention of answering. But I owe her an explanation about Olwyn at least.

'Back in the West, I was taken prisoner by someone we all trusted. I escaped but I couldn't go back to get Olwyn. It wasn't safe for her. And she probably thinks I'm a murderer at this point anyway. But the man who took me is the one we have to fight now. He's the one you should all fear. Not me.'

And I see it then. The concern, the pity, the horror

in Rayvn's eyes. 'What did he do to you?'

She's leading me back towards the cave, and I can't go back there. I won't.

'He drew the battle lines,' I say in a way that shuts down the conversation.

We stand there in silence, and I sense her frustration with me. It hurts that there's such distance between us. Between me and everyone. Just another thing that Gaius took from me when he drained me dry. I hate that I'm losing them all as I'm losing myself. Hate that I can't look for a way back until this fight is over.

Rayvn's right. I am bitter. I've been forced to do so much I didn't want to – leave the children, abandon my friends, lose Bronn. If only I'd never been imprisoned in that cave. I hate myself for ever ending up there. For trusting the wrong person. For allowing myself to get caught. So many mistakes and I paid a heavy price. The heat of shame and guilt rises inside me with the sun.

By the time the bandits' ships start to come into view all around us, changing from specks on the horizon into looming shapes, my heart is beating too fast, the shattered pieces of who I was scratching my insides raw, the magic scorching beneath my skin. I want to peel my own flesh away to free myself of this feeling. It's too much to bear.

There are so many ships. Like an infestation, the

bandits have multiplied, crawling all over the land. They were bred by Adler and fed by the King. And they have destroyed everything good and beautiful in their paths as they've rampaged.

I loathe them as I loathed Adler. As I did the King. As I do Gaius.

Bronn is looking through his spyglass to confirm that they're all there, and though I'm not really paying attention to him, lost in the fever of my malice, I hear him say a name that snatches my attention.

Karn.

He's here, his ship close enough for Bronn to identify him. A man who has slaughtered hundreds of islanders, some for Adler, others merely for his own personal pleasure. I remember the settlement Bronn and I stumbled upon on the Sixth Isle, long ago. The man pinned to the door. The bodies of villagers charred in the stone building. Old and young, women and children, brutally murdered by Karn's men.

Hatred spreads through me like blood in water.

He eluded me all the months I was Viper. He will not do so today.

Bronn is beckoning for me now, and Rayvn escorts me across the deck, but I'm barely aware of being moved. From the corner of my eye I see Torin watching me with concern; he mouths something to Bronn, whose head turns sharply towards me. They can sense something has changed.

And they're right. Because I've finally realised something – I've wasted so much time. I trawled west to raise an army, and when I found a greater enemy, I ran back east to search for more help. But I didn't need an army to destroy the King, and I don't need to wait for one now to destroy the enemy before me.

I *am* an army.

As the thought consumes me, the power takes hold. I am a Mage. One more powerful even than Gaius – he wanted to steal my magic to strengthen his own. I was a fool to think I needed anyone else.

'Marianne?' Rayvn's nervous voice penetrates my ears, but I ignore her. 'What are you doing?'

The last defences that kept the darkness at bay splinter and fall as I snap the irons round my wrists, shattering them like feeble bones.

Bronn shouts something, but I stride past him, pushing him away with my magic so that he's thrown on to the deck. I no longer require incantations. The magic knows what needs to be done and I let it take the lead, exhilarated as it sweeps me along.

The storm is growing now, like it feeds off my hatred and anger. The sky is black, as if night has hurried back, the waves vast and powerful, thunder and lightning crackling through the air. I stand at the prow of the *Maiden* ready to unleash destruction.

Because I intend to crush the vermin. Exterminate them once and for all.

The heat inside me is blistering now as I call forth the power from the deep. The force of it threatens to split my skin as it escapes me, and I cling to a rope to steady myself.

And then I watch as the ocean comes alive with every fearsome creature summoned by the squall. The bandits' ships, which are barely managing to withstand the battering of the waves, are now being attacked from every side by monsters from the depths. A colossal merbeast leaps from the water, its massive jaws tearing the front off one of the ships, and its spiked tail lashing round to sink the remaining half. Three giant serpentsharks are relentless in their destruction, taking down a ship each, feasting on the screaming sailors who have no escape. Twelve huge tentacles wrap themselves round a ship attempting to flee, the head of the vast shadow squid they're attached to emerging moments later to devour its prey.

It's as though a veil has descended before my eyes and I'm looking through smoke and retribution as the magic tightens its stranglehold over me. I've lost all control; my darkness, my anger and my need for revenge are all that's left to fuel the magical carnage.

The violent heavens illuminate the scene every few minutes with flashes of lightning, before the world shakes with the thunder that rolls in its pursuit. One bolt directly strikes the mast of a ship, and it bursts into flames, the fire rampaging through the wood and flesh around it, until the flames meet the ocean and die. It's not only rain pelting down now, but hailstones, as big as a fists, and they explode like cannonballs as they strike, sending planks and splinters of wood flying into the air. The ships untouched by beast or fire are being ripped apart by the savage waves pounding at their sides.

But destruction like this isn't controllable.

Even as I exult in the obliteration of my enemies, I realise with horror that the Fleet has arrived and is starting to be pulled into the devastation. The ship groans beneath me and I hear its cry. The *Maiden* is in danger too, barely able to withstand the onslaught.

I look behind me to see the crew desperately fighting not to get thrown overboard, to secure the ship. Harley and Ana are tying the wheel to the mizzenmast, attempting to stop it from spinning wildly out of control. Sharpe and Rayvn are dropping the sails on the main mast, while Torin and Bronn do the same for the foremast. Ren is screaming orders that the crew struggle to carry out. Raoul nearly gets caught as a wave submerges us for a moment, but then we lift high again, and he's still hanging on, staring at me with complete fear.

'She is the storm!' he shouts over the chaos. 'She will destroy us all.'

Comprehension stops my breath. His prophecy was right all along. I am the wild fury that will devour night and day, earth and sea. This storm was always mine. And I cannot contain it.

With that awareness comes another: pain. It rips through me, the magic tearing me apart as it consumes me. The ecstasy of destruction had dulled my senses, but now it sears me from within as the magic prepares for its next devastating act. A massive maelstrom appears in the seas beneath us, sucking in any bandit ships not already massacred. Soon the Fleet will get pulled in too. And the *Maiden*. And I understand that as it's fed, so it will grow and grow, drinking the oceans, swallowing the land.

'We have to kill her!' Raoul's voice reaches me, as it does the others. 'Before there is nothing left!' He understands better than anyone that I am the storm that will bring the end.

But I know something he does not. He cannot stop me. No one can. In this moment my magic is more powerful than anything has ever been, and I surrender to the inevitability of our imminent demise.

And then in the midst of the darkness Bronn is beside me. When all others are clinging to ropes trying to save themselves, terrified of my tempest, he has risked his life to be with me.

'Marianne!' His voice breaks through my howling magic. 'You have to stop this.'

I turn to look at him, and an ache of longing cuts through the curtain of despair. 'I can't,' I say, and it sounds more like a sob.

My moment of weakness is punished with a lash of magic that flays me from within. My scream mingles with thunder, with lightning. It demands all of me. It destroys me.

All I can see, think, hear, feel is darkness, filled with the fire of hatred – burning, scorching and melting me to nothing.

And then there is a voice, reaching in to save me.

'Remember who you are.' And though Bronn's words are a mere whisper in the noise, I hear them.

'I am vengeance, I am madness, I am ruin!'

'No! You're afraid. Marianne, you're not just angry, you're terrified. And you have every reason to be. It's time to confront it. It's time to accept it.'

It's like his words pierce me, and all the fear I've been holding in spills out like blood from a wound.

'He hurt me,' I say, the words a whimper. 'He hurt me!' The memory of being Gaius's prisoner, his experiment, his victim, smashes into me with more force than the storm crushing the ship. I'm back in the cave, I can smell my blood, my horror, my failure.

The pain is immediate and raw and my screams are lost in the wind. I want to be free of it, but I'm drowning, drowning in fear, anger, regret until I can't remember where I begin or end.

'I'm lost,' I cry, a wave of sorrow crashing over me.

'No, you're not. Come back. Marianne, come back to me.' His voice penetrates the darkness.

And then his lips are on mine.

In the blackest part of my soul, he finds me. He's a float to cling to, a rope to grasp, an anchor to stop me drifting entirely from reach. The smallest flicker of light.

The cave fades as a different memory surfaces. I'm a child again, on the ship, high up on the rigging, hanging upside down, my skirts tumbling around my face. But I'm not afraid. I'm laughing. I can hardly recognise the sound – it's so free, so light. Because I'm with the person I trust most in the world, my best friend, my family, the boy who is everything to me. He will not let me fall.

I thought I'd forgotten what it was like to be her, the girl who laughed, who loved. Who could find moments of joy in the bleakness of her world.

But as Bronn's breath becomes mine, as it soothes my broken heart, I unwrap the remnant of that person, folded tightly into a corner of my mind. And I realise what part of me was missing, what I'd failed to restore when I brought myself back to life, because it had been so cruelly stolen from me. Hope. Gaius had drained it from me in that cave. Surrendering myself to Bronn's blade destroyed any lingering trace.

Now his kiss kindles a spark deep within me. There is still hope. For the Isles. For me. For us.

I am still alive. Despite everything. For all Gaius's efforts, for the King's, for Adler's – I endure. But how can I fight for the Isles if I can't fight for myself? I push away the darkness until light spills in at the edges. For the sake of the girl I was, I will fight.

Strengthened by the light, I battle the magic within me. If I try to use it I cannot hope to keep control. But the old me, the one from before death, remembers how to contain it – it lay dormant within me for years, and must again.

It's only when Bronn's lips lift from mine that I realise the storm has died down – all my anger, all my rage tempered by hope.

And without magic coursing through me to sustain it, my body breaks and I fall to the deck, to the silence of oblivion.

# PART TWO
# ADRIFT

Awareness creeps in like the sun through a cracked door. I am not dead – at least, I don't think I am. But exhaustion chains my body so that I cannot move, cannot even open my eyes. My mind, however, is waking up from the longest sleep, clawing its way through the thick mud of tiredness.

The magic has lost its claim over me. My body feels hollow without it flowing through me, though I can sense it still there, deep down, imprisoned in its dungeon. I can hear its distant cries but am not moved by them. For everyone's safety it needs to stay locked up. I was an arrogant fool thinking I was strong enough to harness magic, when others have succumbed to its call. I was as bad as Gaius, allowing the power to mutate me into the thing I hate the most: someone prepared to destroy everything for their own ends.

I feel ashamed, I feel defeated. But . . . I also feel more like me. The me before Gaius, before the beach, before I became a Mage.

I'm aware of a warmth against my palm and realise there is a hand in mine. I squeeze my fingers round it, welcoming the touch of another.

'Marianne?'

I know that voice, and I scramble faster out of the darkness, wanting to reach the person it belongs to.

'I think she's waking up.'

There's a different hand now, this one resting on my shoulder. 'It's OK,' a new voice says, and it too is familiar. 'We're here.'

I'm not alone. Despite everything, they've not abandoned me.

Finally I manage to flicker my eyes open, though it's like prising panels apart.

Torin is sitting beside me, his hand holding mine, his tired face etched with relief. On my other side Sharpe stands over me, his touch reassuring and firm. My friends.

I try to speak, but though I just about manage to open my mouth, no sound emerges.

'Just rest,' Torin says, leaning forward to stroke my hair. 'You've been unconscious for several days. We were beginning to fear you would never wake.'

Blinking slowly, I try to orientate myself. I'm in the Captain's quarters, lying on his bunk. But the Viper himself is nowhere to be seen.

'Between the two of you, I seem to spend my life hovering anxiously over sleeping bodies,' Sharpe says. 'Perhaps you could both make an effort to keep out of trouble, just for a while?'

Torin smiles and it acts like a salve to my wounded spirit.

'I'm sorry.' The words are barely audible, more of a croak, but Torin hears them, and lifts my hand to press against his chest.

'It wasn't you,' he says. 'You weren't in control.'

It's partially true, but I know it's not enough to excuse what I did. I should have realised sooner how the magic was stealing my body as a vessel to sail on its own tide.

'Was anyone from the *Maiden* hurt? And the Fleet? What happened to the bandits?'

'Everyone on the *Maiden* is fine. The Fleet too,' Torin answers. 'A few of the bandits survived. The Fleet rounded them up and have imprisoned them. Now they're hunting down those who remained on land. All of them will be brought to justice.'

'And the storm?'

'Passed.' Torin pauses. I don't miss the nervous glance he gives Sharpe as he continues, 'Raoul was right, wasn't he? You were the storm? All this time?'

I nod, tears spilling down my cheeks. 'The magic . . . I couldn't control it.'

'But you can now?'

'No. I've simply contained it.'

For the moment. Who knows whether it will find a way to escape? The fuse remains inside me just waiting for a spark.

'So you can't use it?' Sharpe asks, and I know what

he's thinking. *How will we stand a chance against Gaius without magic?*

'Not until I find a way to use it safely.' Which is an oxymoron. There is nothing safe about magic. I've known that all along but hoped I could handle it – after all, I had to try. What a mess I've made of everything. For the first time since becoming a Mage I have no idea what to do next.

As if he can read my thoughts, Torin says, 'Don't worry. We'll find a way without it. It's not over yet.'

I try to sit up, and when I struggle, Sharpe and Torin help, slipping a cushion behind me. The change in position makes me realise something. 'We're not moving.'

'No, we're anchored just off the First,' Torin says. 'There's some . . . business I have to attend to.'

I frown at him, wondering what he means and why he hesitated, and then I realise. 'Your coronation? You delayed it for me?'

'Well, I was hardly going to do it without you. You're the reason it's happening at all.'

Closing my eyes, I shake my head. I don't want any credit for what I did. Not when it was motivated by the very worst part of me.

'We can't change what has been done,' Torin says softly. 'We can only look forward.' He reaches for a cup, and brings it to my lips. The water is warm, but my dry mouth welcomes it anyway. 'How are you feeling?'

'Weak,' I admit. Magic healed my body, and now without it sustaining me, pain stabs through my restored fingers and toes, the bones Gaius broke ache mercilessly, my neck burns where a scar should be, and a wave of fear sweeps across my chest. What if I can never truly recover?

'We can mix you a tonic, if you tell us how,' Sharpe offers, and I am grateful to him for reminding me that there was once more to me than magic. It has been too long since I considered myself a healer.

'Do we have any blackseed or willowdust on board?'

'I'll go and check,' Sharpe says.

'If so, add a pinch of each to a draught of rum,' I add as he makes for the door.

When he's gone, I smile at Torin. 'The best tonic for me is seeing you two happy together.'

'You have a lot in common,' he says, a shadow haunting his voice. 'Both of you have been hurt at the hands of people you trusted.'

'Has he recovered?' I recall too well the way Sharpe shuffled into the courtroom the day the King made him testify against me, his body half broken by torture. 'From his wounds?'

Torin sighs. 'His skin will always bear the scars, and their roots run deep. Is such a thing ever truly recovered from?'

I reflect on the damage inflicted by Gaius and think not.

'But there's no point dwelling on the past. Not when we can hope to shape the future,' he says.

'And in that future you will be King.'

'As soon as you can stand upright.'

'I'll be there, even if you have to prop me up against a wall,' I say, and he laughs. I'd forgotten what it was to feel like this – to feel safe. Not because of an absence of danger – the threat awaiting us hasn't diminished in the slightest. But because I'm with people I love. People I trust. People who accept me just as I am – faults and all. 'I missed you,' I say to him softly. 'I wish things had been different.'

'Like I hadn't been stabbed on our wedding night and kept asleep for months, while you were charged with my attempted murder, sentenced to death and forced to flee West – a place where everything was so much worse, your lover had to kill you so you could become a Mage, only for you to discover your magic was so strong it could consume you and nearly destroy us all?'

'It wasn't a great start to our married life, I'll concede,' I say with a wry smile.

Torin brings my hand to his lips. 'Our marriage would have been happy,' he says, 'in its own way.'

'It would. But we can still have an alliance – the King

of the East and the Queen of the West. The Twelve Isles can be reunited once more even without our marriage.'

Torin's watching me closely now. 'You intend to take the throne then?'

'If we can defeat Gaius? Then, yes, I have to. It's the only way.'

'We have to defeat him.'

I raise my eyes to meet his. 'I don't know how we're going to stand a chance.'

'You mean without your magic? We'll find a way. All of us. Together.' He pauses, looking concerned. 'Will he know you're alive now, from the storm?'

'No, I don't think so,' I reply. 'I don't believe he can sense things happening in the East.'

He looks relieved and I manage to offer him a small smile but it lacks conviction.

The door opens, and I think it will be Sharpe returning with the tonic, but it's Harley who carries the tankard.

'Your commander was otherwise needed,' she says to Torin, pushing him out of the way to come by my side. Torin and I share an amused look, as Harley positions herself to take care of me. 'As are you. Don't you have a coronation to prepare for?'

Torin tips into a polite bow. 'Thank you. I'm sure I've kept everyone waiting long enough,' he says, his eyes sparkling. 'Marianne, I will see you on land tomorrow?'

'I wouldn't miss it.'

'All right, you drink this,' Harley says to me once Torin's gone, like I'm a child and she's my nurse.

I swallow down the concoction Sharpe's made for me and pull a face. It's disgusting.

'Added some bitterwort to it,' she says. 'Good for the spirits, and I'm sure yours need all the help they can get.'

'Well, it's not at all good for the palate.'

Ignoring my complaints, she leans back and folds her arms. 'Yes, that's better,' she says, as matter-of-fact as always. 'You're more yourself. It's your eyes, you know. Before they were like a raging ocean. Now they're still waters again.' She nods her head approvingly. 'Right then,' she says. 'What are my orders?'

It's the last thing I'm expecting her to say. 'Shouldn't you be asking your captain? Or your king?'

Harley frowns. 'You are the one I have always followed, and you always will be. So I'll ask again, what's the plan?'

I do not deserve such loyalty. And the truth is, I don't have much of a plan any more. But I look at her warm eyes, her steadfast belief, and it strengthens me.

'First, we get that crown on Torin's head. And then we train. We need our fighting to match the Guardians'.' I pause as the flaw in even this most flimsy of plans dawns on me. I was going to train them. How can I do that when I can barely stand? All at once I'm overwhelmed, the immensity of the task ahead threatening to sweep me away. I can't think any further than surviving the day, let alone raising an army.

Harley studies me closely, and it's as if she's penetrated my skull to see the doubts and fears that linger within but accepts them anyway. 'What you need now is rest; let that tonic do its work.'

When I open my mouth to object, she holds up her hand. 'Rest. I'll be right here when you wake.'

There's no arguing with her, so I allow myself to close my eyes and soon fall back into a heavy sleep.

I only stir when Harley shakes me. 'You slept like the dead,' she says with a smile. 'But you're going to be late if I let you sleep any longer.'

'It's morning already?' I say, stifling a yawn.

'Aye, and we need you up on your feet, lass.'

And before I can even begin to protest, Harley has wrapped an arm round me, and is pulling me off the bed. My legs buckle, forgetting their purpose, but she holds me up until my muscles remember themselves. Slowly she loosens her grip.

'There now, steady,' she says. 'You can't let them see you falter. Not ever. You're the strongest person I know, so dig deep and find a way to fool them until there's no longer a need, you hear?'

It's an effort, but finally I manage to bear my own weight.

'Right, let's freshen you up.' She helps me out of my filthy clothes, gently washes me with bracingly cold water and attempts to untangle my hair. Someone from the palace has sent down a dress for me to wear, something appropriate for the ceremony, and Harley slips it over my head, guiding it into place. It fits perfectly.

'There,' she says approvingly. 'You'll do.'

The whole process has exhausted me, and I can feel my legs giving way.

'Come on,' Harley says, linking her arm through mine, a gesture that seems purely affectionate, but I know is her way of supporting me without anyone else seeing my weakness. 'It's time to show everyone what you're made of.'

I'm bolstered by her belief in me as we head out on deck, though it's more of a shuffle than a walk on my part. But her words – or maybe it was the bitterwort – have stirred my fighting spirit. And somehow – *somehow* – I manage to push all the guilt aside as I face the crew, lifting my head high as I force one leg in front of the other. My feet hurt, the bones still too fragile to support my body, but I cannot dwell on it. At least I have my toes again. I flex my new fingers and wonder how easily they will grip a blade.

Some of the Snakes stare openly as I pass, some

choose to whisper indiscreetly, but then Rayvn, Ren and Toby are in front of me, and they silence everyone by saluting.

Before I can say a word, Ren steps forward. 'These two will accompany you to the coronation, and the rest of us will remain here and prepare for our next voyage. The ship –' Ren hesitates – 'needs some repairs. Took a battering in that storm.'

He gives me a look that betrays his thoughts, his suspicions. But he does not sell me out to the crew, maybe because he has orders from his captain, or perhaps it's to atone for standing on that beach and making no objection to my murder.

In reply I offer him a nod of thanks. In truth, it will be a relief to leave the *Maiden* for a while, though I wish that Harley could come with me.

Harley shoots Rayvn a glance, and before I know it, my cousin has taken Harley's place at my side, offering me the support I desperately need. All I want to do is collapse to the deck.

I rest my hand on hers in thanks and I watch as Rayvn's stern frown softens. Whatever the difference in me, everyone notices it.

'I'll see you after the coronation,' Harley says to me. 'Try to let just one ceremony pass without disaster, eh?' she adds with an affectionate wink.

'I won't make promises I can't keep,' I reply, trying

to joke, but only exposing my frailty by the crack in my voice. The urge to hug her is strong, but Rayvn is already ushering me away to climb down the rope ladder to the dory waiting to take us to land.

Toby rows the small boat, carrying the three of us away from the *Maiden* towards the harbour. I watch my ship grow further away, and it's a sharp stab to the gut to think how close I came to destroying her. And it was so easy to become that person. All it took was fear and power.

We are all just one misstep away from becoming the villain.

'How do you feel?' Rayvn asks, keeping her voice low, though there's no disguising her words from Toby in such close quarters.

'Better and worse all at once,' I say, affectionately nudging her shoulder.

'Well, my orders are to take care of you, so if you need anything . . .' She lets the thought hang in the air while I try not to feel stung that she needs to be ordered to help me.

But then she nudges me back and says, 'Though I would have done it anyway. We're family, remember?'

After that, I relax and it's only when we reach the First Isle and start our journey through the town that my anxiety returns.

Agony shoots through me with every step, but I

almost welcome it, both as a penance and a reminder that my body is mine alone – the magic remains contained. I'm in control as long as I don't try to use it. Which leaves me where? A Mage without power? Did I really go through all that – put Bronn through all that – for nothing?

No, not nothing, I remind myself. I *did* pass the test and become a Mage. I have the weapon, now I just need to learn how to wield it. The problem is, I think the only person who can help me has cocooned herself away from Gaius. If I can find Esther, maybe, just maybe, she can show me how to control my power. After all, she seems to have found the balance I so desperately crave. And with that thought a renewed sense of purpose seizes me. If I can rebuild my physical strength, then in time I can travel back West. I can find Esther. I can learn to control the magic.

There is still hope.

Torin has arranged horses for us, so I don't have to suffer for too long. Riding the fine-boned gelding reminds me of the last time I was on a horse – a snow mare on the Eighth Isle. I ache for the mountains, for Mama and Pip. A knot of fear tightens as I think of Olwyn and the friends I left behind. Are they all still alive? I glance over at Rayvn and feel comforted to have her with me at least. Does she think of home now, as I do?

A few moments later she answers my question, as she pulls her bay mare beside me. 'Can't wait until this is all over, and we can get back to the ship,' she says. I smile to myself. Of course – the mountains were never her true home. Her heart belongs to the *Maiden* now.

'I'm sure the coronation won't take too long,' I say, having no idea whether I'm right.

'Captain went on ahead the day before yesterday, to begin arrangements, seeing as the King wouldn't leave your bedside,' she says.

So that's where Bronn is hiding himself, is it? He must really want to avoid me if he's chosen party planning over remaining on his ship.

I know how that kiss will have unsettled him. I know because it unsettled me. The ties that bind us will always run deeper than any magic, and he is as essential to me as the blood in my veins. And yet, no matter how much we may wish to erase the past, we cannot. The wounds we have inflicted on one another do not seem to heal. How then do we live?

There is no more time to think of Bronn once we arrive at the palace. It is alive with activity – many islanders have arrived to attend the coronation. The guards are understandably wary of my presence, but I am not the assassin who was here a few weeks ago. My pride won't allow Rayvn to help me, though, and once I've dismounted and handed the reins to a stable boy,

I begin to walk alone, subtly gesturing to her not to assist me. Publicly I do not wish to appear weakened, especially not in front of so many, even if walking on my new toes leaves me feeling both sick and unbalanced.

We're escorted to the open courtyard, where not so long ago I made my vows to the man about to be King. The extravagance the old King had insisted upon at the celebrations had made me uncomfortable, when times of such hardship were being endured. But I see that Torin has not wasted resources on elaborate decorations. It is to be an altogether more understated ceremony.

People openly stare at me as I make my way down the aisle, and I hope my pain isn't obvious. What whispers have they heard about me? What rumours? Do they wonder at having a Mage in their midst after so long? Do they fear me and what I can do? If they discovered quite how compromised I was, would they unleash retribution on me for all my crimes?

I should be relieved to reach my intended position, but I'm standing next to Bronn, who makes no acknowledgement of me at all.

I'm expecting Rayvn and Toby to join us, but only when I search the crowd do I realise they are at the back. I suppose they are not important enough to be at the front. Not like Sharpe and the Viper. Not like me, the ex-wife.

Maybe that's why everyone's staring at me. Wondering

what I'm doing here. Criminal, Viper, Queen – they've been offered many versions of me and I doubt much of the truth has reached their ears.

A few more latecomers arrive before, finally, Torin walks down the aisle, followed by the High Priestess, and then a guard carrying the crown upon a velvet cushion. I try to suppress the memory of removing that exact crown from the King's head, of stealing his mind and turning it to dust. I try to ignore the stab of desire to have that power once again. I try to still the stirring magic that rattles at its bars inside me.

I fail at all three.

My legs go weak, and I'm certain I'm going to fall, but then a hand slips under my arm to hold me up. Bronn doesn't look at me once, but he keeps his arm there through the whole ceremony, long after I require it.

The moment the crown is placed upon Torin's head, I breathe a small sigh of relief. There were many times I doubted we'd get this far, that he would die before having the chance to become King. But now that he is, I feel renewed hope for the East. The Isles once more have a King and a Viper who will defend them. Though the threat growing in the West endangers us all, at least those charged with protecting the people will do just that.

After receiving the crown, Torin turns to address the people – his people – and a hush falls over the crowd.

'We have walked in darkness for too long in the East,' he says. 'Suffering has ravaged our lands, our crops, our safety. Our children's futures. But with my father's decision to abdicate, it's time to return the light to our islands.'

I wince at Torin's version of events; my theft of the King's mind was hardly his decision.

He goes on. 'Your Viper has brought the bandits to justice, and the Fleet will now step in to help each island stabilise again. The mines will work once more, the economy will be revived. Food shortages will be addressed, to ensure everyone receives an equal share. We will return refugees to their homes. We will not cease in our efforts until the peace and prosperity of these islands is restored. That is my solemn vow to you all.'

The crowd breaks into applause and cries of approval ring in the air.

Torin waits until they've died down before he continues. 'I wish I could tell you that such a feat will be easy. But I will not lie to you. Not ever. There is an enemy far greater than the Isles have ever seen, who wishes to destroy all we hold dear. A Mage in the West, who seeks dominance over the Twelve Isles, and would have us live as his slaves. If he lets us live at all.'

A frightened, and slightly confused, murmur replaces the earlier cheer. This may be the first time any of them have heard the West spoken about by someone in authority.

'When I say I wish peace for the islands, I mean all twelve of them,' Torin says. 'I want to reunite East and West – to be as we were so long ago. And to achieve that dream I intend to do three things. Firstly we shall fight this Mage and destroy him. I have pledged most of my Fleet to restore order here, so I shall need an armada to sail West for a battle the like of which we have never seen. For this I need volunteers – men and women prepared to defend our lands.'

Though Torin is giving the best speech I've ever heard, though he's being true to himself and everything he believes, I know where this is headed, and I'm afraid for him to say it.

'Secondly,' Torin continues, 'I intend to ally with the rightful heir to the Western throne, to sever the rivalry between the two kingdoms and begin a new era of cooperation and alliance. And thirdly—' Here, Torin pauses. Because, like me, he knows this will not be an easy thing for the islanders to hear. 'Thirdly I intend for magic to be restored to these isles. For they are sick and suffering, and true peace cannot be achieved until the balance is restored.'

There it is. The whole unpalatable truth. Which has utterly silenced the crowd.

To my horror he is stretching his arm out to me now,

inviting me to join him. I'm not even sure I can.

But I won't let him down, and so I move away from the steadying comfort of Bronn's grip and force myself to join Torin. He gives me an encouraging smile, and takes my hand in his. He raises his eyebrows a little, a sign to ask if I wish to speak, and I love him for it. But this is his moment, not mine. And I'm not sure I could string a sentence together right now even if I wanted to. So I give a barely discernible shake of my head and hope my wince of pain isn't too obvious. His response is to squeeze my hand tighter before he addresses the crowd once more.

'I'm sure you recognise this woman. Marianne. She was once my wife. But our brief marriage has come to an end. Though we care deeply for each other, we have chosen an annulment. My heart lies elsewhere and I intend to follow it to the man I love.'

I glance over at Sharpe and the smile on his face offers me strength.

Torin's not finished yet, though. 'She was also once the Viper. My father accused her of terrible things, none of which were true. She sacrificed everything for the sake of these islands when she was Viper. But she has now relinquished that role. For what you do not know is that she is the only surviving member of the Western royal bloodline. Heir to the throne. A queen in her own right. And . . . she is a Mage.'

My eyes scan the shocked assembly, trying to gauge their reactions. Mostly I see a lot of open mouths. Rayvn and Toby are smiling. Bronn's jaw is as clenched as I've ever seen it and his fingers twitch, ready to reach for his blade should this go badly.

But the atmosphere isn't dangerous. Uncertain perhaps, but people don't seem angry.

'With our partnership the two royal lines are allied once more. The time of the Mage has returned. And together we will bring peace. To East. To West. To all.'

Torin's majestic conclusion is met with silence. And then the strangest thing happens. Someone starts to clap, and then another, and another until the very ground shakes with the sound. Never had I dared imagine such a response, but perhaps the people have been lacking the very thing I was missing too. It shouldn't surprise me that everyone needs hope. And now Torin has restored it.

My legs are dangerously close to giving away again, though, and so I whisper my apologies to Torin. He must see how the blood is draining from my face, because he gestures to Bronn, who instantly comes to my aid, escorting me swiftly out of the courtyard, and into a quiet side room.

I immediately lean against the cold stone wall and slide to the floor, lowering my head between my knees and closing my eyes.

When my strength returns, I look up to see Bronn on the opposite side of the room, staring out of the window.

He looks so very unhappy, and my heart hurts for him.

'Did you know Torin was going to say those things?' I ask.

'No, but it doesn't surprise me. He's honest to a fault.'

'You think he should have kept silent?'

Bronn sighs. 'I think that he shall be a very different King to the last.'

'And you a very different Viper.'

Now Bronn glances at me, and perhaps he thinks it's an accusation about how he claimed the title, and I hurry to correct myself. 'I meant from Adler.'

'A new era,' he says softly, and there's more than a trace of bitterness in his words.

'What is it? What's wrong?' I so desperately want to ease his pain.

But he doesn't answer. He doesn't need to. I know him well enough.

'It's OK,' I say to him. 'I understand why you did it, why you kissed me. You were only doing what you had to do to save your crew. I know the kiss meant nothing to you. You're under no obligation to me.'

Still he remains silent.

Finally he turns to me, his mind seemingly made up.

'I'll do it,' he says. 'I'll go West.'

It's about the last thing I anticipated he'd say, and though I'm the one who asked him to go, begged him to spy on Gaius, now I can't help but feel he's going because he wants to escape me.

'Are you sure?' I don't want him to go. I have sacrificed this man so many times. I don't want to do it again. 'It will be dangerous.'

He steps towards me, closer than I'm expecting. He looks at me intensely and I could drown in his eyes. 'I think I'm in greater danger right here.'

Gently he lifts his hand to my cheek and rests it there for just a moment. I blink a tear that falls to his skin.

And then he's gone. Out of the room. Out of my life.

Torin declared the training camp should be based on the open land of the Fallow Isle and for months that is where I have been, teaching Easterners how to match Guardians in a fight.

It's been a humbling and excruciating experience.

Not only have I had to establish a position of authority and train all manner of recruits to a punishing degree, but I've also had to regain my own fitness. From scratch. Once I could run for a decent length of time, I had to build up my strength, as I could barely lift a sword. My magically restored fingers were as useless as a baby's, and I had to push and push myself just to get them even to grip the bloody handle.

I have vomited, I have bled, I have fainted, but now, as I swing my fist into Raoul's stomach, my eyes blindfolded, I know it's been worth it. I can hold my own in a fight again.

Seconds later Raoul is on the floor, and I'm declared the winner. I pull the blindfold down, and smile at my opponent lying in the dirt as I offer him my hand.

I pull him to his feet. 'No hard feelings?'

'Easy for you to say,' he groans. 'You're not the

one getting a battering. Five rounds now you've been undefeated.'

It's true. My body is close to its old self, and I could almost forget I'm a Mage, were it not for the relentless hum of furious magic that never entirely dies away.

'Maybe next time you'll get lucky,' I say, brushing the earth from his arm.

'Maybe next time I won't fight you.' But he gives me a smile to assure me we're still friends.

And we are – I harbour no ill-will towards him for suggesting I be killed to end the storm, though perhaps I do put a little more weight behind each punch I land on him.

Truth be told, Raoul's been instrumental in setting up this camp. His crew joined him and were among the first to train. I did my best to teach them the techniques of the Guardians even when I was still struggling to stand. From day one we've trained blindfolded, just like Mordecai taught me. Thankfully they learned quickly, and are now teaching newcomers alongside me. After his impassioned speech at the coronation, Torin found himself inundated with volunteers from around the islands, all wanting to fight to defend them. There are nearly a thousand of us now, spread across the fallow ground and divided into smaller subcamps organised by training level.

There is still much work to be done, and I'm not

sure even a thousand soldiers will be enough, but we have the makings of a formidable army. One that can stand against Gaius and his Guardians, against Greeb and the Hooded.

Bronn set sail the very same afternoon as the coronation. Toby returned to the ship with him, but Rayvn had orders to stay with me to assist with the training. While she is an accomplished fighter, I can't help but feel Bronn left her to keep an eye on me. Still, I'm grateful for it, as it was Rayvn who wouldn't let me give up back at the beginning when I didn't believe I could ever be anything other than a pale shadow of my former self. She shouted, taunted, kicked – did whatever she had to, just to make me keep going. No one else was brave enough to take me to task, and to be honest, I wouldn't have regained my skills if I hadn't had Rayvn snapping at my heels.

At night, in the quiet of our tent, we have shared stories, recent and long-past. We have smothered laughter under blankets, we've whispered fears into the darkness, we've held hands in the silence when sometimes the enormity of what lies ahead kept us from sleep.

I have also read her every one of the notes Talon brings back to us from Bronn. They are short, often coded. But sharing them with her eases both our anxieties.

We know their journey west was successful, though

nearly cut short by a tempest almost as violent as my own. We know that Bronn has made contact with Gaius. He made no attempt at stealth, walking straight into the palace, boasting of ending my life and demanding a seat at the table. I can just imagine the scene, the look on the young Prince Rafe's face as Bronn swaggered up to his throne, all charm and danger.

But it's been some time since his last message. Though I'm hoping that's simply because he's infiltrated so deeply he can't contact me safely, until I next see Talon gliding in on the breeze, I shan't really be at peace.

As I walk back through the camp, sipping water, I notice Torin and Sharpe sparring. Torin hasn't been here as much as the rest of us, having many other duties to tend to, but since he's returned this time, I know he's seen the difference in Sharpe. We all have. With everyone training blindfolded, it's been an even playing field, and Sharpe's confidence in himself has been restored.

I watch as he spins fast, sweeping his stick against Torin's legs and sending him flying to the floor. Winded, Torin lies there for a moment, while Sharpe raises his arms in victory. When Sharpe offers Torin his hand to help him up, Torin playfully pulls Sharpe down instead, and the two of them laugh before sharing a kiss.

Grinning to myself, I turn away and start trekking across the churned-up ground. Seeing the two of them so happy and in love lightens my spirits. It reminds me what we're fighting for: the thousands of islanders, all of whom have people they love fiercely. Gaius would seek to destroy them – shatter families, steal children, kill lovers.

But inevitably such thoughts lead my mind to Bronn, and so I make my daily pilgrimage to the cliffs just beyond the encampment and stare out over the ocean, watching the sky for any sign of a vast bird bringing me news.

How I wish the clouds would speak to me, but they remain silent. No whisper from the West.

*Something's wrong.*

It's like a needle tugging a thread of fear through my guts – something's happened to Bronn.

Do I listen to that voice now? When it led me so far astray before? And yet, has it ever spoken anything but the deepest truths? Pleasant or otherwise?

I close my eyes and breathe deeply before turning back to the camp. All I can do is keep going. Keep preparing. Because the air carries the scent of a coming storm, one not of my making. In the wind is the promise of a war, vast and magical. We must be ready.

Today it is my turn to put a fresh group of new arrivals through their paces. Men and women, young and old, from all over the islands, who have come to risk their lives for our cause. I want to embrace them, thank them for their bravery, but instead I'm shouting orders. They'll thank me for it in the end.

I've taken them beyond the camp to a large field on a relatively steep incline, where I have them running up and down on the dry, burnt ground. Much of this isle suffered from wildfires months ago, and the land has still not recovered. The black brambles it's so famous for are charred and brittle, and absolutely no use to healers. The Fallow Isle is sickening every bit as much as the Mist Isle.

My recruits are only another two lengths away from earning a break – though they don't know that – when I see a small cluster of people heading this way. By the looks of them they've come straight off a boat, and I wonder if they are from the Third Isle for their skin is as black as Raoul's.

I jog across the field to intercept them, and offer my welcome.

'We're here to join the King's army,' a young man says to me. In fact, now that I'm closer, I see that they're all young. Possibly too young – I wonder whether I have a bunch of stowaways before me.

'Well, you've found the right place,' I say. 'Come on, I'll show you the way to the camp.'

As we trek through the field, I call out to my recruits. 'Everyone take a break, and enjoy it, because when I return, I'm going to make this morning seem like a gentle walk across the beach.'

I receive a few murderous glances, but most are too exhausted to hate me, and they merely collapse to the ground. I smile to myself, remembering feeling the same way not that long ago. There were times when I wanted to kill Rayvn as much as I'm sure they'd like to kill me right now.

When we reach the camp, I leave the new arrivals with the guards on duty, and go in search of Raoul. I find him sparring with a tall man – one of our volunteers from the Fifth Isle. Once Raoul has used the man's own height to unbalance him and send him crashing to the ground, I call his name.

He shakes hands with his opponent, then runs over to me.

'Problem?' he asks.

'I'm not sure. You tell me,' I reply, and I gesture to where the small group of young people await. 'Do you know them?'

His face folds into a frown. 'What are they doing here?' he mutters under his breath. 'I'll take care of this,' he says and I watch as he goes over and embraces his fellow islanders.

Reluctantly I leave them to it and return to torment my fledgling soldiers some more, but when the day's work is over, the first thing I do is seek Raoul out again.

I spot him sitting away from the fires, lost in thought, throwing his dagger into the air before catching it deftly by the handle, and I take him a blanket and a mug of ale.

He accepts both gratefully, and for a moment we just sit staring out across the land, embraced by the stars.

'What news from home?' I ask him in the end.

'Lilah and Bay are both well.'

I glance at him sideways. 'And the Seers?'

'Still think my coming here was a mistake. They know what happened with the storm, with the bandits. They know the danger you pose.'

I nod in acceptance. They're not wrong. My magic is simply dormant, not gone.

'And those who joined us? Who are they?'

Raoul sighs. 'Our first volunteers from the Third. Turns out my crew and I aren't the only ones unwilling to hide away and leave the Isles to their fate. Others want to fight too. More will follow.' This seems like a positive development to me, but Raul looks unhappy.

'But that's good, isn't it?' I'm confused.

'Maybe. Hopefully. I just don't want this to tear my island apart. We don't need a war between young and old, on top of the one between East and West. I was hoping the violence wouldn't reach the Third.'

I suddenly understand some of his fear. 'You're afraid for Lilah and Bay? If there's any conflict at home?'

He hangs his head for a moment. 'I sometimes wonder why I fell in love. Why I allowed such a weakness to develop. Before Lilah nothing mattered beyond smuggling, selling my produce for the highest price. Now I'm . . .'

When he struggles to find the right word, I help him out.

'The most honourable smuggler in the Isles.'

Raoul groans and I laugh.

'It's not weakness to love,' I tell him. 'It's what makes you strong. You have someone to fight for.'

'Then why do I feel so compromised?'

I reach for his ale and gulp a mouthful before handing it back to him. 'If you think I've got any answers for you, you've forgotten who you're talking to,' I say with a humourless smile.

'Ah yes,' he says, taking a swig for himself. 'Good point.'

We sit quietly for a while, both of us lost in thought. 'Raoul, the first time we met you told me I was the girl who didn't shoot. How did you know that?'

He gives me a wide grin. 'Been wondering if you'd ever ask.'

'There have been slightly more pressing things to deal with.'

'True. Well, it's a simple answer. Someone told me.'

'Who? Who could possibly have known?'

'Someone who was there. A fellow named Gustav.'

In my mind I see the scrawny loner from Adler's crew who got in my way the day the Fourth Isle burned. Who saw what had happened to Cleeve. Who reported back to his captain and condemned many on the Sixth. I'd always assumed he'd died in the West during our battle with the water raptors.

'How do you know him?'

'Saved his life.'

I look sharply at him. 'What are you talking about?'

'Adler threw him overboard after they left the Fourth Isle, blamed him for not killing you when he had a chance. Luckily for Gustav we happened to sail past not even half a day later and fished him out. He stayed and worked for me for a while, before disappearing one day when we were trading on the First. Heard he became a bandit, so he's probably at the bottom of the ocean with the rest of them now.'

'And he told you?'

Raoul nods. 'Got him drunk one night to glean information from him. That was one of the more enlightening stories. Just as well really. Or I probably would have sold you out to the King's Guard that day in the tavern.'

'Then here's to Gustav,' I say, wrapping my hand round Raoul's and raising the mug. 'A weasel and a coward, but a useful one.'

I stay with him for a little longer, until I'm so tired I can barely keep my eyes open. As I rise to my feet, I rest my hand on his shoulder. 'Reach out to your Elders again, Raoul. If they realise that others want to leave, maybe they'll reconsider joining us. Any foresight from them could be the difference between winning and losing.'

From the resigned sigh he gives I can tell Raoul knew it would come to this. For a man who used to live only for his own gratification, he certainly has a lot of responsibility resting on him now.

I pat his shoulder and bid him goodnight, but even when I'm curled up in bed I can't stop thinking about what it would mean if the Seers allied themselves with the King once more. Another link in the chain of stability. And as I think about prophecies, I muse on my own. I went to the Seers and begged them for help, desperate to discover how to destroy Gaius. Why then do I not ask Raoul to read for me again? Do I fear what his rúns would say? Would they still call me the storm that will destroy everything? Or is that now a broken prophecy? Would they offer hope? Or reveal something far worse yet to come?

The truth is, while I do fear the rúns, I'm more afraid of myself, of what lurks inside me, threatening always to be unleashed – which is why I won't be asking Raoul to read for me any time soon.

* * *

The days slip by and still Talon does not appear. His absence is like a festering wound. It causes a sickness to grow inside of me. And though I've tried hard to keep my fears from my friends, one night when we're eating dinner inside Torin's tent after another gruelling day of training, I finally raise my concerns.

'It's been too long,' I say, trying to keep my voice calm and not betray my increasing panic. 'We should have heard from him by now.'

Torin passes me a goblet of wine, and I drink greedily, as if somehow this will help. 'You think something's wrong?'

I don't want to admit the fear churning in my gut, not to anyone. That would make it real. But if Bronn is in danger, I can't stand by and do nothing. 'Yes.'

'Maybe he's too deep undercover even to send a message?' Sharpe doesn't sound convinced by his own suggestion.

'Maybe.'

'What do you want to do?' Rayvn leans gently against one of the supporting wooden poles, looking relaxed, but I know she's as anxious as I am, hating to be separated from her crew, from her captain.

'I want to go and find him.'

'We aren't ready to go west yet,' Torin says. 'The soldiers . . . they're not ready.'

'I know we're not ready to fight yet,' I say. 'But I don't think travelling with the entire army would be the right strategy anyway – if Gaius sees us coming, that could endanger Bronn. It has to be done quietly. Only a few of us should go.'

'I'll stay and get the Fleet ready to sail on your command,' Raoul says.

I smile at him, overwhelmed with relief. 'Thank you.'

'I'll help Raoul,' Sharpe says. 'I'm more use here for now.'

'Well, I'm coming with you,' Rayvn insists, as if I'd had any doubt.

'And me,' Torin says, and I look at him in surprise.

'Surely you of all people should stay?'

Torin reaches for Sharpe's hand. 'I will leave a trusted regent. You know how long I've wished to reunite the Isles, Marianne. Let me fight for my dream.'

'Then it's decided,' I say. 'We'll take a small crew over, and send word when you should join us.'

'And if anything happens to you?' Raoul voices the fear we're all harbouring.

'Then come West when the army is ready. Find the Guardians loyal to me. And be prepared to die before you let Gaius win.'

But as we leave the tent, Torin pulls me back. 'Are you sure about this? It's always been so important to you that Gaius believes you dead. Once we cross to the

West, he'll surely know you're still alive.'

'That time was coming anyway.'

'And your magic?'

I sigh, wanting to be honest with him. 'If it comes to it, I will use it. There is no other weapon against Gaius. But I'm an assassin, Torin. I plan not to be seen.'

I have spent the whole journey west wondering what it will feel like to return. Will the horrors of what happened here haunt me? Will I be paralysed with the same fear? Or will the lure of the magic rise beyond control? After all, the last time I was here, I summoned a water raptor and rode it through the ocean.

But as the coastline of the Twelfth Isle appears on the horizon, the only thing I feel is determination. To find Bronn. To find him alive.

We've gone through all his letters, and tried to trace Bronn's movements. He's been looking for where Gaius may be holding prisoners and, if we've decoded his messages correctly, he's identified three possible locations. One is a temple far inland, heavily guarded; one is the crypt of an ancient ruin; and the third is a tower perched on the northern cliffs. It doesn't sound like he's found any trace of the dank cavern I was held in, with its opening in the cliff face, which means those poor children may still be there, lost and alone.

If he himself has been captured, he might be imprisoned in one of them – and if not, we might find clues to his whereabouts.

After much debate, we have decided the tower is the

best place to start our search – his very sketchy maps are hard to decipher so we can't be sure exactly which ruin he was referring to, and the temple he's only heard rumours of, which is no use to us at all. But the tower on the cliffs, that we can find, and it is there we will begin our search.

Raoul has loaned us the *Nightshade* with a skeleton crew as it's too small to be much use to the Fleet, and it's served us well on our journey. But while the ship was fine, a certain member of the company has taken a bit more getting used to. The royal advisors fought hard against Torin coming with me, much to his annoyance, and the only way to keep everyone happy was to bring his bodyguards. It had seemed like a good solution until I'd watched Braydon step on deck and had to battle the urge to immediately throw him overboard. He's always hated me, gladly condemned me at the trial, and the only reason he still lives is because deep down I knew he always put Torin first. He truly thought I'd tried to assassinate his prince and wanted to see me hang for my crime. But that doesn't mean I wanted to go on a sea voyage with him.

To his credit he had quickly sought me out once we weighed anchor, tried to make amends, but the truth is that even after travelling over the ocean, we continue to regard each other with mutual distrust.

Nevertheless, as we sail close to the land, I know I

don't have time to worry about petty grudges, not when this island is crawling with my enemies. I can only hope some of my allies are still here too.

I've tried so hard to avoid thinking about them, but now it's impossible not to. Did Olwyn, Astrid and Jax remain at the palace believing Gaius to be a force for good? Bronn's brief messages made no mention of them, and I'm not sure what that means. Maybe it means nothing. Maybe it means something. If they were still there when Bronn turned up hailing himself as my assassin, I doubt they would have welcomed him with open arms. Hopefully when I find Bronn, I'll get some answers. If not, then I shall have to go in search of *them* too.

For a wonderful moment I allow myself to daydream. A fantasy of happy reunions filled with laughter and love.

Then I remind myself this is no dream.

Pulling myself back to reality, my attention falls on Torin, who is staring with some amazement at the land we're passing. After all these years of reading and hoping, Torin is finally seeing the Western Isles with his own eyes. Despite the danger ahead of us, he radiates excitement.

'Is it all you hoped it would be?' I ask, walking over to join him.

'It's strange,' he replies. 'I never truly believed I

would come here, but it's every bit as beautiful as I imagined.'

'Don't let their beauty seduce you,' I warn. 'You are not safe here. No one is.'

Torin looks over at me. 'For now. Once you're Queen, you will change that.'

I sigh, suddenly weary. 'Even if I manage to take the throne, change can be slow. The past is not easily erased.'

'Nor should it be. We will not reunite the Twelve Isles by forgetting all that's happened. It's up to us to show them what can be again.'

I reach to squeeze his hand, but don't say what's on my mind. That I cannot even begin to think about something so far away in the future. Torin dreams of allying the islands. I understand; I once did too. But now I merely dream of surviving the day.

The wind is favourable and we tack easily round the coastline, seeking the tower. Not for the first time I'm glad to be in a boat made from nightheart wood naturally imbued with concealment magic. I don't want Gaius to sense my presence here any sooner than necessary. I busy myself with anything I can to keep from being drawn to the water. Because this isn't the Eastern sea. These waters are laced with magic – not just the creatures who dwell in them, or the plants that grow in the deep darkness, but the very liquid itself. It has called to me since the moment we crossed the divide, and I have had to fight to contain my magic ever since. I fear I might dive in and never find the strength to emerge.

It's Rayvn who sees the tower first. 'I think we've found it,' she calls, and I race forward to take a closer look.

There it stands, a lonely stone turret strangled by vines, positioned so precariously on the cliff edge it's easy to imagine it toppling over and into the ocean at any time.

'I think it's one of the old watchtowers,' Torin says, and he sounds genuinely excited. 'Back in the war against the Largeland, there were several of these stationed around prominent peninsulas across the West, topped with braziers that were lit as a way to warn other islands if invaders were spotted. Once the threat was gone, they stopped being used and fell into disrepair.'

Rayvn stares up at it, unimpressed. 'Doesn't look like anyone's been there for a long time.'

'Which makes it a good place to hide prisoners,' I say. 'No one would think to go there, and any sounds might be attributed to ghosts.'

'You think that's where Bronn is?' Rayvn asks, and I can tell she's not convinced.

'I have no idea,' I say, trying not to sound terse, my worry making me snappy. 'But we have to start somewhere – do either of you have a better idea?'

Torin and Rayvn exchange a defeated look and shake their heads.

We find a concealed cove not far from the tower, and drop anchor once we've navigated our way into the shallows.

'Stay with the ship,' I say to my friends. 'I'll go and take a quick look. I won't be long.'

'There's no way you're going alone,' Torin objects.

'With respect, sir, I think she'll be more successful on her own,' Braydon says, clearly not wanting his king to leave his sight. 'She's the most capable of slipping in and out unseen.'

I'm not sure if that's a compliment or a dig, so I ignore it.

'I'll be fine,' I say. 'The more of us that go, the more likely we are to be seen. And if there's trouble, better to lose just one of us.'

That does little to reassure them, so I add, 'But I'll be back. Stop worrying.'

'Let me come, at least,' Rayvn says. 'I can keep watch, cover your back.'

Sensing I'm not going to get my own way, and not wanting to waste time, I agree. But before I leave, I give Torin a hug. 'If I don't come back,' I whisper in his ear, 'don't look for me. Keep going, whatever happens.'

When I pull away, he gives me a searching look, and it's a moment before he nods in agreement.

'Be careful,' he says and I can tell he hates letting me go without him.

'All right, you two, stop fussing,' Rayvn says, grabbing my arm and pulling me away. At this display of typical Rayvn impatience, Torin and I can't help but smile.

We take the dory and row to the small sandy bay. I'm glad that I barely get my ankles wet as we drag it up on to shore, because even in that brief moment the water wraps round me like silken ribbons that are unwilling to let go. Eager to put some distance between myself and the sea, I start the difficult ascent up the cliff, which has no discernible path. Rayvn follows behind, tracking my steps, and I hope that when we return, we're not in a hurry, because climbing up is one thing, but getting back down is going to be another.

It takes every ounce of my focus not to let the memories of this island overwhelm me as we run low along the flat terrain towards the tower. Fear itches beneath my skin, reminding me how I was used, manipulated, tortured – all by a man I trusted. I let the sensation sit there, acknowledge its presence, but keep it at bay. Because I haven't returned as a Mage, or a queen. Today I am a Snake, and I've come for my captain. And Snakes are assassins.

Strike first. Die last.

When we're a ship's length from the tower, I point

to the dense treeline to our left. 'Keep watch from there,' I say to Rayvn. 'Cover me if any Hooded turn up.'

She nods and slinks off, while I head towards the turret.

It would be easy to believe that no one has been in this tower for centuries. But evidence to the contrary is there when I look carefully: the moss slightly compressed by the weight of feet, the torn leaves and broken stems, damaged by a passing blade. One person, at least, has made their way here recently, and for all I know never left.

Gliding my dagger free from my belt, I try the heavy wooden door, and despite the cobwebs and ivy, it opens at my touch. I wince at the creaking hinges, and wait for a beat to see if the noise has alerted anyone. If the Hooded are here, I don't want to announce my presence. But there are no sounds from inside, and so I sneak through the small gap, letting my eyes adjust to the gloom before I begin to explore.

Every floor has only a single room, and every one is empty. But as I ascend the spiralling wooden staircase that wraps round them all, I see signs that, until recently at least, people were living here. Against their will. One room has blood smeared on the floor and the walls. In another discarded shackles and rope litter the floor. And then there's the smell. A faded but distinct scent of stale bodies, sweat, blood and despair.

By the time I reach the top of the tower I've lost all hope of finding Bronn here. Slowly I enter the final room, my blade raised. Unlike the others, this room is furnished: shelves, tables, weapons – and potions. Someone has been brewing them very recently, and, despite myself, I'm drawn to the nearest bench and press my fingers into some ground powder on its surface – a quick sniff of the residue tells me it's lacegrass. It can be used as a sedative, but most healers prefer not to use it as it has unpleasant side effects. Something tells me that whoever was making this potion didn't care too much though. I notice there is a door on the outer wall, and I begin to walk towards it, wondering whether it leads out to access the brazier.

'Marianne?' My heart lurches violently at the sound of his voice and I stagger forward, hardly able to breathe. I never imagined he would be here, not this far from the palace, and it takes every scrap of strength I possess to turn to face him, my fist tightening round my dagger as I do so.

Gaius.

He's the last person I wanted to see blocking my exit, the door shut behind him, and my legs tremble beneath me. No one, not even Adler, has ever terrified me to my core the way Gaius does. I'd thought Adler a cruel man, but Gaius is something else.

For a fleeting moment he looks shocked to see me

too. But he quickly composes himself. 'You're alive,' he says with a wry smile. 'Of course you are.' He shuffles forward, rubbing his chin as he pieces things together. 'You know, I was impressed when you escaped my cave, but making a performance of your death? I didn't think you had it in you.'

I find my voice has abandoned me. *Rayvn.* I think of her with a sudden pang of concern. Did she see Gaius enter the tower? If so, she'll be here any moment to help me and she has no idea who she's up against. Unless they've already met . . . Did he hurt her on his way to me?

'So you're a Mage now,' he continues. 'You finally did what was necessary to pass the test.' He chuckles, a familiar humourless sound. 'You're the one the Viper's been communicating with? Even after he killed you?' Then comprehension dawns on his face. 'Oh, I see . . . it was all staged for my benefit.'

'Where is he?' I hate that my voice shakes, betraying my terror.

Gaius ignores me. 'Your magic is strong, I can feel it.' He sounds mesmerised. 'You've buried it deep, but there it is, contained within you. You fear it will consume you?'

Not as much as I fear it will be consumed by him.

He laughs. 'You went through all that to become a Mage, to match me, only to find you're still too scared to embrace your own power? Oh, Marianne, that's pitiful.'

His taunts ignite my anger. 'Tell me, have you figured out how to heal yourself yet?'

A flash of fury lights Gaius's eyes, but he doesn't rise to the bait. 'One thing I learned during our time together is that while taking your magic didn't allow me to possess your healing skills, it did make my own magic stronger. You're not the only one who's been gaining power since we last met. Have you not realised yet how similar we are?' Gaius is watching me closely. 'You and me.'

'I am nothing like you,' I spit, knowing deep down it's not true and hating myself for it. After my magic was unleashed, I all too quickly turned into a murderous monster like the man before me.

'Lie to yourself if you want,' he says with a perceptive smile. 'But you can't avoid the truth. And what's more, despite your betrayal, despite your disobedience, I'm prepared to welcome you home. Teach you how to harness that magic burning from within. Help you achieve all you desire.'

'My betrayal?' I almost choke on my indignation. 'You took my fingers and toes!'

'Which I see you've restored.' He actually looks impressed.

'All I "desire" is to kill you.'

'That's the human in you speaking, the weak, mortal, powerless girl who has small, meaningless wants and needs. You're more than that now, even if you pretend otherwise. Together we can live for ever. And what's more, so can everyone we love.'

I look sharply at him. 'What are you talking about?'

'You started down this path because those you loved were taken from you. Well, so did I. Like I say, we're the same.'

'You killed your own mother to start down your path,' I remind him.

He shrugs, as though that's merely an inconvenient technicality. 'But that doesn't mean I've not lost people along the way. People I loved. A wife and child, lost to a plague not even my magic could prevent.'

I stare at him. 'You had a family?'

'Once. Centuries ago. Now they lie in a mass grave with many others. Hundreds of men, women and children. Together . . . we could bring them back.'

This conversation is not going at all as I imagined. He's knocked me off balance, and I'm struggling to centre myself. He capitalises on my confusion.

'Aren't there people you would give anything to see once more? To hold? Wouldn't you give up everything to spend one more day with your mother? Your real father? The others you've loved and lost?'

The longing to meet my parents, the desperation

to see Grace again ignites within me, his words fanning the smouldering ember of my grief. I ache just imagining Tomas running through the fields once more while Joren and Clara watch him lovingly. It's a pain that burns, that makes me want to tear down logic, ignore right from wrong. I would give anything to see them again.

'With our combined magic we can do it. Bring them all back. Just as you brought yourself back from the dead.'

But rather than convince me, this only reminds me that I did not resurrect myself as the same person. There are some laws that aren't meant to be broken – and violating them comes with a heavy price. I paid it once to become a Mage, but then it was a necessary cost. Even so, I came back as I crossed the brink, not days, weeks or years later. If I bring my loved ones back, what will they be? Would they be the same people I remember? How could they be? No, I will not do that to their memories. I will not disturb their peace for my selfish desires.

What disturbs me now, though, is why Gaius cares so much? For a lost family? It's possible that somewhere deep inside him is the echo of a man who had the capacity to love. But it's been gone a long, long time. He doesn't care about my loved ones, or anyone else's. He cares only for himself and his own power.

Moreover, Rayvn should be here by now. Something's not right. In fact, nothing is. It's snagging at all my senses.

'The fact you think I would ever join you only proves how deluded you are,' I say. 'I came here for one reason and one reason only. Tell me where Bronn is.'

'Why, on his ship, of course,' Gaius says, and gestures towards the door on the outside wall. 'Sad really, you just missed him.'

I don't trust him, not for a second, and so keep a half eye on him as I walk to the door, which opens on to a balcony that overhangs the ocean. I'm expecting it to be a trick, but there in the distance is the *Maiden*, and if we'd only sailed just a bit further round the coast, we'd have seen her and been reunited with the crew. And I wouldn't be trapped in a tower with the man of my nightmares.

I turn back to face Gaius, my mind starting to process what he'd said before. 'You knew he was communicating with someone.'

Gaius simply smiles and suddenly the fear consuming me is no longer for myself but for Bronn. His cover has been compromised and Gaius is not a forgiving man.

'You intercepted his letters?' Another thought occurs to me. 'Where's Talon? What have you done with my bird?'

'The fate of your sea vulture is the least of your concerns right now.'

I hate that he's right. My fear for Talon can wait.

'When did you stop trusting Bronn?'

'Not as soon as I should.' His eye twitches and I can tell his mistake bothers him. A weakness exposed.

'If you doubted his loyalty, why didn't you kill him?'

'First I had to know who he was working with. And thanks to your visit, now I do. You know me well enough to believe I found a way to infiltrate the Viper's ship. I have everything in place to kill the crew and your precious captain. So you have a choice. Join me, or watch them die.'

My mind's racing. *Think, Marianne*. What am I missing?

I look around the room, searching for what I know is out of place. The empty tower, the sudden appearance of Gaius, the absence of Rayvn. And then it hits me. I should have seen it before. Felt it before. I was so blinded by fear I failed to notice what was right in front of me. Gaius has no shadow. The air around him is still. Rayvn hasn't come racing in after the intruder because she never saw one.

I've no idea how he's done it, what spell he's cast, but I'm certain that I am alone in the room, and that wherever Gaius is, it's not here.

*Why?* I try to connect the dots – the look of surprise

on his face when he first saw me proves he wasn't expecting me. But he was expecting *someone*. He must have put some kind of enchantment over the tower, or perhaps simply in this room, so that he would know if someone trespassed here. In which case . . .

Our eyes meet and I know he's realised I've worked it out.

'Yes, it's a trap,' he says with cruel amusement.

I run to the door. As soon as I open it, the force of the fire rushing up through the tower throws me back across the room and I smash into one of the workbenches. It must have been blazing since I arrived, hidden from my senses until Gaius had extracted all the information he wanted, and I have no idea how he's done this, only that his power is strong.

'Marianne, I do not wish for you to burn to death today,' he says, walking towards me. 'Your magic serves me no purpose when you're nothing but ash. Join me and I shall call back the flames.'

The smoke is flooding the room, stinging my eyes and burning my lungs. But I stare him straight in the face.

'I will never join you.'

And before I reconsider the reckless impulse, I sprint through the room, skid across the balcony, leap on to the railing and fling myself over the edge.

The world disappears beneath me and for a second

my acceleration keeps me moving so that I am flying, a winged creature carrying on the wind. And then I'm hurtling down, down. There's barely time for any thought beyond hoping I've jumped far enough out to miss the rocks, before I hit the water.

The strange echoes of the ocean ring in my ears as I continue to plummet down, hair and weed tangling around my face, my limbs moving in all directions to try to propel myself back towards the air.

Panic consumes me when I look up and see how far I've fallen; I fear I'll never reach the surface in time.

And then the sea sings to me.

*Mairin.*

It calls the name my parents gave me, reminding me of my birthright: as Queen, I rule the ocean as much as the land. There are many things in this world to fear. For me the water needn't be one of them. It doesn't seek to lure my magic from me. It wants to help me.

Kicking with purpose now, I push through the water. I didn't jump from that tower just to save myself. I have to get to Bronn, have to warn him that he's in danger before it's too late.

I reach the surface and the air embraces me like an old friend. I gasp it down, almost drowning on it as I overfill my lungs. As I look back at the tower, the flames greedily clawing out of every window, I realise how lucky I am to be alive. The fall was further than I'd imagined.

Now I need to make my survival count, and I start to swim towards the *Maiden*, anchored out in the distance. I cannot begin to fathom what danger they're in from Gaius, but I have to get to them – quickly.

I'm far from a strong swimmer, but I push my body as fast as it will go, tearing at the waves with every stroke. I'm close now, and start to shout out towards the crew.

'Bronn!' My voice seems to fall flat in the air, and so I try to wave an arm, to draw attention to myself. 'Harley!'

I carry on swimming, calling out as I do, not knowing how much time I have until—

The world explodes around me, the blast ripping through air and water, stripping me of thought and sense, throwing me violently back under the waves. Shock paralyses me for a moment, before I break the surface once more and stare at the horror confronting me.

My ship, my *home*, is a ball of flames – what's left of it anyway. Half of it is scattered in the ocean, torn apart by the explosion.

'Bronn!' Grief is crushing me like lead and I fear I might sink with the weight of despair. 'No!'

I try to swim towards the wreck, desperate to reach

my friends. My family. So many people I love. But my legs don't seem to work any more, and I splash and choke and sob until it seems the ocean has been replaced by my tears. There won't be any survivors. Not from that.

*Bronn.*

The scream that comes from somewhere deep inside me splits through the air, wild with rage and anguish.

I try again to coordinate my limbs, and this time I manage to swim towards the burning wreckage. I know there's nothing I can do, but I go anyway. Because what if? What if Bronn was thrown to safety? What if Harley lies injured, waiting for help? What if Ana needs me? What if Ren is unconscious? What if . . .?

What I find is splintered wood, a leg, broken barrels, an arm, torn rigging, a torso. I sob as I call out for any survivors. But no answer comes.

'Bronn!' I won't give up looking for him. Not ever.

And then I hear it. A faint moan. Frantically I push my way through debris, searching for the source of the sound until finally I see him.

Toby.

He's been half flung on to a floating piece of deck, and he's covered in blood, though I'm unsure if it's his own. When I reach him, he's unconscious, probably due to the gash on his head. But it doesn't look life-threatening and I put my arm round him to stop him sliding into the water.

'I've got you,' I say to the boy, though the fact he's still breathing is as much a support to me as I am to him. A survivor. 'You're going to be OK,' I say, the words sounding hollow to my ears.

I have to keep looking, I have to. If Toby survived, then maybe others have too. But exhaustion is taking over, spreading its poison through my whole body. *Bronn*. I know I have to keep looking for him even as I close my eyes and rest my head on Toby's shoulder, sleep seeking to steal me away from the horrors around us.

I don't notice the boat approaching from behind, or the arms that reach down for me, until I'm being dragged aboard the small vessel. I struggle against my captors with a feral instinct until I see whose arms are holding me.

'Torin?'

'You're alive,' he says, his voice shaking with relief.

Beyond him Rayvn is pulling Toby on board the little dory, clasping him tightly to her.

'I tried to warn them.' I'm trembling from the cold, from the shock.

'I know.' And Torin folds me into an embrace. I cling to him as if by letting go he'll somehow disappear ghost-like into the distance, along with everyone else I loved.

'We left the *Nightshade* concealed while we came to look for survivors,' he says but I'm not really listening.

'I have to find Bronn,' I cry, clutching Torin's arms. 'We have to look for him.'

'I promise we will,' Torin says gently. 'We won't stop until there's no one left to save.' And he pulls me close once more, firmly kissing my forehead.

We search for hours, rowing past bodies, past oblivion, while the smoke from the ship cloaks us with the smell of death.

The wreckage is spread over a considerable distance but Torin doesn't complain once, though his arms must ache from heaving the oars while Rayvn and I scour the water either side, desperately searching for life. Rayvn is the first to find another Snake alive, a young woman named Lena who isn't familiar to me, though Rayvn knows her well. Lena is unconscious, but was saved from drowning by the sheer luck of being thrown on to a large chunk of wood.

Not long afterwards, we pull another body from the water, a man called Stoat, who's bleeding badly from his arm. I'm not sure he'll make it with such heavy blood loss, but I tear a strip of cloth off my shirt and fashion a makeshift bandage nonetheless.

My eyes ache from frantically searching the water, or perhaps it's from the smoke, or maybe the tears burning behind them, because there's no sign of Bronn and part of my soul is ebbing away with the last traces of hope.

‘We should head back,’ Rayvn says, her voice flat with grief.

Torin nods, and starts turning us round with one oar.

I grab his arm roughly. ‘No, no, we need to keep looking. You said yourself, there might be other survivors.’

The look Torin gives me is full of sorrow. ‘We’ve searched everywhere. There’s no one else.’

I stand up with such force the whole dory rocks. ‘No,’ I shout, refusing to believe it. ‘I won’t leave him. Bronn!’ I scream his name across the ocean as if somehow it can reach him where he’s gone. ‘Bronn!’

Rayvn’s arms are tight round me, pulling me down, pulling me back from throwing myself into the water, as Torin begins to row.

‘Please,’ I beg them through heavy sobs. ‘Don’t take me away from him.’

Rayvn cups my face in her hands, fierce as ever, though her own face is damp with tears. ‘He’s gone,’ she says, her voice cracking with pain. ‘Please, Marianne, I can’t lose you too.’

‘Bronn!’ I scream it one more time, as if it were my last breath. And then I have nothing left to fight with, and weep in Rayvn’s arms.

A captain should go down with her ship, with her crew, and mine are bleeding into the depths. I should rest on the bottom of the ocean beside Bronn. Instead Gaius has won. He has taken everything from me.

'We'll avenge them all,' Rayvn whispers as she cradles me. 'Bronn, Harley, Ren, Ana, every one of them. I swear to you.'

But all I can think about is what I'm leaving behind.

A massacre. A graveyard. And the man I loved.

Toby wakes the following morning, as we sweep across the still water, sunlight sparkling off it like stars. The brightness is relentless, as if the world is trying to ease our misery, but for those of us aboard the *Nightshade* it will take far more than calm waters and a clear sky to mend our hearts. If anything ever can.

Once we were back on board the ship, we set a course for the Eighth Isle, where we hope to seek shelter with Mama and Pip to regroup.

Rayvn told me how she had tried to follow me into the burning tower, but the blaze forbade it. How she had raced back to the dory to raise the alarm. How the explosion of the *Maiden* had echoed around the cove and surged through the ocean. How she and Torin had ignored the protests of his bodyguards to come and search the debris. I owe them my life.

Despite my best efforts, Stoat died during the night, his wounds too serious to recover from. We sent him to rest beneath the waves. Lena came round in time to see her crewmate buried, but is suffering with a headache and ringing ears. She's cracked at least two ribs as well, so is resting below deck with Toby.

With nothing more I can do for them, the last threads

that were holding me together have gone and I've fallen entirely apart. I thought I was strong, but I cannot fight the vast, gaping chasm that's opened inside me. Bronn was entwined in every part of who I was, and his death has ripped me apart, the bleeding tatters all that remain.

I have cried until I can cry no more. So now I sit curled on the deck, beneath a blanket that keeps the world outside, while the guilt invades the space inside me.

Because this is all my fault.

I should never have sent them here. I knew the danger Gaius posed but still thought I could outsmart him. My arrogance has cost many lives.

A scream longs to escape me, but I fear its strength, its depth. I fear it would make the ocean rise to the very sky, drowning everything. And I fear even that wouldn't wash away the pain.

Someone comes to sit beside me and rests a gentle hand on my shoulder.

'I've brought you some water.'

When I say nothing, Torin tries again. 'Marianne, you need to drink.'

His voice is taut with emotion and I remove the blanket from my head, looking up at my friend. Dark circles beneath his eyes betray his exhaustion as he holds a cup out to me.

I take it from him and we sit together so that our

shoulders touch but we don't have to directly look at each other.

'*Who will hear my cries o' night? Will it be the stars so bright?*' Torin's voice is a soft whisper as he recites a lullaby. It reminds me of the first time we met, when we were strangers and he quoted a poem to break the ice. '*Or can the moon help dry my eyes? Or will the firemoths soothe my sighs?*'

He pauses, waiting for me to finish the verse.

'*No sweet child, you are alone. Your words are lost, unheard, unknown. For every sorrow left unspoken, your soul does ache, your heart is broken.*'

Torin gives a sad laugh. 'I always wondered what kind of parent would whisper that to their sleepy child.'

I sigh. 'Adler did.'

His hand finds mine and holds it tightly. And for a moment we don't speak.

'Has Toby said anything more?' I ask eventually, my voice hoarse from the day before.

Since he regained consciousness, Toby has barely spoken five words, the shock of what happened and the enormity of his loss taking a toll.

'No, nothing,' Torin says. 'Rayvn's with him and Lena.'

'Good. They'll need each other now.'

'And what do *you* need?'

Oh, Torin. King of the Eastern Isles, and here is he,

propping me up, keeping me going, asking me what I need. I don't deserve him.

I rest my head on his shoulder. *Bronn. I need Bronn.*

Closing my eyes, I concentrate on breathing. It's a place to start. *Breathe in, breathe out.* If that's all I can manage in this moment, it's enough.

And then it comes rushing back. The tower, the *Maiden* exploding, stillness where there should have been noise. And I realise what I need, what I desperately need, is to talk.

So I tell Torin everything that happened from the moment I left the *Nightshade* – the tower empty despite evidence the children had been there, the potion room and Gaius's appearance. I leave nothing out, not one detail, needing to share the horror with someone and knowing that Torin can handle whatever I burden him with. As I speak, I can feel his body tighten with tension, but he doesn't interrupt, not once. He lets me spew out my thoughts in a messy confusion, and listens.

'How did he do it?' I ask when I finish. 'How the hell did he appear in that room, as real as you are to me now, without actually being there?'

'I do not pretend to understand magic,' Torin replies. 'It seems unfathomable.'

'He's grown stronger since I last saw him,' I say. With the magic he stole from me. It's a terrifying thought.

'How do I stop an illusion? One who commands an army of shadows?'

'*You* don't do anything. *We* find a way. But right now, we are weak. Wounded. We need to heal. To just keep sailing.'

I think of Toby, his physical injuries soothed but his emotional ones still raw, of the haunted look that's not left Rayvn's eyes. We are all broken, not fit for purpose.

*Breathe in. Breathe out. Keep sailing.*

And we do. We reach the Eighth Isle undisturbed, anchoring the *Nightshade* just off a north-west harbour. Raoul's crew stay with the ship to make minor repairs while a group of us head towards the mountain. We'll seek sanctuary with Mama and Pip, who I'm hoping will have news of Olwyn. I need to know I haven't lost her too. And maybe, in the still of the mountain air, we will be able to mourn our losses and find some way to piece ourselves back together.

The limited space at Mama's hut means that only one bodyguard can accompany Torin, and of course it has to be Braydon. But he makes use of himself by helping Toby while Rayvn and I support Lena as we trek across the island. We don't speak much; in fact we've barely said more than the essentials since we began our journey, all of us lost inside ourselves. But we are vigilant. We're all aware this island has many dangers, and we can't guess the reach of Gaius's gaze any more. For all we know, the entirety of the West has already fallen to him.

It takes us three days to traverse the island and climb the mountain, every step taking us closer to a refuge that we're all desperate for. We weave through the marram forests, the hollow trunks singing a sorrowful song in the breeze that perfectly reflects our mood. The sandy earth invades our boots, but we ignore the discomfort, welcome the distraction. There's a growing sense that if we can just make it there, just reach the quiet solitude of the mountain air, that somehow everything will be OK. That we will have survived the worst of it.

On the last night we make camp and, as I lie freezing beneath the stars unable to sleep, someone taps me on the back. I roll over to see Toby staring at me.

'What is it?' I whisper, my hand reaching for my dagger.

But there's no danger. Just a tormented boy. 'I saw who did it,' he says softly. It's the first thing he's said to me since he regained consciousness.

'Did what?'

'Set the fuse.'

My blood runs as cold as snow. 'Who?'

'I didn't recognise him. He had barrels of gunpowder. He lit them. Father saw too, raced to stop him. But he was too late.'

It troubles me how a stranger could have got on

board, but right now that doesn't matter. I hear what Toby's telling me. That he saw his father die.

'There was nothing you could have done,' I say. 'None of this is your fault.'

But he's fallen quiet now, and I know he'll be haunted by that moment for the rest of his life. I stretch my arm out and grab his hand, holding it until the sun rises.

The next day, while we walk, I turn over what Toby said in my head. When he's feeling stronger, I'll have to ask him more questions, try to figure out how and when one of Gaius's spies found his way on to the *Maiden*.

As it grows colder, though, and the air starts to thin, all thoughts of traitors disappear. Soon we will be back with Mama, with Pip, with the snow mares. Now the *Maiden*'s gone, this is the last place left I can call home. I want to be there so much it aches.

My pace quickens, and I leave the others – who are moving at a speed that Toby and Lena can manage – behind. But as I reach the familiar copse of ice trees that borders the clearing, my skin prickles with warning.

There's someone up ahead.

Dropping back slightly, I raise my hand, alerting my friends to the fact that we're not alone. They fall behind, apart from Rayvn, who comes up next to me.

'Pip?' she whispers.

'No, footsteps are too heavy.' I slide my blade out from my belt. 'Stay here.'

I creep silently through the trees, listening intently. When I catch sight of the person beyond them, I leap out, tackling them to the ground, landing a good thump across their cheek before bringing my blade to their neck.

'Marianne?'

'Jax?'

I drop my weapon and offer him my hand. The moment he's back on his feet, he pulls me close. To my relief he doesn't seem angry. Does that mean he didn't believe Gaius's version of how Mordecai died? That I killed him and fled?

'We thought you were dead.'

'Takes more than that to stop me,' I say with a strangled laugh. 'I feared Gaius had killed you too.'

'He'd have to find us first.'

Rayvn has come to see what's happening, and when she realises who I've attacked she calls the others to join us.

'Rayvn?' Jax is stunned. 'What are you all doing here?'

'Seeking sanctuary,' Rayvn says. 'What are you doing here?'

'Same thing. Olwyn knew this was our best chance at safety.'

Rayvn's face lights up. 'Olwyn's here?'

'Yeah, up at the house . . .'

Rayvn doesn't wait to hear the rest, and starts running towards her home.

Jax smiles. 'With the others,' he says, finishing the sentence.

'You're all here?' And when Jax nods, my heart lifts – just a little – for the first time since the destruction of the *Maiden*.

Torin is staring at Jax, and I know he's thinking of Grace. Her twin looks so like her.

'Jax, this is Torin, Toby, Lena and Braydon.'

Torin shakes Jax's hand firmly. 'It's an honour to meet you.'

'Likewise,' Jax says. 'I've heard a lot about you.' He turns to me. 'But what the hell are you doing here? What's going on?'

'It's a long story,' I say.

'And one that might be better told in front of a fireplace,' Torin says, his arms wrapped round himself.

'Come on then,' Jax laughs. 'Let's get you all inside.'

As we approach the hut, the door bursts open and Olwyn runs out towards me. I match her pace and we crash into each other's embrace. I can barely breathe she's holding me so tight.

'I knew you hadn't run,' she says. 'I knew that bastard was lying.'

'And I didn't kill Mordecai,' I say, needing to say it.

'We knew that too.' Her voice cracks with grief, and this time I'm the one squeezing her too tightly.

Eventually she pulls away from me, her eyes roaming over my face – whatever she sees causes her to frown. 'You've changed,' she says, and she sounds sad. 'You've suffered.'

Tears rise to my eyes and I nod, finding myself unable to speak.

'Come inside,' she says. 'There is much to say, but let's just be happy in this one moment.'

The others have joined us now, and I make introductions as we walk back towards the hut, Olwyn and I with our arms round each other's waists.

Pip hugs me the moment we make it through the door, followed swiftly by Astrid, before I go to where Mama sits by the fire and take her hand.

'My child,' she says, her voice wavering with emotion. 'I knew you'd return to us.'

'I've missed you.' She seems frailer than when I last saw her.

'As have I. But you're all here now.'

*Not all of us.*

Olwyn is helping Toby and Lena to settle on chairs beside Mama, wrapping them in blankets while Astrid fetches them some water. Pip is curled up on the floor in Rayvn's arms. Braydon stands close to Torin, who hovers in the doorway, an outsider looking in, and I stand up, wanting to pull him into the fold.

'Everyone, this is Torin. King of the Eastern Isles. And my best friend.'

Mama reaches out her hands, and I gesture for Torin to go to her. When he does, she grips hold of him, and bows her head.

'To think, the King and the Queen are both here, under my roof. I am honoured.'

'You are kind, but I am the one who is honoured,' Torin says. 'Thank you for letting us take shelter in your home.'

'I'm not sure we have space for everyone,' Olywn says, looking around the full room. 'Jax was already sleeping on the floor.'

'The floor is good enough for all of us,' I say. 'We just needed to see you – we can't afford to stay too long.'

Mama chuckles. 'That's what you said last time.'

'We don't want to cause you any trouble,' I say. 'I had no idea you'd all be here, though I'm very glad you are.' And I smile at Olwyn who's now sitting on the arm of a chair, leaning into Astrid whose arm is round her. They look closer than ever and it's a spark of light in the darkness.

The silence is warm, comforting, but it can't last for ever. It's Olwyn who's brave enough to break it. 'So . . . what happened to you?' she asks. 'One minute you were there, the next, you were gone, Mordecai was dead and everything changed.'

Jax clears his throat. 'As much as I want to hear this, I should get back outside. No one's on patrol.'

'I'll go,' Astrid says. 'It's nearly my turn anyway.' She leans down and kisses Olywn lightly. 'You can fill me in later.'

We allow them a moment to sort themselves out, Astrid piling on layers, while Jax sheds them, and then once Astrid disappears outside, an expectant silence falls over the room. I realise, with some dismay, that I'm going to have to relive all the horrors of the past few months. My time in the cave, how Gaius broke me into a thousand pieces. How Bronn came to my rescue by killing me. How I lost myself to the magic and became the monster I always feared I might. How Bronn saved me again – this time from myself. How he died. How they all died. And how I'm as lost as I was the first time I stumbled blindly into these mountains.

Though even the memories are traumatic, I tell them everything. I realise that apart from Torin no one knew all that had happened, and I see Lena and Toby wince more than once at the part their captain played, when they believed him guilty of a crime he hadn't committed. Even Braydon has the decency to look horrified.

When I'm done, Olwyn looks at Jax. 'It's worse than we feared then.'

'What did you fear?' I ask. 'What happened after he took me?'

Jax sighs. 'When the alarm was raised that Mordecai was dead, Gaius summoned us to a meeting with the council, and told us that you were responsible. He said that you had gone to him for help to cover up what you'd done, and when he'd refused, you'd fled.'

'Were you taken in at first?' I so desperately don't want to have been the only one duped by Gaius.

Olwyn comes over to hug me. 'His lies about you were the thing that raised our suspicions. After that we saw the dynamic change quickly, could feel Gaius's loyalties shifting back towards Rafe and his advisors. Arlan and Eena could sense it – they relished it. It immediately became dangerous for those of us who had given you our allegiance and the Guardians loyal to Rafe were sent out to find you. Everyone was baying for your blood.'

'We all kept our heads down, hoping you'd return, mounting our own search for you when we could. But you'd disappeared without a trace. And now we know why,' Jax says.

*They didn't give up on me.* Gaius had lied about that as well as everything else, stealing the last scraps of hope I'd clung to in that prison. I never should have believed him.

'And then the Viper showed up.' Olwyn glances

at me apologetically. 'Sorry, Bronn. Claiming he had killed you, and offering his services to Gaius and the Guardians – for a price, of course.'

'What did they say?' Even though the mention of Bronn's name is a stab at my heart, I'm wondering how Gaius reacted to that.

'He brought welcome news. With you dead Rafe had nothing to fear any more. But Arlan sent Bronn away. You may have noticed they don't like Easterners too much over here.' Again Olwyn smiles her apologies.

'After he left, there was nothing standing in their way,' Jax says. 'They crowned Rafe. He is the King.'

I thought such news would hurt, but honestly, after everything else, it barely touches the sides. I'm too numb to care.

'But Bronn didn't leave,' I interject, confused. 'He was working with Gaius.'

'Then Gaius must have struck his own deal with him. We didn't see him again,' Olwyn says.

Yes, that's exactly what Gaius would do. Keep Bronn all to himself.

'So why did you leave? What made you come here?' I'm trying to piece everything together without asking too much. Dwelling on anything related to Bronn is unbearably painful.

'Rafe decided that the Guardians were insufficient

protection. He ordered that we let word out to the Hooded that they would be well rewarded should they come and fight for the crown. No questions would be asked about the whereabouts of the stolen children, no past grievances would be held against them.' Olwyn makes no attempt to disguise her contempt.

'He's working with the Hooded?' I can't quite believe it.

'Yep,' Jax says. 'Rafe has built an army of mercenaries. Those of us who objected were hugely outnumbered, and we knew that if we stayed, sooner or later we'd go to bed one night and not wake up.'

'How many of you left?'

Jax shrugs. 'Hard to say. Maybe as many as a hundred? We've spread out all over the West, but we still have ways of communicating.'

'But there's not much to say,' Olwyn sighs. 'Now that Rafe has the Hooded, we're massively outnumbered. We can't fight them – and with Gaius on their side . . . Well, what chance do we have anyway?'

'The only chance,' Rayvn says, and she's angry. 'He killed my friends. My family. It can't just be me who wants to make him pay.'

'Of course not,' Jax snaps, temper fraying. 'I've lost people too; you're not the only one who's suffered.'

'It's not a competition,' I whisper.

Olwyn sees my distress and tries to calm things.

'Well, what can we do?' she asks her sister. 'How can we make things right?'

Rayvn's eyes glint with determination. 'We fight. Marianne has an army training back in the East. Soon they will join us, and then the battle for the West – for the Twelve Isles – will begin.'

My Western friends weren't expecting that and turn to look at me, astonished. I see the hope in their faces, and the room starts to spin. They want me to tell them I have a plan, that it's going to be all right, that we're going to defeat Gaius and the Hooded, but I can't. Right now I can barely keep the thick night of grief from closing in on me, can hardly keep the rushing tide of panic at bay.

'I . . . I . . .' Words fail me. 'I have to get out of here.'

And without a backwards glance I flee the hut, the cold mountain air hitting me like a wall as I run across the clearing before I sink to my knees in the deep snow, my chest burning as I struggle to breathe. Spots dance in front of my eyes and my vision starts to fade, my head spins, my balance fails. I close my eyes, wondering what's happening to me. I can't be dying – why then does it feel like I am?

A soft muzzle gently nudges my face. One of the snow mares has come to find me.

*Breathe in. Breathe out. Keep sailing.*

I'm aware of the warm breath of the mare and match my own to hers. Slowly the crushing anxiety subsides and the world feels steady beneath me once more.

'Hello again,' I say quietly, stroking the mare. As my heartbeat slows to a normal rate, I open my eyes.

She's as beautiful as I remember, gentle and strong, wise and ancient. The dominant mare who brought me home long ago. I press one palm to her neck, the other to her mouth, and her lips brush my skin.

'How are you?' I ask her. 'Been keeping Pip out of trouble?'

She nods her head and whinnies.

'Good.' And something like the ghost of a smile haunts my lips.

When she nuzzles me again with a gentle nicker, I sigh. 'I'm not doing so well. I don't think I can do this any more.'

It's surprising how easy it is to be honest with her. Maybe it's because I know she'll keep my secrets safe.

The mare paws the snow, and throws her head about, gesturing to the higher ground. She wants me to go with her.

'OK,' I whisper, scrambling on to her back and winding my fingers into her mane. I trust her absolutely.

And with a small rear the mare spins round and canters across the clearing. The icy air rushes past, burning my skin, scouring my soul. I expect the mare to slow before we reach the rock face, but she doesn't. Instead she leaps up on to it, climbing with an ease and speed I wouldn't believe if I wasn't with her. I should be terrified, as the world dangerously disappears beneath us, but I'm not – maybe because I trust the horse completely, maybe because I just don't care what happens to me any more.

The higher we go, the thinner the air, but strangely I find myself able to breathe properly for the first time since the *Maiden* was destroyed. It's beautiful up here in this hallowed place where humans have never dared venture, where magic dances like snow on the wind. When we reach the summit, the mare comes to a halt, breathing hard but happily, and I lean down to wrap my arms round her neck.

'Thank you for bringing me here.' She knew I needed to be alone for a while. Away from the pressure and responsibility. Up here, with only a horse and the mountains to witness, I can be a girl who's lost the boy she loves. A girl who's lost her family. A girl who's desperately afraid.

I want Harley to hug me and tell me it's going to be all right, that I'm tougher than I look – and then to laugh at my mad plans.

I want Ren to stand beside me, with his gruff exterior and loyal heart, and pledge to cut down my enemies where they stand.

I want Ana to laugh in the face of danger and set a course towards it with a flourish.

I want Bronn . . . I just want Bronn.

And I cry.

At first it's just a few slow tears, but then I start to sob, then wail, until a scream rips me from navel to neck, spilling my grief like guts over the mountainside.

I'm not sure how long it takes, but slowly my cries start to subside.

I cannot stay here for ever. I cannot bring them back. I cannot fall apart. I owe them all more than that.

Patting the mare, I sit up and take a deep breath, as if resolve is something I can inhale. 'Thank you. We can go back now.'

Her descent is slower, more careful, and I have time to take in the view. We're so high up that everything below looks insignificant and small. Which is how Gaius sees the Isles and the people who live here. My hatred for him is going to have to fuel me while I have nothing else. I gently feel for the magic contained within me, checking it's still safely locked away. My anger mustn't unleash it – not until I'm ready at least.

It's when we return to the clearing that I realise what my next step must be. Find Esther. Last time I was in the mountains, she tried to reach me in my dreams. I need to listen in case she tries again. But even if she doesn't, I have to discover where she's hiding. She's my last hope of harnessing this magic that I sacrificed so much to acquire.

The mare carries me almost all the way back to the hut where Torin stands in the snow waiting for me with a blanket.

I slide down from the mare and pat her again. 'See you soon,' I say to her and she presses her head against mine before prancing away towards the rock face.

Torin comes to wrap the blanket round my shoulders, a smile on his face. 'Olwyn said it was a sight to behold, a queen riding a snow mare, and she wasn't lying.' I slip my arm through his as we walk back to the hut. 'Did it help?' he asks, and I hear the concern in his voice.

'Not really,' I say, wanting to be honest with him. 'But I'm not giving up.' The icy embrace of the mountain as I poured out my grief has brought me enough peace to carry on.

'Do you want me to send word to Sharpe to bring the Fleet?'

'No, not just yet,' I say. 'I have one more thing to try before we take the fight to Gaius. But you should still write to Sharpe. Tell him what's happened. Tell him you love him because it can never be said enough.' He smiles sadly at my words, hugging me tighter.

Then I explain about Esther, and how I hope the magic of the mountains will help me locate her. 'And in the meantime let's make contact with the other Guardians and tell them our future plans too. Because to win this fight, we won't just have to be good.' And I fix him with my most determined look. 'We'll need to be exceptional.'

The days pass and I fall quickly back into the routine here. And yet my grief only seems to grow more acute, sharpening against the vengeance I carry inside me. Though I'm with people I love, I'm consumed with loneliness. Though I smile, there is no light behind it. I do my best to keep my mind distracted from nightmares but cannot escape them when I close my eyes, and so I try to sleep as little as possible, occupying myself by working either in the hut, training, or on patrol.

Several things become noticeable to me during this time. One is that Pip and Toby have struck up an unlikely friendship. It shouldn't be surprising, considering neither of them have ever had the company of others their own age, but something about the sweetness of their innocent bond catches me off guard. When we first arrived, Toby was lost in himself, the death of his father a silent burden, but Pip made an effort to draw him out, making sure he ate and talking to him even when he wasn't able to talk back. One day I watched as Pip rolled up her trouser leg, causing Toby to blush – until he saw the scar left by the ice lion and the blush changed to awe. They shared war wounds and since then I have rarely seen them apart. Inside, they sit in the corner, reading the small collection of books Mama has. Outside, they throw snowballs at each other, and build ice houses. Their laughter is magic; it illuminates the mountainside.

They remind me of how Bronn and I used to be. Children growing up in a dangerous, cruel world that seeks to snatch happiness from them – and refusing to let it do so. Defying life to hold them back.

But it also reminds me of the children I left in the cave, their laughter stolen, their hope gone, their futures drained. Cold, nauseating guilt burrows in my gut whenever I think of them and I have to push the memories aside. I couldn't help them then. I must find a way to help them now.

The only other person who seems not to find any joy in Pip and Toby's youthful play is Jax. He's angrier than I remember him being, his fuse shorter, his voice quicker to rise. I understand. He's frustrated. Always he's asking me what my plan is, when we're going to leave, where we're going to go. But I simply don't have answers for him yet.

'I'm sick of the cold,' he shouts at me one day when we're fetching wood for the fire. 'It's crept into every part of me, I feel infested by it.'

I pat his arm. 'It's not for ever.'

He sighs. 'I'm sorry. I'm just fed up. I want to fight.'

'We will,' I say. 'And it will be bloody and brutal and when it happens you'll be glad we had this rest.'

'I want it over. Want what's best for the Isles.'

'I know. And I know you want vengeance. I understand. For Grace, for Mordecai. You will have it, I swear.'

He looks at me strangely then, lost and lonely with something buried beneath that I can't identify. Fresh sorrow blooms in my chest.

'Look, why don't you start to make contact with the other Guardians?' I say, unable to bear seeing him so low and wanting to restore some purpose to him. 'Let them know that we're here, that we have more soldiers coming and that they should ready themselves for a fight.'

'Thank you,' he says, releasing a deep sigh. 'I'm sorry, I didn't mean to be—'

'It's fine. We're all on top of each other here; it's not surprising you're beginning to get frustrated.'

But the next time I'm on patrol with Olwyn and Rayvn, I tell them of my concerns, that Jax doesn't seem himself.

'He's just been cooped up for too long,' Olwyn says, as we talk under the night sky, the snow lightly falling around us.

'We all have,' Rayvn agrees. Having escaped the

mountain once before, she's longing to be back on the water again and I often hear her talking with Torin about where there might be a place for her in the King's Fleet. With the *Maiden* gone she's desperate for a new crew.

'Astrid knows him best,' I say to Olwyn. 'What does she think?'

'The same as me,' she replies. 'He's taken it hard, that's all. He's lost his cousin, and the Guardians – everything he's ever known. It's just taking some time for him to adjust.'

That I can relate to, and so I drop the subject, instead enjoying spending some time with my own cousins, talking into the small hours, even as the snow falls more heavily around us, and the wind starts to whip up.

'I haven't missed the blizzards,' Rayvn growls, pulling her face scarf higher up so that only her eyes peep out. 'Give me a storm any day.' She glances over at me. 'Well, apart from your one.' But her eyes sparkle and I know there's a smile lurking beneath that scarf.

'Tell me more about the East,' Olwyn says to Rayvn, raising her voice to be heard over the wind, and, as they talk, I start to drift away from them.

Because I can hear something.

Closing my eyes, I concentrate, trying to focus. For a moment it's gone, but then there it is again. A voice. Calling my name.

'Which direction is this weather coming in from?' I shout at the others, interrupting their conversation. I think I know, but I have to be sure.

'From the south,' Rayvn calls back. 'South-west maybe. Why?'

'I have to go,' I say, running to them.

'Go where?' Olwyn looks confused. 'What are you talking about?'

'To the Seventh Isle.' And something akin to excitement stirs inside me. 'She found me. Esther found me.'

Cloaked in perpetual gloom, the Shadow Isle really does live up to its name. The absence of light would be unnerving, were I not a shadow myself. Since setting foot on the shore, I've felt like this island has been drawing a cold, uncomfortable truth from me. Here, I finally accept what I had been trying to fight in the caress of the mountains: that I exist simply to finish what I started. That once Gaius is dead and peace restored, I will no longer care what happens to me. The loss of Bronn and my family of Snakes is a grief too heavy to bear.

The whole island thrums with a haunting power, the remnants of a time long ago when magic wasn't forbidden or feared. But now the magic is buried under the stench of its own decay, the island a pitiful echo of a former world.

What better place for Esther to cocoon herself away, safe from the prying gaze of Gaius? No wonder she fled the Eighth to hide here.

I trudge through the swamp, imagining it was once a vibrant jungle, rather than the unpleasant wilderness it is now. Corpse-like trees with crooked backs stoop to peer at me as I pass through, slimy vines hanging from their branches like entrails that I have to brush aside. Somewhere out of sight birds call to each other, their song a menacing laugh, and I can't help feeling I'm the butt of their joke. The fool who wandered willingly into this deadly environment. It's almost as if the whole island is holding its breath, waiting to see if I'll survive or fall victim – as surely many others have before me.

But so far I've seen no sign of the shadow demons rumoured to dwell here, the spirits that men on the Eighth Isle hoped to appease with my sacrifice. Maybe people were simply hearing the howls of sorrow drift over the ocean from the heart of this island and misunderstood the cries.

Despite the fact that it's cold, beads of sweat trickle down my back. I press on uncertainly in search of Esther, hoping she'll call out once more to guide me to where she's hiding. Instead I see a bone, a small leg bone from some kind of mammal. And then I spot another and another, leading me to a pile leaning up against a rotting tree. I step closer for a better look. The bones are unblemished, no sign of scratches or teeth marks, which is strange. Normally some scavenger or other would pick them clean, but these look as untouched as when they rested beneath flesh.

I turn to move away . . . and find I cannot. My foot is stuck fast, and I realise with horror that the bones have lured me into a bog. And I'm beginning to sink.

Swearing, I try to pull myself free, only causing the bog to tighten its grip. By the time I manage to wade near to the bank, I'm waist deep in thick, ravenous mud, but I'm close, so close to safety. If I stretch, I can almost reach the tree roots at the edge to pull myself out.

Suddenly and painfully something grabs my foot and yanks me backwards, deeper into the swamp. The force of the movement squeezes the air from my chest, and the marsh reaches my shoulders, but it's panic that crushes at my ribs as whatever has hold of me coils tighter and higher up my leg, threatening to pull me under entirely, away from light, from air, from life.

If I could, I would thrash about, but my limbs are imprisoned in the heavy sludge. Breath has abandoned me, replaced by the suffocating certainty of death.

And then, smashing through the mire, a fearsome creature appears, worm-like with two bulging eyes that are nothing but empty dark caverns. Its long neck weaves high above me and in a moment of horrifying clarity I understand I'm being held by the other end of this monster, just before it lifts me up and out of the bog.

Still firmly squeezing my leg with its tail, the swamp-worm dangles me above its head, like I weigh nothing. Its mouth opens, widening abnormally so that its whole head seems to expand, multiple snake-like tongues darting out to taste the air, gliding over a circle of razor-sharp teeth, long and needle-thin.

And with a jolt I realise why none of the bones piled by the tree have marks on them. This creature swallows its food whole and spits out what's left. If I don't do something, I'll be the next addition to the pile.

Twisting and turning my body, I manage to reach my belt, my fingers searching for the knife that should be there – but it's gone. It must have been pushed out as I sank beneath the swamp. Hope gives way to despair as the swamp-worm begins to lower me towards its jaws, the stench of rotting flesh rising to meet me. I thrash and writhe, desperately trying to free myself, but to no avail.

When I'm close enough for the tongues to lick me like flames, I make a final attempt to save myself, grabbing hold of the mouth and using all my strength to push against it. I've stopped myself from disappearing into the darkness, but now I'm stuck here, and soon I'm screaming with the exertion and the pain of being forced in while still trying to force myself out.

I'm making so much noise that I don't hear the twang of the arrow loosing from the bow or the rush of it flying through the air. I have no warning anything is coming until it lands in the back of the swamp-worm's head. The creature bellows in pain, relaxing its grip on me as it rears away, so that I fall back into the swamp, trading one prison for another.

A second arrow lodges deep in the swamp-worm's

bulbous head, and though not fatally injured the huge creature decides I'm not worth the risk, and submerges once more beneath the murky soup of death, leaving me frantically searching for who just came to my rescue.

Slinging her bow over her shoulder, my hero approaches, holding out a long branch for me to grab.

We both have to stretch, but eventually my fingers curl round the wood and, as soon as they do, she pulls me with a strength I wouldn't have believed she possessed towards solid ground. I crawl out, collapsing flat on the damp earth, gasping for air.

She sits beside me. 'Steady now. You're safe.'

I blink up at her. And then I start to laugh, relief making me giddy. Esther looks far worse than I remember, older, thinner, but I've never been happier to see her. 'Where did you learn to shoot like that?'

'I'm old, not incompetent,' she says with a wry grin as she offers a hand to help me up. 'I wondered when you'd come looking for me.'

'I would have come sooner but things have been a bit –' I search for the right word – 'challenging.'

'Tell me everything,' she says. 'But not here. This swamp is dangerous.'

I follow Esther without question. She has kept hidden from Gaius's gaze for her whole life, and survived everything this lethal island has to offer. Under her protection I actually feel somewhere close to safe.

She leads me through the dank wilderness, brushing spidery vines out of our way as she picks a deliberate and invisible path through the shadows, avoiding unseen dangers. Low, eerie noises drone through the air, a sound of knotted grief and endless heartache that strikes a chord with my own. I don't bother to wipe away the tears that silently run down my cheeks.

We walk for almost an hour, though it's hard to judge the passage of time as the natural light barely breaks through the trees, until eventually we reach what looks like a wall of vines. In fact, it's more like a curtain, as Esther lifts them for us to pass through, revealing a hidden clearing beyond. Nature has provided her with a tent; the leaves carpeting the ground are dry in here, not the soggy, limp ones out in the swampland. Branches and twigs have woven through the roof and edges of this little nook, strengthening its structure, and piles of moss offer comfort and warmth. Blankets made of grasses and vines are strewn on the ground, and a jolt of recognition passes through me. They are what I saw in my dreams, the cocoon that Esther was safely encased in.

I sit on the floor as Esther pours me a glass of unappealing water, cloudy and grey, and offers me a handful of brown seeds.

'They're safe,' she says, seeing my expression. 'Boiled swamp water and seeds from the moldwort plant.

Wouldn't recommend you eat any other part of the plant, but they're nutritious.'

It's only polite to try them, and I am ravenous, but the moment I put the seeds in my mouth I regret it. They are dry and bitter and taste like dirt.

Esther smiles. 'I said they were nutritious, not delicious.'

The water isn't much better. Apparently swamp water tastes like swamp water no matter what you do to it.

And yet afterwards I feel refreshed and ready to tell Esther everything that's happened since we last crossed paths. It takes a long time, so long that we're sitting in almost perfect darkness by the end, apart from the glow of the fire she's started in a small pit in the ground.

'You called me here,' I say when the tale is told. 'Please tell me you have a way to help.'

Esther sighs. 'I hoped I could, but now I'm not so sure. Nothing is as it was,' she says.

I frown in confusion. 'You can teach me how to use my magic to fight Gaius.'

'Child, I would teach you everything I know if I thought it would make a difference. But you're a Mage. You know how to use your magic, have wielded it far more powerfully than I've ever managed to. What you're really asking is how to use it without losing yourself. And there . . . I cannot help you. To my knowledge there has never been a Mage who has succeeded in such a thing. I doubt there ever will be. And the stronger the Mage, the more absolute their fall. I've always known you had the potential to be the most powerful Mage of our time. And the most dangerous. Given how quickly you lost yourself to the magic, when for most Mages it destroys us slowly over the years, I'd say I was right.'

Shame burns inside me, but I'm not ready to give up just yet.

'But you're a Mage, and you've not lost yourself.'

The look she gives me breaks my heart. 'You think I've found balance? I am nothing like the woman I was. I have used my magic to control, to manipulate, and lost much of myself to it. Now I use it as little as possible, only when necessary and only for protection. And still it eats away at me, Marianne. Dissolves me from within. Magic isn't meant to be contained. We all pay a price for using it in the end.'

'Why did you offer to teach me then? All that time ago on the Eighth Isle?'

Esther laughs humourlessly. 'Because back then you were like one of these moldwort seeds. Small and ready to grow. I owed you more than I could ever give, but that was all I had to offer – a place to take root. Instead you've been taught by that devil Gaius, and now you've grown too fast, too wild. You are like this island, overflowing with magic that rots it from within. I am sorry for it.'

My eyes flash as fiercely as the flames reflected within them. 'You're sorry? What use is that to me? I can't fight Gaius with your apology!'

I regret raising my voice instantly. Without Esther I'd be nothing more than another pile of bones in the swamp graveyard.

But she sees my guilt and brushes it away. 'No, you're right to be angry. There's nothing fair about this. Gaius has to be stopped. But if you can't control your magic, you're more of a threat to these islands than he is.'

My anger came first, but it's disappointment that follows, crushing me under its weight. I'd been so certain finding Esther was the answer to my problems. I teeter on the brink of my despair, wanting to weep in the face of yet more adversity.

With a deep breath I pull myself back. If I can't give up, I must push forward. Maybe Esther can't help me in the way I'd hoped, but there must be more I can learn from her.

'Tell me about your magic,' I say, reflecting on how little I know about Esther, despite our lives being bound since before I was born.

She stares at the ground. 'I can communicate, unlock the mind. Reach inside people's heads, see their memories, call them to me. You know that better than anyone.'

That's true. In dreams, across islands – always Esther has drawn me to her or warned me when needed.

'Do you know how Gaius managed to speak to me in the tower then, without actually being there?'

'I have my suspicions,' she says with a heavy sigh. 'His magic alone, even increased by taking yours, would not be enough. He's not naturally inclined to that type of magic. He would have needed enchantments, spells . . .' Her eyes meet mine. 'A blood sacrifice.'

'What? Some sort of ritual?'

'Yes,' she says. 'I imagine wherever Gaius really was, he was standing over a disembowelled body, the life force flowing directly from that person to him.'

'You mean his victim would have been alive?'

'When he spilled their intestines? Yes. They would have died fully aware of what was happening to them.'

It's a grim thought, but Gaius has always done whatever it takes to increase his own ability.

I think again of his obsession with bringing back the dead. Whatever he says, it's not just because he wants to see loved ones again. Perhaps he considers it the ultimate mark of strength? And maybe he's right – once he can control mortality, once death no longer means the end, there is nothing more for him to master, his powers absolute. He will be unstoppable.

*You controlled death.*

The thought cuts through me like a sharp blade.

A reminder that *I* could be unstoppable too. If I just let the magic back out.

Shaking such temptations away, I try to refocus on our conversation. 'If Gaius does that again, is there a way to sever the connection?'

She nods. 'If he's there because of a blood offering, I believe that by making one of your own, you could break the link.'

'I won't hurt anyone for magic,' I say. Not again.

'You'd only need to hurt yourself. Spill your own blood and his spell should hold no power over you.'

Hardly an appealing prospect, but definitely preferable to being in a room with Gaius.

'I wonder . . .' Esther muses, talking more to herself than me, but I leap on it nevertheless.

'What? What is it?'

For a long while Esther says nothing, her eyes narrowing in thought. 'There is something, but there is much to consider. I need to think – and to rest. Ask me again in the morning.'

Even as we settle for the night, I can hear her muttering under her breath. She sounds as if she's arguing with herself and is still doing so when I fall into a troubled sleep.

By the time dawn breaks Esther seems to have made her decision.

'I think there is one thing I can offer you,' she says, handing me some more of the repulsive moldwort seeds. 'But it won't be easy.'

'I'll try anything you can teach me.' I screw my face up as I chew, grateful despite the taste.

'It's not teaching, exactly,' she says. 'But there is a way for me to impart my magic to you, a way to show you how to call to others. It might be useful in the fight ahead. If you're willing?'

'Yes, anything,' I say honestly.

Her lips press tightly together. 'You can take some of my magic. Taste it, dissect it, learn from it.'

I shake my head. 'I can't take your magic, that's what Gaius does.'

'No, he *steals*, I'm offering. I trust you.'

When I still don't say anything, she says, 'You are not him, Marianne. No matter what you fear.'

The prospect terrifies me. But when she holds out her hand, I take it, trembling. Her other hand rests on my head and the moment she starts to offer her magic, white heat surges through my skull. My heart pounds as my own magic shrieks inside me, begging to be let out. The urge to drain her power from her, to drink her dry is sudden and strong, and it would be so easy. She's practically put her neck against a blade and asked me to cut it open.

I fight the impulse by focusing on the unfamiliar

sensation. While my own magic heats my blood, Esther's prickles inside my head, an altogether unique feeling. Not unpleasant, but not comfortable either. Her magic is straining to take its natural path, reaching out beyond me – it's as if my mind is expanding, too big to fit inside its prison, seeping outwards, searching . . .

*Bronn*. There's only one person my heart calls out to, only one person I long to have by my side. But no magic can reach him.

I push Esther away, wanting it to stop. I didn't come here to think of him. I came here to escape. To move on.

She looks at me in confusion. 'What happened?'

It's only then I realise that I'm crying. 'Nothing. You were right, this was a bad idea.'

Esther shuffles away, but doesn't take her eyes off me. 'You were tempted to take it all, weren't you?'

I brush my cheeks with my sleeve. 'Yes.'

'But you resisted. How?'

'I'm not sure. I was focusing on what the magic could do . . . and then it led me to someone I loved.'

She claps her hands together to emphasise her point. 'And that's why you will find a way to defeat him. Because Gaius doesn't love. Which means he doesn't know how to protect. That's your advantage. Same as it was with Adler.'

'The man I love is dead.'

'That doesn't mean you can't still fight for him. For all of them. Death is only a temporary separation. The love doesn't die with them. This is the most valuable lesson I can teach you,' she says, sounding suddenly weary. Gifting me a little of her magic has clearly taken a toll. 'It's up to you now.'

She's right. My love for Bronn will never die, but not everyone I love is gone. There are people still depending on me, who believe in me. And I believe in them. If these are our last days, I want to share them with the people I love.

I'm gripped by a fresh sense of urgency. 'Come with me,' I say to Esther. 'Stand with me against Gaius.'

She looks tired, like she knew I would ask but hoped I wouldn't. 'I'm an old woman. What use would I be in any fight?'

'You're a Mage. You'd stand a better chance against him than most. What have you got to lose?'

'My life,' she says. 'I have spent decades preserving it and I'm in no hurry to throw it away.'

'You've spent a lifetime *hiding*,' I remind her gently. 'From others, from your magic, from yourself. You've made yourself an exile from everyone and everything. Are you truly telling me you're happy? That you enjoy being alone in this place?'

'At least I'm alive.'

'This isn't living,' I say softly.

For a moment I think she might reconsider, but then she bows her head. 'I'm sorry, Marianne. I've done all I can. I wish you well, truly.'

I take her hand in mine and squeeze it. 'I understand,' I say. 'And I'm grateful for what you've done for me.'

When I reach the vine curtain, I pause and turn back to her. She looks lost, haunted by her past. I wish things could be different, that fate hadn't dealt her such a cruel hand. I hope one day she finds some peace. 'Goodbye, Esther.'

I venture out into the dangers of the island once more, but the truth is, I feel an affinity for it now. Esther was right, I do have a lot in common with this grim place. Both troubled, both feared.

And both deadly.

By the time I've returned to the Eighth Isle I'm wishing I'd tried harder to convince Esther to come with me. I'm not sure I should have left her alone on the Seventh, especially after she saved my life – again.

I can't help thinking about what she said, about how she was nothing like the woman she once was. I wonder how the magic has twisted her, who she used to be before. Even with her attempts to use it as little as possible, only dabbling in the occasional potions and protection spells, has its damage spread through her body like a disease? If I cut her open would I see the path it's carved like an infection? Or would every part of her be tainted, poisoned by the irresistible seduction of power? Then I think of my own insides and shiver at what I'd discover.

But would there even be any sign of the magic's damage when I've been hollowed out by sorrow, left empty so there is nothing to absorb the raw ache of grief? Fear gnaws at me always; anger inflames me constantly. For every bruise I bear on my skin there are a hundred more beneath and they hurt. *I* hurt.

And now I must also learn how to quieten Esther's magic, buzzing in my head like a dull ache, beating

Bronn's name like a chant, crying out to him over and over.

I walk across the island, tormented by my thoughts, until the rising of hairs on my neck silences them. My senses sharpen into focus. I'm being followed. I've taken every precaution to keep myself concealed, knowing how dangerous this island can be, yet somehow someone's done the impossible and found me.

My skin burns with the anticipation of a fight, nausea swooping in as I consider who it might be. Has Gaius used magic to seek me out and sent one of the Hooded for me? Could I best them this time, or would they use my weaknesses against me once more? Do I dare use my magic should it come to it? One thing is for certain – I won't be taken prisoner again. I will fall on my own sword first.

I scale the nearest marram trunk, using the thick foliage to conceal me from my pursuer. Time for the hunter to become the hunted.

A figure wearing a travelling cloak, the hood pulled up, passes slowly beneath me, and my breath catches. The build, the gait – they're both so familiar, and jolt my grief to the surface.

I force it away, refusing to be distracted. It isn't him – he's at the bottom of the ocean. I'm just seeing similarities because I've been thinking of him. I wait for the stranger to move far enough away, and then I lightly jump to the ground.

Though I make no noise, the person turns at my movement, and I see his face, though it's hidden in shadows.

Time stops.

It *is* him. Not a ghost, not a figment of my imagination. He's standing before me, as I real as I am, his breath a faint cloud on the cold air.

'You're alive?' My voice is half-whisper, half-sob. And I drop to my knees, unable to do anything beyond drown in the relief flooding me.

Then Bronn's kneeling beside me, his fingers tilting my chin to make me look at him.

I drink in every familiar detail of his beloved face, the scars, the lines, the curve of his lips. 'I thought you were dead.'

'Not yet,' he says. 'Not today.'

I throw my arms round his neck, holding him tight. I thought I would never feel his embrace again. Slowly his arms enfold me too, and the forest watches as two broken souls are momentarily mended.

'How? How are you here?' I murmur into his neck, my lips brushing against his warm skin.

'I've been looking for you,' he whispers.

'How did you know where I was?'

'I just knew. It was like you were calling to me.' And his arms hold me a fraction tighter.

Esther's magic worked. Somehow I succeeded in summoning him to me. But even though that's astonishing, it pales in significance compared to the fact that Bronn is here. Alive.

When we eventually release each other, our intimacy leaves us both a little shy. Momentarily we'd dropped our defences, the walls we'd built between us these past months ripped down, leaving us exposed in the rubble. Bronn looks nervously around. 'We should keep moving,' he says.

'Come with me,' I say. 'I can take us somewhere safe.'

I want to reach for his hand. I need his touch to remind me he's real, not a phantom. Maybe he's feeling the same because his fingers graze against mine and neither of us makes any effort to move apart. I stare at him as we walk in silence, fearing that if I even blink, he'll blow away like dust on the wind. 'How are you alive?' I ask. 'The ship . . . the crew . . .'

He stops and pulls me into a sudden embrace. 'I know. We'll avenge them all, I swear to you.'

His fierceness allows me to crumble, and to both my horror and relief I start to sob uncontrollably, the river of grief breaking the dam I've built inside me. He says nothing, just holds me while I mourn our family.

'How will we avenge them?' I look up at him, my face damp, hair plastered to my skin. 'I don't know how to fight Gaius. I have no idea what to do.'

Bronn takes my face in his hands and his façade is stripped away. He hides nothing from me and in this moment he is as broken as I am. 'I don't know either. I don't know if we can beat him.'

His truth hurts. I've never heard Bronn admit anything close to defeat and his raw pain stokes my need to protect him.

I thought he was dead. Had to exist in a world where I believed him gone. It was the loneliest I've ever been. But somehow he's come back to me.

And I will do anything – *anything* – not to lose him again. I will tear this world apart if I have to, and the next.

I rest my hands on his, determined, fierce. 'Strike first.'

I see the shift in his eyes, watch them turn to steel like my own. 'Die last.'

Just like that, we're Snakes again. Assassins. Prepared to fight, scrap, claw until the very end, until we are bloodied, battered, beaten – but together.

He brushes a strand of hair away from my eye. 'I heard you scream my name,' he says, a sad smile pulling at his mouth. 'That's how I knew you were here, in the West.'

'What?' A wave of guilt consumes me. 'You were in the water? But we searched and searched!'

'No, I wasn't on the ship.'

Now I'm just confused. 'But Toby never said; he believed you were dead—'

'Toby's alive?'

I nod. 'And Lena. No one else made it.'

'Harley did. She was with me.'

Tears spring to my eyes. 'Harley's OK?'

'I didn't say she was OK, but she's not dead.'

'Tell me everything. What were you doing?'

'I was on my way to the tower.' As he talks, we start walking again. 'Gaius had summoned me there, said he wanted to discuss something. I left Ren in charge of the *Maiden* but Harley insisted on coming to watch my back. There's no reason Toby would have known we'd gone; I didn't tell anyone else.'

The pieces slot easily together. 'Gaius's trap was for you. That's why he was surprised to see me. So what happened? Why didn't you make it to the tower?'

'Sheer luck. Harley fell, hurt her ankle badly; she couldn't walk. I couldn't leave her exposed, so I took her somewhere safe and was on my way to the tower when I heard the explosion. By the time I got anywhere near it was too late. But I heard my name. I heard you. And once I realised you were here in the West, I knew there was only one island you'd flee to.'

'Where's Harley now?'

'In a settlement on the Twelfth Isle. Gaius has no reason to believe she's still alive. I said I'd make contact when I could.' He frowns. 'How did he blow up the *Maiden*? With magic?'

'No, Toby saw someone lighting fuses. Said he didn't recognise him. Could you have had a stowaway?'

Bronn's forehead creases with fury. 'I think when it comes to Gaius, anything's possible.'

'Was it all for nothing? Everything we went through? Making you responsible for my death, so he would trust you?' *Did I destroy us for no reason?*

'No,' Bronn says fiercely, holding me by the shoulders. 'It worked, for a while at least. He did trust me. I've heard things, learned things. Including something he's not aware that I know. I found the cave.'

It takes me a moment to realise what he means, and when I do, horror and relief grip me in equal measure. 'You mean *my* cave?'

Bronn nods. 'I know where he's keeping the children.'

Something like hope rises inside me, purpose galvanising me as my eyes lock with his. 'Then what are waiting for? Let's go and bring them home.'

By the time we're close to Mama's hut we've formed the skeleton of a plan. It's felt like a lifetime since we schemed and plotted together, and it reminds me who I am, who I want to be: the girl who was the Viper, fighting injustices one at a time, with the boy she loved at her side. In so many ways that girl is dead, but perhaps slowly I can find my way back to being something close to who she was.

The prospect of returning to the cave is one I avoid dwelling on. If I'm honest, the thought of going anywhere near that place where I was dismantled – physically, psychologically and magically – makes bile rise to my throat, leaves my hands shaking, my heart pulsing, my body weak. But I must confront my fear for the children I abandoned there. For their sakes I must make amends.

And I won't be alone. Whatever else happens, I will have my friends with me.

The wind is whipping up as we approach the ice tree copse that signals I've made my way home.

'Brace yourself,' I say. 'You're about to be very popular.

Bronn shrugs. 'I'm used to that.'

I smile to myself and whistle out a tune, so that whoever's on patrol will know it's me coming back, and then we weave through low-hanging branches to cross on to the snow mares' land.

I'm not sure who will be out here to greet us, but I'm pleased when I see it's Torin. He's heading our way and, as I emerge from the treeline, he raises his hand in welcome. And then Bronn appears beside me and Torin stops. For a few seconds, he just stares at us before he starts to run awkwardly through the thick snow.

Bronn laughs and runs to meet him with a huge bear hug.

'We thought you were dead,' Torin says, his disbelief an echo of my own. 'What happened?'

'It might be easier if we save that story until we're all together,' I say, still slightly bemused at the closeness between the two of them.

'Of course,' Torin says, coming to pull me into an embrace. 'It's so good to see you both. Get into the warm, and I'll go and fetch Rayvn – she's out on the high plain. Then you can tell us everything.'

And with a final hug – Bronn in one arm, me in the other – he's off again, leaving me to escort Bronn up to the hut.

'When did you two become so close?' I ask.

'After you became Viper, before the wedding. We talked a lot.'

'What did you two have to talk about?'

'We have a shared cause. One that we love and will do anything to protect.'

I nod as we reach the door of the hut, pausing outside. 'Of course. The Eastern Isles.'

He glances over at me for a moment, a slight frown creasing his forehead. 'No. You.'

And he opens the door before I can say a word, though my heart has grown wings and taken flight in my chest.

When Toby sees Bronn, he leaps to his feet, flinging himself at the man he has always idolised.

Bronn holds him tightly for a long time, knowing how much Toby has lost, how much they both have, and offering what comfort he can. When they finally release each other, I start making the many introductions and have barely finished when the door is flung open. Rayvn stands there, her mouth parting, a gasp of delight escaping it. She's in Bronn's arms in a heartbeat, clutching him as if he might otherwise disappear.

He returns her embrace and a glint of jealousy tarnishes my happiness. I look up to see Olwyn's face falling. She's seen it, as she sees everything: her sister is in love with the same man I am. Her eyes meet mine, and I can offer her nothing but a sad smile. Someone is going to end up hurt.

As if suddenly aware of how exposed she is, Rayvn pulls away from Bronn, and smiles awkwardly. 'Captain, I thought you were dead.'

'I should be,' he says bitterly. 'I should have gone down with my ship.'

Torin has followed Rayvn in, shutting the door, and watching me closely. He's seen how Rayvn feels about Bronn too and he's worried about how I'll react. With a pang of sorrow I realise that beneath all Torin's love for me there is something else now too. Fear. No matter what I do, or say, I can't take back what happened in the East. Those that matter most to me will always be afraid that I will once again lose myself to the storm.

I offer him a smile, but I can tell it's unconvincing.

'I know you all want to hear Bronn's story,' I say, my happiness sounding forced even to my ears. 'Why don't I take over patrolling while he fills you in?'

Grabbing one of the furs by the door, I avoid the eyes that I can sense are watching me. After all, I have my own tale to tell too – they need to know what happened on the Seventh Isle.

'Let me keep you company,' Torin says.

'If you want.' I'd rather be alone but can tell I'm not going to get a choice.

Taking a spear, I head out into the cold air, stabbing the blade into the ground as I walk.

'What did the snow ever do to you?' Torin teases, coming up behind me.

'Would you rather I take my frustration out on you?'

'Bronn's alive,' he says, confused. 'I thought you'd be happy.'

'I am,' I say a little too forcefully. 'Of course I am.'

'Then what's wrong?'

I say nothing, just twist the weapon deeper into the snow.

Torin sighs. 'Tell me what happened with Esther.'

So I do, and, when I'm done with my story, I tell him Bronn's, ending with his discovery of the cave.

'Then we have a chance,' Torin says. 'A chance to help those children.'

I nod. 'And I'm glad of it. Truly.'

Torin waits and when I don't continue he coaxes me along. 'But?'

'I was wrong about Esther. I thought she'd managed to stay true to who she was, that she was proof there was hope. But I was wrong.' I stab the snow hard again. 'If I don't use my magic, no matter what we do, no matter how hard we fight, we'll lose. And if I do? I'll lose myself.' I breathe deeply, fighting to stay calm, even though I tremble.

After a moment's silence, Torin shoves his own spear into the ground and leans on it. 'What does your heart tell you to do?'

'Listening to my heart has only ever got me into trouble.'

A smile spreads across his handsome features. 'Marianne, you are many things. Impetuous, stubborn, and, yes, you make mistakes. You're human. But you're also brave, loyal and smart. And of all the people I know, you are the most determined to do the right thing. Even if it often goes spectacularly wrong.'

'You know what I've done. Back in the East. I killed a lot of people. I nearly killed you all in the storm.'

'But you didn't.'

As if I can take any credit for that.

'I hurt your father.'

Torin meets my guilty eyes with his own. 'I wanted you to hurt him. Does that make me evil as well? Possibly. Look, none of us is perfect. But if there's one person I would be willing to trust in all this, to lead us to free the Twelve Isles, it's you.'

His words warm me, but I know what I saw behind his eyes back in the hut. 'You're afraid of me. How can you fear me and truly believe any of that?'

His shame is obvious, rolling over his expression like a storm cloud. He hadn't realised he'd betrayed that thought. 'Yes,' he admits, 'I am afraid. Your power, your magic . . . it's something I don't understand. It's beautiful and deadly. But the truth is I'm more afraid *for* you. I want to help you – we all want to help you. And what I see is my friend struggling, terrified, hurting.'

Tears sting my eyes. I've never understood what I did to deserve this man in my life.

He steps forward and pulls me into a warm embrace. 'You can do this, Marianne,' he whispers into my ear. 'I know you can. Sooner or later, you will figure out how to match Gaius and destroy him. And until you do, we will fight with everything we have. Together.'

I hold him tight, wanting the moment to last a little longer, because I know once I break free from the comfort of his arms, there's no turning back. No more talking, no more resting. It will be time to prepare for war, time to finally put our plans into action. Starting with rescuing the children I never should have left in the first place. One way or another the fate of the Twelve Isles must be decided – whether I'm ready or not.

I pull away, resting my hands on his shoulders. 'You're right,' I say, and my words bite into the cold air. 'This world's going to burn anyway. Let's be the ones to light the match.'

# PART THREE
# ALIVE

Unsurprisingly the cave is on the Twelfth Isle – and close to the palace. Of course Gaius would want it to be somewhere within easy reach, somewhere he could slip away to without being missed.

But discovering how close I had been to my friends hits me hard.

It's no more than an hour's ride from where my ancestors lived to the ruined remains of an old settlement high up on the cliff. Bleak and deserted, the old buildings stand empty and half decayed, silent guardians of Gaius's secret underground lair.

On our way, Jax told us all he knew about its history. Apparently, long ago, a deadly plague swept the island, and it was believed that the disease originated from this village, for its residents were the first to die. Later on, when the body count became too great for individuals to be buried on their own, it was chosen as the location for the mass graves – the fields were opened like wounds and corpses were brought from all over the island to be dumped and buried in them. As if the earth itself was infected by these bodies, the trees above died, the earth dried, and soon no one could live there – even if they'd wanted to. As the years passed, so the ghosts multiplied, until no one would set foot near this haunted stretch of coastline.

A perfect place for Gaius to choose.

And though I haven't voiced my suspicion to my friends, I can't help but think this might be where Gaius's family are buried. I wonder if he chose it not just for its privacy but to be near to his loved ones – even after all this time.

We arrive under the cover of darkness, with our plan firmly in place. Tonight we must work seamlessly together in silence, using nothing more than looks to communicate.

Bronn is leading the mission, a Viper assassin doing what he does best. The rest of us know the parts we are to play. Prowling across the barren scrubland, I glance to my right. Torin is beside me, his jaw locked with tension but eyes burning with determination. To my left Olwyn stays close, her dark hair swept back, her expression fierce. Bronn, Astrid and Jax are approaching from the other direction, but I cannot see them because they don't wish to be seen.

We're all heading for the same building, one of the few still standing, though half its roof has collapsed. Torin peels off as we get nearer, then Olwyn, both of them positioning themselves to cover other potential exits on this side of the building. As I pass one of the windows, I peer in, wanting to be sure of what's waiting inside. It's just as Bronn said and the relief I experience is undeniable. There's no room for the unexpected tonight. I reach the front door, just as Bronn does.

*Everyone in place?* I ask him simply by raising an eyebrow.

He nods. The building is surrounded.

I take a breath and he gives me a look, asking if I'm ready.

I am.

He kicks the door hard and we're in before the two men sitting at the table even look up from their card game. Targeting one each, our daggers slice through their necks before they've managed to stand and they slump forward, spilling their warm blood over the table.

The others join us moments later. Jax guards the door as Bronn kicks away a rug on the floor to reveal a trapdoor. Together, he and Torin pull it open, Astrid aiming a crossbow into the hole, should anyone be there. But only a black chasm waits to swallow us whole.

My heart is beating too fast, imagining how I was carried down here unconscious by the Hooded. Had they lowered me gently? Or thrown me in? I suspect I know which it was.

There isn't time to linger on the thought though, as Bronn is disappearing down the ladder and I know I must follow. The only one staying behind is Jax, who will remain to ensure there are no unwanted surprises.

I hesitate, and Torin rests his hand on my shoulder. He knows I'm afraid. But I can't be the reason we fail, and so I smile briefly at him to convey my thanks and then start to climb.

I'm expecting it to be pitch-black, but there's a slight glow coming from below, though I still have to feel for rungs with my feet until I'm nearly at the bottom. When I touch solid ground and turn to see Bronn waiting for me, I realise the tunnel has torches burning all the way along it, lighting the path for whoever might be passing through. I look at Bronn with concern.

If the torches are lit, there's a good chance someone else is using the tunnel.

He returns my look with a grim one of his own. He's thinking the exact same thing.

Within moments Torin, Olwyn and Astrid have joined us, and we start our journey through the tunnel. From this point on we're going blind. None of us knows how long this tunnel is, if it leads directly to the cave I was imprisoned in, or how many guards might be waiting for us when we get there.

The prospect of coming face to face with Gaius here is almost more than I can bear. I can only hope that Astrid's information, from a Guardian friend still within the palace walls, proves accurate, that Gaius is currently there at all times on Rafe's orders – which would explain why he's been relying on magic to take him elsewhere.

The tunnel is long, winding slowly down deep into the island. It's hard to tell the direction we're going, but I would suspect we're adjacent to the coastline, or maybe snaking inland slightly. With an icy shiver I wonder whether we're beneath the mass graves, whether the weight of a thousand skeletons lies above us.

Suddenly Bronn stops walking and holds his hand up to tell us all to follow suit. He points at me and I creep over to join him. I can hear it then, the sound of voices. We aren't alone down here.

He gestures to warn the others and then slowly, in total silence, we carry on.

My grip is too tight on the handle of my dagger, my palm slick with sweat. My body is screaming at me, loath to return to this place, and I'm having to ignore every survival instinct I possess to keep one foot moving in front of another.

We cautiously approach the end of the tunnel as it widens into an open space. Ahead, four hooded figures are guarding the entrances to two further tunnels that lead out of the clearing, their backs to us. Our attack is swift and deadly. Bronn breaks the neck of one man with a single movement, while Torin and I target the throats of two others, and Astrid fires a bolt from her crossbow through the fourth guard's back, piercing him right through the heart.

My hand is shaking as the blood drips down my

blade, and Olwyn gently touches my shoulder, gesturing behind us with her head. I know she's offering to switch places, to let me drop back if it's too much, and I appreciate it. But now that I'm here, I need to keep going, to confront this living nightmare if I'm ever to be free of it.

Bronn points to the tunnels, shooting a questioning glance at me, silently asking which one we should take. And I know the answer, because there's a reason my hand is trembling. I recognise this place, remember being dragged along here by Gaius's men. The tunnel on the right leads to where the children were kept. The tunnel on the left leads to my personal hell.

We head right, braced for more guards, but our path to the cavern remains clear. Bronn's first in and immediately stops, his arm dropping to his side. Confused I join him, and then I understand.

The cages are still there. Row upon row, just as before. But they're nearly all empty. Only a few remain inhabited, the bodies inside slumped and lifeless.

'He's moved them,' Bronn says, and after the last half an hour of silence, it's jarring to hear his voice echoing loudly in the cave.

'He knew we were coming.' My voice is the faintest whisper. It's as though the walls are closing in around me.

'Not necessarily,' Torin says, drawing up beside me.

'He might have moved them for another reason and we were just too late.'

Olwyn is staring in horror at the cages. 'Are they still alive?'

'If he's left them, probably not,' I say, and my voice sounds distant. The same crushing panic that threatened to undo me in the mountains is enfolding me now, fear obliterating even my breath.

Bronn's hand steadies my arm, as if he can sense my legs are starting to buckle. 'Check them all,' he orders the others, as he manoeuvres me to the wall, and lowers me to the ground.

'Breathe,' he says softly. 'Slow and deep.'

I try to speak, only to choke on the air trying to force its way in, and the tightness squeezing my chest is an acute agony.

'It's OK,' Bronn says and he takes my hand and presses it to his chest. 'Feel that? Focus on it. Let your heart beat with mine.'

His pulse is strong and steady. Like him. And slowly the thick panic dissipates, lifting the weight from my body and allowing air to fill my lungs once more. My sight steadies and I meet his concerned eyes.

'I'm sorry,' I say. 'I don't know what happened.'

'You've returned to the place you fear above all others,' he says. 'I'd have been more surprised if you didn't have a reaction.' When I still look stricken, he adds, 'You have nothing to be sorry for.'

'Marianne!' Astrid's cry interrupts us, and we're both on our feet instantly.

'What is it?' I ask, running up to her.

'She's still alive,' Astrid says as she frantically tries to open one of the cages.

'Here,' Olwyn says, gesturing for Astrid to move out of the way before she smashes her spear down on the lock, breaking it free.

I'm beside them now, reaching into the cage for the thin, limp body. The girl can't be more than six or seven, a fragile little bundle, her breath ragged, her skin sallow.

Sensing our presence, her eyes flicker open and I recognise in them the same terror I once had when Gaius came for me in my cage. She shrinks away, a soft whimper escaping from somewhere deep inside of her.

And my heart breaks.

'It's OK,' I say to her. 'I'm not going to hurt you. My name is Marianne and I'm here to take you home.'

I have no idea whether the girl believes me or not, because she slips back to oblivion before she can say anything else. Gently I slip my arms round her and lift her from the cage.

'Let's get out of here,' I say, not wanting to stay for another minute. We cannot help the others – death having spared them any more suffering – and the rest are gone, snatched once again beyond our reach. I don't know how we're going to find them, but that's a problem for another day. Right now, I just want to put as much distance as I can between myself and this underground hell.

We all know the next part of the plan. Not back out through the settlement – we'd thought travelling with the children would give us away. We hadn't anticipated leaving with only one. Instead when we reach the clearing where we killed the guards, we turn into the other tunnel, the one that leads directly to my former prison. My mind screams for me to run away but I keep going, the helpless, suffering child in my arms giving me all the strength I need. But even as I run, I sense something's not right.

The cave hasn't changed much since I last saw it, though to my dismay the smaller cages I emptied of creatures have been refilled. The stench is worse than I remember.

My eyes can't help but drift to it. My cage. The prison where I was broken into pieces by my enemy. Olwyn wraps her arm round me as Torin says, 'Bloody hell.'

Bronn has followed my gaze to the cage too, his fists balled tight.

At least it's empty.

I pass the sleeping girl to Olwyn and head for the nearest cage, which is home to a cowering rodent. I open the door and lift it out, hating how its tiny body trembles with fear. Gently I set it on the ground and watch as it darts off, before opening the other cages. Gaius has replaced all the animals I released last time, but that won't stop me doing it again. No one reminds me that we're in a hurry; they all help free the creatures, who scuttle away, disappearing into any crack and crevice they can find. Today nothing will be left behind.

When we're done, I wordlessly press on to our exit, only to realise what's been nagging at the back of my mind. I know this cave. Know how the light falls in shadows on the walls. Night or day, torches or not, I *know*. And even at night, moonlight should be catching on the damp trickles of water down the stone.

It's too dark.

And now I see why. The opening that I escaped from before has been blocked up, a huge pile of rubble separating us from where Rayvn and Toby are waiting, along with the rest of the crew, on the *Nightshade*.

'No, no, no!' I scream at the stones, frantically clawing at them.

Torin grabs my arm. 'Stop, Marianne. It's no use.'

'What do we do?' Olwyn asks.

'Back out the way we came,' Bronn says. 'Come on, let's go.'

But before we've even left the cave, Jax hurtles in.

'We've got company,' he says.

'How many?' Bronn is completely calm, completely focused.

'Half a battalion. Judging by the wagons they're escorting, they're here to move something.'

'He wants the rest of them,' I say, looking at the empty cages. But I know he wants more than just the creatures we released. I run to the cupboards beneath his work area, trying to block the memory of being dragged here to be carved up.

When I open the door, I'm unable to hold back my bile and lean over to retch on the floor. Astrid and Torin run to join me, and both recoil in horror at the sight.

The jars with my fingers and toes are still there. Waiting. Preserved magic for whenever he wants a boost.

'Are they yours?' Torin asks in a whisper.

I can only nod. This is what he's sent men for. And I will not let him have it.

If Bronn is perturbed by the sight, he doesn't let it show. He's the Viper on a mission. Success is his only objective.

'Jax, how long until they get here?'

'About ten minutes. We need to hurry.'

'The exit's blocked,' Astrid tells him.

'So how the hell do we get out?'

'We fight,' Bronn says. 'If we meet them in the tunnels, they won't be able to come at us all together. We might stand a chance.'

'Wait.' For the first time since we arrived here my voice is confident, strong. Because one of the things I learned in this place was that Gaius is not the kind of man to leave anything to chance. Everything he does has been planned over centuries. In the palace he had endless secret passages. He would never, ever only have one way out of this, his most special place.

'There's another way out,' I say.

'You never mentioned it before.' Bronn is confused.

'I never thought about it before. But I am certain there *is* one. We just have to find it.'

Bronn instantly adapts his plan, putting all his trust in my instincts. He turns to Astrid, throwing her his pistol.

'You and Jax head up the tunnel, shoot at the rock, see if you can create enough rubble to block the way without bringing the whole lot down on us.'

They nod, and run off to blast the tunnel. Then Bronn turns to me. 'Where should we be looking?'

I know there's no other way out of this cave, so there's only one place left. 'Try the walls in the other cave. He's got a secret door there somewhere, I just know it. I'll be there in a minute. There's something I have to do first.'

I can tell none of them wants to leave me. With his

most commanding stare, Bronn says. 'Five minutes. And then I come and drag you out myself.'

As they go, I'm already putting my plan into action. I lift Gaius's large cauldron and set it on the floor. I start grabbing his notes and books from the cupboards, pulling them all out. Something clatters to the ground, and despite my hurry, I pause. Staring up at me are two things I never thought I'd see again: my mother's brooch and my compass from Grace. They would have been in my pocket when I was captured. I assumed Greeb had taken them, but here they are. For some reason Gaius kept them for himself. A link to his past perhaps? A trophy to remember the royal family he betrayed? I reclaim them defiantly, and then I throw his papers into the cauldron, along with his wooden tools, his jars, his potions and lastly, the bits of my body. I won't let him take anything more from me. I grab a torch from the wall and throw it in. The preserving alcohol catches light immediately, so that flames soar greedily upwards, devouring the food I've provided.

For a moment I watch. Watch parts of myself burn. Part of the old me. A strange pain stings beneath my skin, like the magic within me can sense the loss of the magic thrown to the fire. And with a horrid certainty I know Gaius will feel it too. He will know I'm here and what I'm doing.

We have to go. Now.

I sprint towards the other cave, not giving mine a backwards glance. I decided once before I wouldn't die there. And I won't today.

Jax and Astrid are clearly doing their part. Distant blasts are making the whole underground world shake and quiver, but I don't stop until I'm with the others, who are systematically testing the rock surface.

'Anything?' I shout.

'Nothing yet,' Torin replies and I can hear his panic beneath the surface.

The urge to throw myself against the wall and start randomly feeling for something is strong, but I take a breath. And I think. Where would Gaius conceal an exit? If I know him the way I think I do, it won't be anywhere obvious. He wouldn't want anyone else knowing his secrets.

My gaze drifts around the cave. It's huge, far bigger than mine, and at the far end is a small pool of water standing before a natural stone archway. I head towards it, noticing distantly that Jax and Astrid have entered the cave covered in dust.

They've bought us some time. Not lots, but hopefully enough.

It would be possible to skirt the edge of the pool, but I don't bother, going straight through, getting wet up to my knees. Beyond the pool and through the arch there's an alcove hidden from view. It's a dead end.

'I've already checked there,' Bronn calls out to me, but I'm not listening.

Because though it seems the cave walls are unremarkable, my magic can detect something my eyes can't.

A door.

I press my hand against the wall, and instantly recognise the traces of magic that linger from when Gaius created it, the slight cracks, the inconsistency in the stone now obvious. It's a jolt to be reminded of how magic feels, how it lights up my body from the inside. I've been fighting it for so long and now it calls to me, begging me to give in once more, to reignite the power within me.

*Soon*, I promise it. *Soon*.

I push. The wall moves inwards, revealing a dark, narrow tunnel.

'Over here!' My voice bounces around the cave.

They're with me in seconds, Torin carrying the girl, who's still deeply asleep.

Bronn looks at me sharply. 'How did you know?'

'I know my enemy,' is all I say, and then take the spare torch that Olwyn holds out for me. 'Come on.'

We venture quickly into the darkness, with no idea where it's taking us or where we might emerge. Rayvn will have seen our escape route was blocked, so should have moved the *Nightshade* somewhere safe until I can send word. I just hope that this tunnel doesn't lead inland towards the palace. I imagine surfacing into a room surrounded by Rafe's Guardians. Or, worse, into Gaius's private chambers.

Still, we have no choice. Behind us lies certain death. The way ahead still has hope.

The tunnel seems to be on a slight decline, the ground smooth and worn, well trodden. The air is stale and musty though, so I keep my breathing shallow, not wanting to inhale too much of it.

After what feels like an eternity, I see a change in the light ahead, and a gust of cold sea air rushes to welcome me. Thank goodness. We're still near the coast.

I start to run now, desperate to escape the oppressive walls, craving more of that cleansing fresh air. I can hear the others close behind me, as moonlight illuminates the path, coaxing us out into the open.

As I emerge from the tunnel, I can hardly believe my eyes.

The passageway has led us to the side of a cliff, overlooking a tiny cove. There is a treacherous pathway carved into the rock that winds down to the pebbled beach below. The cove is surrounded by large rocks jutting up from the ocean, making access extremely difficult.

It would be a dead end, but waiting in a small dory, being tossed about by the waves, is a man.

He raises his arm and shouts up at us.

'Thought you might need a ride!' And Raoul's familiar laughter rings through the air.

I have so many questions, but all of them must wait until we've safely scrambled down the cliff and waded out to the small boat, where Raoul takes the girl from Torin before we climb aboard.

Immediately we set about helping Raoul row through the labyrinth of rocks, Bronn standing at the bow and shouting navigational orders, all of us desperate to put as much distance between ourselves and the island as possible.

'Where's your ship?' Bronn asks, as if Raoul's appearance is the most natural thing in the world.

'Anchored in a cove not far to the south.'

'We need to send word to Rayvn,' Olwyn says.

'Already done,' Raoul says, and I cast him a sideways glance.

He just grins back. He's enjoying this.

Once we're past the rocks, and into the open sea, it takes about twenty minutes for us to make our way round the coast. We don't talk, the others saving what energy they have to take turns rowing, while I cradle the child in my arms. Her pulse is weak, but steady. If I can get her somewhere safe, feed her, treat her with tonics and let her rest, I'm hopeful she will make a full recovery.

And then she can tell me where home is so I can safely return her. I cannot do it for the others, but I damn well will for her.

Eventually we round a peninsula and there it is. *Storm Promise*. The ship Bronn and I sailed West in all that time ago. It feels oddly good to see it again. Even as we approach I can tell that Raoul has brought a decent crew with him, and my questions multiply.

A ladder is thrown over the side for us to climb and we tie the girl to Bronn's back to keep her secure while he makes his way on to the ship.

As soon as we're all on board, Raoul pulls up the ladder and shouts orders to his crew. 'Let's go! Weigh anchor and quick about it!'

Within seconds the ship is shifting through the water. I don't care where we're going right now, as long as we're moving. Olwyn and I gently release the girl from Bronn and then I look up at Raoul.

'She needs somewhere warm to rest.'

He nods. 'You can use my quarters.'

'Can you take her?' I ask Olwyn. 'I need to speak with Raoul.'

'Of course,' Olwyn says, giving me a smile. Now that we've survived our mission, her relief is showing, and I smile back to show I feel the same way.

Then I'm on my feet and wrapping my arms tightly round Raoul.

'It is good to see you, my friend,' I say as I squeeze him. But when I release him I add, 'Now, would you like to tell me exactly what you're doing here?'

His smile is as wide as ever. 'As a matter of fact, I would. Come on.'

He stretches his arm out to invite me to join him, but when Bronn, Torin, Jax and Astrid make to follow us, he stops.

'I'm sorry,' he says. 'What I have to say is for royalty only.'

For a moment I think he's joking but then I realise all trace of his smile has gone. He's deadly serious.

'You can trust them,' I say, but he's not budging.

'You and Torin only,' he says, and it pains me to turn to the others and ask them to give us privacy. Jax and Astrid seem unconcerned, but I can tell it bothers Bronn to be excluded.

I give him a look, trying to convey I'll share anything important with him later, but whether he translates it correctly, I'm not sure.

Raoul leads us below deck, right down through the ship to the storeroom. He pushes the door firmly shut behind us and lifts a lantern off the wall to place it on a barrel, gesturing for us to sit round it on piles of ropes and old sails.

Torin arches an eyebrow. 'Think this is private enough?'

'Trust me,' Raoul says. 'You'll understand soon.'

I meet his gaze and know what he's going to say next. There's only one way he could possibly have anticipated we'd need his help. Only one reason he'd want to speak to me and Torin alone.

'The Seers sent you.'

He nods. 'There were too many people from the Third Isle wanting to join your fight. They realised they couldn't ignore what was happening any more and the need to protect their own islanders eventually outweighed their desire to hide. And so the readings began with renewed earnest. Looking outwards instead of inwards. Agon had a vision not long after you left the East. He saw you emerge into a hidden cove, saw your despair at being trapped while your enemies closed in. Visions like these are rare, even for the Elders. Normally the visions are like the readings, subject to interpretation. But this was different and Agon knew it. As soon as he told me, there was no question I would come. We consulted the rúns again and again until we felt we had the right coordinates and then I set sail immediately.'

He glances at Torin. 'With Sharpe's permission, of course. He sent this for you.'

And Raoul pulls a letter from his pocket and hands it to Torin, who looks at it with undisguised longing, before tucking it into his jacket, saving the intimate words for later.

'Thank you,' I say to Raoul. 'You saved us back there.'

'My pleasure. Nice to smuggle my friends rather than goods for a change.'

But I also know Raoul wouldn't have insisted on just talking to the two of us if there wasn't more to tell.

'What else did the rúns say?'

Our eyes meet and I see behind his excitement, there's also worry.

'I have two prophecies for you. One is from the Elders.'

Torin looks over at me in anticipation. This is his first experience of hearing a prophecy from the Seers. I'm hoping it won't be his last.

'*Fear not the dead. But when spectral servants rise, beware their master. For he is close to his ends.*'

Raoul is watching me closely. 'Any idea what it means?'

'Gaius wants to bring his family back from the dead,' I say, my voice flat. 'But he hasn't the magic to do it, not yet anyway.'

The prophecy makes it sound like it's only a matter of time, though. And when he's powerful enough to do it, he'll be invincible.

It's not the best news the Seers could have sent, but nonetheless, the warning is welcome. I've broken prophecies before and perhaps if Raoul continues to consult the rúns, they will show me how to combat such a threat.

Which leads us to the other prophecy. 'Who is the second one from?'

'Me.' He shifts slightly, suddenly awkward and uncomfortable. 'I read for you once before, as you might remember.'

As if I'd be likely to forget the words that led him to scream that I should be killed before I destroyed them all. 'I do.'

To his credit Raoul gives me a guilty smile. 'I kept reading for you and the message stayed the same, over and over. Until suddenly it changed. Just the smallest shift, but I thought you should know.'

I wait expectantly, my pulse starting to race. I'm not sure I want to hear.

'You remember the old prophecy, don't you?'

'*A storm is coming. A wild fury that will devour night and day, earth and sea, until all that remains is sorrow. Fear her, face her, destroy her.*' I quote the words that haunt me, a constant reminder of the devastation I am capable of wreaking.

Raoul nods. 'For so long, whenever I read for you, I got the same as before. *Fear her, face her, destroy her.*'

'And now?'

'*Fear him. Face him. Destroy him.*'

My insides gape with hollow fear. All along a part of me had hoped there might be another way to defeat Gaius, that perhaps the Seers would illuminate another path. But there it is. Stark and unavoidable. I have to face him. And I have to destroy him.

'Please tell me you bring some remedies along with your warnings,' Torin says, perhaps realising I'm unable to form words, the heavy tug of fate paralysing me.

'I'm sorry,' Raoul says. 'Warnings are all I have, but they're better than nothing. I'll keep reading and communicating with the Seers. If we can help, we will.' He places his hand over his heart and bows his head towards us. 'The Seers of the Third Isle pledge their allegiance once more to the King of the East and the Queen of the West. Our foresight is yours.'

Though we may be sitting in the gloom of a small storeroom in the bowels of a ship, the atmosphere crackles with energy. Something lost has been restored, no longer forgotten. Despite everything, a little flame of hope flickers inside me. And, just like that, I know what I need to do next.

'Where are we heading now?' I ask Raoul.

'We're on our way to meet the *Nightshade*,' he says. 'I'm keen to be reunited with my ship. After that, I await your orders.'

'Once we're all together again, set a course for the Ninth Isle,' I say. 'I have questions for the dead.'

* * *

On the morning the *Nightshade* arrives at Blood Island, the sunrise is so vibrant that it looks as if the red of the island has bled into the surrounding waters. We're sailing into the same harbour as the last time we were here, and recalling Mordecai's warning that ships were often stolen from the Ninth, we're taking no chances. Raoul intends to anchor the *Nightshade* out of anyone's reach, and he will leave crew aboard to guard her. Only a few of us need go on land. Astrid has been assigned to help me, and the others are going to stock up on supplies while we have the chance.

I've spent the journey here tending to the girl. While she slept, I brewed tonics with the few ingredients on board, and when she was awake, I helped her swallow them down. She still hasn't spoken a word, but, as the days have passed, she's stopped shrinking away from me when I touch her. I've talked to her. Nothing important, nothing that will overwhelm her, nothing about the cave. Instead I told her my name, I described the plants I used in the tonic. I told her about Talon, about the snow mares, about every beautiful thing I could think of. When the weather was fine, I carried her on deck, to let the fresh air cleanse her and the sun warm her. I think she liked being outside after all her time in the cave. I know how that feels. And so I sat with her, partly to keep her company, but also to plan what I must do next.

Though Raoul's arrival was undoubtedly welcome, as is the restored allegiance of the Seers, the messages he brought with him are frustratingly vague. Or horribly specific. Depending on how you look at them. When Gaius achieves his goal of bringing the dead back to life, he may well be invincible. And I have to stop him.

The only person I know who's ever successfully raised the dead is me. I did it once for myself, yes. But I had done it before that too, thanks to a blood curse. When I summoned the spirits of the dead on the Ninth, it wasn't through any skill or knowledge, but simply because a cruel king once bound their souls to the island and to the royal bloodline. I have no idea what magic was involved that Gaius might seek to replicate. Nor do I know how it can be undone. So I intend to do the next best thing. Ask those who were raised.

My friends know little of what I intend to do, because last time I came to this island and raised the dead all hell broke loose. I doubt anyone's keen to experience that again. All I've said is I need to go there. They know me well enough by now not to press further.

In truth, they've all kept their distance from me since the cave, as if seeing a glimpse of what I endured has tainted their thoughts of me. Perhaps it's pity that I see in their eyes now. Maybe horror. Either way, I don't want any reminder of what I endured, so I'm happy for them to stay away.

When we caught up with the *Nightshade*, we had a reshuffling of crew. Sharpe's letter to Torin had revealed the Fleet was ready to sail at our command, and so Torin sent back the order for them to make their way to the divide between Eastern and Western waters. Braydon has taken the *Storm Promise* and her crew to meet them, and those of us on the *Nightshade* will join them once we're done on the Ninth Isle.

The war is coming.

We're dropping anchor when Rayvn seeks me out. I'm preparing a sleeping draught for the girl – I don't want her to wake up while I'm gone and be afraid.

'Are you OK?' Rayvn asks, coming to stand beside me.

'I'm fine, why wouldn't I be?' As if I don't remember what happened the last time I came to this island.

For a moment she doesn't answer, and I can tell she isn't sure how to ask what she really wants to.

'It must have been awful returning to the cave,' she says, and I realise why she's here. She's drawn the short straw and has been sent to help me confront my demons.

'You've been talking to the others.' I don't bother to hide my irritation.

'Only because they care. They said it was soulless. Awful.'

I slam my hands down on the table, screwing my eyes shut, not wanting to even think about that place.

She flinches and I instantly feel guilty.

'If they care so much, why are they avoiding me?'

Rayvn frowns. 'They're not. You're the one who's keeping away. You've been separating yourself at every opportunity. We just wanted to give you space.'

I look at her in surprise. Is it possible that's true? That it isn't their pity I fear, but my own shame? Because when they saw the cage, I'd felt exposed, raw. As vulnerable and weak as when I was trapped there.

Overwhelmed, I sink to the floor, shaking my head. 'I should never have gone back. We were too late anyway.'

Rayvn nods at the sleeping girl. 'Not for her.'

'I should have found a way back sooner,' I say, panic rising at the memory. 'Should have figured out a way to save them. Or maybe I shouldn't have left at all.'

'You did what you had to, just like you've always done,' she says. 'If you'd stayed, you'd be dead along with the rest of them.' She pauses. 'In truth, I think the others are battling their own guilt.'

'What for?'

'Well, Olwyn feels terrible that she didn't look harder for you. Torin regrets starting the whole chain of events by underestimating his father. And Bronn? Well, he wishes he'd never let you go to the West alone.'

'But that's ridiculous,' I say softly. 'Olwyn couldn't possibly have known where I was, Torin was lying on his own deathbed, and Bronn only ever did what I asked.'

'Exactly. Guilt isn't logical,' she says. 'I just wanted you to know that we're here for you – I'm here for you. If you ever need to talk. What you went through? No one recovers quickly from that.'

*If they ever do.*

'Thank you.' And with an effort I manage to meet her eyes for the first time, not bothering to blink away my tears. 'I'm not OK,' I finally admit. 'I haven't been for a long time. I may never be again.'

She takes my hand and we sit in silence until it's time to go.

When we row over to land in the dory, my focus is solely on the island and what I need to do. Without using my magic. There is no time to reflect, or to mourn what I've lost. There's always more to lose.

Bronn, Torin and Raoul are fairly relaxed as we come alongside the small jetty and leap off the boat, securing it with a rope and paying the harbour master. Jax, Rayvn and Olwyn, on the other hand, are more than a little tense. One by one they disembark until only Astrid and I remain in the boat.

'Are you coming?' Olwyn asks, and there's more than a hint of hope in her voice that I've changed my mind.

'You all go on,' I say lightly. 'We'll meet you back here later.' I don't want everyone staring at me when I do this.

She smiles at me, and Rayvn nods her encouragement, before they walk off.

When they've started their journey towards the settlement, Astrid steps on to the jetty and then looks down at me. 'Ready?' She holds out her hand.

With a deep breath I take it and step up on to the land.

Immediately I feel it. The island sings to me, the bond of the land's curse to my royal blood strong. I can see the magic as clearly as the landscape itself. It shimmers off the ground in shades of red, a crimson mist swirling at my feet. A wave of fear sweeps over me and for a second I am certain that my magic will be released from its prison. But after a moment my tension eases. The magic is humming through me, but it's not free.

Because though I hauled my magic back deep inside me to save everyone from the storm, I am still a Mage, a lifetime away from the inexperienced girl who came to this island before.

Astrid looks at me cautiously. 'Are you OK?'

I smile at her. 'Yes. All in control.'

'Good.' She doesn't disguise the relief in her voice. 'So you want me to take you somewhere remote?'

'Yes please. I don't want anyone to witness this.'

That doesn't seem to reassure her, but she starts walking anyway. 'This way then.'

Initially we take the same path through the island as I did last time, but it's not long before Astrid deviates from it. We fall into step as she leads us up away from the settlement and off the track.

'You and Olwyn seem happy,' I say after a stretch of comfortable silence.

Astrid smiles. 'We are.'

'Do you love her?' I know I'm being nosy, but I don't care.

Now Astrid gives me a sideways glance. 'I do. Very much.' And then she sighs. 'Makes it harder, I think – loving someone. Before I had nothing to lose. Now I have everything.'

I slip my arm through hers. I know precisely what she means. 'Try to think of it as having someone to fight for.'

'I would die for her,' Astrid says, her voice fierce with devotion.

'Let's hope it doesn't come to that. I want to see you both happy together for a long time.' And I squeeze her arm. 'What does Olwyn think about me returning here?' I ask after a moment.

Astrid laughs. 'She's about as keen on the idea as the rest of us. Do you want to share what you're up to yet?'

'I need some advice, that's all.'

'From the dead?' Astrid gives me a knowing look.

'Don't worry, it'll be fine,' I say airily and she laughs again.

'It's a good thing we all trust you,' she says as we approach the edge of a forest.

It's strikingly red. Most of the trees are the same type as those along the main road, bright scarlet twisted trunks and weeping, feathery red branches. But interspersed between them are others: golden trees, their flaxen branches praising the skies; deep yellow trees with thin trunks and pale sun-coloured puffs of leaves at the top; trees with burnt orange trunks, their leaves every shade of copper.

'Oh!' It's breathtaking.

'It's known as the flame forest,' Astrid says. 'While it's beautiful, it's also supposedly haunted, so no one ever comes here. We shouldn't be disturbed.'

The forest only grows more captivating once we're safe under the canopy. There are as many types of moss growing over stones and fallen logs as there are colours of trees. Russet ferns brush delicately against the trunks.

Astrid leads me further in until we reach a clearing. 'Will this do?'

'It's perfect, thank you.'

I settle myself in the hollow, while Astrid hovers nervously nearby.

'Do you want to stay while I do this?'

She shakes her head. 'I'll keep watch.'

'Thank you.' I'm glad she doesn't want to be here, because this is something I'd rather do alone.

When she's gone, I let my fingers hover above the red earth. I can hear the whispers of the dead, though not their words. Their blood sings to mine, bound by my ancestor's magic.

And I plunge my hands into the forest floor.

'You've come back.'

I look up to see the warm, smiling face of my grandmother beaming at me. I did it. I managed to summon her – and her alone. I spring to my feet to embrace her tightly.

'Dearest one,' she says, stroking my hair. 'Oh, you have suffered since last we met.'

I pull away, and she rests her palm against my cheek. My tears spill on to her skin, almost as if she is conjuring them from me.

'And you've changed.' She frowns. 'You bear so much weight on your shoulders.'

My voice seems to have shrivelled in my throat.

'Come,' Baia says. 'Tell me what you need and why you are here.'

She leads me to the base of a tree, and we sit together, sheltered by leaves and companionship.

'I'm a Mage,' I say, hardly knowing where to start, and finding that's what comes out first. Despite everything it's cost me, I realise I want my grandmother to know what I've achieved. Because I'm proud and I want her to be too.

'I knew it. You're not the same as you were before.

You're stronger. More powerful.' She hesitates, her smile fading. 'But broken too. You've been hurt in many ways.'

Closing my eyes, I take a moment, just the briefest one, to experience such maternal love. It is everything warm and comforting, and I want to weep for my past self, for the child who was denied it.

But there isn't time for self-pity. There's too much at stake.

When I open my eyes, I'm a weapon once more, ready for battle. 'After we last met, I was tortured by the man who hunted my parents. Gaius. He's a threat to everyone and I have to stop him. That's why I'm here.'

Baia's face shifts from horrified to vengeful. 'How can I help you?'

'I need to understand what happens when I call you back from the dead,' I say, with an apologetic smile. She nods encouragingly and I go on. 'When I use my magic there's always a command and a physical sensation, usually heat. But because of my blood tie to the curse, when I summon you it happens with barely a conscious thought. I have to unravel how the process works – to prevent Gaius from using similar magic himself.' I don't mention the prophecy, not wanting to scare her.

Baia sighs. 'I'm sorry, my dearest one. Such things are far beyond my comprehension. My skills lay in healing, not magic.'

My eyes widen with excitement, momentarily forgetting the imminent threat of Gaius.

'You were a healer?'

'I was. And a very good one at that.'

Beyond my delight to learn that I share something in common with my grandmother, I hear the unspoken warning in her words. 'But?'

She smiles wryly. 'But it was the death of me.'

'You caught a disease?'

Baia chuckles. 'No. Nothing so simple.'

'You don't have to tell me if you don't want to,' I say, suddenly aware that she might prefer not to dwell on how she died.

She sighs. 'I will tell you anything you wish. But you may not like the truth you learn about me, Mairin. It is bloody and messy and doesn't have anything close to a happy ending.'

I reach for her hand. 'I'm beginning to think those don't exist.'

She squeezes my fingers. 'All right then,' she says, sighing deeply. 'Well, the first thing I should tell you is that to become a good healer, a truly effective one, you need to understand what it is you are doing. How the body works. The truths hidden beneath skin.'

I look up at her sharply, my heart quickening its beat. 'You mean . . .?'

Baia's face reveals her discomfort. 'Yes. In order to

learn, I opened the dead to discover their secrets.'

My excitement continues to rise. 'I did that too!'

It's clearly not the response she's expecting. 'You don't judge me?'

'Not at all. I tried to understand the reasons our bodies behave as they do, but my subjects were limited to rodents, birds, a she-wolf . . .'

She laughs and claps her hands together. 'Oh, how wonderful!' Her laughter fades quickly, though. 'Sadly most people aren't like you. One day I was caught and those who discovered me didn't see what I was doing as a way to help the living. They accused me of terrible things, saying that a shadow demon from the Seventh had possessed my spirit and urged me to murder and defile people for my personal gratification.'

I can sense the unhappy ending looming.

'After tending to them for years, delivering their babies, nursing their sick, mending their bones, my neighbours turned on me in a heartbeat. I was dragged through the settlement, tied to a post, flogged and then stoned until my body was broken beyond repair.'

'Baia!' I had no idea my grandmother had suffered so greatly, and I want to run to the settlement and raze it to the ground to avenge her.

'They acted in ignorance and fear,' she says, and there's no hate in her voice, just acceptance. 'As so many do.'

'I wish I'd been there; I could have saved you.'

'You would have got yourself killed; no doubt people would have considered you my apprentice,' she says with a soft smile. She rests her hand gently on mine, her eyes glistening with affection. 'So you're a healer too?'

'You sound surprised.'

'I suppose I am. Heir to the throne, a Mage and a healer? Is there anything more I should know about you?' She chuckles but I'm not laughing.

'Add assassin and killer and that's about it.'

Her forehead creases with concern. 'You speak as though it's bad to have so many skills.'

'It makes it hard to know which of those things I am.'

'Why must you only be one? Why can't you be all, even if those things do not easily coexist? Complicated can be beautiful.'

When I don't answer, she carries on. 'You came here looking for help. Perhaps I can't give you exactly what you want, but remember what I said. To be good at something you have to understand it. You want to succeed in stopping this Gaius? You need to understand him. You want to harness magic? You need to understand it. You want to know who you are? You need to understand yourself.'

'How?' A small word, a huge question.

'If I knew I'd tell you. I cut things open, dug deep

for answers. You'll find a way too. And when you struggle, take solace in nature. It's grounding and steadying – and magic *is* nature. Perhaps you'll find your answers there.' She pauses. 'But if I might ask for your help in return? As wonderful as it's been having a chance to meet you, I want to rest. We all do.'

I lower my head. 'You want me to break the curse.'

'Our spirits are tired. We ache for peace. Not from you, dear one,' she adds hurriedly, perhaps seeing the guilt on my face. 'From the curse. We are trapped, restless. Not a part of this world, not a part of the next. We long to be set free.'

'I don't know how.'

'Your blood is what summons us, it must be able to free us too. I know you can find a way.'

'I will, I promise.' I manage a sad smile. 'Though I wish we could always talk together like this.'

'You don't need me as much as you think you do,' she says. 'You just need to believe in yourself. The answers are already there, waiting to be found. And you will find them.' She takes my hand. 'I have something I want to give you. Buried beneath the solitary thistled tree, just outside the settlement where we first met, is my journal. It has all my notes, my sketches, everything I learned about healing, about the body. They're yours now. Just dig beneath the patch of earthweed and you'll find it.'

'Thank you.' My heart swells at such a gift.

'Good luck, dear one,' she says, squeezing my hand in farewell.

With a deep breath I close my eyes and release her spirit. When I open them again, she's gone, the connection severed instinctively, with less than a thought. For a moment an aching emptiness consumes me, but slowly it fades and I'm able to face leaving the clearing and go in search of Astrid.

She's not far away and smiles when she sees me. 'Did you get what you needed?'

I consider this for a moment. I didn't get the answer I was hoping for, but the love I received from my grandmother has strengthened my faith in myself and my plans. 'Yes, I think I did. Before we join the others, can you take me to the solitary thistled tree? Near the settlement?'

She guides me back through the forest and, perhaps sensing my mood, she doesn't ask any more questions about what just happened. My mind is replaying the conversation over and over, especially the part where I promised Baia that I would find a way to break the curse. Though I have every intention of keeping my word, I'd be lying if I said I wanted to. Every selfish instinct longs for her always to be there for me to call upon. A safe person, a safe place. I can hardly bear the thought of giving that up.

When we emerge from the forest, we make our way down into a valley, at the bottom of which grows a single tree.

'That's the one,' Astrid says. 'What now?'

'Got anything to dig with?'

She gives me a quizzical frown and I just laugh as I start walking again, wanting to reach the thistled tree as soon as possible.

It's a strange-looking thing with a gnarled thorny trunk and thin spiky branches bristling with prickly crimson blooms.

The ground beneath it is loose, sandy and stained pink. I kneel down next to the crisped leaves of earthweed at its trunk and start clawing at the dirt with my hands. As my skin meets the earth, I have to consciously resist summoning the dead.

'Want to tell me what you're looking for?' Astrid asks.

'A book. My grandmother's book.'

'Any particular reason she buried it?'

'Because it's full of things that frighten people. Full of things that got her killed.'

'Sounds about right.'

I look sharply up at Astrid but she's smiling and I relax slightly. 'Maybe it runs in the family?' I say with a grin, as she kneels to join me.

A few minutes later, my fingers brush against

something hard. 'Did you feel that?'

Astrid nods, and together we prise out a small wooden box and place it on the ground between us.

It's rotting away from years of being damp beneath the earth, but I can still make out a motif carved into the lid, and I trace over it with my fingers. A flower twining round a tree. I hesitate. The contents of this box are no ordinary treasure. They are dangerous, and they are precious. And now they're mine.

I lift the lid.

A dried sprig cut from the thistled tree is resting on top of a cloth bundle. When I start to unwrap it, I realise the cloth is an old shawl and stare at it with a strange longing. And then I reach the book, lovingly swaddled in the folds of material. Bound in leather, it's well worn, and when I start to turn the pages, my heart does a little skip.

My grandmother was a skilled artist. The diagrams, the drawings, the detail – it's as if I were looking at the real thing. And the descriptions! Full explanations accompany every picture, and I cannot wait to get back to the ship, curl up in a nook and devour Baia's life's work.

It's almost a physical pain to place it back in the box. But the others will be waiting for us, and I doubt Astrid wants to sit here and watch me lose myself in the minutiae of human anatomy.

The box just fits into my satchel, and when I'm done, Astrid, who's been refilling the hole, dusts her hands off.

'Shall we?' I say, and then she grins. 'What?' I ask.

'You did it,' she says. 'You came here and controlled your magic.'

Her words take me by surprise. 'Only the curse's magic, I haven't used my own,' I say, but she shakes her head.

'You unleashed something terrible last time you were here, but not today. You're more in control than you think. You should be pleased.'

But before I have time to wonder if she's right, if there is more to what I've achieved today than I realised, a scream carries to us on the wind from the settlement on the other side of the hill.

It's quickly followed by others until it sounds like all the world is shouting, screaming. Dying.

Astrid looks at me, her face taut with fear. 'Olwyn!'

We start running without another word, towards danger, towards our friends. I can't quite imagine what's happened – perhaps some sort of tavern brawl that's spilled on to the streets? Maybe the crew aren't even part of the fight taking place. They may already be safely back at the ship.

But by the sinking of my gut I know that they're there, in the heart of trouble.

As we reach the brow of the hill that looks down over

the settlement, we finally see what's happening, and stare in disbelief.

The Hooded. They're here, in plain sight. And they're fighting to kill.

Astrid and I sprint towards them, searching the crowds for those we love. I see Torin locked in battle with a hooded figure. I see Olwyn spearing one through the guts.

And then I see Bronn. He's fighting three men, wild and fierce, but he hasn't seen the man running up from behind him, sword raised.

My world seems to slow down.

I can't save him. Not from this distance. I cannot possibly make it in time. I have defied death, I have withstood torture, but in this moment I have never felt so helpless.

And then Rayvn sees it too. She runs, fast and focused, cutting down everyone in her path. I cry out her name to stop her, though I know she can't hear me, even as I fly down the hillside, and can do nothing but watch as she flings herself into harm's way. Her spear blocks the blow, and for a moment I think she's going to be all right, but the hooded man has a second blade, and he plunges it into her stomach.

'No!' My scream echoes around us as I fall to my knees.

Bronn has killed the men he was fighting and now

he spins on his heels, bringing his blade round in an arc, cleanly separating the head of Rayvn's attacker from his body. He hovers over her, protecting her from further harm, but they're under such fierce attack that Bronn can't do anything more than keep fighting back the hordes, while Rayvn's blood pools around her.

They're both going to die. They're outnumbered; they're overpowered. What are the Hooded even doing here? Instinctively I know it's for me and my rage threatens to undo me, the tempest of my magic banging at the cage I keep it in.

Without a second thought I smash my hands into the ground and summon them – the dead. Instantly I am surrounded as thousands of souls cover the hillside, called to fulfil their duty to me.

As one we look at the massacre happening beneath us, and my heart turns cold with malice.

'Kill them.'

At my command the dead roar into action and we pour down the hillside together like a lethal waterfall, destroying everything in our path.

My army cut them down with ease, so quickly the Hooded don't know what's hit them until it's their blood flowing along the street.

My sword slashes through arms and across torsos as I hack my way to my cousin. Bronn is still keeping watch over her, killing anyone who gets close, but the enemy is already thinning as I fall to Rayvn's side and grasp her hand.

'You're going to be OK,' I say, putting pressure on the gaping wound in her stomach that spills her life on to the island. 'I won't let anything happen to you.'

Olwyn and Astrid have joined us now. Olwyn cries out as she kneels on the other side of her sister, and clutches her right hand tightly. Astrid joins Bronn in forming a defence around us, but it's not necessary; the dead won't let any harm come to me.

'What did you do?' Olwyn gently chides Rayvn, her voice tight with grief, while I battle against her blood loss, frantically trying to stop it and failing.

'I'm sorry,' she says. 'I had to protect my captain.'

'Because you love him.' Olwyn smiles with such affection at her sister that a solitary tear spills down Rayvn's cheek.

'Yes.' Her eyes flick to mine, and I see her shame, her guilt. 'I'm sorry.'

'You have nothing to be sorry for,' I say.

The battle is over. The dead have fulfilled the command I gave them, and are now standing idly, waiting for the next. In a moment Jax and Torin are with us, bloodied, bruised, but alive. Torin pulls his shirt over his head and offers it to me to help stem the bleeding. He can see what I can. That I'm losing the fight.

Bronn comes to sit beside Olwyn and she moves slightly out of the way for him.

'You shouldn't have done that,' he says to Rayvn, his voice barely more than a whisper.

I turn away, wanting to give them a moment together.

'I had to,' she says, though I can tell she's struggling to speak at all. 'I couldn't let you die.'

And then I see them. The faint wisps of life starting to leave her body.

I don't even think. Don't hesitate for a moment. Instinctively I reach for the threads, because she's my cousin and I love her. It doesn't matter that I'm not supposed to be using my magic; it doesn't even occur to me. All I know is I can't lose her.

A hand wraps round my wrist, distracting me. I look down to see Rayvn, shaking her head as best she can. 'No,' she says, her voice weak. 'Marianne, don't.'

'I'm not going to let you die. I can stop it; I can save you,' I say, aching to knit the life back to her body as I once did for myself.

'You already did save me,' Rayvn says. 'When you freed me from the mountain and set me adrift on the ocean. I wouldn't trade a moment of it.' She stares up at Olwyn and Bronn and smiles. 'I loved living. I loved it.' She turns her gaze back to me, her eyes beginning to cloud over as she fades away. 'But it's time. Let me go now.'

A hand touches my shoulder, and I look up into my grandmother's face, which is filled with sorrow.

'You have a gift, Mairin. But nature has laws. And even Mages have to obey them. You of all people should understand the cost of breaking them.'

And with sudden clarity I *do* understand. No one can be brought back. Not even me. Always something is left behind on the other side. I felt it in myself on the beach the day I became a Mage, that I was no longer the same. I thought it was just the loss of hope. Now I see that it was far more than that. My spirit straddles life and death, most of me here but some of me there. Death cannot be cheated. It keeps something for itself, and the cost is high.

With Lilah it was her memory; who knows what it might be for Rayvn. I cannot force that price on to anyone else, no matter the power at my fingertips. I have to learn to let go.

My grandmother smiles at me, offering me courage to do what is right, not what I desire.

I look at Rayvn. 'Sail onwards and know you were loved,' I say, gripping her hand tightly.

Olwyn scoops Rayvn into her arms, cradling her, whispering words of love as her sister slips away.

But though grief shreds my heart, I know there is something I have to do before I can give in to it. Because there is no way I'm letting Rayvn be tied to the curse, trapped as Baia has been. As they all have. I'm fighting for peace in the islands, and the dead deserve it as much as the living. They have more than fulfilled their duty today.

Baia is right about my blood being the key, so there's only one thing for it – I bring my dagger to my left palm and slice into the skin. Instantly my blood rushes free and I press it to Rayvn's, pooling in the ground already soaked with the blood of those who have been killed today. The blood of the living, the blood of the dying, the blood of the dead, all mingled together.

Royal blood made this curse. Royal blood will surely break it.

Heat burns through my hand, up my arm, angrily coursing through my body. The curse doesn't wish to be destroyed; it is deep and ancient, forged with bitterness and fury. I think of the King who conjured it out of petty cruelty and weak magic. And I know I am more than a match for him and his legacy.

*You will not have her. You will not have any of them.*

The heat is trying to consume me, to neutralise me, but I resist, forcing it from my body and back into the ground. It hurts, as though I'm being scorched from the inside out. My screams ring like a distant sound. All I can focus on is succeeding.

As the last remnant of heat is expelled, a blast beneath the ground sends me flying backwards, the island shaking to its core. For a moment everything is still. And then Olwyn's wail pierces the air, an agonised cry of despair.

When I look up, the dead have gone. And so has Rayvn.

We bury her at sea. It's not even a discussion; we all know that's where she'd want to rest.

Breaking the curse weakened me – I had barely the strength to stand – but I have no regrets. As we made our way back to the ship, I could sense that the whole island was different, like it had breathed a sigh of relief. The ground shimmered more brightly, the air tasted sweeter, but I was left with an emptiness. There would be no more opportunities to see my grandmother, my only link to the life I should have lived, had Adler and Gaius not conspired to steal it from me. And yet what is the point of death if it does not separate us entirely? We are not meant to linger – a truth I am finally accepting.

*Where does that leave me?*

This is the question that has haunted me since we set sail. To have finally realised that some part of myself waits on the other side to be reunited with the rest makes me wonder what I am. Living or dead? Real or ghost? Without having passed my test and become a Mage, I wouldn't be here at all – and how did I thank the magic that sustains me? I shut it away, afraid of my own power.

After we commit Rayvn to the ocean – wrapped in a sail lovingly stitched up by us all – we take ourselves off to different corners of the ship, craving the privacy to weep without being seen.

I long for darkness and find my way to the storeroom, wanting to lose myself in the shadows. The loss of Rayvn has broken us but there's little time for repair. Raoul has set us on a course for the Eighth Isle, where Olwyn and I will break the news of Rayvn's death to Mama and Pip, and afterwards we will continue on to the East–West border to reunite with Sharpe and the Fleet. Always we have to keep moving forward, though we leave so many behind. With each of them lost, so is a part of us. Maybe we're all straddling that great divide between life and death, perhaps I'm not so different after all. Our hearts break, and death takes the fragments as payment.

It's Bronn who seeks me out. We've barely spoken a word to each other since we fled the cave, and when I see him moving through the shadows towards me, I realise how much I've ached for his presence.

It's so gloomy down here without a lantern that even when he sits next to me I can barely see him. But we've spent enough hours alone together in the dark for it not to matter.

'I'm sorry,' he says after a while. 'It should have been me.'

'It shouldn't have been either of you,' I say in a rush of anger. 'What the hell were the Hooded doing there? How did Gaius know where we were?'

'Perhaps he's doing what Adler did when you escaped him, sending men out to every island, knowing he'll find us eventually. There are only so many places we can hide.'

'Maybe,' I say, though their presence felt more than coincidental.

I sense there's something else he wants to say and don't rush him; I'm not sure I want to hear what it is.

'That cave,' he says eventually. 'When I saw the cage he kept you in . . .' He sighs. 'There's no shame in being afraid.'

I can't hide anything from him. He saw my fear when it fed my magic, he saw it when it debilitated me in the tunnel.

'There's shame in being weak.' My voice is bitter, as I remember Adler forcing me to cut myself to purge such frailty.

'You don't really believe that,' he says. 'You know better than anyone that fear can be a strength. It makes you fight for what matters, because you fear losing it.'

'And what are you afraid of losing?'

'I've lost almost my entire crew. I don't have much left.'

I can't help feeling that isn't really an answer, but

before I can press him further, he says, 'Your magic is breaking free, isn't it?'

I'm so stunned, I whip my head round to look at him, even though all I can make out is his outline. Because he's right. Despite all my denials, of course I used magic on the Ninth; I couldn't possibly have broken the curse without it. 'How did you know?'

'I know you,' is his reply.

Did he realise before I did? That every day I'm back in the West, I lose the fight to contain it. There's too much magic in the land, in the sea, in the air here, calling to *my* magic like a lost lover.

'It's seeping out of me. I can't stop it,' I say quietly.

'And you're afraid of what you might do?'

'You saw what happened last time.'

For a moment he doesn't say anything. 'You may have to do it again.'

'What are you talking about?'

We seem to have moved closer to each other, our shoulders now brushing.

'If we cannot find another way to defeat Gaius, are you prepared to do whatever it takes to destroy him?'

'If I unleash my magic now, I could destroy everything.'

'I think one way or another that's a risk you may have to take.'

A chill spreads through me like a fever. *I am the*

*storm. Fear him. Face him. Destroy him.* Is that what the prophecy means? Does winning against Gaius still mean the islands lose?

'You don't think we can win?'

'It's a war,' he says. 'No one wins.'

He shifts his weight and I know he's about to stand up and leave, but I don't want him to go.

'I'm sorry,' I whisper into the gloom.

He stills. 'What for?'

'Once, long ago, I promised I would never ask too much of you, that I wouldn't take advantage of the way we feel . . .' I catch myself. 'The way we *felt* about each other. But I broke that promise. I knew I had to sacrifice myself to become a Mage, and that was my choice, but I also sacrificed you, sacrificed us, and that wasn't my choice to make. I'm sorry for hurting you.'

His silence roars like the stormiest of oceans, thundering with unspoken thoughts and emotions.

But all he says is, 'I'm sorry too. I have spent a lifetime hurting you, intentionally or not.'

I turn my head to face his and dare to reach my hand to his cheek. His skin is warm and rough with stubble. 'Perhaps we should stop living in the shadow of regret.'

Now his head turns, so that I can feel his breath upon my face. I lean into it.

'You think we can escape our pasts?' He's so close that his lips brush against mine, sending shards of heat to nestle in my stone heart.

'We're assassins,' I say, my voice breathless. 'We can always find a way out.'

'And yet I cannot seem to escape you.' His hand meets mine, and when our lips graze each other's this time, neither of us pull away.

We're both hesitant, both unsure, but I know it's going to happen. One slight tilt of my head and I will be kissing him and he will be kissing me and the end of the world be damned.

'Marianne?' The sound of someone calling my name has the same effect on Bronn and me as if we'd been stung by a venomray. We jump apart. 'Are you down here?'

'Yes, what is it?' I have to clear my throat.

I can make out Jax standing in his lantern's light. 'It's the girl,' he says. 'She's talking. And she remembers her name.'

For the briefest moment, I linger beside Bronn. I don't want to leave him. But I cannot stay. I try to shrug off what just nearly happened as I hurry up to Raoul's quarters, where the girl has been staying, finding her with Olwyn and Astrid.

When she sees me, recognition flickers in her face and she almost manages a smile.

'How are you feeling?' I ask, coming to crouch in front of her.

'OK,' she says, her voice thin from lack of use.

'Do you remember much of what happened?'

She blinks and nods, the fear on her face entirely familiar.

I touch her arm to reassure her. 'It's all right, you don't have to think about it. You're safe now.'

Her gaze meets mine, and in her eyes I see reflected all the horrors she's endured – that we've both endured. It breaks my heart.

'What's your name?'

'Dala.'

'It's nice to meet you, Dala.'

She glances around uncertainly. 'I'm scared. I want my mummy.'

'I know,' I say, stroking her hair. 'But we're all here to look after you. I want to take you home; do you know where that is?'

Her eyes pool with tears and her lip trembles as she shakes her head.

'Don't worry, we'll figure it out.'

'What about your family?' Astrid asks. 'Can you tell us about them?'

'The bad men hurt my mummy. She wouldn't move.'

I glance up and meet Olwyn's eyes, the horror of what happened to Dala only growing.

Ever so gently I ask, 'Was that when the men took you?'

Dala nods.

'What about your father? Sisters or brothers?'

She shakes her head and this time her tears fall. I move to sit beside her and slowly fold her into the crook of my arm.

'You have us,' I say. 'We'll take care of you. I swear it.'

'I've never been on a ship before,' she says. 'Is it safe?'

The truth is nowhere's safe, but fortunately Olwyn speaks before I can.

'Once we show you how everything works then it won't seem so frightening, I promise.'

Dala considers this for a moment and then nods. 'I'm hungry,' she says, and I take it as a good sign we've reassured her enough that she's ready to eat again.

'I'll get you some food,' I say, and head down to the small galley to find some supplies.

To my surprise Bronn and Torin are there, and while Torin greets me with a smile, Bronn avoids meeting my eyes. I wonder whether he's thinking about my lips as I'm thinking of his.

Wanting to escape the awkwardness as quickly as possible, I focus on grabbing food, selecting some of the fresh fruits the others bought at the settlement today before the chaos hit. They won't last long, so need to be eaten quickly. After everything Dala's been through she deserves only the best, and so I choose the small pink ones that look especially sweet.

'Oh, these are summer suns,' Astrid says when I bring them back. 'I used to pick these when I was a girl.'

Olwyn's eyes suddenly fill with tears, and she turns her head away. I wonder whether she's remembering when she was a girl, playing with her sister in the snow, and thinking how she'll never do so again. Nostalgia and grief are a potent combination.

I rest my hand on her shoulder, offering her what comfort I can. It's little enough.

Later that night, when Dala is safely settled to a calm sleep, my friends and I gather on deck to drink to Rayvn's name.

'To the fiercest, most loyal sister I could have hoped for,' Olwyn says, raising her mug of ale high. 'To Rayvn.'

We drink to that.

'To Mordecai,' Astrid adds.

Jax stands up. 'To Grace.'

Toby follows suit. 'To my father.'

'To my crew,' Bronn says, rising to his feet.

Torin, Raoul and I look at each other sadly. As one, we stand. 'To all we've lost on this journey,' I say. 'There have been too many.'

We all drink to their memories, but as we sit back down, Torin meets my eye. He's thinking the same as me. That there will be more before the end.

* * *

When the Eighth Isle finally comes into view, the heavy dread that's been lodged in my chest sinks deep into my stomach. The prospect of having to break Mama's heart and crush Pip's joy is one I do not relish. But if I'm dreading it, that's nothing to what Olwyn must be feeling.

Because we're not planning on staying long, we anchor near where Jax and Mordecai did the first time they came to the island, where the climb up the mountain is difficult but quicker.

We decide only a few of us should go, to avoid overwhelming the family, and Bronn and Torin volunteer to accompany me and Olwyn. Toby's keen to join us, and I agree, thinking his presence might go some way to comfort Pip. Astrid also wants to come, but Dala needs one of the three of us to stay for reassurance. She doesn't really trust anyone else yet.

There's a pensive silence between us all as we row across to the shore, the boat bouncing on the choppy waters. When we're in the shallows, Bronn leaps out, the ocean rising to meet his waist, and tows us up on to the sand. We shoulder our satchels and climb out of the boat.

But the instant my foot connects with the crystal beach, pain hits me hard and I drop to my knees. Olwyn and Torin rush to my side.

'What is it?' Olwyn asks.

I meet her eyes, full of concern, and see my own reflected back. 'Something's wrong.' This island has always welcomed me with its light and warm magic, but now there's only a gaping darkness. 'We should hurry.'

The mountains are the heart of this island, and I can no longer hear their beat. There's just a hollow silence, and as I run I try to reassure myself that if anything too terrible were to have happened, I would have sensed it. My magic would have sensed it.

*Not if he used concealing magic. Like you did.*

The thought is unwelcome. The hut in the mountains is the closest thing I have to a home in the West. I want to get there faster; I don't want to get there at all.

We scramble up the same unforgiving path that we descended when Mordecai and Jax returned me to my ancestral home.

I reach the outskirts of the land first and at the sight in front of me horror strikes like a blade. For a moment I can't move. It is Olwyn's cry that brings me to my senses.

'Keep her away,' I warn Torin, pointing to Olwyn and Toby. 'Don't let them come any further.'

He wraps his arms round Olwyn, and sinks into the snow with her as she drops to her knees, her scream splitting the air.

To protect her from discovering precisely what has

caused the devastation before us, I shall have to do it myself.

The closer I get to Mama's hut, once such a happy place, the redder the snow turns. I walk past the dead horse whose slit neck has emptied to turn the white world crimson. I can do nothing for it. I walk straight into the shell of the home I once loved, now ravaged by fire. The smell of blood and smoke clogs my nostrils and I gag. But though I sweep the entire building, there is no sign of Mama or Pip.

I'm going to have to fall deeper into this nightmare to find them.

Back outside, Bronn is waiting for me, his expression grim. Toby is with Torin, who is still cradling Olwyn and whispering to her, offering comfort for a pain that cannot be eased. But I want answers for her. She needs the truth, however terrible. And it is going to be terrible.

'Did you find them?' Bronn asks.

I shake my head. 'We have to keep looking.'

'I can go on my own,' he says. 'You don't have to do this.'

'Yes, I do.'

But he's right beside me as I continue my search. We don't get far before we both stop in our tracks.

'Merciful seas,' Bronn says, while I just stand frozen, unable to breathe or think or speak.

Behind the house, in the place where once the herd

descended to bow to me, is the scene of a slaughter.

The bodies cover the ground, the only movement coming from manes and tails catching in the breeze.

In front of them all, cut down where she made her stand, is Mama.

Her spear has rolled slightly from her hand, her grip weakened by death. Her other hand rests on the bloom of black staining her dress, where the fatal wound has already dried. Her unseeing eyes stare upwards, her expression startled and sorrowful all at once.

She died doing what she was born to do. Protecting the snow mares.

I stumble towards her and kneel at her side, gently closing her eyes with my fingertips. She didn't stand a chance, but I love her more than ever for fighting to her last breath. I want to sob and wail, but they are not my tears to cry. The last thing I want is for Olwyn to see this massacre, and so I scoop Mama's frail body into my arms, and carry her to where my friends are waiting.

Olwyn's howl almost undoes me entirely, as I lower Mama to the ground beside her.

She takes her grandmother into her arms, burying her face in Mama's hair as she sobs.

Toby looks up at me questioningly. 'Pip?' he asks softly.

I shake my head. 'Bronn and I will keep looking.'

Resting my hand on Torin's shoulder, I say 'Find a shovel and start digging. We need a grave.'

Heading back to where the herd lie butchered, I wonder what is to be done with their bodies. We cannot possibly hope to bury them all. I fear we shall have to burn them, a prospect that fills me with dread. But it cannot be worse than the horror of walking through the corpses, searching for a small girl. Because, as I approach the carnage, I realise the bodies have been mutilated.

If there had been any doubt who had done this, there is none now. It wasn't enough to kill them; he had to take parts, as he always does, to feed him at a later date.

Gaius has killed the snow mares and stolen their magic.

Grief and rage propel me forward, my need to find Pip growing, though I have no hope she'll be alive. I just want to be able to leave this place.

It's when I see the leader of the herd, the mare who first befriended me, that I finally crumble.

He has taken her legs. All four of them. Presumably, as the dominant mare, her magic was the strongest, the most potent. The sight of her beautiful body so disfigured is more than I can bear. I don't bother to wipe the tears that fall away as I force myself onwards, desperate now for any sign of Pip. But she is nowhere to be found.

When I have trawled my way through every last inch

of the flesh, bone and blood, I cry out in frustration.

Bronn joins me. 'What do you want to do?'

'I have to find her.' I look up at the mountainside. 'Perhaps the fight extended further than this. I'm going to climb up. You stay here, make sure we haven't missed her. And then help the others.'

I scramble up the rock, trying to ignore my shaking hands, trying to forget that the last time I came this way was on the back of the mare, flying into the sky. There are no signs of fighting, or trails of blood, but I push forward, not knowing what else to do, where else to search, because Olwyn will not rest until she knows the fate of her younger sister.

I keep going, though my fingers are turning to ice and my eyes cannot stop seeing the horrors beneath me.

Exhausted, I rest my head against the stone. How long have I been climbing now? It feels forever, and it feels pointless. The fight clearly did not reach this far.

There's only one thing left to try. Magic brought Bronn to me when I thought he was dead; perhaps now it can lead me to Pip. Closing my eyes, I bring her face into my mind. Pip. *Where are you?*

My head prickles at the use of Esther's magic, which I now claim as my own. The strongest sensation sweeps over me, and it takes me a moment before I realise what it is. The trace of magic that runs in Pip's veins is calling to mine. For once I don't fear the way my magic stirs inside me, instead I embrace it, following it like an invisible path. Though I slip and stumble, I eventually find myself in front of a crack, where a concealed cave lies burrowed into the rock itself. Like I always knew it was there.

'Pip?' I call into the darkness.

For a moment I think maybe I've made a mistake, that only sheer chance brought me here, but then there's a movement in the shadows.

'Pip? It's Marianne. You're safe,' I say, and, seconds later, a small body flings itself into my arms.

'I'm sorry, I'm sorry,' she says over and over again as I hold her tight.

'You have nothing to be sorry for,' I say, wishing I could protect her from the horrors, knowing I can't.

Pip pulls away from me, and my eyes scan her for any sign of injury. Other than shock and grief, she seems unharmed, though the vibrancy of her bright white hair seems to have dulled.

'I ran,' she says, silent tears falling. 'I'm supposed to protect the herd, but I ran.'

'If you had stayed, you would be dead,' I say. 'There was nothing you could have done.'

'I could hear them,' she says. 'Their screams. They carried on the wind.'

I pull her close to me again. 'I'm sorry you had to go through that alone,' I say, stroking her hair.

'I'm not alone,' she says to my astonishment, taking my hand in hers.

She leads me deeper into the darkness until I smell the warmth of horse hair and life, mingled with fear.

'I brought the foals with me,' she says, though it is too dark for me to see her any more.

The relief is so great, I could cry.

'How many are there?'

'Fifteen, I think,' she says. 'I'm not sure. I couldn't protect them all.' Tears pool in her eyes.

'Pip, you are a true protector of the snow mares. Without you there would be none left to protect.'

'But I ran away,' she repeats, and her voice trembles.

'Sometimes running is the bravest thing you can do. It can take more strength to survive than to die.'

Her hand slips into mine. 'What happens now?'

'I need you to be brave a little longer,' I say, though I hate asking it of her. But I cannot bring her down the mountain yet, not when such a sight remains. Not even her worst imaginings will come close to the reality.

'I need you to stay here with the foals, until I'm certain it's safe for you all to come out.'

Her panic is obvious, even in the darkness, and I seek to reassure her. 'I'll send Olwyn to stay with you.'

'Olwyn's here?'

'Yes,' I say, knowing that Olwyn's presence will bring both comfort and pain, for Olwyn will have to break the news about Mama and Rayvn. The cave can swallow their tears. 'Can you do that for me? Will you wait?'

'OK,' she says, and I hear how hard she's trying to stay strong.

'I promise it won't be for long.'

Leaving her is awful, but I cannot hide from what needs to be done. The mares have already been picked apart by one vulture, I won't abandon them to other scavengers.

As I carefully climb back down the mountain, the implication of what has happened truly dawns on me.

Gaius has the power of the snow mares. An ancient strong magic flowed in their veins, and he has consumed it. How can I stop him now? I cannot hope ever to wield so much power.

And then I'm hit by another thought. After all these centuries of their location being concealed by magic, how did he find them?

I think of how the Hooded knew where we would be on the Ninth Isle. How Gaius has uncovered the secret of the snow mares. It cannot be coincidental.

We have been betrayed.

We stay in the mountains only for as long as it takes to clear the carnage. Once I took Olwyn back to Pip, I set to work building a huge pyre on which to burn the dead horses. It took all four of us – Bronn, Torin, Toby and me – to carry the more complete carcasses to the flames and after long, hard hours of gathering up dismembered limbs and entrails, the fire now burns fierce and foul. The smell is unbearable and several times I spit up bile. The air that was once so sweet is now polluted with death, and as we inhale it, our bodies become infected with the bitter taste.

Torin and Olwyn had buried Mama when I was up in the mountains, while Bronn and Toby determined what was salvageable of the hut. The stone walls are pretty much all that's survived, and they are black with soot.

We take out debris and throw it on the fire as well, and all the while I'm wondering how we can possibly leave Pip here.

I lean against the wall to catch my breath. Even though we're in the snow, sweat trickles down my back.

'The roof will have to be completely remade,' Torin says, coming to join me. 'Perhaps we can bring up some old sails to use as a makeshift shelter for now?'

'This hut endured for generations,' I say in a whisper.

'And it still stands,' he reminds me gently. 'What's gone can be rebuilt.'

'By a twelve-year-old girl?' I give him a doubtful look.

'Maybe she should come with us.'

I shake my head. 'She won't leave the foals.'

'What do you want to do then?'

Bring the fire to Gaius. Destroy him the way he's destroyed this hallowed place. My magic is singeing my insides, so fierce is my need for vengeance.

'It's not up to me. This decision is for those bound to their duty. We'll ask Olwyn and Pip what they want to do.'

Torin nods in agreement, but he doesn't move. Instead he says, 'There's something else bothering you. What is it?'

I sigh. 'I think we have an enemy among us.'

He frowns. 'What do you mean?'

'I think someone's communicating with Gaius. Feeding him information, like the fact that we were going to the Ninth Isle, like the location of the snow mares.'

'He didn't already know where they were?'

'He would have come for them long ago if he had. There are enchantments around this place, protecting it, masking the magic.'

'But he knew when you were here,' Torin points out. 'Isn't that why he sent Jax and Mordecai all that time ago?'

'Maybe he sensed my presence before I reached the protective magic? His magic and mine aren't so different, so perhaps that's how he recognised it.' A truth that shames me.

'No one in our group would be working with Gaius,' Torin says.

'Maybe it's one of the crew. Gaius managed to infiltrate the *Maiden*; who's to say he didn't do the same with the *Nightshade*?'

Torin pulls a face. 'He would have had to have some foresight to do that—'

'He does have bloody foresight!' I scream, suddenly unable to bear it all any more, and pressing my hands to my ears as if they can block out the horrors. I take a breath and remind myself this is not Torin's fault. My voice is softer when I add, 'I don't have any answers, all right? I don't. All I know is he's always ahead of me, he's always behind me, he's *everywhere* I go.'

Torin pulls me to his chest and holds me tight. 'It's going to be OK.'

It would be so easy to dissolve in the safety of his arms, to crumble away and scatter on the wind. I remember the spark of hope that ignited the day Bronn kissed me and calmed my storm. It's dying out now. It's hard to feel hopeful in the face of such relentless loss. And as it dies, so the magic bleeds ever more from its prison.

I pull away from Torin, rejecting his comfort. 'No, it won't.'

I'm not sure it ever will be again.

I fetch Olwyn and Pip as the sun starts to set, and we manage to make it back to the relative safety of the clearing before darkness blankets the mountains. The foals follow us down, all huddled together anxious for reassurance, scared by what has happened to their herd, their mothers.

We make a fire in front of the hut and sit close together round it for warmth. When Bronn asks them what they want to do next, Olwyn doesn't hesitate.

'I'll stay here with Pip,' she says, nudging into her sister. 'I'm not leaving her alone.'

It's precisely what I expected her to say, but I'm disappointed nonetheless. I shall miss her company, her wisdom, her steadiness.

'What about Astrid?' Torin asks.

Olwyn blinks back tears.

'She'll understand,' Bronn says softly.

'We can bring you anything you need from the ship,' Torin adds. 'Supplies, tools?'

'We'll manage,' Olwyn says. 'We always have. You

need to make haste to the Fleet.' Her eyes meet mine, the flames of the fire reflected in them. 'You need to make him pay for this.'

I hold her fiery gaze and nod. 'With pleasure.'

'Then we'll leave at dawn,' Bronn says. 'We should all try to get some sleep. I can take the first watch.'

'No, I will.' I can't sleep anyway. 'And when we return to the ship, not a word about the foals surviving, understand?'

They all look at me, astonished.

'I don't know who we can trust.' I know they think I'm wrong, so torn apart with grief that I'm looking for someone to blame. I don't care. 'If there's even the smallest possibility that someone is feeding information to Gaius, we can't risk him knowing there are still mares left alive. He'll come back to finish what he started.'

Bronn and Torin exchange a glance, but they agree. I'm not sure if it's just because they don't want to upset Pip by arguing with me, or if they genuinely think there's a possibility of a spy in the ranks, but it doesn't matter. All I care about is keeping the remaining herd safe. And, if I'm honest, making sure Gaius can't take their power too.

Because he has more than ever now, his own infused with the magic of the mares. I didn't know how I was going to defeat him before.

Now I stand no chance.

* * *

At first light, as we prepare to set off, I notice Toby is quieter than usual. In fact, he was quiet last night too, I'm not sure he slept any more than I did, and I worry that the horrors of yesterday are haunting him still.

'Are you all right?' I ask him, softly so the others won't hear. 'It's OK to be upset—'

'No, that's not it,' he says. 'I mean, it was awful, but that's not what's wrong.' He looks at me with such seriousness that I see his father in his features for the first time.

'Then what is it?'

'I want to stay,' he says.

'What? Stay here?'

He nods. 'I'm good at carpentry, I can help Pip rebuild her home. I can help her protect the foals too. And if I stay, Olwyn doesn't have to. Let me stay.'

I look at his determined face and smile to myself, wondering whether he's been missing the mountains ever since we left.

'Come on, let's talk to the others,' I say.

When Toby's explained to everyone, Bronn asks, 'Are you sure this is what you want?'

'The sea has never been my home. I'd be happy here with Pip,' he says, turning to her and adding, 'if you'll have me.'

Pip smiles her agreement, but Olwyn doesn't look

convinced. 'It should be me here,' she says. 'I should never have left in the first place.'

'You'd be dead alongside Mama if you'd stayed,' Pip says, and we all know she's right. 'It's not your duty any more; it's mine. I think I've earned the right to decide my future. My place is here, and your place is with Marianne. Toby and I will be fine.'

Olwyn stares at her little sister for a moment, and then wraps her arms tightly round her. 'I'm so proud of you, Pipit of the mountains, guardian to the snow mares.'

'I'm proud of you too,' Pip replies, and she seems so much older than her twelve years. Aged by what she's endured.

Our departure is slightly delayed as Olwyn talks Toby and Pip through everything she can think of, from advice on how to cut the marram trees correctly to thatch the roof, to best places to hunt for food, to how to harvest and grow frost roots. Pip already knows all of it, but she patiently lets her sister speak. It's what Olwyn needs to do before she's able to leave.

'I will be back,' Olwyn vows to her when there's nothing else left to explain. 'We will fight, we will win, and then I'll return. This is not goodbye.'

'I know,' Pip says. Then she turns to me, and that's when I truly see how much she's changed. The girl she once was died in the cave in the flames of her own fear. But she has been remade from the ashes. I know how that feels. Her expression is now as hard as if it were carved from mountain rock. 'Avenge them, Marianne. Make him suffer for what he did.'

Though I doubt I can do what she asks, though I'm already accepting we're heading into a war we barely stand a chance in, I cannot rob her – or those who fight with me – of all hope. An army who believes they'll be defeated have already lost. And so I say, 'I will,' with every ounce of confidence I can muster.

We descend the mountain in silence and though my heart is heavy to leave them behind, I can't help but feel that Toby and Pip are where they're meant to be. Just as Olwyn was meant to come with us.

By the time we're back on the *Nightshade*, I'm bone-deep exhausted. So much has happened in such a short space of time, so much horror. Olwyn is buckling under the weight of her grief, and the crew is subdued as we set a course for the East-West divide.

My way of coping is to devote my energy to Dala. Our newest member of the crew has lots to learn, and so I begin to teach her what she'll need to know. She still doesn't talk much, and often withdraws into herself. When that happens, I stop whatever we're doing and hold her in my arms. I can imagine why she slips away into the safety of her mind – I know better than most how haunting the memories of the cave can be. I often wonder if she was Gaius's prisoner at the same time as me, if she was one of the children I left behind. But such a thought only awakens my guilt and so I continue to do what I can now, as if by caring for her I'll atone for my sins.

If I have other motives, they're equally selfish. Dala doesn't ask anything of me, while the expectations of everyone else are suffocating. They fear my magic and rely on it simultaneously. And all the while I want to scream at them that it won't be enough to match the ancient, powerful magic Gaius has stolen from the mares.

When I'm not with Dala, I burrow myself away in my hammock, reading Baia's book by candlelight. It enchants me every bit as much as the magical texts I took from Torin's castle all those months ago. I'm particularly drawn to the intricate sketches of blood vessels, the way veins weave and branch out through the body, like streams from a river, carrying the blood wherever it needs to go. Something about the images strikes a chord with me, lingering like a half-forgotten dream. They nestle reassuringly in my mind, instilling a strange calm in my otherwise chaotic thoughts. Perhaps it's the connection they give me to my grandmother or maybe it's simply that it helps to have a reminder that some things endure beyond death, that legacies can last.

The days pass until finally, on the horizon, we spy the Fleet of Eastern ships waiting for us. In an effort to channel my nerves into something productive, I scrub the deck as if it were Gaius himself and I could scour him from existence.

I've been working all morning, my fingers red and raw, when a mug appears in front of my face. I look up to see Jax standing over me.

'Though you might appreciate a drink,' he says. 'You've barely stopped since you woke.'

I sit back on my heels and take the water from him. 'Thank you.'

'We should reach your friends in the next couple of hours,' he says, coming to kneel opposite me. 'You must be looking forward to seeing them.'

'I am.'

Jax raises his eyebrows. 'But?'

But then we're out of time. We'll sail towards the fight awaiting us, because we have to stop Gaius, and we're as ready as we'll ever be. By now he must know we're coming. That I'm coming.

I decide not to burden Jax with my concerns. 'Nothing, I'm just tired. How are you doing?' I'm not only trying to change the subject; I realise I've not spoken to him properly since we were up in the mountains together seeking sanctuary with Mama, when he was angry and frustrated.

'Me? Ready to fight.' His lips curl slightly at the corner, a cross between a snarl and a smile.

I know he's been making contact with many of the other Guardians for the past few weeks, and that they are covertly congregating on the Twelfth, ready for us to join them and march on the palace. He's been an essential linchpin in organising the troops and I thought having a role to occupy him would calm his troubled spirit. But I still sense a discontentment in him.

'Do you dislike being at sea as much as being up in the snow?'

He pulls a face. 'Is it that obvious?'

'You miss him, don't you? Mordecai.'

Jax takes a long swig of his own drink and sighs. 'We used to do everything together. Since we were boys. He was my brother in all but blood. I wish we hadn't been forced to . . . part ways.'

I reach out and touch his arm. 'When this is all over, you can restore the honour of the Guardians and put things back the way they should be. For Mordecai and for Grace.'

'That's precisely what I intend to do,' he says, before gulping down another mouthful.

I stand up and rest my hand on his shoulder to offer comfort. 'Thanks again for the drink.'

Tidying my bucket and brush out of the way, I wipe my hands on my shirt, and go to the bow of the ship, where Torin and Bronn are talking.

They pause when they see me coming.

'How are your strategies coming along? All in place?'

'Pretty much,' Torin says. 'We'll sail with the Fleet to the Twelfth, join with our allies, and launch our attack on the palace.'

'And we're not expecting any trouble on the way?' Bronn has asked me this before, but he's not one to leave things to chance.

'No, the West has no real fleet, only a few ships. In the ocean, at least, we're stronger,' I say. On land, on the other hand . . .

'Then we'll have plenty of time to brief the other ships and give them maps of the island before we land,' Torin says.

Jax and Astrid have provided us with detailed charts of the landscape, to help the Eastern soldiers familiarise themselves with it, and their help has been invaluable. We're not sure what we'll find when we reach the Twelfth Isle – but I think we can safely assume that Gaius will be expecting us. If we have a spy, our movements will have been passed on. What's hard to know is how he'll react. Will he be waiting for us and cut us down before we've begun? Or will he be patiently biding his time at the palace and let us come to him? My money's on the latter. He would definitely allow us to trek across the island, exhaust ourselves, drain our supplies. It would suit him to be a hunter luring his prey into a trap.

We continue to firm up details and discuss tactics as the Fleet looms ever larger on the horizon. There are more ships than I thought there'd be – at least forty – and pride swells inside me. The Easterners want to fight for their islands, for their lives. And, just as quickly, my pride is swallowed by fear. Have I rallied them only to lead them to be slaughtered? Am I making Gaius's life easier for him?

Raoul brings the *Nightshade* alongside the *Storm Promise*, and boarding planks are set up to receive visitors.

When Torin sees who's waiting there, he practically runs across, and sweeps Sharpe into his arms. They laugh and kiss, and their reunion warms my dull spirits.

They come back to our ship, Sharpe resting his hand on Torin's shoulder to lead him safely over the planks, and are followed by Braydon and several of Raoul's crew who were left behind in the East to continue helping with the training. They've now been appointed commanders of different flanks within the Fleet.

Hugs are exchanged, introductions are made, and after Torin gives the order to set sail for the Twelfth, we sit down for a thorough debriefing.

Sharpe tells us how, with the bandits wiped out, things are relatively stable in the East. For now he has appointed an interim governor for each island to keep them safe. But when Torin returns home, he intends to implement a council, much like the one he used to have with banished advisors on the Sixth Isle. There will be a representative chosen from each island, by the islanders, and they will work together for the prosperity of all.

His reign will be nothing like his father's. That is, if there are still islands to rule.

While the bandits are no longer a threat, Sharpe brings other, less welcome news. The islands are continuing to sicken, disease spreading through the soil itself. What crops remain are wilting or rotting, and uncontaminated water is becoming increasingly hard to find. Healers are struggling to meet the demand for medicine, and people have begun dying. Inevitably it is those with little who are suffering first, but no amount of riches will save any one of us if the land we rely on perishes.

No wonder we've had so many volunteers join the fight – it's this or wait to starve.

I shuffle uncomfortably at the thought of what awaits me back in the East. Even if I find some way to defeat Gaius, then I still have to return magic to the islands. How I'm supposed to overcome that impossible challenge is a problem for another day.

'How skilled have the soldiers become?' Bronn asks Sharpe.

'Enough. I'd have preferred more time, but here we

are,' Sharpe replies. 'We've balanced every squadron with those more talented and those less so, to give each their best chance.'

'We've fought the Hooded,' Torin says, and his voice drops at the memory. 'They are exceptionally talented, ruthless and hard to beat. What lies ahead won't be easy.'

'Tell us everything about their fighting style,' Sharpe says. 'Best we be armed with as much knowledge as possible.'

While Torin and Bronn fill them in on our battle on the Ninth Isle, I glance over at Olwyn to see how she's doing. She's paler than usual, her lips pressed tight together. Reliving the day her sister died won't be easy for her. Astrid is clearly thinking the same thing, because she quietly slips her hand into Olwyn's, their fingers entwining for strength.

My gaze drifts from them to the others, watching how alive they all seem, how animated. How determined. I wish that Rayvn was here and Harley. Ana and Ren. The *Maiden* should be leading this fleet with her fearless crew. Maybe then I wouldn't feel so detached, like I'm a mere observer of events rather than an integral participant.

Still, I smile when I'm supposed to, nod when it's required, offer my voice when it needs to be heard. And all the while I cannot shake the inescapable truth – that I'm no better than an executioner surveying my victims.

* * *

The Fleet makes good time sailing towards the Twelfth. The ocean causes us no confusion, and I take that as a positive sign, that at least we have the will of the islands behind us.

I'm deep in conversation with Bronn and Torin about our current state of supplies across the Fleet, when something beyond me catches Bronn's eye. He's staring in horror and I trail off mid-sentence.

'What,' Bronn says, 'the bloody hell is that?'

I turn to follow his gaze and my mouth falls open. On the horizon, where there should be nothing but the outline of land against the expanse of sea, there is a wall of orange. A vast fire that's spreading across the surface of the water and heading this way.

Gaius.

If the fire hits us, the whole fleet is going to be destroyed. If we run, then the fight is as good as lost. If running's even possible.

'Hold your course!' I shout to Raoul, who's at the helm, and to anyone else who can hear me.

Bronn grabs my arm. 'We can't sail through the Mage's flames.'

I pull free from his grasp. 'And we can't outrun them either. He hasn't sent them to scare us. He means to destroy us.'

'Then what exactly do you intend to do?'

I hear his unasked question. Do I dare use my magic given what happened last time? I may not have to – there is something else I could try, though I have no idea whether it'll work. But there's not a lot of time to plan when a magical fire is racing to incinerate you.

'What I always do. Probably something stupid.'

To my utter astonishment, he grins. 'Sounds about right. Meanwhile we'll keep heading towards the blazing inferno.'

For a moment everything that's happened between us disappears. He's just the boy I knew, and I'm the girl I was, and we're teasing each other, believing in each other. It gives me all the strength I need.

I give him a smile of my own and then run to the bow of the ship and dive into the sea.

The water enfolds me, like an icy embrace, and I slowly exhale, letting the sudden quiet calm me. It's strange to think I once feared its darkness so much. I thought to dwell here was to be lost, but now, in the heavy stillness, I seem to find myself. Though I can't use my lungs, it's as if I can finally breathe.

I cannot speak beneath the surface, but I do not need words. Thoughts are enough. The question is, will they be answered?

My plea ripples out through the depths, a cry from my heart carried on the currents. I call until my lungs burn with the need for air.

What will I do if they don't come?

But then I sense a shift in the water and I'm lifted up on the waves, crashing through the surface, and I catch a glimpse of the look on my friends' faces before I'm carried away.

A look of sheer awe.

I glance to my right and then to my left and I'm not surprised. It's not every day a herd of sea stallions gallop across the ocean. The roar of their hooves thunders in my ears as we storm across the water, a shifting tempest of flesh and froth. I'm realise I'm riding the same stallion who saved me the day I jumped from Gaius's cave. His strength, his sheer force of nature, gives me the courage I need, and I lean forward against his watery mane to urge him on.

He needs no encouragement – none of them do. Their pace is fierce, their determination evident in every crashing motion as they swallow the sea beneath them. The fire is an abomination to them as much as me, an unnatural and cruel act of magic, summoned from stolen power.

I can feel the heat as we grow closer, and the stallions toss their heads and flare their nostrils in defiance. The absence of smoke from the fire is abnormal, but it lacks nothing in ferocity. My skin is hot, my hair singeing, but I don't flinch, clinging to the silken, wet mane as we plunge forward, one unstoppable force barrelling towards another.

And then we collide.

All I can hear is the violent hiss of water quenching flame as the stallions overpower Gaius's hellfire. Some scream out as they evaporate for ever, and I can do nothing but hold on as we tumble and crash through the blaze, two forms of elemental magic waging war against each other.

The water douses me, protecting me from the fire, and I snatch air when I can. Despite my precarious situation, I'm confident that for all the power Gaius may have accumulated, he is still no match for the raw strength of the ocean.

We plummet through the dwindling fire and I feel a glimmer of triumph. But when we emerge on the other side, my stallion rears up in fear, the remaining herd suddenly stationary, halting their charge.

Because the wall of fire wasn't just there to savage us. It was also there as a screen, to hide what was behind it, and that sight freezes me to my core.

Gaius has raised a fleet. Literally *raised* one – from the very depths of the ocean. Every ship ever sunk in these waters has been brought back and patched together with magic. Commanding these skeleton ships are those who died with them, corpses in varying states of decay.

I know the ship leading this death fleet. It's my ship. The *Maiden*. Rebuilt in a muddled, broken way, she's a shadow of what she once was.

And staring down at me from her bow, strips of flesh melting from his bones, is someone I never thought I'd have to face again.

Captain Adler.

The stallion needs no encouragement to spin and gallop away from this nightmare. We race back towards the Fleet, as panic steals my breath.

How are we going to fight against the dead? On the Ninth Isle, they were indestructible – but they were on our side. Now they serve our enemy. Gaius has an army we cannot defeat; he intends to stop us today, halt our opposition before we can reach land.

Strengthened by the magic of the snow mares, he's finally gained the power he needed to raise the dead – even if they are putrid corpses. He's growing ever closer to his ultimate aim.

The stallion takes me right to the *Nightshade*, and lifts me up so that I can jump on to the deck. The water horses are retreating, fading back into the waves. Now it's just us against the dead.

'What the hell is going on?' Raoul shouts. 'I thought you said they didn't have a fleet!'

'They didn't,' I say breathlessly. 'Gaius has raised all those lost at sea and their ships.' There are gasps of horror, and my eyes meet Bronn's. 'Including Adler. On the *Maiden*.'

Bronn's expression barely shifts, but I see it in his

eyes. The same cold dread that's gripped me since the moment I saw those ships.

'What do we do?' Olwyn asks, matter-of-fact as ever.

'They may be dead, but we can still blow them out of the water,' Sharpe says. 'Send word through the Fleet to ready their cannons.'

'Would be good if we had any,' Raoul says with a wry smile. 'I built her for smuggling, not bloody battle.'

'Then we'll have to rely on hand-to-hand combat,' Torin says to Raoul, offering him a sympathetic pat on the shoulder. 'And hope you built her to last.'

The *Nightshade* might not be a warship, but plenty of the others are. And Sharpe's suggestion could work – we can't kill the dead, but we can take them apart bone by bone.

Everyone hurries off, shouting orders, preparing themselves for an impossible fight, but I grab hold of Olwyn's arm. 'Find Lena, take her to Dala, I don't want her alone during this. And make sure they stay below deck.'

Olwyn nods and runs off and, as soon as she's gone, I step close to Bronn. 'If he's brought everyone back—'

'Then our crew will be among them, I know.'

'It's not really them,' I say. 'If you see them, don't hesitate. Cut them down.'

His jaw is set tight with tension. 'Any bright ideas

how to get us out of this?'

My own magic thrashes wildly inside me, begging to be set free. If I release it now, there may be no opportunity to use it on Gaius. It could devour me whole. But if I do nothing, will we even survive?

'There might be others who'll help us,' I say, a thought forming in my head.

Bronn knows me too well and the colour drains from his face as he realises what I intend but just as quickly he steels himself. 'Do it.'

'Cover me, OK?'

Bronn nods, and calls Torin and Sharpe over. Together they form a protective circle round me. I haven't got long. The noise drifting over from the ghost fleet is eerie and sinister, a battle cry that's more like an echo, faded and worn. But the beating of blades on shields is real and menacing enough.

I'm chilled by the thought that if we die now, we might rise back up and fight for our enemy. To think I could kill my friends at Gaius's command is a grim prospect.

The sound of our cannons being fired is deafening, the smell of gunpowder choking the air. It won't be long before their ships are close enough for them to board us, and then things are going to get brutal quickly.

I daren't use the language of the Mages, or any other kind of incantation, not when my magic is already hard enough to contain. Instead my blade glides effortlessly across my skin as I reopen the cut I made on the Ninth Isle, so that blood blossoms at the surface. I don't need much, just enough to let my magic reach them. But before I can do anything else, the deck shudders. The first enemy ship has reached the *Nightshade* and the roar of battle surges up around us.

'Hurry!' Bronn shouts at me.

Trying hard to block out the chaos surrounding me, and the sound of my friends hacking through rotting flesh, I lean over the side of the ship and whisper, 'If you can hear me, I beg of you. Help us. Ancient creatures of the deep, save us, please.' And my blood drops down into the water.

Nothing happens.

'Marianne!'

Slamming my fist hard on the deck in frustration, I pull out my sword, and spring to my feet. We're going to have to do this the hard way.

The *Nightshade* is crawling with the dead, and the fighting is frantic. I wield my sword through limbs, but even after I sever one corpse's head, still she keeps fighting. And they're not just attacking *us*. To my horror I realise they're targeting our ship too, cutting ropes and smashing the decking.

'We need to drive them back to their ship,' I call out. 'Before they destroy ours.'

In my peripheral vision I see Astrid shooting the dead down from the rigging of other ships with her bow, so they fall into the water. It's a good plan, buying us a bit more time at least.

'Throw them overboard if you can,' I shout to anyone who can hear, as I fight my way across the deck to her.

'How far is your bow's range?' I call as I approach.

'I can reach them,' she says, pointing to the ships behind those closest to us.

'Can you make fire arrows?'

She gives me a wicked grin as she realises what I'm asking.

'Oh yes,' she says, and I guard her while she sets to work.

While I dismantle the remains of every dead soldier that approaches us, I spare a thought for the islanders on the other ships. They've gone their whole lives never experiencing any magic, and now they're battling it. I wish I could have warned them this was coming. Although how, I wonder as I slash my blade through a skeletal leg, severing brittle bone, could you ever be prepared for this?

Astrid's arrow whistles through the air and I glance to see its impact. It hits the foremast of her target which bursts into flames, fire quickly spreading across the wooden deck. The dead don't bother trying to put it out, and at first I think it's because they lack the intelligence of the living, but then I see them walk through the flames, until they're fully alight, and still they keep coming. If they reach our ships, the Fleet will burn. We've just turned them into fiery weapons.

How can we stop them?

Before I can consider my tactics any further, an explosion to my right makes me jump and instinctively crouch for cover. When I stand up, I see that one of our Fleet is sinking fast, the crew jumping into the sea, abandoning ship.

'What happened?' I shout to Bronn who's running towards me.

'The *Maiden*'s firing cannons.'

'We have to stop them. Take Torin and Raoul, get to that ship on fire, and do whatever you can to stop them spreading it to ours. I'm going to the *Maiden*.'

Before he can argue, I'm already running, mapping a route in my head. The ships are close now, all packed densely. Every few steps I have to pause to sweep a corpse out of my way, but soon I'm on the ship that boarded us. I need to run its full length to reach the next one, and I dodge and weave through the bodies that seek to cut me down. When I make it to the stern, I launch myself through the air and just make the distance to land on the neighbouring vessel. There are a lot of dead sailors waiting for me, so I grab the line hanging from the top of the mast and cut it free.

I swing across the deck, my sword slicing through anyone in my way, and immediately jump to the next ship. I have to fight my way across four more before I reach my destination.

The *Maiden*. My home. Only it's nothing like the ship I knew. The wood is rotting, draped in weed, and the smell of death clings to every part of her remade shell. The sails are shredded, blowing in the ill wind. The crew – *my* crew – look more human than many of the dead, having died so recently, but that's only more distressing. The body of what was once Ana raises her cutlass towards me, her face missing chunks where it's been nibbled by some sea creature, the bone on her right hand showing, and it breaks my heart.

*It's not her.*

Still I can't bring myself to cut her down, and so I dash past, having discovered one thing the dead do not possess is speed. My only aim is to reach the gun deck and stop them from firing any more cannons.

But I don't get far before I skid to a halt. Blocking my way, as if he anticipated this move, is Adler. Armed with a massive club.

'Well, that's new.'

In response he bares his teeth and roars, before swinging the club at me. I have to dodge quickly out of the way, but as soon as I've regained my footing, I make my own attack. I swerve to avoid his next strike, but then tip my balance forward and bring my blade to slice across his middle.

He doesn't even flinch.

'Fine,' I say, 'I can do this all day.'

His response is to aim for my head, but I manage to slide out of the way, only to find myself face to face with Ren.

He's vicious in his assault, pummelling me with blow after blow that I struggle to block. He's pushing me towards Adler.

Throwing all my weight at him catches Ren off guard, and he stumbles backwards, falling on to a grappling hook hanging from the rigging and impaling himself. He tries to pull away, but it only tears at his flesh, slowing him down to give me enough time to escape and return to Adler, to face him on my own terms.

'I killed you once, you bastard; I can do it again.'

He bellows defiance, the smell of putrid flesh wafting from him, and I throw my blade into my left hand, leaving my right one free to catch the club handle as he brings it down.

It's heavy – even dead, Adler is far stronger than me – but I'm more determined. With the club temporarily halted I sweep my blade hard across his arm, severing it at the elbow.

The club falls to the ground, still gripped in his hand.

'I'll take you piece by piece if I have to,' I growl at

the man I once called father.

This time when he roars it's like a shriek in the air, a call to arms, and all the crew close in on me. Suddenly I'm confronted with my own personal nightmare.

They back me into a corner so that my options are to jump ship or stand and fight them. I'm not sure how many I can take before I'm overpowered.

I'm still agonising over my decision when something hits me hard, flinging me across the ship. Winded, I look up from where I lie on the deck, wondering what's going on – and then I cry out with relief.

The water raptor who carried me East has finally answered my call, her tail knocking me out of the way to protect me from the acid she's now breathing over the carrion crew. I don't know whether it's the magic in her venom, or just the toxicity, but their bodies hiss and dissolve, flesh melting, bones crumbling to ash. I feel a pang of remorse for my old friends and have to remind myself that they were already dead.

The raptor looks towards me and I throw my hands up in welcome. 'You came!' A massive wing unfolds and she extends it to where I sit, inviting me to come aboard. I scramble up until I'm sitting high on her head.

'Thank you,' I say. 'You saved me.'

In return she screams out into the air, a sound to burn fear into her enemies' hearts. Her wings lift high before smashing down on to the *Maiden*, snapping her in half so that slowly the ship begins to sink. I close my eyes. Seeing her succumb to the ocean once was already more than enough for me. Instead I focus on what must be done.

'Target the dead – you're the only weapon we have,' I say. 'But don't hurt the living; they're on our side.'

She shrieks out again, and I think she's trying to tell me something until I feel the ocean shift beneath us, and see the ships around us bobbing about like cotton reels. And that's when I realise she's not talking to me.

Her mate marks his arrival by scooping up a shipwreck in his massive jaws and crushing it between razor-sharp teeth.

And then, all around us, the creatures of the deep begin to emerge.

A ship on my left is being enveloped in the thick smooth body of a vast eel-like beast, which winds its steel-grey coils tightly round the vessel before it sucks it back under the water, bubbles the only thing remaining on the surface.

To my right there's a cast of giant crabs, their pincers more like blades, that chop and slice through the corpses with a scissoring motion.

A shoal of huge fanged fish are attacking from all angles, leaping from the water to snatch as many bodies as they can in their mouths before they submerge once more.

My Fleet is bolstered by this unexpected assistance from beneath, their spirits renewed, and I watch as more and more of them manage to push bodies into the water, to let the creatures deal with them.

But from my vantage point I can see we've had substantial losses. The *Maiden* took out at least four ships before the water raptor ended her unnatural reign of terror, and the corpses have spilled plenty of blood. The water has turned a murderous pink.

For all the extra help we've got, the armada Gaius has raised is still greater in size than ours, and the danger still very much real. I could ask the water raptors to position themselves between the two fleets, but then our people on the enemy ships will have no way back, and though the raptors try to be targeted in their attacks, their venom tends to spray indiscriminately.

And all the while, as I'm thinking what to do, the water raptor beneath me is causing devastation – smashing, burning, crushing. I remember what it was like to be on the receiving end of their strength and power, and am endlessly glad they're on my side this time.

Then a deafening crack of thunder makes me jump, and the whole world shudders. The water raptor flaps her wings in protest.

'What the hell was that?' I shout. Fearing a new threat, I look around for the source and discover that the dead have all fallen where they stood, returned now to what they truly are.

What's more, the ships are starting to sink, retreating back to the seabed.

'Get back to our ships!' I scream to the living, cupping my mouth. 'Hurry!'

Some of my people are scattered widely through the armada and stand no chance of getting back in time. Before I even say a word, the raptor hears my thoughts, and takes flight. I cling to her feathers as she swoops down, scooping my drowning fighters on to her wings before depositing them safely back on our ships.

And that's when I see her. Some distance from all the chaos, in a small boat, her hands still raised from unpicking Gaius's magic, is Esther. She came.

Once the water raptor has safely rescued all those still alive, I ask her to carry me through the water to Esther. I slide down her neck and hop on to the boat, which rocks on the waves the raptor has created.

Esther smiles at me as she lowers her arms.

'What changed your mind?' I ask, relieved beyond belief to see her.

'Someone told me that the time to hide was over. She was right.'

But she looks pale and drawn, and she reaches her hand to her head.

'What is it? What's wrong?' I ask, rushing forward to

put my arms round her to steady her.

'I haven't used my magic like that in a long time. It's exhausting.'

'Come on,' I say, 'let's get you to my ship.'

The water raptor lowers her head to allow us to clamber on, and then she carries us over to the *Nightshade*, where Torin and Bronn rush forward to help Esther down.

When I'm back on deck, I turn to the water raptor and bow. 'I am in your debt. Again. Thank you.'

She bows her head, before uttering a guttural cry to her fellow sea monsters, who, on her command, return to the deep once more, taking the last traces of carnage to the seabed with them. With one final ear-piercing shriek the raptor too dives beneath the waves, and peace is restored to the ocean.

Ignoring all the cheers of victory sweeping through the Fleet, I hurry to Esther's side. Torin's already fetched her some water and is now hunting for a blanket to keep her warm.

'You tamed the water raptors?' Esther asks with a grin. 'Trust you to be the first.'

'Me? You're the one who undid Gaius's magic.'

'At some cost to myself. He's grown very powerful,' she muses.

I sigh, reluctant to explain the reason. 'He slaughtered the snow mares and stole their magic.'

Esther stares at me in horror, and I nod to confirm the awful truth.

'To steal such potent and ancient magic has amplified his own,' she murmurs, 'enabling him to do things far beyond his previous capabilities.'

'The Seers sent a prophecy that said if he managed to raise the dead, then the war was lost.'

'Don't despair just yet,' she says. 'He's nearly there but not quite. Didn't you notice how the dead behaved? These were simply puppets. They did his bidding, yes, but they were not the people they once were. There are only two ways I know of to *truly* bring back the dead, and both have been achieved by one person alone. One was when you brought yourself back to life to become a Mage – a gift unique to you. The other is the curse of the Ninth Isle.'

An icy trickle of understanding glides over me. The Blood Isle. The attack from the Hooded. It was all a trap.

'I raised the dead there not long ago.'

Our eyes meet and she knows what I'm saying. 'He wanted you to do so. Wanted to sense the magic, learn from it.'

Just like I wanted to learn about Esther's magic. 'Well, he's succeeded, and grown powerful enough to use the dead as vessels.'

'As vessels, yes, but he can't bring them back fully.

Not yet anyway. This was a rehearsal,' she says, confirming my worst fears. 'He's honing his skills.'

And then our time really will have run out.

Before I can say anything more, Astrid comes running up, out of breath, her face full of fear.

'What's the matter?' Torin asks.

'It's Olwyn and Jax,' she says, her voice trembling. 'They're missing.'

We made camp just days ago, after the Fleet limped towards the Twelfth Isle and reached her shores. There was no army waiting for us, no resistance from Gaius at all. Which means he wants us to come to him, for reasons I'm sure we'll find out soon enough. But I'm certain he knows we're here.

Weighed down by our losses, exhausted from battle, we traipsed to where Guardians loyal to their true calling have been gathering ever since Jax made contact with them.

Several hundred of our people were lost at sea. Olwyn and Jax included. There are daily patrols going out on the water searching for survivors, while others comb the beaches, but so far none have been found.

I'm not sure if it's because I can't bear to be crushed under any more loss, or if I'm just in denial, but I cannot believe they're gone. Accepting that I've lost Olwyn and Jax on top of everyone else might just be enough to unravel the threads of my control and undo me entirely.

Astrid distracts herself by caring for Dala, who is happy to be on dry land again, but I know Astrid's just doing her best to hold herself together too.

Both of us are hoping for something we know deep

down can't happen. But hope is a strange thing. An invisible anchor to which we cling when logic and reality would suck us into an abyss, drowning us in despair.

Our camp is in a clearing on the outskirts of a vast forest. We estimate we have close to four thousand soldiers in total, and it's been a colossal task setting up tents, managing supplies, organising weapons – all of which had to be transported inland from the Fleet.

Together with the Guardians from the East, Torin, Bronn, Sharpe and Raoul have been discussing our battle strategy. I probably should be with them, but instead I've been going into the forest with Esther. Because I know there is only one battle left to fight. The one where we march on the palace and destroy Gaius and his army of mercenaries. No doubt Gaius will have convinced Rafe and his advisors that I am coming to claim his crown, and so we anticipate being met with every soldier they've got. Which will be more than we have. So I need to be ready.

Standing against Gaius's magic has drained Esther's energy, and I recognise the war waging within her now. The magic wants to be let loose again, wants another turn at being in charge. She needs to gather her strength before we travel, and while she does so, she's helping me as much as she can.

'For you to harness your magic you need to stop being scared of it,' she'd said to me the first time we came out into the quiet of the trees. When I'd opened my mouth to object, she'd held up her hand. 'I know you have good cause. But you were a youngling then, a brand-new Mage, filled to the brim with anger and fear. It's no surprise you nearly destroyed everything. Now you've had time to settle into your new skin. You feel it, don't you? The difference? Being a Mage is not the same as being human, perhaps more so for you than anyone.'

I had already told her about how I was incomplete, not dead but not entirely alive, and she hadn't seemed surprised. 'Death isn't a boundary lightly or easily crossed. As Gaius has been discovering for centuries.'

To help me try to relax into my power, we sit for hours in the peace, and I listen to the magic inside me. To start with I could only hear a rattle, a roar, a rage, as if my magic were smashing against the bars of its prison. But as the time passes, I realise what a mistake I've made. That sound isn't the magic. It's me. My head, my heart, my internal war eternally waging. My panic, my terror, my pain. The magic is at the centre of it all, humming gently, reminding me it's ready whenever I am. And slowly I start to hear it over the clamour of everything else, the siren-like call, the hum of magical power. It's saved my life before, freed me from the cave, even enabled me to bring most of my spirit back from the dead. It is something to respect, as much as to fear.

Close to nature, where the roots of the trees beneath me are full of their own life-sustaining magic, it is easier to find the balance.

In the evenings my friends fill me in on their conversations and deliberations of the day, so that I know what is to come. We will stay at this camp for one more night before we start the journey across the island. Bronn has sent word to Harley, and she will join us en route. It's a reunion I'm anxious for, to see her safe and have her back where she belongs. Scouts report that Gaius is rallying his army, recalling all the Hooded spread out across the islands to fight alongside the Guardians still loyal to him and Rafe. His numbers are greater than ours, especially with recent losses, but we are fighting for our homes and loved ones, while they fight on orders. We must hope it gives us an edge. For what other choice do we have? Run home and suffer a slow death on the sick islands? Or wait for Gaius to come for us? No, we will make our stand, fight for the islands, or die in the attempt.

That evening I'm gathering wood from the forest to keep the fires burning all night, when the sense that I'm not alone prickles up my neck. I draw my dagger as I spin round, just in time to see the huge bird sweep down through the trees and I hold out my arm for him.

'Talon?' I cry with shock. 'You're alive!'

Barely, though, by the looks of him. The sea vulture

has clearly put up a fight against his captivity. His once sleek wing feathers are torn, and both fresh blood and scabs are visible from where he's battered himself against something – probably his prison bars. He's desperately thin, and his eyes, once so bright, are now dull.

'What has he done to you, my love?' I murmur, refraining from stroking him in case it causes pain.

He makes a small sound, more a croak than his usual beautiful song and my heart breaks. Of course Gaius wouldn't have killed him. A sea vulture is too valuable a commodity.

'I'm so sorry,' I whisper, as he breathes heavily on my arm. His flight has exhausted his weary body. I rest him down on to the ground and sit beside him. That's when I realise he's not here because he's escaped. He's carrying a message.

I take it from him, and open it with trepidation. I'm fully expecting it to be from Gaius, but it's not. It's from Greeb. She has Olwyn and Jax and will set them free in exchange for the treasure she really seeks: me. If I go willingly and alone, not only will their lives be spared, but she promises she will deliver me to Gaius dead, so he cannot torture me.

I stare at the note for several minutes, trying to take it in. Olwyn and Jax are alive. No doubt deliberately taken during the fight for this very purpose, as bargaining chips.

Talon nudges me gently, and I look down at him with pity. No one – sea vulture or human – should be a prisoner of these people.

'How did we end up here?' I whisper to him. 'How has it all gone so wrong?'

His dark eyes meet mine and I realise he's given up. He has nothing left to fight with. And I can't bear it. I can't keep losing those I love.

I reach my hand out, ever so gently resting it on his chest. Listening closely to the beat of magic that rings alongside my pulse, I allow a little of it to rise up and flow from me to Talon. My breath catches at the soar of energy as heat pulses through my fingertips and into the bird.

It's an effort to stop – it's only when I sense that Talon has had enough and that any more would hurt him that I stay my hand. Afterwards I'm breathless, empowered by what I've just done, a reminder of the good my magic can achieve. Talon stretches his renewed wings and flaps them hard. This time his cry is as rich and full as it ever was.

'You have been a loyal friend,' I say, choking slightly with emotion. 'Your service is more than done. It's time you flew free.'

He nuzzles me one final time, a wordless goodbye, and then he soars up into the sky and disappears from my sight.

I sit for a moment, alone and sad. And then I rise to my feet because I know what I have to do.

Once everyone but the night watch has gone to sleep, I slip into the tent which Bronn shares with Raoul. I crouch low beside Bronn, but his knife is at my throat before I know it. When he sees it's me, he quickly removes it, frowning in confusion. I put my finger to my lips to warn him to be quiet, and gesture for him to follow me.

Without a word I lead him into the forest and only once I'm sure we're alone do I hand him Greeb's note.

I watch his expression darken as he reads it, and when he has, he looks at me. 'You're not actually thinking of going, are you?'

'Of course I'm going,' I say. 'Right after we've come up with a plan.'

Because I'm done making the same mistakes. I'm done putting my trust in the wrong people. There's no way Greeb is going to let Olwyn and Jax go, no way she won't hand me straight over to Gaius. So I'm putting my trust in myself – and in Bronn.

He watches me closely for a moment, a faint hint of a smile forming. 'What did you have in mind?'

'I'm going to have to go alone, or they might kill Olwyn and Jax before we can reach them. But you can follow me, scout out the location, find an entrance, break in and rescue us.'

He doesn't like it. 'That very much depends on them not killing you all the moment they have you.'

'Greeb won't kill me.' I'm certain of that. 'If she hands me over to Gaius, she'll be rewarded. And my magic is worth a lot more with me alive than dead.'

'If she's lying about giving you a quick death, she could be lying about everything else too,' Bronn says. 'She may not have them at all. Or they might already be dead.'

'It's possible, but it's a risk we have to take. If there's even the slightest chance Olwyn and Jax are there, we can't leave them. We can't.'

'And you think we can make it out alive? Just the four of us? They're not great odds.'

'We can't afford to trust anyone else, not when we still don't know who the spy is. And anyway, how hard can it be for a couple of assassins and two skilled fighters?' Now I'm the one who smiles.

'Just like old times, huh? Like when I rescued you from the King.'

'As I recall, I kicked your ass and then let you come with me.'

'Yeah, well, my memory's a little hazy,' he says with a grin.

'You're getting old.'

'And yet you want my help.'

'No one else to ask.'

His eyes are sparkling and I know mine are too. But just as quickly our humour falls away, replaced by the seriousness of the situation.

'What if I can't find a way in?' he says.

'I'll use my magic if I have to. I won't stand by and watch them die, Bronn. I can't bear to lose anyone else. I won't.'

His jaw clenches as if there's something he wants to say, but the moment passes. Instead he nods. 'Fine. When you do leave?'

I sigh. 'Now. There's no time to waste.'

'I won't be far behind,' he promises, and as I leave, he calls out, 'Be careful.'

It's hard walking away from him, but I pull Olwyn and Jax into my mind and they strengthen my resolve. *I'm coming for you.* And once they're safe, I'm going to kill Greeb.

The message gave instructions for where I should go, and I follow them through the night, guided by stars that are scattered across the sky like fallen breadcrumbs. Day is breaking when I finally make it, weary from my sleepless night.

My path leads me to a dusty valley flanked by long-dead trees, decayed to barren trunks now home to burrowing insects and cadaver crows. They may be the only things living in this abandoned place.

At the far end is an ancient temple. Once it might

have looked ethereal, its stone pillars decorated with ornate carvings, but it has crumbled over the years, and withered with neglect. It is beautiful, forgotten and heavily guarded.

Two things occur to me simultaneously. One is that it's going to be close to impossible for Bronn to sneak in undetected, but the other is more pressing. Bronn identified a temple as one of the places Gaius kept the children. What if this is it? Even if Bronn could sneak in and the four of us escape, how could I leave more children behind? Just thinking of Dala's face, of her wide-eyed fear, makes my heart hurt.

Bronn will reach the same conclusion and he'll share my dilemma. And we have no way to communicate. I'm just going to have to trust him. Because the guards have seen me, and there's no going back now.

I raise my hands in surrender as I approach the temple, conscious of every arrow pointing at me.

The vast door opens and I'm greeted by five members of the Hooded.

One of them steps towards me, rope raised, and reaches for my hands.

I don't object, allowing him to bind my wrists, though the rope fibres are unexpectedly coarse and irritate my skin almost like a burn. Once I'm secured, they escort me through dimly lit corridors until we reach a hall. Long ago, I imagine that Mages gathered here to honour the nature of the islands, perhaps they knelt at the ornate altar and gazed up at the tapestries of the Isles. But it's been many years since this place was used to worship anything but wealth. And the woman who glorifies it beyond life itself, Greeb, waits for me now.

Olwyn and Jax are gagged and bound beside her. Dried blood frames Olwyn's brow, and Jax's chin is bruised, but the sight of them comforts me. They're alive.

Greeb smiles at me. 'It's been a long time, Marianne.'

'I would have preferred it to be longer.'

'I confess, I did not think you'd come.'

'Your note gave me little choice. And I'm here, as you demanded, so you need to let them go. A trade, as you promised.'

Greeb moves to Jax, and starts to untie his restraints. 'Never let it be said I'm not a woman of my word,' she says, and instantly I'm on edge. I didn't think she would actually release them. If she does, if she keeps her word, that means she's going to kill me too. Bronn won't be here in time and I brace myself to use my magic if necessary. 'But the truth is,' Greeb continues, 'I didn't send you that note. None of this was my idea.'

A worm of unease burrows into my gut. 'Then whose was it?'

Greeb removes the gag from Jax's mouth. He spits out the fibres caught on his tongue, before meeting my gaze. 'It was mine.'

The world falls away from me.

I should have seen it.

Why didn't I see it?

'I knew you would come for Olwyn, your beloved cousin. And for me, Grace's twin. You're too blind to see what is so obvious to your enemies, that your love for others makes you weak.'

His words echo the ones Adler once taunted me with. I think I might be sick.

I meet Olwyn's gaze, and see my thoughts reflected back in her wide eyes. How could he betray us?

'How long have you and Greeb been working together?' I ask, though I have some idea.

'Since your return,' Jax says. 'All those years searching for you, and for what? A hot-headed girl who couldn't decide what she wanted. What made you worthy of being Queen? Once I confided my concerns to Gaius, he brought Greeb and me together.'

The extent of his treachery is an acid burning through my guts. 'You told Gaius to send the Hooded after us on the Ninth. You told him where the snow mares were. You let him slaughter them!' My voice rises in a crescendo. 'Mama welcomed you into her home and you betrayed her!'

'I gave him another weapon,' he spits back. 'Not that he needs it now he has you. Greeb wasn't sure you would come, but I knew if you were offered a clean death in exchange for our lives, you wouldn't hesitate to hand yourself over.'

'Well, that's where you're wrong,' I say, wishing I could kill him where he stands. 'I'm not here to hand myself over.'

Greeb smiles at me. 'If you're thinking of unleashing your own magic, be advised. Your wrists are bound by no ordinary rope. Gaius made it himself and enchanted it, so that if you use your magic, it will pass into the rope to be stored until he can claim it.'

That's why it burned when it touched my skin. I curse myself for not sensing what it really was as my chest tightens with panic. This is all going wrong fast – there is nothing I fear more than returning to Gaius.

'That's what I thought,' Greeb says, sensing my defeat. 'Nothing but a pathetic child in the end, are you?'

I can't wait for Bronn. Though I'm heavily outnumbered, I have to fight, even if my hands are bound. I will not go so easily to my fate. Before anyone can stop me, I spin swiftly to my right, sweeping the sword from the scabbard of the Hooded at my side, and following the circle round to slice the blade through three stomachs as I go. The surrounding Hooded swoop in and descend on me and I slash and cut, and maim and kill with impunity.

Jax's voice cuts through the chaos. 'Enough!'

The Hooded fall back, and I see the knife Jax is holding to Olwyn's throat. So this is why they included her in their plan. She is here as collateral, to stop me from doing this very thing.

'I have no qualms about letting you watch her die a slow and painful death,' Jax says. 'So do carry on if you wish. But if you want her to live, I suggest you surrender now.'

The sword clatters to the floor as I raise my hands. And then the Hooded descend on me, beating every part of my flesh they can find, and I curl to the ground, spitting out blood as I fall. It's minutes of agony before a heavy blow strikes my head and I slip into the glorious oblivion of darkness.

When I come round, I'm still in the same hall, only I'm leaning against the wall, out of the way, while the Hooded rush busily about.

The ropes remain tightly round my wrists, but they've not bothered with any further restraints. They know they don't need to. I will not retaliate if it means they hurt Olwyn and I can't use my magic to defend us either. They've rendered me utterly impotent.

'Are you OK?'

I turn my pounding head to my left to see Olwyn propped up against the wall too. Unlike me, her feet are bound as well as her hands, which are behind her back.

'I'm fine, are you?'

'I will be once that bastard is dead,' she says.

I blink away the pain behind my eyes and try to focus. 'What's going on? What's everyone doing?'

'Getting ready to move out. Think we're going back to the palace.'

To Gaius. There's no way Bronn's going to be able to sneak in here with so many people guarding us – that plan is lost. *Think, Marianne.* I've got to do something but I have no idea what.

Jax strides towards us and we glare at him with shared hatred.

'Ah, good, you're awake,' he says to me. 'I wasn't sure you would be.'

'What do you want, Jax?'

'Well, we're going on a little journey, one which you won't be returning from, so I thought we should clear the air between us first.'

'What's there to say? You're a traitor.'

He feigns an injured expression. 'That depends on your point of view.'

I look at the man I believed was my friend, my family, and wonder how he deceived us all. 'You know Gaius doesn't care about restoring the bloodline? The Guardians are his pawns as much as the rest of us.'

'You think I care about the Guardians any more?' His light, cocky tone has been replaced with sharp, deadly anger. 'They forced us into a life of servitude, and for what? One side would pick that idiot boy king, the other, you.' He pauses and looks down at me with contempt.

Ignoring the insult, I say, 'And you think Gaius is a better alternative?'

'The best thing for the Isles now is to have someone take charge. Provide a fresh start. Create a new order.'

'And, let me guess, you and Greeb have been promised power and riches in this new world?' The look on his face answers my question. 'Anything he promises is a lie,' I say. 'He doesn't want to rebuild the Isles; he wants to destroy them. He'll feed on them until he's drained everything dry, and you and Greeb will simply be his puppets, little more than the dead corpses on the ships who had no choice but to do his bidding.'

His reply is to kick me in the guts. I bite my tongue so that blood fills my mouth, which I spit directly at his feet.

'What did I do to make you hate me so much?'

His eyes narrow. 'You even have to ask?'

For a moment I don't know what he means, and then it hits me. I stare at him, hardly believing it. 'This is about Grace?'

'Because of you my sister is dead!' He shouts the words at me, and I wonder how long he's wanted to say them.

'Grace is dead because Adler put a bullet through her head. Adler, who was working for Gaius.'

'She put her trust in you. She believed in the wrong person.'

'What would you know? You left her.' My anger rises now and I'm on my feet, hissing the words, but he points his sword at Olwyn, warning me not to come any closer.

'Quite the temper,' Jax says, though I sense fear beneath his bravado. He knows I could hurt him given half the chance. 'How you've convinced so many to follow you, I'll never understand. Even after nearly wiping out your own islands with your uncontrollable magic, they still remain loyal.'

'You'll never understand friendship because you've never had it.'

'I had a true friend,' he shouts, his face suddenly in mine. 'And you took *him* from me too!'

'I didn't kill Mordecai . . .' I shout back, but even as I say it, my voice trails off, the horrifying truth dawning on me. 'But you did. Didn't you?'

'You gave me no choice!'

'He was your best friend.' My voice is small, as the depths of Jax's betrayal grow ever darker.

'Just like Grace he chose the wrong person. I tried to convince him that he should question his faith in you, that a Viper-raised Easterner couldn't be trusted, but all I succeeded in doing was to create doubts in his mind about me.'

Oh, Mordecai. 'That's why he came to my room that night? To warn me about you?'

Jax scoffs. 'Imagine his surprise to find Vorne and me helping Gaius ransack your room instead.'

'How could you?' I can hardly bear it.

'He shouldn't have been there. I didn't want to do it, but I had to persuade him that things weren't what they seemed before he ran and raised the alarm. I was the only one who could get close to him.'

'To drive a blade through his heart.'

'Because of you. So, you may ask why I let Rayvn die? Why Mama? Consider us even.'

My gaze drifts to Olwyn, and I see the tears staining her face. Her pain stokes my own.

I turn back to Jax. '*You* killed Mordecai. Blaming me doesn't change that. And you can hand me over to Gaius for whatever he's promised you, you can watch as the rest of us are cut down by the Hooded, you can even live out your days in pampered, indulgent luxury, but I swear to you that truth will haunt you. It will rot you from the inside out until you die alone, festering in your own sins.'

This time he hits me so hard I fall back to the floor, coughing, my lungs unable to take in air properly.

'This is a war,' he says, crouching to speak softly into my ear. 'There's always two sides. One that wins and one that doesn't. I simply picked the right one. And you, dear Marianne, have chosen poorly yet again. One final mistake to mark the many others you've made. That will be the legacy you leave. Failure. Total, abject failure.'

With a final kick to my stomach Jax stands up and straightens his shirt. 'They're all yours,' he says to a group of Hooded who have been hovering nearby.

They roughly pull Olwyn and me to our feet and start

to drag us through the temple. I manage to turn and give Olwyn a tight smile that convinces neither of us.

When we reach outside, I'm astonished to see so many wagons and carts. Greeb really is emptying house. I look around for any sign of Bronn, wondering whether he's watching from a distance, but only the cadaver crows stare back at me from the dead trees. Olwyn and I are split up, and I'm bundled on to the back of one of the carts. To my surprise Greeb comes to sit beside me.

'Gosh, you look awful,' she says with disdain.

I don't bother to dignify that with an answer. I'm too busy looking around for Olwyn, wanting to make sure she's still OK.

'Your cousin is over there,' Greeb says with a sigh, as if I'm so predictable it bores her. 'Jax is keeping her company on our journey.'

'What will you do to her once you've handed me over to Gaius?'

'She will be given a choice. Join us or return to her cell. But I'll let her live if she behaves herself, I give you my word.'

'Your word means nothing.'

'Oh, come now,' Greeb says. 'You're a woman of the world. We simply do what we must to survive. That's as true for you as it is for me. We just have differing perspectives on how to achieve that.'

'Tell yourself whatever you need to sleep at night,' I say.

'I'll sleep well when Gaius pays me for delivering you,' she says. 'I made a fair amount the last time – I can only thank you for escaping so I could earn even more today. Strange to think that you are the most valuable commodity on all the Twelves Isles. You should be flattered.'

'It's a real honour.' I don't bother to hide my sarcasm.

The horses start to pull our carts away, forming a long and vast convoy of covered wagons and Hooded, both on horseback and on foot. If Bronn's stayed to see this, he'll have to abandon any plans of a rescue. Or perhaps he's already gone for help. Either way, for now we're on our own.

As the cart bumps along the track, I glance over at Greeb and see her necklace has fallen free. She notices me staring and pulls it all the way out.

'You remember this? I told you I liked it enough to keep.' She doesn't bother tucking it away again, letting Torin's wedding present to me hang there as a visual taunt. I want to strangle her with it.

I ignore her for several hours but all I can think about is what's waiting for me at the end of this journey. Eventually my rising anxiety gets the better of me and I can't bear the silence any more. 'What's in all the wagons?'

'The rest of my delivery to Gaius, of course. I've been guarding them for a while now, ever since he started to question the Viper's loyalties. Now it's time to return them to him.'

My throat seems to constrict; my chest tightens. 'The children? The children are in those wagons?'

'I'll be glad to be rid of the brats,' Greeb says dismissively. 'Gaius insisted they were fed and watered and it's been far too much effort.'

As if she'd lifted a finger herself.

My mind casts around for options. What can I possibly do?

Greeb chuckles. 'You're still trying to work out if there's a way you can save them, aren't you?'

'They're *children*.'

'And the island is overrun with them. No one will miss a few.'

'Their parents might.'

She shrugs. 'Not really my concern.'

'You have no heart.'

'And you have too much. See where it's got you.'

I turn my head away, unable to bear looking at her. It's taking every bit of self-control I possess for my magic not to take over, so deep is my anger, so great is my fear.

When the company comes to a halt, I think nothing of it, until one of the Hooded rides up to speak to

Greeb, whispering something I can't hear that makes her forehead crease with concern.

Everyone's on edge and their nerves spike hope into my heart.

*Bronn.*

A whistle pierces the air and then a dozen of the Hooded fall from their horses, impaled by arrows through their hearts.

'We're under attack,' Greeb shouts. 'Guard the goods!'

She launches herself at me, and I try to fight her off, but she's surprisingly strong. When I feel the sharp scratch of a knife at my throat, I surrender.

Greeb pulls me to my feet, her arm tightly round my neck, her blade threatening to split me open like a soft fruit.

'Hold your fire or your beloved queen dies!' she bellows to the hidden threat.

For a moment the world falls still. Some of the horses shift with anticipation. A whinny slices the air.

And then the army – my army – swarm in from every direction, roaring their battle cry. The sudden onslaught causes Greeb to hesitate, and that's all I need to make my move. I thrust my elbow back, catching her right beneath the ribs and the blade drops from my neck, trailing a shallow cut with it. I spin round and double-punch her in the face, hearing a tooth crack beneath my knuckles. But Greeb has not become as powerful as she is by sitting idly all day. She can fight every bit as well as the other Hooded. Quickly rallying, she strikes my shoulder, then my nose. Her fists fly fast and find all the bruises that Jax had already left on my body as if she had a map. When she kicks me hard in my guts, I stagger backwards, towards the far end of the cart, and when I look up she has a pistol raised, pointing right at me.

'I know Gaius wanted you alive, but I think he'll just have to make do,' she says. But before she can pull the trigger, Bronn appears from nowhere, leaping on to the cart and burying his sword deep in her side.

She stares at him in surprise. 'The Viper, I presume?' And a feeble laugh escapes her lips as she stumbles, before collapsing at his feet.

Bronn turns to me and I daren't believe he's real. I'm about to speak when he tackles me, throwing us out of the cart, covering my body with his own as we hurtle to the ground, the arrows that were aimed at me grazing his back as they fly over us. We fall further still, rolling down into the ditch beside the road, until we finally come to a stop, lying in the dirt, Bronn on top of me.

Time seems to stop, obeying only us. I stare at Bronn, his face close to mine, and for once it is utterly unguarded. I see nothing but love, and a fierce protectiveness that brings unbidden tears to my eyes. Despite everything, his heart still beats with mine.

'You're here.' My voice breaks with endless emotion as I breathe the words.

His beautiful, familiar face burns down at me with honest intensity. 'I watched you die once. Never again.'

I pull him to me, our lips crushing passionately together, and though death surrounds us, we defy it in each other's arms.

When we reluctantly break apart, he looks down at me, as vulnerable and exposed as I've ever seen him.

'Are we in this together?'

He's asked this question before. Then I answered with a lie, breaking his heart and leaving him for the West. I will not lie again. Not to him. Not ever.

'Yes,' I breathe, curling my fingers into the fabric of his clothes, not wanting to ever let go. 'Always.'

'Then let's get out of here.'

Bronn cuts the rope from round my wrists. My skin is raw from the unnatural magic woven through the fabric. Gently taking my hands in his, Bronn pulls us both to our feet.

'Strike first,' he says with a smile.

I press my forehead to his. 'Die last.'

We climb up out of the ditch and I jump into the cart to reach Greeb's lifeless body. My fingers find

Torin's necklace and I snatch it from her neck, tucking it into my pocket.

'The wagons are full of children,' I tell Bronn as I leap back down and assess the chaos. 'You've got to free them.'

'What are you going to do?'

'Go after our spy.' I turn to him. 'It was Jax.'

Anger blazes in his eyes and he nods. 'Kill the traitor.'

And pressing one last kiss on my head and a dagger into my hand, Bronn runs towards the wagons, leaving me to look for the man who betrayed us.

But instead my gaze falls upon Torin, and my heart leaps to my throat. He's locked in a brutal exchange with Vorne, the amber-eyed assassin sent by Gaius to kill me, who once left Torin fighting for life. Knowing how skilled Vorne is, how vicious, I forget about Jax for a moment. I can't let Vorne hurt Torin again. I won't. I run fast to help my friend but before I can reach them, Torin swipes his blade below Vorne's knee, and the assassin stumbles for just a second. It's enough, though, and Torin snatches the advantage, driving his sword hard into Vorne's guts, then kicking him to the ground. As if he can sense me watching, Torin turns and our eyes meet. A small nod is all the acknowledgement we give the moment – that score is settled.

I have another still to resolve, however, and resume my search for Jax. Instead I see Olwyn, fighting back to back with Astrid, and relief rises inside me to see her safe. Does that mean she killed Jax? I keep scanning for him and then – there he is. Olwyn may have escaped him but she didn't kill him. He's leaping on to a horse, and setting off at a gallop, away from the fight. There is no way I'm letting him escape to report back to Gaius.

I sprint to the nearest horse and swing myself up. Bronn's calling after me, but his words are lost in dust as I set off at pace in pursuit. I can hear nothing but the thunder of my horse's hooves as we fly across the track, and I push him further and further, my mind focused on one thing only – catching Jax. We're closing the distance, and as we round a bend, I'm near enough to be choked by the clouds of dirt left in his wake. I stretch forward, my hands high up the horse's neck, willing him to give everything he's got, and perhaps he's enjoying the race, because he finds something extra and closes the gap a little more. Enough that I can take the dagger in my hand. Enough that, as I steady my breath, I can take aim. Enough that, when I throw, my dagger lodges in Jax's thigh as I intended, and he falls, hitting the ground hard.

I pull my horse to a halt as soon as we reach him, jumping off before we've even stopped and striding over to where Jax lies.

'Going somewhere?' I ask him, wondering how it came to this.

He looks up at me, and in his hate-filled face there is nothing of the friend I once knew.

'Grace would never forgive you for this,' I tell him.

'Then it's a good thing she's dead, isn't it?' he spits back.

Anger flares inside me. 'Get up!' I shout. 'Get up and fight me, you coward.'

Jax looks angrily at the blade protruding from his leg, before turning his gaze to me. Slowly he starts to rise to his feet, as if unable to bear the pain, but then, so fast I almost miss it, he pulls the dagger from his flesh and swings it at me, almost slashing me across the stomach.

I leap back just in time, and quickly regain my footing. I don't have a weapon beyond my fury but I'm certain that'll be enough.

My fist finds his cheekbone and I feel it shatter beneath my force. He spits out a mouthful of blood, before trying once more to stab me with the blade. But this time I kick it from his hand, and in the split second while he considers his next move, I elbow him in the neck. Though blood ebbs from his thigh like the tide, he fights as if he's not even grazed. We've both been trained by Guardians, but this is different. This is personal. We're relentless – attacking, defending, blocking, breaking. He targets my guts because he knows I'm still sore from his previous beating. I target his wound, which must burn like fire, but even as I do so, my heart breaks that he's done this to us.

He rolls along the ground to avoid my fist, and snatches up the dagger, coming at me with it once more.

'You can't win,' I say. 'You're bleeding too much. I hit an artery.'

Jax bares his teeth at me. 'Then I'll take you with me.'

This time when he slices the blade, he catches my arm, cutting it – though not deeply. He lunges again, frantic now, but his blood loss is slowing him down. I'm slowing down too. I'm exhausted; I'm in pain. We're both giving everything to this fight but it's taking more than we have.

He cuts me several more times, a swipe here, a lash there, but they're flesh wounds, nothing more. And when he makes a mistake, relying on his injured leg to support his weight, he falters, and I swoop. Smashing my right hand down on his wrist, I make him drop the blade, allowing me to catch it in my left hand and plunge it into his chest.

Jax stares at me and blinks. He looks furious.

'You were my friend,' I say through the tears that have started to fall. 'I would have fought with you to the end.'

'I was never your friend,' he says, bitter to the last.

'And you will die. Soon Gaius will destroy you.'

With a scream of rage I twist the blade and silence him for ever.

I fall into the dust next to him. My body hurts from the cuts and bruises Jax has left as his legacy. The wounds to my heart have done the most damage, though. I trusted Grace's twin as I had her, and that was my mistake. I was blind to what he really was. Am I to blame for the deaths his betrayal caused? I let my heavy eyelids close, desperate to escape if even just for a moment, welcoming the darkness, recognising it as a friend.

The sound of approaching hooves has me sitting up, ready to fight again, but the moment I see who it is, I relax, wincing at my aching body.

'I've got you,' Bronn says, his strong arms scooping me from the ground. I let him carry not just my weight, but everything else that burdens me. He lifts me on to his horse before sitting behind me, and then sets off at a gentle walk. He doesn't say anything at first, he doesn't have to. He understands me well enough to know how I'm feeling. I simply rest my head against his chest and breathe in the steadiness of him, and when he absently leans to kiss my hair, warmth blooms inside my cold heart.

He murmurs softly into my ear, letting me know that the battle was won, that everyone I love is safe, and that even now they're returning to the camp with the children. His words unknot the last of the tension binding my lungs, the air suddenly easier to breathe.

We ride for hours, our bodies pressed close, firm yet tender, a silent act of affirmation that all we've done to each other is forgiven. That in this violent and angry world we find peace when we're together. That we are as essential to one other as the blood in our veins.

When we finally make it back to the camp, Bronn lifts me from the horse and carries me to my tent. My body aches, and I'm shivering, but it's the sadness that threatens me most. The loss. The betrayal. And there is still so much to fight against. What do I have left to give?

Bronn lowers me to the ground and wraps a blanket round me before leaving the tent. I haven't moved by the time he returns with water heated by the fire. He pours it into an old tin bucket, repeating the process until the small tub is full.

Then he kneels beside me, and lightly brushes my cheek with his finger. I look at him then for the first time since he lifted me from the ground. His eyes are as sad as mine, the grief we bear too great to simply blink away, but they also shine with such fierce love that I could weep. So many times I thought I'd lost him. Now I finally understand. The ties that bind us together run deeper than any magic and cannot be broken.

Slowly, gently he starts to undress me. Sometimes his fingers graze my skin and though the air is cold, they trace a path of fire. His eyes never stray from mine, and when I'm naked, he carries me to the water and lowers me slowly into it. Its heat burns and then soothes my broken skin, as Bronn washes me with such tenderness it makes my heart ache. He has seen my body before, has touched every part of it, but there is something so beautifully intimate about him respectfully and lovingly tending to my wounds.

When I'm clean, he holds my hands as I step out of the tub, and quickly wraps a blanket round me to keep out the chill. Not that I feel the slightest bit cold any more. The very air crackles with love, with devotion, with desire.

Bronn's shirt is damp from bathing me, and he pulls it over his head. I move my fingers to his chest, tracing over the many scars that I could find with my eyes closed. He has a few new ones since we last shared this kind of intimacy, and I rest my fingers on them for a moment, making them familiar to my touch.

His hands find mine, entwining, and as he runs his thumb over my skin, my heart, body and soul spark to life at his caress. Slowly we step towards the pile of blankets on the floor, our bodies moving as one, and as we lower ourselves down, he folds me into him, his strong arms taking care not to hurt my wounds.

Not one word passes between us as we lie together that night. But a thousand are spoken. And as I finally fall asleep, my head resting on his chest so that it rises and falls with his slow breathing, I feel a momentary peace I haven't had in years. I'm where I belong.

The next morning we make preparations to leave camp. There is no avoiding what is to come. Gaius is waiting for us, and we're as ready as we'll ever be.

Besides, now that we have several hundred children with us, supplies will quickly dwindle, and space is non-existent.

We're leaving the children here along with a substantial guard to keep them safe. Not that I think Gaius will bother with them just yet. He'll be hoping to eliminate us in battle and then claim them at his leisure. Still, they need to be looked after.

While everyone else prepares to move the encampment across the island, Esther and I mix potions to strengthen the children's weak bodies. In time I hope they will learn to live with the memories and move forward with their lives. And, of course, we intend to reunite them all with their families once we return. If we return.

Those of us not staying will start the long journey across the island today. It will take several days to march on the palace, and there the fate of the Twelve Isles will be decided. I look around at the men and women I'm leading into battle and am filled with pride. Gaius's army is made up of mercenaries and enemy Guardians. Mine is made up of those who want to protect their loved ones and their homes. Astrid has been recruiting fellow archers to form their own group. Plus, we have Esther. Two Mages against one definitely pushes the odds in our favour. We can do this. We can defeat him.

I seek out Dala before I have to leave. She clings tightly to me and begs me not to go.

'I will come back,' I say, and, though I hate making promises that are impossible to keep, I know I'll do my damnedest to keep this one. 'In the meantime stay strong just a bit longer for me, OK?'

She gives a small nod and I kiss the top of her head. 'I'll see you soon.' And I turn away so she can't see the tears pooling in my eyes.

I head over to join Bronn, who's tightening the girth on his mare. He smiles at me, and then gestures to another horse. 'Do you feel up to riding?'

'Yeah, I'll be fine.' Though I'm still sore from my fight with Jax, it's nothing compared to what I've been through before.

I can't bear to think about what would have happened without Bronn's quick thinking. Once he saw the temple, he suspected it was the one where the children were being kept. He knew no one would be able to sneak in or out. Fortunately he'd had the foresight to bring horses for our escape. He galloped back to camp and raised the alarm. By the time he returned with reinforcements, we'd already left the temple, but were moving slowly because of the wagons. My friends easily tracked and caught up with us.

Gaius may have nearly recaptured me, but he failed. And it's strengthened my resolve. I want to live. I want a future with Bronn. I want to win.

Though I leave the children with a sense of trepidation, it's good to finally get on the road. I'm ready to end this one way or the other.

The weather is on our side, calm with a gentle sea breeze sweeping across the island: not too hot, not too cold. I find myself basking in the company of my friends. Being with them reminds me what I'm fighting for. *Who* I'm fighting for.

On the second day of travelling, Torin and Sharpe ride up beside me, gesturing for us to pull away from the others slightly.

'What's wrong?' I say, always fearing the worst.

'Nothing,' Torin says quickly. 'We just want to talk to you about something.'

'Of course, what is it?'

Torin smiles. 'I've asked Sharpe to marry me. You know, if we're still alive after all this.'

I cry out with delight and several people look at us in concern until I signal to them that everything's OK.

'I said "yes", by the way,' Sharpe says with a grin.

'We wanted you to be the first to know,' Torin says.

'I'm honoured. And thrilled. And we have to win now.'

'Not for the islands but for a wedding party?' Sharpe raises an eyebrow. 'Interesting priorities.'

'I don't think it's unreasonable for me to want one celebration where I'm not there against my will, or barely able to stand.'

'You make a fair point,' Torin says, as I lean across to hug him as best I can on horseback.

They share the news with our close circle of friends that night, and as we all sit round the campfire, I drink in the warmth. Not from the flames but from the people. Torin and Sharpe positively glow; Olwyn rests her head in Astrid's lap while Astrid absent-mindedly strokes her hair; I nestle in the crook of Bronn's arm, half listening to him talk with Raoul, half drifting into sleep, feeling safe and content. We all know what's coming, what lies ahead, but for this brief night we're together and we're alive. It's a good way to end a day.

The following morning, though, the mood is sombre. We know it's our last day of travelling, that tonight will be our final camp. Beyond today lies the end of everything we've fought for. One way or the other, the fate of the Isles will be decided – and our own.

My gaze roams over my army. There are soldiers, smugglers and Seers. Farmers, sailors, assassins. Guardians, royalty, Mages. I'm still not sure how we managed it, but the people of the Isles have come together to fight for their freedom. I only hope I'm not leading them to their deaths.

The clearing where we set up camp is less than an hour's march from the palace. Our scouts have reported that Gaius has two camps of his own, one within the crumbling walls of the palace and one just beyond. I wonder who his army fights for – Gaius or King Rafe? What have they been told is their cause? Protect their king? Save their Isles? Annihilate the enemy?

Esther has positioned herself at the edge of camp, away from everyone else. She's not used to being surrounded by so many people. I take her some broth and sit with her for a while, noting her weariness.

'I'm too old for this,' she says with a sigh. 'Traipsing across islands.'

'After tomorrow, you can rest in all the luxury you could ask for,' I promise her, mustering a confidence I don't truly feel.

She offers me a sad smile in return and then surprises me by saying, 'I tried to teach your mother magic, did you know?'

I nod, slightly thrown by the mention of my mother. 'I did wonder.'

'She was very special,' Esther says, her eyes glazing over with memories. 'She was from the Song Isle and had a voice that seemed to float through the air, brushing your skin like silk. The world was never sweeter than when she sang. Your father . . . Oh, they were so in love. They needed help I was happy to give. It was a gift to spend time with another magical person. But while your mother was talented, she wasn't powerful like you. Her magic was quite specific. It –' she searches for the right word – 'comforted people. She had a way of soothing troubled spirits, easing suffering. I told you once she had peace in her heart, and I meant it. She was a kind, sweet soul, with magic to match. She sought my help to use her magic to protect you, and we tried. Tried to twist it, change it, manipulate it, but while she carried you inside her she wouldn't allow herself to reach within her own darkness, afraid it would spill into you. Once you were born, her teaching resumed, and she was starting to make some progress.'

'And then Adler showed up.' I know the rest of this story.

Esther stretches across to rest her hand over mine. 'She wasn't afraid of her magic. She wasn't afraid of who she was. She was almost entirely fearless. Except when it came to you. You were the person she fought for, from the moment you grew in her belly to the moment she died. Take courage from her, child. Her blood flows in your veins. If she was able to find peace with her magic, so can you.'

I turn to look at her, a tear spilling down my face. 'And will you manage to find peace?'

She considers this for a moment. 'Over the years I've been warped by many things. Anger, fear, guilt, magic – they've all twisted me into someone I hardly recognise. I share the same name as the woman I once was, but she's barely a memory any more. Using my magic against Gaius, though? Fighting back? Beginning to repay my debt to you? It's like I'm waking up, rediscovering what it is to live. But peace? That may take a little longer.' She squeezes my hand. 'And as for *you*? Stop trying to find yourself, Mairin of Vultura, Star of the Sea. You already know who you are. You just need to remember.'

Sensing she's tired, I take her empty bowl, brush an affectionate kiss on her cheek and bid her goodnight. As I make my way back through the camp, a booming voice cuts across the evening air.

'And what mad plan with near certain death have you got for me this time?'

My heart leaps and I run into Harley's arms. She squeezes so tightly, she crushes the air from my lungs but I don't care.

'You made it,' I say when she finally releases me.

'Are you all right?'

'Well, the settlement Bronn left me in was no palace, but my ankle's all healed if that's what you mean.' That's her way of saying the loss of the crew is still as painful for her as it is for the rest of us.

'Wouldn't be a proper fight without you there to tease me when it all goes wrong,' I say.

'Fighting the dead on the water would have been far more enjoyable with Harley there, I agree,' Bronn says, coming to join us and hugging her. 'Good to see you again.'

He throws his arm round my shoulder, and Harley's eyes narrow.

'Does this mean you two finally sorted things out?'

I smile up at Bronn, who brushes a stray strand of hair from my face. 'Yes,' I say. 'All is good.'

'About time too,' she says, folding us both into another enormous hug.

While Bronn takes her off to find food, I head for our tent, wanting to be well rested for tomorrow. The tension is showing among the ranks, the eve of battle fraught with nerves and fears. Conversation is sparse, and I'm not the only one retreating to bed early.

I'm still awake, though, when Bronn joins me some hours later, and it's only when I'm curled up in his arms, the steady beat of his heart a lullaby to my own pounding one, that I finally drift to sleep.

At first I dream of nothing, but slowly a figure forms in the darkness, thin like mist.

*Marianne.*

It's Esther. She's reaching out to communicate with me, and I know that however she's doing this, it's taking everything she's got. Her pain is so acute it cuts through the vision.

*Forgive me.*

In my dream I reach urgently out to her. 'What is it? What's wrong?'

*They took me. The Hooded. He's hurting me, Marianne. He's stealing my magic.*

Her voice is weak, fearful. But even in her agony, she's trying to warn me.

*I'm sorry. Make him pay.*

And then all I can hear are her screams until they abruptly end in a hollow silence.

I wake with a cry, tears already streaming down my face. I'm sitting up, Bronn's arms are round me, and he's staring at me with concern.

'What happened?'

'It's Esther,' I say, hardly bearing to say it. 'She's dead. Gaius killed her.'

'Not possible,' Bronn says. 'She's in the camp.'

I shake my head. 'No, the Hooded were here; she's dead.' And he has her magic. *He has her magic.*

Bronn is on his feet, rushing outside, and I can hear

him raising the alarm, getting people to look for Esther. They won't find her. Grief is quickly giving way to fear, all hope I may have carried for our success ebbing away. Gaius now has his own power, the power of the snow mares *and* the power of Esther. I don't stand a chance. None of us do.

I'm shaking, frozen with terror. He'll kill them all, rob me of everyone I love and then he will keep me in his cave once more until my bones turn to ash. The mere thought paralyses me.

*NO.*

The voice within screams, snapping me out of my panic. I will fight with everything I've got before I let that happen.

Bronn rushes back into the tent, his face tight with concern. 'She's gone.'

I barely listen to him, my thoughts racing. 'He sent Hooded to the camp and they went unnoticed, which means he could have taken any of us. He could have taken me. The fact that he didn't means he's up to something. He has something planned for this battle, something that makes him certain he's going to win. Something he needed Esther's magic for.'

I fear I know what it is, and can hardly dare contemplate it. Because I know precisely what he's been building towards this entire time.

'What can I do?' Bronn asks.

'Hold my hands,' I say. 'I need you to ground me.'

As soon as I ask, he does it, the warmth of his touch a balm on my breaking heart.

'What are you going to do?'

I close my eyes. 'I'm going to spy on that bastard.'

Esther found a way to warn me at considerable cost to herself in her final moments. She wasn't just doing that to let me know what happened to her. There's more at stake here, and so I'm going to have to try something new. I'm going to have to find a way to use her magic.

I already know I can – I called out to Bronn without trying, and I found my way to Pip. It's just about harnessing it differently.

I focus until the strange prickling sensation builds inside my head, like an itch beneath my skull. It's not natural to me, this magic, but nor did I steal it. Esther gave it to me to learn, and now's the time to use it. I summon the image of Gaius into my mind and focus on him. I want to be where he is, but I don't want him to know I'm there, and that's where I let a little of myself into this magic. My assassin training, my need to be invisible. I hold it as closely as I do the thought of Gaius.

It's like I'm walking through the darkness of my thoughts, mist dancing round my ankles, coiling up my legs and body until it surrounds me, and then I'm no longer walking in nothingness, I'm walking on grass. I can feel the damp earth beneath my feet as if I were really there. I'm climbing a hill and the place looks familiar. It's the settlement where the mass graves are.

Just ahead of me, Gaius is kneeling on all fours, his fingers knotted in the dirt as he mutters incantations. He's speaking in the ancient tongue of the Mage and I recognise the words.

*Glyda. Rysa. Lifya. Dauran byndi nei ykr mermri.*

Return. Rise. Live. Death binds you no more.

I feel the shift immediately. An immense tremor of magic flows through the ground, weaving, tangling, curling its fingers round whatever remains of the many buried there.

The exertion is taking a toll on Gaius. I can see he's straining to hold his position, his eyes pinched tightly shut, but he doesn't waver, doesn't give up.

All my own senses are screaming for him to stop, that he can't do this, that he mustn't. But I'm not really here, I'm simply an observer with no power over what happens.

And then energy soars up from the ground, throwing me backwards and almost severing the link I've made. The sound is unbearable, a screech, a wail, but from thousands of voices all at once, ripping the air to shreds. My hands fly to my ears, desperate to block it out, but it's sharp and savage, penetrating right through me.

When I look up, the fields are full of people.

He did it. He brought them all back.

Gaius has also been thrown to the ground, and now he struggles to his feet, and I see in his face the shock, the awe at what he's finally achieved.

It would be impressive if it weren't so horrifying. Thousands of bodies, who moments ago were bones and dust, are now restored to life, as perfectly as if they'd never died – physically at least. The screams have trailed off, but somehow the silence that descends is even more sinister. The dead stand there, unmoving, as if dazed – or else awaiting their orders.

'Ryla? Nell? Freel?' Gaius limps towards the crowd, searching desperately to find the three people he's done all this for, and I understand how massively I've underestimated his longing to see his family again.

'Ryla!' He cries out her name once more, and slowly a woman turns to face him.

I can tell it's his wife from his expression. I've never seen him look like this. Overjoyed and grief-stricken at the same time.

'Ryla, I've brought you back to me.' I expect his voice to be broken with emotion; instead it rings with triumph. But the woman stares at him, unseeing, and I know everything is wrong.

Two small children stand behind her, one boy who looks no more than two, and a girl of about six. Their eyes are as wide as the moon, and as unsettled as a storm.

'My dear ones, how I have missed you.'

But still they say nothing and the air crackles with imminent danger. I think Gaius senses it too, his immediate happiness to see them starting to give way to apprehension.

'Ryla, say something, anything. I have done all this for you. Defied death itself for *you*.'

She starts to scream then, a sound of pure rage spewing from the deepest part of her spirit. The children copy their mother, and soon the noise spreads across all the souls ripped from their resting places. They're angry, so, so angry, at having been disturbed.

'No,' Gaius says, shaking his head. 'Please, you're back. We can have the life we once had, only more. You will live at the palace; you will wish for nothing.'

But Ryla's screams intensify and she starts snatching at her hair in desperation, as if somehow that can relieve her distress.

'You can have anything you want – just tell me what you want!' Now Gaius is shouting too, and I've never seen him like this, vulnerable, uncertain.

The dead woman starts clawing at her skin, as if she can peel this physical body away, and when Gaius tries to stop her, Ryla pushes him off with an unnatural strength. He lands hard, bewildered, devastated.

I wonder if this ear-splitting racket is horrifying him as much as it is me. He crawls across the ground, his stick forgotten, and stretches a hand up to his wife.

'Please, Ryla, come back to me.'

This time her scream turns to a roar as she throws herself on to him, her hands squeezing tightly round his neck. I think she may succeed in doing what I have so longed to do, and actually kill him, but then I watch him raise his deformed hand and lower it swiftly through the air.

Ryla and the children disappear. He's let them go.

But all the other dead remain, and they're still furious.

Gaius sobs into the dirt, an utterly broken man. He's learned the hard way that what is lost can never truly be restored to us.

Slowly he lifts his head and I watch as the devastation on his face mutates to bitter fury. Where before there was always calculated control, he now abandons it all for reckless chaos. His eyes glint with the fire of a man who's about to burn the world down. A man with nothing left to lose.

I sever the connection, hurtling back through my mind until I'm returned to the tent, gasping for breath. Bronn is still beside me, steadying me.

'We have to wake everyone up. We have to go now.'

'What are you talking about?'

'He's ready to end this.' I remember the look on Gaius's face and dread grips my heart. 'He's sending his army now. Including the dead.'

Bronn's eyes widen with alarm. He's on his feet in an instant, issuing orders to the camp.

We'd gone to bed almost fully dressed to be ready for action, so I only have to pull on my boots and my belt, before arming myself with daggers and a sword. I grab a pistol too for good measure, though on the battlefield it'll only give me one shot as there'll be no time to reload.

Bronn hurries back into the tent to fetch his weapons. 'How the hell has he raised more dead?'

'By adding Esther's magic to what he's already stolen. He's accumulated exceptional power.'

Bronn hears the fear in my voice and stops what he's doing to come to me. He takes my hands in his and presses his forehead against mine. 'You can do this.'

I shake my head. 'I can't beat him.' I whisper this confession, trusting him with my weakness for the first time since we were children.

Bronn moves away slightly, his eyes searching mine. 'Maybe you can't. Maybe today we lose. Maybe this is the day we die. But whatever happens I will be right there with you, fighting, clawing, scratching until the breath is gone from my body. If we go out, we go together.'

A tear spills down my cheek as I nod. 'Together.'

He brushes the tear gently away. 'Now let's go and take as many of those bastards with us as we can.'

Hand in hand we leave the tent, and head out into the frantic activity of the camp. This is what we've been preparing for, everyone knows where to go and what to do. Raoul and Harley will lead a flank to the west, Astrid and Braydon one to the east. The main army will be broken into four divisions, led by Bronn, Olwyn, Torin and Sharpe respectively. They will approach the palace through the dormant Fire Fields, the wide valley scarred with deep fissures that periodically vent gas. It's a dangerous route, but the most direct one. My mission is to infiltrate the palace, find Gaius and somehow stop him.

We march on my ancestral home, focused, determined and ready to storm a castle.

But it soon becomes clear we're not going to get that far.

Gaius's army is already waiting for us. High up on the hillsides of the deep valley are his men. Hooded on the left, Guardians on the right. And below them, filling the Fire Fields, are the dead.

'Looks like Gaius wants this fight to happen here,' I say to Torin who's come to a stop beside me.

'There go all our strategies,' he says, staring at the

vast size of our enemy with dismay.

Bronn shakes his head. 'We can make this work. Raoul, you and Harley take your troops up to face the Hooded, Astrid and Braydon will handle the Guardians.'

They break away, and start to make for their new positions. That leaves the rest of us to face the corpses.

'I don't think they will be quite like the dead we fought at sea,' I tell my friends. 'They're a lot angrier. And less puppets, more captives being forced to fight. Expect the unexpected.'

'Marianne, there's a valley full of dead people waiting to kill us. It doesn't get much more unexpected than that,' Torin says with a grin.

And then we're all smiling and it helps. Because if you're going to stare death in the face, there's no better way than being surrounded by friends.

'Let's do this,' I say.

'Strike first!' Bronn bellows at the top of his voice.

'Die last!' comes the thunderous response from our army.

And then we charge.

We run full pelt into the Fire Fields that I had so longed to explore the first time I saw them. This wasn't quite what I'd had in mind.

Gaius's armies stand their ground as we roar towards them, the very island trembling with our stampede. As I sprint towards the thick wall of bodies, I try not to think about the enormity of the full task ahead, focusing instead on one immediate target: the soldier in front of me, already dead for over two hundred years. He's probably a little rusty.

My steel meets his, and there's more force behind it than I'd expected, but whoever he was before he caught the plague, he was no trained warrior. My sword easily finds its way past his, into his soft guts, but though he grunts he still keeps fighting. I lunge again, but no matter how deeply I cut him, he doesn't bleed and he doesn't surrender. Maybe he can't.

'I'm sorry,' I say, knowing none of this is his fault. He should be at rest. But I do what I must, and sweep my sword through his neck, severing his head and pushing his writhing corpse to the ground. He may not be fully stopped, but he'll struggle to harm anyone else as he crawls on his belly.

Body after body I have to maim and dismember just to slow them down, and soon my own body hurts from the intense exertion.

As I fight, I'm trying to locate Gaius. But there's no sign of him, nor of King Rafe and his advisors. They're keeping out of the way somewhere safe no doubt, relying on the others to protect them. Cowards to the last.

And of course the dead are not the only perils of being in the Fire Fields. When I reach the first fissure,

I skid to a halt. It's fathomlessly deep, and wide. I should be able to make the jump but I can't be certain. Still, it's the only way forward. Taking a run up, I leap, just clearing the distance, only to be attacked immediately by a walking corpse. I manage to use his momentum against him and flip him down into the bottomless crevasse.

'Use the vents!' I bellow to my fellow fighters. 'Throw the dead down!'

Before I can say anything else, another enemy soldier comes at me. I manage to knock her off balance so that she stumbles backwards into the deep hole – only to reappear moments later, carried up on the gas that bursts violently through the fissure. Her skin is melting in the heat as her body is thrown high, and then her burnt corpse falls back as the gas subsides. Judging from some of the screams I heard, she wasn't the only one caught in the blast. I do not want to die like that.

Some of my soldiers are trying to climb round the edges of the valley to push their way through without having to try to clear the fissures, but the rock surface there is loose and more than once I see an unsuspecting soul slip and plummet into an abyss.

What's more, bodies are falling from above us, people who have been flung off the perilous cliff in the fighting raging above, and after I see someone knocked to the ground by the weight of a dead Guardian landing on them, I resolve to keep well away from the sides of the valley.

The truth is there is no good way through, and still the dead come at us, an ever-rolling wave of malevolence.

From behind me I hear someone shouting, 'Duck!' and I instinctively obey. Seconds later something swoops over me and crashes into the dead man running at me. It takes my brain a moment to believe what it's seeing. A whole flock of sea vultures has descended from the sky like a pestilence, pecking and tearing at the faces of the dead. And the one in front of me I would know anywhere.

'Talon! You raised your own army?'

He replies with an ear-splitting shriek and I laugh in sheer disbelief.

'You are the best of all birds,' I say, watching fondly as he shreds my would-be attacker to pieces before moving on to another.

For a blissful moment I think the momentum has swung our way and that we might actually stand a chance of winning.

But such moments never last.

The Hooded and the Guardians have started throwing lines down the cliffs into the valley and are descending them, leaving my fighters up high, and starting to outnumber us in the Fire Fields. They're targeting the sea vultures, shooting them with pistols, throwing knives, and I cry out as their beautiful bodies fall from the sky.

'Talon, get away from here,' I scream at the loyal bird, but he ignores me as he always has.

One of the Hooded who's made it down into the valley is lining Talon up in his sights, and I sprint to intercept the man, crashing into him just in time to send his shot away from the vulture. We're both lying on the ground, and I punch him in the nose, slashing his exposed neck with my blade.

At least the living actually die. The dead never give up, even as bits of them hang off.

'We need to get more of our people down here,' I shout to anyone who can hear, but I can't see Bronn or Torin, or any of my other friends and my heart hollows with fear.

There's no time to worry about what's become of them, as I fend off attack after attack from the newly arrived Hooded. A quick glance up at the ropes alerts me that more are coming, but then I realise something. It's not only the enemy making their way down. It's my army too. I recognise Harley and some others as they lower themselves down the ropes and relief rushes in at the prospect of reinforcements.

No sooner do I feel this spark of hope, though, than I realise that the Hooded still up on the cliffs are hacking at the ropes. They're going to let my people fall.

'Target those men!' I shout, running forward and raising my pistol. One shot is all I've got. I'm going to make it count. Holding my breath, I take aim, and pull the trigger.

The Hooded slashing at Harley's line drops almost instantly through the air, smashing to the canyon floor.

Others are now following suit, trying to shoot the other Hooded down, but while some succeed, others don't and the first of the lines are severed.

Screams fill the air as my soldiers plummet to their deaths, bodies breaking on impact. I can hardly bear to watch, frozen in horror and unable to help. I think Harley at least is going to make it, but then someone takes the place of the man I shot, and with one clean slash cuts Harley's rope.

She snatches at the air, as if she truly believes she can climb it, even seeming to float for a moment, but in the end there's nothing to save her, and she dives and spins before snapping her back on the rock that awaits her on the ground.

I cry out, but the sound is lost in the chaos. I close my eyes, fighting back my grief. Not Harley, not now. Not after everything we've survived together. When I open my eyes again, I'm fuelled entirely by rage, slashing and hacking at anyone who dares to cross my path. I catch sight of Bronn fighting two dead people at the same time nearby, and seeing him alive offers me some hope. To my left Olwyn is busy impaling a Guardian, and behind me Torin and Sharpe are back to back and taking on a circle of living and dead.

They're still with me. I'm not alone. And so I keep going, though my legs are heavy, though my arms ache, though I'm covered in blood.

When I find myself facing a huge man who towers above me and must have weighed three times as much as me in life, I groan. 'Oh, come on,' I mutter as I swing my sword, only for him to grab it in his fist, not caring that it slices through his flesh.

With my left hand I snatch a dagger from my belt and bring it down to sever his hand at the wrist. He simply growls at me.

He may be huge, but he's not nimble, and I buzz about him like a fly while he tries to swat me away, until I'm able to find the right angle to separate his head from his body. For a moment I don't think even that's going to be enough as he still lurches towards me, but then he falls, knocking me down with him. His heavy torso lands on my leg and I'm trapped. I realise that I've dropped my weapons when I fell and they're all slightly out of reach. My fingers grasp for the handle of my dagger, which is closest, but though I can brush it, I can't quite grip it.

The sense that I'm being watched makes me glance up. An enemy Guardian has spotted me and with a smile raises her pistol. I'm an open target.

I try one last time to grab the dagger, but she pulls the trigger first.

And then Talon swoops between us, his wings raised protectively, and her shot hits his chest. He drops dead in front of me.

'No!' I cry, and with one painful effort I finally reach the dagger and fling it at the Guardian. It lodges between her eyes, killing her instantly.

'Talon.' I shuffle to cradle the massive bird in my arms, his intelligent eyes now glassy and empty. 'I'm so sorry.'

Bronn has spotted me and is running to help, heaving the great headless weight off my leg.

'He saved me,' I say, tears swimming in my eyes.

Bronn hugs me close just for a moment. 'He always loved you most. That's why I sent him West, when you left me. I didn't want you to be alone.'

I stare up at him in shock. 'That was you? You sent him?'

'Think he would have gone even if I hadn't.'

I furiously rub my eyes with my sleeve. I cannot be blinded by tears now. I have to focus. 'How are we doing?'

'We're taking a lot of losses, but so are they.'

'Then we have to keep going.' There's no alternative.

'Is that . . . Raoul?' Bronn says, squinting into the distance.

I turn, fully expecting Bronn to be wrong, but there's Raoul, covered in blood and heading for us, trying to get our attention. He must have made it down one of the ropes, or come the long way round.

We start running towards him, but there's a fissure between us and he's closer. There's no reason he shouldn't make the jump, but as he launches himself up, someone throws a dagger that lodges squarely in the back of his thigh and his face contorts with pain as he stumbles forward. With his leg compromised he slams into the side of the crevasse, just managing to cling to the edge by his fingertips.

Bronn and I race as fast as we can to grab his hands, Raoul swearing like the smuggler he is.

'Hold on,' I shout as we strain to pull him up and out of the fissure. When we've hauled him to relative safety, I move round to where the blood is running down his trousers. I pull off my belt and tie it as a tourniquet to slow the bleeding.

'You're going to live,' I say, patting him on the shoulder. 'If we can get you out of here.'

'Just pull the bloody thing out, will you?'

I'd rather leave it until I could safely do it, with bandages, a needle and thread. But he's going to have to hobble off this battlefield or die here. We can't carry him over the fissures, but he might have a chance if he stays at the side of the valley.

Bronn has gestured to a couple of our men to come over, and they hurry to us.

'Rip your shirt sleeve; I need a bandage,' I say to one of them, while Bronn protects us from an incoming attack.

'Is this going to hurt?' Raoul asks.

'Not a bit,' I say, and I quickly glide the blade out of his leg.

Raoul cries out and swears at me. 'You liar!'

'Don't ask stupid questions then,' I say, wrapping the makeshift bandage round the wound, tying it tightly.

'Let's get him up,' I say to the other soldiers. It's an effort, but soon Raoul is standing, his forehead glistening with sweat. He takes a deep breath before he's able to speak.

'I came to tell you we're getting massacred up there, and it's the same on the other side by the looks of it. I was going to suggest we pull all our remaining troops down here to make a final stand.'

'Do it,' I say with a nod. 'I'll come and fix you up if I'm still alive later.'

'And if you die?'

I give him a wry smile. 'Then I'll see you on the other side.'

'Reassuring as ever,' he says, before grimacing as he puts weight on his leg.

He nods and limps off, the other two supporting and guarding him.

There's nothing more I can do for him, or the troops up at the top. But I can help Bronn, and so I rush to fight at his side, battling back the unrelenting dead.

Arrows fly overhead, cutting down a group of Hooded who were running towards us, and I look up to see Astrid shouting orders to our archers on the cliff edge, who are already loosing another round of arrows at our enemy.

The noise is awful: steel, screams, the moans of the dying, the cries of the sea vultures, the hiss of the gas bursts. The clamour of brutality and misery and finality.

And then, from nowhere, a horn cuts through it all, instantly stilling the dead. The horn rings out again, and we all turn to look at the far end of the canyon. There, where the Lightning Tree stands proud, carrying a white flag of peace, is Gaius. With him are the King, the royal advisors and a small army at their back for protection. It would appear they want to talk.

A third horn blast seems to be the order for the Hooded and Guardians to fall back, while our soldiers look around, confused.

Torin and Sharpe run over, and then to my relief Olwyn is there too, a deep cut on her head but otherwise intact. I hug her fiercely.

'Think he wants to surrender?' she asks.

'No,' I say, narrowing my eyes as I stare in Gaius's direction. 'Arguably we're the ones losing. I have no idea what he's up to, but it has to be some kind of trap.'

'It would be dishonourable to ignore the white flag,' Torin says, and I can't help but smile at him.

'Let's go and find out what he wants,' Bronn says.

'I doubt anything he has to say will be worth hearing.' The fact that Gaius has yet to unleash a scrap of magic in this battle worries me. He's waiting for something. I just don't know what.

'I'm not sure we have a choice.' Sharpe tosses his blade easily from hand to hand.

A nagging sensation in my gut tells me this is a very bad idea, but I agree with my friends. To do nothing is not an option. And Gaius knows it.

'Fine,' I say. 'Let's go.' But I catch Olwyn by the arm. 'I want you to stay,' I say, my voice low so only she can hear.

Confusion creases her forehead. 'Why?'

'Because I don't trust that old bastard an inch, and I want someone to stay behind who I *do* trust. Someone who can lead if . . .' I don't want to say it, but we both know what I mean. If we don't return.

There was a time when Olwyn would have argued with me, but now she sees her exclusion for what it is: an absolute endorsement of my respect for her. I have chosen her above all others to carry on our fight should we fail.

She pulls me to her in a tight embrace. 'Come back, do you hear me?'

I give a sharp nod of my head, not trusting myself to speak. I won't lie to her. When I turn away, I don't look back, not wanting to acknowledge how much this feels like goodbye.

The Seer's prophecy rings loud in my ears. *Fear not the dead. But when spectral servants rise, beware their master. For he is close to his ends.*

But Raoul's is even louder. *Fear him. Face him. Destroy him.*

I lead the way towards the Lightning Tree, Bronn, Torin and Sharpe just behind me. In any other circumstances I would feel invincible. But the old man awaiting us is anything but weak.

When we're close enough to talk, I stop and weigh up my enemies.

King Rafe is swamped by armour in an attempt to keep him protected. Arlan and Eena stand close to him, as do the swarm of bodyguards. As if the only reason I've crossed this wasteland is to try to kill their king.

'What do you want, Gaius?' I am in no mood for preamble.

'Gracious as ever I see,' he says with a humourless chuckle. 'We're here to negotiate your surrender.'

‘Then we have nothing to discuss,’ I say. ‘Because, I swear to you, we didn’t come here to lose.’

Gaius casually steps towards Rafe, draping an arm round his shoulders.

His eyes blaze at me, my growing sense of unease keeping me alert. ‘You can keep fighting if you wish, and condemn more of your people to die. This battle means nothing to me. You think I care if you fight the Guardians or the Hooded? The dead? That I require their victory? You know better than that. Remember what I told you back in *our* cave. That everything I have done . . . *everything* . . . has been to bring in the reign of the Mages. Forgive me, the Mage. The islands are mine, no matter what you do.’

Confusion spreads across Arlan and Eena’s faces, though Rafe is too foolish to realise what Gaius is saying. But I see the way his arm tightens about Rafe’s shoulder, and I know we’re in trouble.

‘What do you want?’ I’m not asking as the leader of an army. I’m asking Mage to Mage.

His response is an action so fast that I can barely take it in. A movement of his hand and Gaius snaps Rafe’s neck. The boy falls to the dirt. Gaius’s face contorts in an evil smile.

Eena screams out, but Gaius holds her back with a raised palm, his power unfurling. Tracing his finger through the air with a cutting motion, the skin on Rafe’s neck opens, and his blood spills on to the dry ground.

My mind is racing. A royal blood offering. Why would Gaius need it? He's already exceptionally powerful; what would he need . . .?

The moment I understand, I shout at my friends. 'Fall back. Now! Run!'

Gaius flashes me a wicked grin and then raises his hands.

I raise mine at the same instant, my magic surging to the surface without a second thought, and it ploughs into Gaius's.

As our powers collide, I can sense his intentions. He's trying to awaken the Fire Fields. Not just to command the fissures to spew flames instead of gas, but to turn the whole valley into an ocean of fire. We'll be incinerated – that's why he lured us here. He intends to wipe us all out in seconds. There's only so long I can hold his power back, I just hope it's enough for my friends to reach safety.

Gaius himself exists in his own protected sphere, but he's left the others behind him exposed. He'll let them perish too, would welcome their deaths. He no longer needs the royalty, the Guardians or the Hooded. In fact, by fighting them we've only helped him. Less mess for him to clean up afterwards. That's why he's let this whole needless battle unfold. A pantomime simply to entertain him.

It's clear now that Gaius intends for there to be only one survivor today and then he will bend the Twelve Isles to bow at his feet.

I'm struggling to withstand the magical onslaught – my magic, still so new and untested, is a fragile barrier compared to Gaius's ancient tsunami. The pain of holding back the tide is excruciating, and I can sense my defences will soon be breached. I glance over my shoulder to see that the last of my people are making it safely out of the Fire Fields. Good. Now I just need to get myself out.

Slowly I take a step backwards, and another, my legs trembling with the effort of holding Gaius's power at bay.

'You'll never make it,' he taunts. 'The sacrifice is made. The blood spilled. The Fields will awaken. And when you're dead, I shall drink your magic dry.'

Behind him, the Fire Fields are already roaring to life, the flames shooting fiercely up from the fissures and engulfing any Guardians in the near vicinity. Gaius releases his hold on Eena, and she seizes the opportunity to rush forward to pull her dead son into her arms, wailing with loss. Arlan does precisely what I'd expect him to; he runs. But there's no escape, and the ground cracks beneath his feet, wide enough for a whole new burst of flames to soar up and devour him. His screams harmonise with Eena's cries for a moment, before silencing for ever.

Gaius locks eyes with mine and grins. He's having fun. Then he turns to look at Eena with contempt. Fire forms in the palm of Gaius's clawed hand and he launches it at her. She throws her body over Rafe as her hair and skin burn, even though he's dead, her maternal fierceness unwavering to the end, until she collapses on top of the boy she was devoted to.

There's only one person left for him to play with. Me. And I can't take much more of his magic's assault, my own buckling under the pressure. It's clear I don't have the power to match his, let alone overthrow him. So I do the only thing I can. Run. With one hand held back acting as the merest shield, one hand raised in front to clear a safe path, I sprint back through the fields, fleeing his vitriol and the destruction he's wreaking. Behind me, the Fields are burning, and I'm only just staying in front of the spreading furnace, the heat licking at my heels. The valley is long and I'm nowhere near the end, flying over fissures seconds before they erupt.

I'm weakening, my feet tripping as I run out of energy. Not only is Gaius overpowering me, but using my magic while keeping it at arm's length, afraid to embrace it fully, is an unnatural exertion, and I realise I'm not going to make it. I dive behind a boulder and crouch there, as all around me the world burns.

This is how it ends then. Hiding, afraid, alone. I have failed them. All of them. I cannot win.

And then I see him. His strong arms glide down a rope hanging from the clifftop, as he attempts a way back in to this firepit, avoiding the fissures. Gaius senses him too and directs a river of flames towards him.

With a flare of defiance I send my magic to crash into it, holding it back long enough for Bronn to reach the valley floor. He sprints towards me, keeping low, and I hold my protection around him until he slides to the ground beside me.

'You came back.'

'I never really left. I told you: we do this together.'

We grip each other tightly, the inferno raging around us.

'I can't fight him,' I say. 'He's too powerful.'

'Marianne, he is a thief. He's lived his whole life on stolen time and magic. But you? You have never needed to use or hurt others to be powerful, and you don't need to now. You simply have to ask.'

He presses his lips to mine, soft and warm, and I realise what he's doing. He's willingly offering me some of his own strength, and it passes between us as a promise. The strength of our love.

And that's when I finally understand.

I've been trying to fight Gaius, like for like, while never truly embracing the magic, too afraid it would consume me, as it did him, as it has all of them before.

But I am not them. I am not Gaius.

It's time for me to accept myself for who I am – all of me, even the darkness gathered at the edges.

I've long been warned that no one is strong enough in mind and body to resist the seduction of magic. But that was wrong.

I *am* strong enough.

I am the Viper. I am the Queen. I am a Mage.

And I will stop him.

'Stay here,' I say to Bronn. 'Whatever happens, do not move.'

Our eyes meet for a moment, and I know he sees my determination because he smiles.

'Give him hell.'

He leans in to press a fierce kiss on my forehead, before flattening himself against the rock again.

I burrow my fingertips into the earth, close my eyes and for the first time since that day on the beach when I became a Mage, I truly and completely invite the magic in.

The heat is sudden and welcome, and my body delights at the infusion of power. Just as quickly the darker part of myself flares up to meet the magic. And I let it. But this time I harness the darkness. Yes, the magic is wild, but so am I. Always have been. A healer on a ship of assassins. A killer with a conscience. A queen without a throne. Alive and dead. Always a contradiction. It's why I can be a conduit to the magic in a way no one has ever managed before, because I understand it.

*Help me.*

I think the words, not needing to say them out loud. I implore the islands I have loved my whole life, the land I want to protect. I beseech the ocean I've sailed on, respected and feared. I call to the sky that's watched over me through both calm and storm. If I fail, Gaius will eventually destroy them all, and they deserve to be part of this fight.

For five long heartbeats nothing happens, just a silence filled with anticipation. But when their answer comes, it strikes fast. Shooting in through my fingers and feet, the raw energies of nature surge through me, so fiercely I can barely breathe, threatening to tear me apart.

Pure magic.

I have feared it because I feared myself. What I might become. But I'm no longer afraid of what I am. I simply accept it. And I find that I'm enough.

Strong enough to be the vessel and not be destroyed. Brave enough to give everything for those I love. Flawed enough to accept I'm both good and bad and never simply either. Vengeful enough to end this war.

I am a warrior. An assassin. A Snake.

Ancient, elemental magic surges through me, waiting to be released. We are allied against the same enemy.

I rise to my feet and turn to the far end of the Fire Fields.

I am the storm. I have feared him. Now I face him. And I will destroy him.

Even from a distance I note the flicker of surprise on Gaius's face. Perhaps he senses the new power surging through me. Or maybe he just sees the absence of fear. Either way, he intensifies his attack. The flames shoot higher, and he rains down fireballs around me.

I don't flinch as I stride towards him. Waves of the ocean's magic quench the flames as they reach for my skin, the earth's magic smothers their eagerness to feed. The wind blows them away from me and I am untouched.

I'm vaguely aware of being watched from above. Both armies know there's only one real battle that matters – the one happening in this valley of death.

Still the magic builds, the immensity of nature slowly being unleashed. The sky grows dark as clouds gather around us, a perfect storm building to aid my fight. Behind Gaius, the Lightning Tree hums with energy. The bolts that destroyed it, held for years within the earth, suddenly erupt, flashing violently from its charred trunk to strike directly at Gaius. He struggles to stay upright under the force of the attack.

I cannot help but smile. I am not the only one with a vengeful heart. I am not the only one wronged by this man. He has angered nature itself.

When the lightning subsides, Gaius turns to me, and this time, for the first time, I glimpse a hint of fear in his face. Where it belongs.

But just as quickly it's gone. Even now he considers me weak compared to him. 'You think this is enough, Marianne? I have the magic of *two* Mages and the snow mares. Until you're prepared to do what is necessary, you are no match for me.'

His words echo another man's, spoken to me long ago. A man who underestimated me and paid the price. Gaius has made the same mistake that Adler once did. Gaius thinks me too good, too kind to sink as low as him. He forgets I was raised in darkness by his Viper puppet and I have done some unspeakable things in the name of revenge. Gaius and I share a common magic. I have used it to restore life; he has used it to take life. But if Gaius thinks he's the only one evil enough to steal magic, he's wrong. I *am* prepared to do it too.

Just once. From him.

Today the assassin shall become the thief. No longer will he be the only vulture feeding off others. But *his* will be the final carcass. I, Mairin of Vultura, will strip him of all the power he's ever stolen. And then I will destroy him.

Raising my hands, I call out to it, the magic that doesn't belong to him. My ancestors', his caged creatures', the children's, the snow mares', Esther's . . . mine.

And it hears my call.

Eager to leave the body Gaius has imprisoned it in, the stolen magic starts to break free. I can see its threads snaking out from his chest, as clearly as when life leaves a body, and I coil my own magic around the tendrils. But this time I don't try to restore them, I snatch them hard, ripping them from him and pulling them fiercely into me.

I can barely stand, the force is so staggering. But the magic of the Isle steadies me and the air supports me gently beneath my arms, and so I am able to withstand the influx of yet more magic.

Like two frozen statues, unable to move in the storm, Gaius and I face each other, his features etched with horrified comprehension. By draining the magic from him I'm draining his life, for without it he would have died two hundred years ago. His skin pales first, then tightens, until it's nothing more than a thin film stretched across muscle and sinew. They melt away on the wind, exposing the bone beneath. There's nothing to protect his skeleton as his body collapses in on itself, organs disintegrating away to nothing, until even the bones themselves begin to crumble, turning grey and then to ash.

And at the last, nothing remains where Gaius stood but a pile of dusty cloth.

There is no time to dwell on his demise, though. The

magic soaring through me is too much to withstand any longer.

Falling to my knees, my arms outstretched, I whisper to it. I thank it for saving us. And I set it free.

My scream disappears on the wind as sheer energy bursts out of me, returning to land, sea and sky. As it did when I first became a Mage, the magic drowns me, filling me up from the inside out. I can do nothing but let it flow from me, for I will not harness it or try to control it.

The greatest lie ever told wasn't that the magic was gone, but that it belonged only to the Mages. It belongs to everyone and no one. Joren knew it, Tomas knew it. Now so do I.

When the magic has returned to the land, ocean and sky, I fall to the ground, exhausted. But not empty. Some has chosen to stay with me.

The warmth of power still tingles through me, though I have no strength to move. I know what I must do, where this last bit of elemental magic belongs and how to finish what I started. And contentment spreads through my veins alongside the magic as oblivion rushes to meet me.

The ocean wind blows sweet and soft on my face. On the horizon is the familiar silhouette of land, a welcome sight after our long journey back from the West in our small ship.

I sit at the prow, a blanket wrapped round me, and drink in the view, happy to let Bronn do all the work by himself for a moment. I may be glad to see land, but it has been wonderful to be alone, just the two of us at sea.

Soon enough, we will have to go back West. For a start I need to be crowned. And once I am, I shall name Olwyn as my regent, to rule in my stead when I cannot be there – which will be a lot. Astrid has already been made Captain of the Guardians, and much like the Snakes did long ago, many who fought for Gaius have humbly begged forgiveness and asked to join our side. Astrid's advice on who should be pardoned has been invaluable. But the Guardians no longer exist to protect the bloodline. They exist to serve the people.

I intend to do precisely the same as Torin – to create a council representing all the Western islands. All voices will be heard, not just the powerful. It will take time to restore the peace, to undo the legacy of Greeb and the Hooded. But we will.

The Guardians set to work immediately, returning the stolen children to their homes. All but Dala. Since her family were gone, Olwyn and Astrid asked her if she wanted to stay with them – they will now raise her as their own, their family complete. Bronn and I stopped briefly at the Eighth Isle to let Pip and Toby know all that had happened, and were relieved to find both them and the foals thriving. In time the herd will grow again, when the sea stallions return. But for now there is peace in the mountains.

Torin sailed East ahead of us. Before he left, he declared himself Captain of the King's Fleet, having resolved not to reign from within the stuffy walls of a castle. He wants to be out there, with his people, keeping them safe, and hearing their concerns. His first act was to lead the surviving Fleet home, to reunite them with their families. Once he and Sharpe are married – a ceremony that will take place before I return West for my coronation – Sharpe will spend his time alternately watching over the castle and sailing with Torin. Raoul made a full recovery from his wound, mainly because not long after I'd woken safe in Bronn's arms at the end of the battle, I used my magic to heal all our injured. Raoul came back East with Torin and Sharpe, to be with his beloved Lilah and Bay. I hope to see them all soon. Because Raoul and the Seers, now pledged to the King once more, will be relied on to watch for any trouble brewing in the shadows. As will I.

After all, I'm not just Queen of the Western Isles. I'm Mage to all twelve. But first, before duty reclaims me once more, I have a promise to keep.

'We'll be there within the hour,' Bronn says, as he releases the sail.

I look over at him and smile. Once we have finished our duties in the East, he will return West with me, to stand by my side when I accept my crown. Afterwards, he will stay and help me raise a fleet of my own. Meanwhile Raoul has promised to build him a new ship, one that can be a true successor to the *Maiden*. Bronn has already told me what he intends to name her. The *Rayvn*. It's the perfect tribute to the woman who loved the ocean above all things.

The Twelve Isles will once again share a Viper – like their Mage, he will serve them all. Which means for long stretches of time I can escape to sea with the man I love.

When we reach the island, Bronn anchors our ship in the shallows. 'Are you sure you don't want me to come with you?'

I nod. 'This is something I need to do alone.'

He laces his fingers through mine, pulling me close until our lips meet, spreading heat through me that has little to do with magic. 'Take all the time you need. I'll be here, waiting for you.'

'Then I shall hurry back.' And I give him one last kiss before I sit on the side of the boat, swing my legs round, and drop into the water. I swim until it's shallow enough to wade towards land.

The Fourth Isle.

Even after all this time, I easily find my way across the island to the cottage where I was so happy. Always this place will have a pull on my heart. Much like I left a part of myself behind when I died, so too a part of me remains here. I pay my respects at the grave where Joren, Clara and Tomas lie together, and then I head to the fields where flowers of all colours once grew, where Joren first opened my eyes to magic and, most importantly, where I learned how to be accepted. To be loved.

I swore I wouldn't return to this island unless it was to restore its magic. Today I hope to fulfil that oath.

Kneeling on the ashen ground that was once carpeted with flowers and is now as barren as the Fire Fields, I close my eyes. Baia told me on the Ninth Isle that to heal people you first have to understand how the body works. The same is true for the islands.

It's time for me to learn.

My fingers sift through the dusty earth and I allow the magic inside me to connect with the island. At first I sense nothing but darkness, emptiness, a loneliness I'm all too familiar with. Only when I delve further do I understand why. Buried deep – pitiful and shrivelled – is the heart of the root system of the Eastern Isles. Millions of magical threads bound together, which once fed out to the other islands to sustain them like the roots of a tree. After King Davin of the East banned magic, these roots withered and faded, and when Adler scorched what little remained of the magic, they slowly began to die. Their death spread through the intricate system like a rot, poisoning all magic in its path. I can see it as clearly as if I'm looking at one of Baia's drawings of veins and arteries, only here it's a map of how the islands lived and breathed. Some part of me had begun to understand it when I saw her sketches, but finally my eyes are fully open.

Now these roots have perished. It's no wonder crops have been failing and animals dying – the islands cannot thrive without this beating heart.

I summon the residual magic that I've been carrying since the battlefield, the magic entrusted to me by nature, which chose to stay with me for this very purpose, and release it into the earth. Instinctively I guide it towards the threads – it's similar to when I have tried to restore life in the past, only now there's no sense that I'm defying the rules. It's almost as if everything I've ever done has prepared me for this very act. My love of healing, my magical skill, my connection to the islands. I weave and untangle, unknot and bind together, restoring, mending. And the magic runs through the roots, breathing life back into them, until eventually I hear the heartbeat of the islands start once more, first a soft flutter, then a hum. When the only magic left inside me is my own, I gently break the connection with the land and open my eyes. Nothing looks different, but I sense that nothing is the same.

And when I brush my hand across the ash, I see it. Peeping up through the lifeless dust, is a small green shoot. Fresh, lush, alive.

Tears fill my eyes. 'Your flowers have returned,' I whisper to Joren, hoping he can hear me wherever he is now. 'They will bloom again.'

The magic of the West, gifted to the East, binding them together once more. The Twelve Isles reunited – not just in name but in essence.

My own magic dances inside me, at ease, balanced. For the first time in my life I know who I am and welcome it. I no longer fear the power that dwells within me, I delight in it. I'm ready to rule, to serve, to defend. But mainly I'm ready to live.

Soon I will return to Bronn, and our next adventure will begin. I hope it will be less eventful than our last, but something tells me that's not the life we're meant for. Still, no matter what lies ahead, I can't wait to share it with him.

The wind returns, curling round me like an old

friend. My magic rises in response, and though it remains tethered to me, it carries on the breeze, flying upwards, spiralling, twirling. I close my eyes and let the magic carry me across the land, over the sea, and I sigh with contentment.

I'm everywhere. I'm nowhere. I'm free.

# ACKNOWLEDGEMENTS

To have one book published was a dream come true. To have a whole trilogy out in the world is beyond all I could have hoped for. It's been the best three years and I'm full of mixed emotions to reach the end of Marianne's story. I wouldn't have made it here at all though, without an amazing, talented group of people around me, and they have my eternal thanks.

Davinia Andrew-Lynch, the best agent a girl could ever want. Seriously. The. Best.

Lena McCauley, my editor, who utterly understood my characters from day one. I cannot imagine anyone more perfect to have helped me tell their stories.

All the fantastic team at Hachette – thank you for everything. Extra special thanks to Becci Mansell, Natasha Whearity, Naomi Berwin and Emily Thomas. And my undying gratitude to Samuel Perrett for designing three exceptional covers.

Where would I be without my wonderful writing community friends? There are so many of you I can't possibly mention you all by name, but you know who you are. Special shoutout to Kat Dunn, Connie Ashpole, Rosie Talbot, Menna van Praag, Amy McCaw, Lucy Powrie and Mich Kenney. Thanks also to Steph Elliot, Charlotte Burns, Sarah Withers, Tsam Potts, Sarah Corrigan, Imogen Gray, Jenn Faughnan, Paige Harris, Beth Saunders and Asha Hartland.

My wonderful Vitriol crew: Lorraine Wotherspoon, Sifa Poulton, Rose Gant, Katherine Wilson, Kelly-Ann Davies, Emily Mitchell, Amy Rush Da Silva, Nikki Sidaway and Hollie Wilson.

All my gorgeous family, I love you. I have to single out my incredible Mum for extra praise, for reading everything I send her and for spending hours with me pouring over grammatical minutiae.

Joe, Kara, Odette – I'm so grateful you're my people. Love you always.

It's been a tough year for everyone, and all the support I've received has meant more than ever. Endless thanks to every single blogger, bookseller, reviewer, librarian, teacher and reader who's helped fly the Storm and Sorrow flag in any way. Thank you for joining me on this amazing journey.

Bex Hogan was raised on a healthy diet of fantasy and fairy tales, and spent much of her life lost in daydreams. Initially she wanted to train as an actress, but she quickly realised her heart belonged to storytelling rather than performing, and soon after started creating stories of her own. A Cornish girl at heart, Bex now lives in Cambridgeshire with her family.

Follow her on Twitter @bexhogan
or visit her website at bexhogan.co.uk.

THE EPIC
ISLES OF
STORM & SORROW
TRILOGY

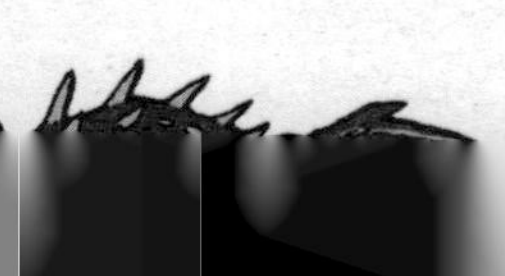